Submissive Secrets

ZANE MENZY

SUBMISSIVE SECRETS

Crashing Hearts Book Three

CHAPTER ONE

Christmas Eve

It had been three weeks since Keegan lost his virginity to a supposedly straight man and *joined the club*. If Damon had been straight before that night in the cabin, he couldn't claim to be entirely so now. Not after the way Keegan had fucked him so intrusively; spilling raw passion between the sheets in the form of sex sweat and sticky cum.

Keegan found the whole thing almost contradictory. It felt like he had become a man while making Damon somehow less of one. The nature of their hook up was dubious to say the least. There was no denying that Keegan had tricked Damon into doing it. He had been like a sexual monster in virgin's clothing. What had started as innocent questions, soon morphed into curious physical exploring leading to Damon's face buried in a pillow with his arse up in the air, waiting to be taken... *hard.*

The pairing was all sorts of wrong. Keegan was barely eighteen and Damon was thirty-seven. Admittedly, Damon looked young and hot for his age. Oddly, Keegan had never known just how dick-stiffening attractive this man really was until that fateful night. His gym-chiselled chest, short brown hair and moss-green eyes all combined to give him a beauty not many of God's creatures could claim.

What made it particularly bad wasn't the age-gap but who Damon was—which perhaps explained why Keegan had never viewed him in a sexual light. He was Keegan's father's best mate. Matthew Andrews and Damon Harris had been best friends for twenty years and while Keegan had grown up barely seeing his globetrotting father, he had grown to know Damon very well. Damon would swoop into town every few months to check how Keegan and his mum were doing. It was like Damon's job to turn up and remind Keegan how awesome his busy and selfish father was.

Secretly Keegan was relieved that his father didn't visit. His reception would not be a warm one. Keegan's mum tolerated her ex but Keegan's grandparents were not fond at all of anyone from the Andrews family who they openly referred to as being "basic."

Damon's routine visits through the years made him a sort of surrogate uncle. It was this role—and his status as a close family friend—that made what they did together so scandalous. Still, none of that took away just how damn hot it had been using Damon and treating him dismissively.

As Keegan now sat at home in his bedroom, half-heartedly playing an online game, he felt a shiver tap his spine as he remembered how brutal he had been. He had shown Damon no mercy in the cabin that night by the lake. On a small rickety bed, he had peeled away Damon's clothes and dignity, layer by layer, until the man was left naked and without pride. The whole ordeal had been unflinching and raw with carnal wanting. It wasn't love. It was fucking. Pure undiluted fucking.

Keegan was shocked by his own actions and how ruthless he could be in that moment. That moment where his cock did all the thinking and showed him how capable he was of being commanding and in charge. But the most shocking part of the experience wasn't his self-discovery for sadistic tastes but Damon's acceptance of submission. After all the wriggling, reluctance and gritted teeth, Damon let go of his body and had submitted to what was being done to him; gasping in pleasure, wanting more, begging to be made an example of.

Keegan had obliged. He wanted nothing more than to teach the older womanizer a lesson. The man who paraded as a surrogate uncle figure, always claiming to be Keegan's mate, deserved all of it. He had needed to pay for what he had done.

The night before the cabin trip had been Keegan's

eighteenth birthday party. It was supposed to have been one of the defining nights of his life when his girlfriend Tess said she would be giving him the best present of all. Sex! But it wasn't to be. In the middle of the chaotic evening Keegan had lost sight of Tess, only to find her later hidden in the shadows hooking up with Damon. Keegan hadn't said anything. He had run off in shock before they spotted him.

He had planned to try and block out the scummy betrayal. Pretend it never happened. He loathed conflict and he did not see how he could bring up what he had witnessed without causing some sort of major drama. He probably could have erased it from his memory eventually had he not woken up the next day to be hijacked with a boy's weekend away. As part of his birthday present, Damon was taking him away to stay at the Lakes Forest Park. Just the two of them.

Driving for miles only to be cooped up in a small cabin with the same man who had just fucked his girlfriend felt more like a punishment than a birthday present. Being stuck in the middle of nowhere with the arrogant prick proved too much. Keegan's emotions were so freshly bruised from what Damon had done that he let his mind go to some dark places and those places were what set the whole event in motion.

Later that evening when Damon crawled into bed, half-naked and drunk, Keegan's dubious desire came out to play and make Damon pay for robbing him of his first-time. If Keegan couldn't have Tess then Damon's arse would have to fulfil the cherry popping honour.

As great as it had felt reducing Damon to little more than a fuck-hole, Keegan didn't expect what came after he came. *The guilt.* An avalanche of the ghastly emotion seized him immediately once he ejaculated in the condom buried deep inside Damon's arse, Keegan began to cry. Regardless of what Damon had done, it didn't seem to warrant such harsh vengeance. It didn't matter how Damon had seemingly enjoyed it...*eventually.* That didn't stop Keegan feeling like he was a monster. A monster who had gone too far.

Damon had heard his crying and was like a fucking

knight in shining armour to the rescue, he made Keegan hop back in the same bed and he cuddled him, kissing him, telling him it was all okay. He assured Keegan we all make mistakes. The tenderness of their bodies wrapped together was oddly healing and it did help Keegan calm down enough to fall asleep beside Damon's warm body.

Keegan got up from his seat and went to close his bedroom door. All this reminiscing of his raunchy evening was bringing on his hundredth hard-on of the day. He toddled back to his chair and brought up a web page to look for porn and beat one out.

GAY DOM FUCKS SUB he typed into the screen. This was his new porn preference. He had always had a tendency to watch BDSM videos but now it was exclusively gay content. No more hetero sites, just full on same-sex fucking and sadistic attitudes.

Before sleeping with Damon, Keegan had been confused. Unsure what he was or what he wanted. He had been dating Tess for two years while also carrying lecherous thoughts for his best mate, Liam; the black-haired, blue eyed stud whose every inch of his five-feet-eleven height was a thing of pure beauty. Keegan hadn't been sure just what the feelings were about—until Damon.

Admittedly, he would jack off every day thinking about what Liam's cock would taste and feel like in his mouth, but he wasn't convinced these queer feelings were real. It was probably just some weird phase that would pass. He didn't want to be any different from his mates. But now Keegan knew he was different. He wasn't the same as his mates. Thanks to Damon, answers were given and secrets had been made between the sheets. He didn't want others knowing this side of himself existed. That this was who he was.

Only Damon knows my secret.

Keegan scrolled through the list of videos appearing in his search results. He clicked on one with two twinks as the stars. One blond, one ginger. He felt a bit vain admiring the blond boy who bore more than a little resemblance to

Keegan with his pretty face, olive skin and slim frame. The boy's large cock even looked the same—eight inches of thick flesh.

The ginger boy was tied to a tree, his face grinding against the bark while his smooth back and arse were left exposed. The blond boy tickled him, taunting his ginger lover with threats about how hard he was going to fuck him against the rough surface of the tree. Keegan grabbed hold of his dick, groping it to life. He imagined himself in his doppelganger's shoes, taking charge and having his wicked way. Keegan briefly wondered if the two boys would feel as weird after fucking as he had with Damon. They at least had the luxury of being on a film set and could walk away after somebody shouted "cut." That hadn't been the case for Keegan and Damon.

When Keegan had woken the next morning in the cabin it had reeked of sex. A strong, stuffy smell that was quite unlike anything he had inhaled before. He slipped Damon's draped arm free of his naked body and rolled out of bed. Damon's snoring told him his surrogate uncle was well and truly locked in slumber. Keegan stepped over the used rubber on the floor and quietly got dressed, letting his first-time sleep in. Closing the cabin door gently behind him, Keegan had gone for a walk around the lake, trying to clear away some of his still-lingering guilt. With traces of spunk still glued to his skin, Keegan had felt like a murderer with blood on his hands.

By the time he had returned to the cabin, Damon was awake and sitting having a coffee at the small table beside the kitchenette. Fiddly small chat ensued but to Keegan's relief—and immense gratitude—Damon didn't mention any of what had transpired between them. Try as they might to act normal, it didn't work. The small chat never went beyond tricky short sentences like, "Nice day outside by the looks."

Keegan's anger with Damon had vanished for what he had done with Tess. The older man had earnt his forgiveness. But sex had caused a new kind of rift. An awkwardness Keegan had never experienced. He had known this man his whole life but the moment he breached the friction of Damon's arsehole had made them become strangers.

After Damon finished his coffee he asked if Keegan fancied going home a day early. He answered "Yes" in a heartbeat. The relief on Damon's face was palpable. Keegan assumed that Damon feared his arse being on the block for a second night in a row if they stayed. They packed up their belongings at lightning-speed and jumped in Damon's car to come home. The whole way Keegan sat in the passenger seat in complete silence. They didn't look each other in the eye. As Damon dropped him off outside his house they still didn't say a word. They swapped knowing glances at one another. A look that translated so clearly it didn't need subtitles; *we will NEVER speak of this!*

Keegan was getting close to reaching his climax, his hand slipping up and down his spit-lubed rod at a furious pace. The blond boy had slapped the ginger lad's arse so hard his cheeks were redder than his hair and now his arse was being fucked with vicious intent. Keegan's mouth creaked out saggy gasps as he was about to spurt his load.

Screeeeeeeeech. The high-pitched noise of his mum's car tires told Keegan she was home.

He let go of his cock.

Fucking hell!

Annoyed at being robbed of an orgasm, Keegan slipped his erection back under his pants and shut the porn off, willing his cock to go down. He quickly brought up a clean google page just as his mum's footsteps sounded down the hallway's wooden floor.

A soft tap emitted from behind his door and his mother asked, "Is it okay if I come in?"

Keegan faked a laugh. "Yes, Mum. I ain't cutting up the bodies of my victims."

His mother opened the door and poked her head in. She had just gone and had herself a haircut. She walked in, smiling, waiting for some sort of compliment at how amazing her hairdo looked. "What do you think?" she asked, touching the side of her freshly-dyed and barely chopped hair.

"It looks really nice," Keegan said, despite hardly noticing a difference. Her hair still hung just past her shoulders and the colour she had gotten was the same colour she always got. A sort of honey blonde that was her natural hair colour—the same as Keegan's.

"Thank you, darling." She narrowed her eyes, trying to make out what was on his computer screen. "What are you looking up?" she blurted. She went and stood beside him with an almost whimsical look on her pretty face.

Keegan shuffled his seat closer to the desk so his pointed crotch would be hidden. "Oh, nothing. I was just about to look up some of the courses at Auckland Uni," he lied.

"Yes. You're running out of time, Keegan. You need to hurry up and make up your mind. If you're not going off to study then you'll need to start looking for work if you plan on staying around here and getting a flat in town."

Keegan frowned. "What makes you think I'll go flatting?"

"Wouldn't you want to? I assumed you and Liam would go find a flat together," she said, tugging on her hair. "You don't want to stay at home living with me, surely."

"You sound like you want to get rid of me."

"Not at all, darling. You're welcome to stay as long as you like. I just know that when I turned eighteen I couldn't wait to get away from the nest and be independent." She stepped over to his bedroom window, inspecting the overgrown backyard and changed the topic, "I don't suppose you could mow the lawns for me today, could you?"

"I thought you had decided to pay someone to mow them?"

"That was when I thought you were fully decided on moving to Auckland to study. Why waste my money when my big strong son can mow them for me?" His mother flashed him a cheeky smile.

Keegan rolled his eyes as he gripped hold of one of his tanned biceps on show in the loose singlet he was wearing. "I don't think my skinny arms count as big and strong."

"Maybe not," his mother sighed. "But your labour is free."

"Okay. But I am going to visit Liam soon and when I come back I'll mow them."

"Thank you." Keegan's mother looked delighted to hear that the jungle of a lawn would finally be taken care of. "It will be nice to have outside looking good for when Damon arrives this evening."

"Damon," Keegan replied in a shrill voice. "What's he doing coming here."

"It's Christmas Eve. You know he comes for Christmas most years." She narrowed her eyes, furrowing her brow.

"But why this year?"

"I know you find him annoying but do try to be nice," his mother soothed. "He does try his best by you. Remember how generous he was for your birthday giving you what he did."

"Sorry," Keegan said, jolted by his mother's sentence. "What do you mean?"

She gave him a funny look. "The money he gave you. That was very generous of him so do try to be nice. He may give you some more for Christmas."

"Oh, yeah." Keegan rested back into his seat, calming down his minds worry that his mother knew their secret.

"Anyway, I'm going to go put up this pesky Christmas tree."

"Christmas is tomorrow. Why bother." Keegan laughed.

"Because Santa won't bring your presents if he doesn't see the tree up."

"We can't have that can we," Keegan said sarcastically.

"Anyway, if you hear me scream and a loud crashing sound then that will be the tree and the raggedy old angel falling down on top of me."

"The angel isn't raggedy," Keegan said defensively on behalf of the angel that felt like a family heirloom.

"Maybe if you had bothered to help me put the tree up in the last five years, you'd know that she looks like she's been getting chemotherapy."

Keegan laughed then asked reluctantly, "Would you like me to come help?"

"No, it's fine. You can be spared Christmas tree duty if you promise to have those lawns mowed before Damon gets here." She gave him the sternest look she knew how, which wasn't all that stern.

"Consider it done." Keegan nodded.

"Thank you, darling. Now I'll leave you to get back to researching university." His mother chuckled. "And don't worry I will stomp loudly if I have to come ask for any help. I know how much boys like to be left alone when *researching* their future."

"You're so embarrassing. I am not looking at anything like what you're suggesting."

"That's good. I would hate to have a blind son with incredibly hairy palms." His mother laughed and walked away.

Keegan rolled his eyes. He may have found his mother's pathetic attempt at humour funny had he not been shocked by the announcement Damon was arriving.

He must know this will be a fucked-up storm of awkward.

"Fuck," Keegan mumbled to himself as he gripped his stubborn erection in his pants. Instinctively he knew that Damon's visit was going to be every bit as hard as what was in his hand.

CHAPTER TWO

Damon threw the old, worn travel bag onto the couch. He ripped open the zipper so he could start filling it with presents he had bought for Marie and Keegan. This festive trip south of the Bombay Hills to visit mother and son was not going to be easy. Truth be told, he didn't even want to go. After what had unfolded in the cabin between him and Keegan it was going to take every ounce of strength for him to try and act normal.

What the fuck is normal anyway?

That was a perplexing question for a straight man who had been used like a sex toy by another male half his age. Damon had done his upmost to dismiss what they had done, sweeping the memory like dirty dust under some invisible rug in his mind. But try as he might, he still couldn't erase the feeling of committing some sort of moral crime. As soon as he had arrived back in Auckland to his bachelor pad, he threw himself into his work and drunken nights out, getting laid with as many women as possible, desperate to try and salvage some heterosexual pride.

His pride may have taken a severe rogering but it had done some good. It had freed him of guilt. Guilt he had carried for years. Kegan's father was the only other male Damon had ever been intimate with, and he hadn't been kind about it. Damon and Matt may have remained best mates ever since those early days but Damon had always carried around a secret guilt about the way they had gotten to know each other and the way he had treated Matt. What Keegan did had help erase some of his guilt. It may not have been Matt who exacted the revenge—not that such a nice guy ever would—but his son without knowing had done a good fucking job of it with his young cock that was just as big as his father's.

To be on the receiving end of such selfish passion had been infuriating, knowing he couldn't escape Keegan's wishes. The part Damon was most ashamed of was that a buried part of him had—for the briefest of moments—enjoyed it. He hadn't enjoyed the pain, or the derogatory demands—of which there were plenty—but what he had enjoyed was the strange sense of freedom. In the strangest way, it almost felt liberating being pinned beneath Keegan's young body drilling his arse. In that most submissive of moments Damon had been laid bare with nothing left to hide.

When Damon had gone *that way* in the summer of his youth he had been an arrogant rich kid who abused his position of so-called power by encouraging Matt to do him sexual favours in return for friendship. Damon had been the one in control. The one calling the shots. Back then it had been all about getting his end away, about finding fulfilment. Only one time—the last time—he was intimate with Matt had it been tender and loving. Not love in a sexual sense, just love from one friend to another.

How the fuck can I look Marie in the eye after what I did with her son?

Damon sighed, pinching the tip of his nose with his fingers. He shuddered thinking about it. It had been hard enough trying to look Matt in the face when he had returned from the trip with Keegan to the cabin. He considered Matt family and therefore Keegan was family, which made the whole thing feel uncomfortably incestuous.

I got fucked by a boy I am supposed to be a role model to. He used to call me uncle for fuck sake!

Damon wandered to the bathroom to grab his razor and toothbrush. As he returned to his bag on the couch, he heard a series of friendly knocks at the door. A quiet rhythmic thumping that was so polite in tone he knew who it would be.

Matty.

Damon ran a hand through his hair, bracing himself to act like everything was okay. He strolled over to the door and put his game face on. "Matty," Damon said with a big smile. "Come in, brother."

Matt was in his running gear of black shorts and black t-shirt. They were damp and his limbs dripped with perspiration. These clothes had become his second skin of late as he had taken up running and gyming, desperate to get into shape since his wife, Karina, and two step-sons had left him.

Matt offered a feeble wave, puffing heavily. He walked inside and took a seat on the couch beside Damon's bag. He leant forward grabbing his knees, catching his breath.

"You look like you're having a heart attack, Matty."

"I feel like it too," Matt said, rubbing the back of his neck. He glanced down at the open bag. "Are you heading down to see Keegan and Marie?"

Damon walked into the open plan kitchen. "Yep. I am heading down this evening." He grabbed a glass from under the sink, holding it up in the air. "Fancy a water, old man?"

"Fuck yes," Matt heaved out. He lay back into the couch, his breathing slowly returning to normal levels.

The way Matt was sprawled out in his gym gear made him look just how he did back in high school days when all he ever woe was baggy black clothing. He still had those sleepy blue eyes and pale skin. His black hair was no longer shaggy and aside from the specks of grey on his side burns, Matt still looked the same after all these years. Matthew Andrews may now be a successful accountant running his own firm, living in an executive house in their home suburb of Port Jackson but in Damon's eyes, Matt would always be the lovable lad from *poverty peak*.

"Here you go," Damon said, extending his hand out to pass Matt the tall glass of water. He nestled down in a chair across from where his mate was sitting. Matt gulped down the water greedily, drinking the entire lot. "Looks like you needed that," Damon said.

Matt wiped his quenched lips. "Sure did. I'm absolutely shattered."

"I guess you are getting old," Damon teased.

"Ha. We're the same age in case you had forgotten. Thirty-seven."

"Yes, but you're six months older than me, Matty. It makes quite a difference." Damon grinned.

"Wow." Matt rolled his eyes. "Six whole months."

"Anyway, why are you still trying to kill yourself with all this fucking running."

"I'm trying to lose the last of my fat." Matt lifted his shirt up and patted his sweaty tummy, which was not fat at all.

"What are you talking about," Damon exclaimed. "You're not fat. You're nice and normal."

"The goal is to try and get myself some abs. I would like to say I had a six pack at least once in my life before I died. And not the kind that I keep in the fridge."

"You don't need abs. You're fine just the way you are." Damon didn't understand Matt's obsession with needing a defined stomach.

"Considering I'm a soon to be divorcee on the wrong side of thirty, I think I am gonna need to look better than just fine if I want to meet anyone." Matt shook his head. "Ideally, I'd like to end up with a body like you."

"Matty, it's gonna take more than just running around the domain to get like this. You gotta be religious with your workouts and stop eating so much shit food." He gave his pal a playful wink. "And figure out a way to inherit my genes."

"There isn't much I can do about changing my gene pool." Matt tipped back the glass to feed his mouth the last remaining drips.

"You don't need to change your gene pool. You don't even need to have a body like mine. You have something even better."

Matt put the glass down and frowned at Damon. "What's that?"

"A fat wallet and pockets full of real estate," Damon said plainly. "You have money, Matty! You don't need to look like a fucking movie star as well."

"Ha—" Matt chomped down on his own laughter. "I

ain't gonna have that much if Karina decides to try and get at my assets. She could get the house and half of everything."

"Do you really think she will?" Damon knew this was something his mate worried about, but after years of knowing Karina she didn't strike him as the type of person to take Matt to the cleaners. Besides, the woman had her own career and money, not to mention she had moved back to her native England. Getting a slice of Matt's financial pie seemed more hassle than it was worth. "Even if she does take half of everything, you're hardly going to be broke are you?" He shot Matt a condescending glare. "Are you?" he prodded.

"I guess not," Matt mumbled.

"You'll be fine, mate. You're the most resilient fucker I know."

"It's not the money I'm worried about." Matt sighed. "It's being on my own again. It's been so long since I've been single... I'm not used to it."

This was true. Matt had been with Karina eight years. Since dating Marie at university, Matt had never been without a girlfriend for more than a few weeks. This past six months was the longest time he had ever been without a partner. Damon on the other hand enjoyed being single. He was so accustomed to his selfish life he couldn't fathom the thought of sharing it, whereas Matt couldn't handle the idea of not having anyone to share his life with.

Damon felt terrible for his best mate not being able to see Karina's kids. He had helped raise both boys and even though he wasn't their biological father, he had certainly treated them like they were his own. It was a sore point. After breaking up with Marie and returning to Auckland, Matt had never forgiven himself for losing contact with Keegan. The decision may have seemed sensible at the time to a barely turned twenty-year-old with big dreams, but Damon knew that it was one that Matt had grown to regret more and more as the years had gone by.

It was *this* decision and snowballing regret where Damon had come in to act as a male role model for Keegan. Marie's family loathed Matt and he never tried standing up for himself to try and prove them wrong about any of their unflattering notions about him. As much as Damon loved his best mate, Matt was a chicken shit. He didn't rock the boat and he kept his distance, scared to make a scene. After a couple years of barely seeing his own son, it wasn't the fear of making a scene that kept Matt away but his embarrassment for not trying harder.

This is where Damon stepped up to the plate. He had made a promise to Matt when they became friends that he would always stand by him. Through right and wrong. While Matt was busy studying, getting on with life in Auckland, Damon offered to visit Marie and see how Keegan was doing. Matt was grateful and accepted Damon's offer. The visits became a regular thing and soon he was driving down every few months to see how Marie and Keegan were getting on.

Marie's family were nice people at heart and were nothing but lovely to Damon, but then they knew Damon came from a *decent* upbringing and even when Matt had achieved his own wealth and good-standing they never saw him more than the trashy kid Marie made the biggest mistake of her life with.

"Look, mate. You'll be fine. Being single isn't all that bad," Damon said soothingly. "You'll be able to come out with me. I'll be your wingman." He raised his eyebrows, trying to get an excited reaction out of Matt. "We will have a fucking blast."

"You reckon?"

"Yeah, man. For sure." Damon got to his feet, picked up Matt's empty glass and walked towards the kitchen. "Trust me, Matty. You'll be fine."

"Yeah, I guess you're right."

"Of course, I'm right." Damon put the glass in the sink, glancing back towards his friend.

"Maybe if Keegan decides to move up up he can join us," Matt said, sounding hopeful.

Hearing Keegan's name made Damon's arsehole twitch.

I don't think your son is going to be joining us in the hunt for women.

Damon forced up a smile. "Maybe. But do you really think an eighteen-year-old is going to want to hit the town with his dad?"

"I used to hang out a bit with my dad at that age."

"To be fair, Matty, your dad is one cool cat and you had no fucking mates 'till you met me."

Matt laughed. "Yeah, he is one cool cat for sure. Speaking of which I get the luxury of having Christmas lunch with him tomorrow. I just hope he doesn't try and bring a date."

"Has Glen been chasing the old girls down at the tavern again?"

"Like a greyhound chasing a rabbit."

Damon laughed. "That old bastard gets more action than me."

"I don't think anyone gets as much as action as you." Matt focused his bright blue eyes on Damon. "Have you got any favourites so far this month? I reckon you should start releasing a calendar of your conquests."

"Uh… no. It's been a quiet month on that front," Damon said, ignoring the joke. Images of Keegan naked in his arms blazed his mind. He cringed trying to dismantle the vision as a hot stab of lust went through him.

"Maybe you're finally growing up," Matt said.

"Fuck, I hope not. That might encourage the grey hairs to start growing."

"You already colour your hair so maybe they have."

"Piss off," Damon chuckled. "I don't dye my hair."

Matt wagged his head. "Anyway, I better head off and continue getting this Greek God body I'm after." He stood up and made his way towards the door. "Merry Christmas and I'll come see you when you get back, okay?"

"Sure. Merry Christmas, Matty."

"Oh, and Damon?" Matt poked his head back in the door.

"Yeah?"

"I know it's not your responsibility but if you can…

could you please try and convince Keegan to move up. I think it would be good for him... and me." Matt smiled softly, a look that was almost painfully sad. He waved and disappeared out the door.

"Fuck sake," Damon muttered to himself. He knew he would have to do his best to convince Keegan to move up. It was really the only reason he was even heading down. It would make Matt the happiest guy alive if Keegan were to move closer. And Damon wanted only good things for his best mate—even if the best thing was one incredibly fucking awkward situation for Damon.

CHAPTER THREE

The summer sun shone down with menacing delight, scorching the land as if it were a savoury scone. The breeze coming in off the Tasman Sea was insignificant and offered little relief to the humidity in the air. As Keegan drove along, he could hear the melted and sticky tar squirting beneath his tires.

He was not looking forward to mowing the lawns if the day stayed hot like this. If he was being sensible he would have mowed them before going to visit Liam, but then Keegan wasn't sensible. Not when it came to Liam. Nothing got in the way or came before his best friend and secret crush. After his night spent with Damon, Keegan was under no illusion now as to which direction his cock pointed. It pointed towards men. Especially men called Liam Corrigan.

This self-knowledge was a relief and a concern at the same time. The relief came from no longer being sexually confused. The concern stemmed from feeling on the outer with his friends. Liam, Skippy and Tony all chased after girls and Keegan knew in his heart of hearts he would never date girls again. It was a part of his life that was closed. A chapter that had come to an end after returning from his trip with Damon and breaking up with Tess.

He was exhilarated about what lay ahead but he was scared what his mates would think if they ever found out. And this is where the pain of an aching heart came into it. The only way he could ever have Liam was if he told Liam about himself. But then he knew that ran the risk of Liam taking things badly.

Would he disown me as a friend?

Keegan hoped not. Liam was a nice guy. The best guy. He wasn't narrowminded but how would he feel finding out that his best mate had the hots for him? That his best mate had imagined a hundred different ways of fucking him? That his best mate had even snuck a pair of his freshly worn underwear and pressed them to his face to jack off with.

Fuck I'm weird. Who does that?

Keegan cringed remembering the incident. He liked Liam so much that he would stoop to any level to have a piece of him. Even if the *level* was a warm, musty smell staining Liam's underwear.

Liam had never done or said anything that remotely indicated he was into guys. Girls loved him and he was crazy about them in return. The closest Keegan had ever gotten to sharing his truth with Liam was the night of his birthday when they were drunkenly sprawled out on the roadside together; he had copped a feel of Liam's crotch and left him the brightest love bite in history on his sexy neck.

Liam had just gone with the flow, offering himself to Keegan as a birthday wish. The best wish he could ever have been granted. The problem was Liam was so drunk that he didn't even remember it happening. The next day when Liam had showed Keegan the bright red love bite on his neck, Keegan didn't dare enlighten his mate who was responsible for the unsightly mark. He just played dumb and felt grateful for such a lucky escape from a premature outing.

It had taken a whole week for the love bite to fade. Liam had had to hide it whenever he left the house, wearing high collared shirts buttoned all the way up, sweating profusely in the heat of summer. Each time Keegan spotted it, he would have tingle of joy knowing it was his mouth that had planted such eye-catching passion on Liam's smooth neck.

Keegan could see farmland in the distance, which meant he was getting close to his destination. Liam lived with his parents on the edge of town just before suburbia gave way to grassy paddocks. The Corrigan family home was only a few years old. It was made of deep-red bricks and had four large bedrooms. The windows were tinted; the type that acted like a mirror on the outside to give the occupants the best sort of privacy. Being so far out of town meant they had a large section. Liam's mum had spent a small fortune turning it from a muddy mess into a well-established garden to appear older than its young age.

The huge yard reminded Keegan of his father's house in Port Jackson just north of Auckland. He had visited it once four years ago—the last time he saw his father—and was blown away by how beautiful it was. The mini mansion was situated right across the road from the beach and as lovely as the home was, it was nothing in comparison to the two-and-a-half-acre section it was built on. A small part of him was curious to go visit his dad again one day just to explore the maze of gardens, bush and lawns.

When Liam's house came into view, Keegan slowed down and parked his car up outside. A sense of relief came over him to see Liam's parents vehicles were not in the driveway.

I will get him all to myself!

Keegan slammed his car door shut and raced towards the front door, excited to lay eyes on his sexy best friend. He didn't bother knocking and walked right in. Keegan was so focused on seeing his pal he didn't even see Liam's older brother Joel in the hallway 'till he walked straight into him.

"Shit. Sorry, Joel." Keegan took a step backwards. "I didn't see you there."

Joel cast him a stormy glare. "I guess that happens when you barge into peoples homes without knocking." He rubbed his hands down the front of his white singlet that showed off his impressive arm muscles. He glanced over his shoulder towards Liam's bedroom. "If you're looking for my loser brother, you'll find him tossing off in his room." Joel pointed with his finger. "Off ya go," he said arrogantly.

"Umm, thanks," Keegan said, feeling uncomfortable. Joel was a slightly shorter version of Liam but more muscular. He came equipped with the Corrigan male traits that his father and younger brother both had. Dark hair, baby blue eyes and handsome faces with finely etched cheek bones. While Liam and his father were nice guys, Joel was just an arrogant prick who deserved a punch in the face, Keegan thought. He stepped around the frosty Joel and made his way towards Liam's bedroom and tapped on the door.

"Yep," Liam hollered back.

"It's Keegan."

"Come in, bro."

Keegan opened the door and stepped inside the curtain-pulled room. Immediately his nostrils were filled with a whiff of sweaty unwashed clothes. The room was stale and in desperate need of fresh air, but Keegan didn't mind. After all, this was Liam's smell and he would wear it as cologne if he could.

Liam sat shirtless on the edge of his bed, wearing track pants and white socks. He hitched his eyebrows up at Keegan and smiled.

"What you up to?" Keegan asked, sitting beside him.

"Fuck all. I just finished doing my workout." Liam pointed to the weights on the floor. It seemed he was keen to catch up with his older brother in the muscles department. He raised his arm up and flexed his bicep, giving it a small peck. "These guns are loaded and ready to fire."

Keegan laughed. "And who will you be shooting at?"

Liam's lip curled into a smile. "You!" He leant across, grabbed hold and tried to bury Keegan's face into his armpit.

Keegan burst out laughing, *reluctantly* pushing his friend away. He rubbed his face but it didn't wipe away his giddy smile.

"How come Joel's here?" Keegan asked, spouting out the first thing he could think of.

"He had a fight with his flatmate or something so he's moved back home 'till he finds a new place."

"True," Keegan mumbled.

"Yeah. Hardly surprising though. The arsehole fights with everyone," Liam said bluntly. He bent forward tugging on one of his white socks. Suddenly he lurched up, clutching his side. "Fuck that's sore still."

"What's that?"

"My side. I think I pulled a muscle yesterday at training." Liam said, rubbing his flank just above his hip.

"Ouch."

"Yeah. It ain't made me a cripple or nothing but it's a bit tender." Liam scooted backwards and rest back into his pillows, stretching his long legs down the length of the bed.

"Would you like me to kiss it better for you?" Keegan joked, secretly wishing he could kiss Liam better.

"Aww, what a sweetie," Liam said in a half-giggle.

"That's me... a sweetie."

Liam gave him a cursory glance. "I bumped into Tess in town yesterday. She told me you two had split." He stared at Keegan with a look that was hard to decipher. "Why didn't you tell me you had broken up?"

"I haven't really had a chance to tell you," Keegan lied. He had purposely not said anything, hoping he could pretend to be one of the boys just a bit longer under the guise of having a girlfriend.

Liam narrowed his eyes, suspicion slipping in. "You've seen me nearly every day since your birthday and she said that you broke up with her after your trip away with your uncle."

"Damon's not my uncle," Keegan snapped a little too abruptly, not wanting any family tie chained to the man who had taken his virginity. "And yeah. We split up when I got back."

"Then why didn't you say anything?"

"I didn't want to bother you with it."

"Keegan, I'm your best mate, you're supposed to bother me with shit like that."

"I guess." Keegan felt himself blushing.

"So how come you broke up?" Liam asked.

"Lots of reasons."

Oh, and she fucked another guy, the same guy I ended up fucking.

An awkward pause drifted in the room, forcing Keegan to elaborate "We'd been together a while and with school ending it just felt like maybe a fresh start was what we both needed."

"That makes sense," Liam said. "And you're okay about it?"

"Yeah, I'm fine. I think it had been coming for a while."

"Are you sure?" Liam frowned.

"Yes, Liam. I'm fine." Keegan smiled at his best mate, glad for his concern.

"Good. Because if you're not then you can tell me, you know?"

"I know."

Liam stuck his tongue out slightly, wetting his bottom lip. "You can tell me anything. You know that right?"

Keegan's stomach clenched. "I know I can," he croaked in a whisper.

"And there isn't anything else you want to tell me?"

Keegan shook his head. He began thinking the worst, wondering if Liam knew his secret. "I can't think of anything else. Why's that?"

"It was just something Tess said to me. That's all."

"What did she say?" Suddenly Keegan found himself sweating, worried what the hell Tess could have said.

Liam didn't answer.

"Tell me what she said?" Keegan glared, waiting for an answer.

Liam tilted his head, thinking it over. "I'll tell you if you kiss my sore spot better like you said."

"Excuse me?"

"Kiss me better and I'll tell you what she said." Liam flicked his eyes down towards his hip. "You did offer."

"Umm, and I was joking," Keegan groaned. "I'm not kissing you. You're all sweaty from your workout."

"Yeah, but I don't smell bad. Promise." Liam circled his finger around his skin where the injury was. "One little kiss and I'll tell you what Tess told me."

"Don't be a dick. Just tell me what she said." Keegan pretended to sound more irritated than he really was, secretly wanting to kiss his friend even if it was just a quick peck above his hip.

Liam's eyes smouldered, daring Keegan to kiss him.

Keegan swallowed a moan. "So if I kiss you better,

you'll tell me what Tess said?"

Liam nodded, smiling.

"Okay then, egg." Keegan lay down and placed his face by Liam's hip. He gently kissed his friend's damp skin. "There. I kissed it better. Now tell me."

"I don't think you got the right spot," Liam said tauntingly. "I think you should kiss all the way up just to make sure you get everywhere."

Keegan felt his groin buzz with excitement at what he was being asked to do. He knew Liam was taking the piss and having a laugh but it didn't stop him finding the moment slightly erotic. Thankfully not erotic enough to spring a boner. "All the way up?" Keegan asked.

"Yep. From here to here," Liam said, running his finger from his hip to just below his armpit.

"Fuck sake," Keegan muttered, pretending to find the situation funny. He pressed his lips to Liam's warm hip again and trailed tiny kisses up his flank, dabbing his lips along his mate's salty skin. *Fuck you taste good.* Keegan went all the way up, stopping only when his cheek collided with the damp hair in Liam's armpit. "I kissed you better—all the way up—now tell me what Tess said."

"Well done, Andrews." Liam smirked, looking impressed. "That was a little bit sexy. I almost wanted you to keep going."

Keegan blushed. "Really?"

"What do you think?" Liam said, not giving away if he were being sarcastic or not.

Keegan stared back, searching beneath the surface of the moment.

Is this my chance to make a move?

Liam crossed his arms and squinted, breaking the questionable moment.

Keegan quickly spat out, "So what did Tess say?"

Liam took a deep breath like he was about to deliver earth shattering news, "Absolutely... fucking nothing." He burst out laughing.

Keegan sat up and whacked Liam in the leg. "Then

why'd ya make me kiss you like that, dick?"

Liam unfolded his arms and shrugged. "Dunno. I guess I just wanted to see if you'd do it." He scuttled forward to the edge of the bed, planting his feet on the floor and stood up.

Keegan took advantage of his mate having his back to him. He admired Liam's defined back muscles and firm rump that prodded the seat of his pants.

Liam walked over to a small bookcase against the far wall of his room, he grabbed his laptop that sat on the top shelf. He strolled back and sat down next to Keegan, switching the laptop on. "Okay. That whole kiss thing was just a joke, but I do have a serious request. And if you're game enough to kiss me like you just did, then I'm hoping you're game enough to help me with what I'm about to ask you."

"This sounds interesting."

"It is interesting... but it's a little bit gay." Liam coughed nervously.

"Gayer than what I just did?" Keegan felt his stomach drop to his toes.

Liam nodded. He typed his password into the computer to bring up an internet search page. "Fuck, bro. This is kinda shame. But remember me telling you about that website... Crashing Hearts?"

Keegan vaguely recalled Liam showing him it. It had heavy material from memory. While Keegan got off on sadistic attitudes, Liam loved porn that was sadistic in any sense and preferably to the extreme. "The one with people being tied up and whipped and shit?"

"Yeah," Liam said in a bland tone. "But it isn't all about that. They have a whole heap of other stuff. Amateur videos, online diaries. Mild to wild."

"Okay. And what does that have to do with me?"

"I've started uploading my own videos. Talking about some of the shit I've done with chicks around here. Stuff like that."

"You what? You're online, telling people what you do

25

and who with?"

Liam laughed. "Settle down, Captain Sensible." He shot Keegan a warm smile. "I don't say real names and I don't always tell the truth."

"So you have made an online video diary where you spout off a bunch of lies based on wet dreams you've had?"

"Got it in one." Liam winked. "Fuck. If I told them the truth they'd hardly be impressed, would they?"

"I dunno. You score quite a lot."

"Yeah, but none of the girls around here are up for anything too kinky," Liam said bitterly. "You know what I mean."

"True." Keegan didn't know what he meant.

"After I posted a few videos, I started getting messages from people. Saying they liked my stories and thought I was hot and sexy."

Keegan nodded. Liam would get messages like that. He was sex on legs.

"So I kept them happy and started flashing my abs at the end of each video." He tapped his stomach. "Anyway, I have moved on to posting videos of me working out. Letting them watch me do sit ups, press ups, lift weights. Shit like that."

"And they like this?" Keegan added shock to his voice. He didn't hold it against anyone for wanting to watch his best friend work up a sweat.

"Yeah, man. They go fucking crazy for it. But I noticed it wasn't so much the girls getting all worked up, it was all the guys."

"Gay guys?"

"No Keegan. Straight men," Liam said sarcastically. "Of course gay guys, doofus."

"Okay, and?"

"One of the features of the site is you can have premium accounts. Ones where people have to pay to view your videos."

Keegan felt dizzy. He knew where this was going. "So you have started a premium account?"

"Sure have. Take a look." Liam loaded up his accounts home page. The screen became filled with photos of him shirtless in a variety of workout positions. One shot in particular was especially horny, Liam sitting on a chair in nothing but a pair of tight briefs with his legs spread open wide.

Okay as soon as I get home I am signing up for this page.

Keegan flicked his eyes to the username so he could look it up later when he got home. "Your name is Kurt?"

"Yep. Kurt Knox." Liam laughed at the name. "I thought it had a certain... quality to it." He smiled like he was proud of himself. "What do you think?"

"Sounds sort of porn starrish, I guess." Keegan looked across at the short bio Liam had made about himself.

Hi Everyone. My name is Kurt. I'm a kiwi guy with a wild appetite for anything to do with sex. Mild to wild. When I'm not working a shift at the fire station I like to post photos and videos here of me working out and sharing naughty stories. Check out some of my free pics and if you like what you see you can sign up for my pay to view videos and you might just sneak a peek at my 9 inch cock.

Keegan burst out laughing.

"What's so funny?" Liam asked.

"You saying you're a fireman with a nine-inch cock."

"I can't just say 'oh I work in my mum's bookstore' that ain't exactly sexy."

Keegan looked down at Liam's crotch. "And the nine inches?"

"Okay, I may have rounded up a bit." Liam smirked, groping himself.

"Yeah, by four inches."

"Piss off." Liam nudged him. "I'm bigger than that."

Keegan was dying to ask Liam how big exactly but that felt like crossing a line. "I'll take your word for it."

"Maybe it does look like nine inches though. They say the camera adds ten pounds." Liam waggled his eyebrows.

"That they do." Keegan grinned. "So how much

money have you made so far?"

"Only fifty bucks," Liam sighed.

"Better than nothing."

"Yeah, but if I had hotter videos then I could charge more and make more money."

"And you want me to help?"

"If you think you can handle it," Liam said cautiously. "You can say no and I'll understand but anything we make I'd go halves with you, bro. Straight down the middle."

Keegan felt his throat constrict. "Why me?"

"You're my best mate, aren't you? Who else would I ask. And you're a good-looking guy," Liam said matter-of-factly.

"You think?"

Liam rolled his eyes. "Yes, Keegan. You're attractive. There I said it." He leant across and ran a hand through Keegan's hair. "With ya cute little blond curls and those sweet, pretty brown eyes," he said in a girly voice. "Not to mention your sexy tan." Liam dropped his hand to Keegan's forearm, stroking seductively with his fingers. "Your milkshake brings all the boys to the yard."

Keegan laughed, flicking Liam's hand away. "Thank you." Liam's compliment felt so fucking good, he almost thought he could fly home.

"So you'll help me?"

"Yeah, why not." Keegan rubbed his hands down the legs of his pants. He would love to do stuff with Liam even if it was pretend. He just hoped his true desires didn't come out and expose a very real attraction. "What sort of stuff did you have in mind?"

"I will have a think about it," Liam said. "But the more we do the more money we can make." He hitched his eyebrows up at Keegan. "Whataya say, big boy?"

"Isn't that you, Mr nine-inches?"

Liam looked him up and down. "I spose mine would be bigger."

Keegan coughed. "Whatever."

"I'm only joking, bro. For all I know you could have

an anaconda in ya pants." Liam cocked an eyebrow. "Unlikely. But I guess I'll find out."

"Excuse me? How far are you planning this to go?" Keegan asked, trying to sound scared at the idea of two men doing stuff together.

"Don't get too worried. I ain't exactly expecting us to nosh one another off and bum fuck."

"Okay." Keegan felt disappointed.

"Sweet, bro." Liam nodded enthusiastically. "I guess we will both be busy doing the family thing tomorrow for Christmas but what about Boxing Day? Will you be free to come around then and help me out?"

"Yes," Keegan answered a little too quickly. "I think so." He would be making sure he was free come hell or high water.

CHAPTER FOUR

Matt sat down with a beer on the comfy sofa, staring around the ridiculously large lounge that felt too big for just one person. When he had bought this waterfront home for himself, Karina and her two boys, it had been as close to perfect as he could have hoped. It felt like a victory. He had grown up at the south end of town in what had then been known as *poverty peak*. A small collection of streets that housed former state homes where the seaside suburb's poor were congregated.

A lot had changed since the nineties though. Poverty peak was now every bit as expensive as the rest of Port Jackson. Progress had swarmed in like a flesh-eating disease, stripping away the old weatherboard homes and their poor inhabitants, replacing them with overpriced apartments and affluent young families.

Matt's father was one of the cash-starved residents pushed out when the house he had rented for nearly twenty years was auctioned off. Had it happened only a year or two later, Matt would have been in a position to buy the house for his father to stay in, but unfortunately that had not been the case. Instead, Matt bought his father a smaller, more affordable unit closer to the centre of the village. Even though it wasn't the old family home, it had been such a privilege to give something back to the man who had sacrificed so much for him growing up. The day he handed his father the keys to the unit, telling him he didn't have to worry about rent anymore, was the only time he had seen his father cry aside from the death of Ricky, Matt's big brother.

Of course, his father had insisted on paying something, so Matt set up a savings account and had his dad pay a small amount into it each week. He didn't need the money but it made his father feel better that he wasn't being given a complete handout.

Matt's own home reminded him of the house Damon grew up in. It wasn't quite as large as the Harris household but it was every bit as grand. Matt and Karina however had never kept it to grand levels. Matt and his ex-wife didn't agree on much but one thing they did agree on was letting a home look *lived in*. Neither of them had any interest residing in a place that resembled a show home.

They had loved the house for its nice furnishings and its unrivalled sea views. A short stroll across the road and they could step foot on the beach It had been perfect for Karina's boys, Mason and Lance, they had become regular beach bums, spending everyday they could going for a swim or boogie boarding. Mason had been three and Lance five when Matt met their mother during his time working in London. Karina—an accountant also—worked in the same firm and after a couple months of swapping flirty looks a whirlwind romance began and in no time Matt and Karina were inseparable. By the end of that year they were married and eventually came to New Zealand.

He embraced the family role wholeheartedly and deep down he knew this stemmed from the guilt of not trying harder to stay in touch with Keegan after he had split from Marie. At first, the marriage with Karina was great and everything was exciting but after a few years it became evident they were different people and wanted different things. Finally, six months ago Karina made the decision to return to London. Overnight Matt went from a noisy house with a wife and two kids to being all on his own—again. In his twenties, he had gone from relationship to relationship but at thirty-seven he felt scared to go out and explore the dating pond.

Damon had tried to talk him into using Tinder but he didn't like the sound of meeting someone based on the swipe of a thumb. Where was the romance in that? There wasn't any. And romance was something Matt craved. He wasn't like Damon who would fuck anything that moved, and if it didn't move then Damon would probably push it just so he could fuck it. That wasn't Matt's style; he wanted to give his partners more than just one night and orgasms.

The last time he had been single he was still in his twenties and although he never possessed the vitality guys like Damon had, Matt had always managed to have his own share of admirers. He just hoped whatever it was he had going for him back then was still going for him. It wasn't going to be easy to get out there and mingle. He was an introvert in an extroverted world—a terribly lonely thing at times.

Aside from the dark nights of the soul brought on by an empty and lonely heart, Matt was bored. So fucking bored. The boredom of coming home to a dead house had been making him stay late at the office. He had been running his own business advisory service in Port Jackson for the past two years and had staff to do the nitty gritty work but in a bid to keep his mind busy he was more than happy to do this bottom-feeder work.

He had even resorted to running and exercise as an outlet for his boredom. As much as it was to try and get into shape it was also an excuse to drop in and see Damon. Matt would drive all the way into the city just to run around the domain until he was ready to visit his best mate. He felt bad for dropping in unannounced nearly every day, but Damon insisted he didn't mind. Matt hated the idea of being some sort of burden but seeing Damon's face always made him feel better. The guy was like medication designed to reduce pain and sadness.

Sometimes when he was alone on days like this, Matt wondered if this was karma coming back to bite him in the arse for being such a selfish idiot when he and Marie broke up and he left behind a life with Keegan. He could say he felt forced into the decision—Marie's family had been plenty horrible to him—but Matt knew the truth. He had wanted to break away. Chase his dreams that had felt lost forever when he became a father at just nineteen.

These dreams had been more than dreams. They were a twisted sort of revenge. A way to prove to the arrogant pricks here in Port Jackson that he was every bit as good as they were. After leaving Marie he came back and finished his study, got good grades, got that great internship, saved up the money to go overseas travelling and establish a career in a top accounting firm. He did it all. He had achieved his dream. His success.

Yet, sitting as he was, alone in a fancy house, he couldn't help but wonder if his definition of success had been all wrong. He had helped raise another man's kids while neglecting to ever get to know his own child. Matt had resented his mother when she abandoned him and his father, but at least she had waited 'till he turned 18. She didn't leave before he was even a year old and still in nappies.

Matt sipped back on his beer, washing down his guilt.

You fucking deserve feeling like this Matthew Andrews, you arsehole.

He wiped his nose as he felt the start of tears tingling in his eye sockets. He felt bad sending Damon down to do his dirty work. He tried reassuring himself that this was the best option. Damon knew Keegan. It probably wasn't a stretch to say that Damon had been more a father to the boy than Matt ever had been. He prayed that Damon could convince Keegan to at least come back for a holiday. Maybe then they could get to know each other a little better.

Matt knew Marie's family would have done nothing but bad mouth him through the years and other than a handful of short visits he was never there to defend himself against their slander. But Matt had Damon on his team and he knew Damon would do anything in his power to help him out. Aside from his own father, Damon was the only person Matt knew he could truly rely on and who would never betray him.

I'm counting on you buddy.

The phone suddenly blared through the house, startling Matt from his pity party. It rang and rang with a loud volume of urgency. He took a moment to steady himself so that he didn't sound too sad or drunk when he answered. He swaggered his way to the kitchen and found the phone laying on the bench.

"Hello," Matt said, doing his best to sound together.

The sunniest voice he had ever known answered back, one he hadn't heard for far too long. "Heeeeey, Matty Pie. Guess who?"

Matt laughed, instantly happier. "Jason!"

"Got it in one," Jason said. "How is my poverty peak sister?"

"Brother," Matt corrected.

"Whatever," Jason dismissed. "What are you doing right this instant?"

Matt looked around the quiet kitchen. "Nothing much."

"Good so we can have a drink together."

"Umm, I would love to but I can't exactly go jump on a plane and fly to Sydney just this moment."

"No, silly. I'm home. In Aotearoa. I'm at my Mum's place."

Matt felt his mood skyrocket. "You are?"

"Mmm hmm, girl. Get your best frock on cos I'm coming over. I have BIG news!"

"You do?"

"Yip. I'm coming RIGHT now to this ridiculously flash house of yours my sister has told me all about, so get your arse ready for a big night." Jason paused and giggled. "Okay, that probably sounded all sorts of wrong. I don't mean I am going to fuck you. What I meant was—"

"It's okay, Jason." Matt laughed. "I know what you mean."

"Phew. Thank god. I'd hate to get a poor boy's hopes up. See you soon, doll," Jason said, followed by a kissy sound before he hung up.

Matt knew he better prepare himself because he would soon go from a lonely house of one to entertaining a friend whose personality was as loud as a crowded stadium.

CHAPTER FIVE

The sun beat down mercilessly on Keegan's shirtless body as he pushed the mower over the untamed lawn in the backyard. The grass was thick, messy and a dirty-green colour, cutting it short resembled shaving Oscar the Grouch. Amidst the screaming throttling of the mower, nothing could come close to drowning out the filthy thoughts in his head about making a video with Liam.

Even if they didn't touch each other and it was just a mutual wank of some kind, it would still be fucking hot. As he pushed the lawnmower around in wobbly lines, Keegan's mind mulled over endless questions.

Will Liam get naked? Will he ask me to be naked? I wonder how he strokes his cock?

In Keegan's fantasies Liam's cock always spurt thick white streams of spunk... usually all over his face. He imagined the crown of his mate's dick to be thick and glistening, a beautiful member worthy of being attached to a king. A king who could surge pleasure like a cresting wave and ravish the shoreline of Keegan's body. A king who could fuck, and be fucked, like a monster. The daydream was intoxicating, so much so that he could feel the tip of his dick leaking drops of precum from the anticipation. He knew that as soon as he finished the lawns the first thing he would be doing was have a shower and taking care of the rigid need within his pants.

Just as Keegan spun the mower around at the final strip of shaggy lawn, he lifted his chin and saw his mother standing on the deck, holding a glass of wine. She waved her free arm excitedly, a large smile painted across her face. Keegan wondered the reason for her looking so happy, then he saw the reason appear behind her. His throat tightened.

Damon!

The sweat on his body turned cold at the sight of the man who had claimed his virginity. Damon stood stoically, his arms folded, wearing a pair of white shorts and a black polo shirt. His eyes were shielded behind a pair of black shades and his tanned strong limbs almost glimmered in the sunlight. His dark-brown hair was cut shorter than normal, making him look even better in Keegan's opinion.

The deed they had done had gifted Keegan x-ray vision and he looked over knowing exactly what Damon's body looked like under the clothes. He bit down on his lip, trying to shake away the image of Damon's dick, which he knew hung slightly to the left when soft. Keegan turned the mower off and dropped to a squatting position pretending to tie up his shoe laces so he could hide his Liam fueled erection.

"Look who's here," Keegan's mother called out.

"I can see," Keegan replied, staying low to the ground.

"Hey, K dog," Damon said, his tone light, dry and inexpressive.

"Me and Damon are just gonna sit down for a wine. Come in and join us when you're finished, darling." Keegan's mother took a sip on her glass then turned around and led Damon inside to the lounge. Just before Damon disappeared out of sight he looked over his shoulder and snapped Keegan still staring at him. Damon quickly flicked his sun-glassed gaze away and followed Keegan's mum inside.

Keegan grabbed his crotch, begging his cock to calm down. He started up the mower again, finishing off the final strip of lawn before emptying the catcher. The late afternoon sun was beginning to dip, leaving a red tinge to the sky. *Red sky at night, shepherds delight*, Keegan thought. A rare event so close to Christmas. Christmas in New Zealand may have been a summer time affair but it usually had rotten luck, often landing on windy or rainy days.

He stayed outside a few minutes after locking up the mower in the garden shed. He took a few deep breaths, composing himself for the inevitable socialising with Damon inside. He suspected it would be a difficult task for both of them. They had not seen or spoken to each other since Damon dropped him off home following the creation of their big secret.

When Keegan walked inside he was glad to see his mum and Damon buried in one of their usual gossips, catching up about days gone by. He took the chance to go jump in the shower, get washed and put on a fresh change of clothes. When he reappeared in the lounge he was greeted by his mother who had a cold beer waiting for him.

"For you, darling," his mother said. "Thank you for doing the lawns."

Keegan hitched his eyebrows up and took a swig of the cool beer that oozed down his dry throat with medicinal smoothness.

"I was just asking Damon if he had any photos from your boys' trip away," Keegan's mother innocently said. "I was keen to see some of the hijinks you both got up to."

"We didn't get up to any," Keegan replied speedily. He quickly realised how defensive he sounded. He laughed, trying to cover up his odd response. "Just saw the lakes and mountains."

"Sounds a rather tame trip." Keegan's mother looked across at Damon.

Damon said nothing. His sunglasses shielded his eyes and whatever thoughts he was having. The man usually talked confidently, filling any room with a sense of his own importance. Not today. Not this trip.

Keegan's mum rambled on, none the wiser to the tension in the room. Any niggling suspicion he had ever had about Damon and his mother hooking up in their younger days was ruled out in that instant. She didn't seem able to see what Keegan could see. The nerves. The awkward posture. The guilt. Intimate details that Keegan could see so clearly because he and Damon had been just that. *Intimate.*

Keegan felt bad. He wanted to tell Damon it was alright. That he would never whisper a word of what happened. That he was grateful for what Damon had let him do and even more grateful for the reassurance after the deed when Keegan had broke down crying.

Ring, ring. Ring, ring.

Keegan's mum stood up and raced to the phone on the kitchen bench. The way she took a breath like she was swallowing patience meant it could only be one person. Keegan's grandmother. His mum stood there nodding her head for the duration of the short call and finally said, "Yes. Okay, Mum. I'll be there soon." She rolled her eyes and hung up the phone.

"What did Nana want?" Keegan asked.

"Apparently she has placed an online order with the supermarket in town here but forgot to click delivery and she has no way of picking it up in time." Keegan's mother groaned aloud while pulling at her blonde hair. "I swear it's moments like this I curse them living out in the country."

"I can come with you," Damon said. He shifted to get out of his seat.

"No, Damon. You stay here. I don't want you rushing around for my mum after the distance you just travelled."

"I really don't mind," Damon said, standing there looking desperate to tag along.

Keegan's mother rushed around looking for her keys. "Don't be silly, Damon. Stay here and have another drink and unwind a bit. I'm sure Keegan can keep you entertained for an hour or so."

Keegan felt his face blush. He looked across at Damon who took a deep breath and reluctantly sat back down.

"I'm off. I should be back in an hour or two. You two boys have fun." She jangled her keys in the air and rushed out the door.

Keegan smoothed his hands over the knees of his jeans. He flicked his eyes to the floor, staring at Damon's shoes, letting his gaze crawl the length of Damon's body before meeting his face with a twitchy smile. Out of nowhere, Keegan felt a familiar feeling grip his instincts. The same feeling that hurled him head-on to Damon's cock the night in the cabin. Mere seconds of being alone with his father's best mate had unleashed the same dubious desire.

"So, K dog. How have you been?" Damon asked, finally removing his sunglasses to reveal his moss-green eyes.

Keegan nodded. "Pretty good." He looked down at Damon's toned legs on display in the white shorts he was wearing. They looked sleek with sweat from his long drive in the summer heat. Keegan's heart skipped a beat and his mouth dried up wanting to quench a very different type of thirst. He wanted so badly to just lean over and touch Damon. Feel him up again the way he had the night he lost his virginity. Make the same mistake all over again.

"Have you decided what your plans are for next year?" Damon asked. His voice made Keegan raise his eyes again.

"Umm. I'm still not sure to be honest." Keegan ran a hand through his honey-coloured locks. "It's probably too late for uni now so I will probably stay here and work for a year."

"You could move up to Auckland and stay with Matty. He would love to have you stay. There is way more work to be found up in Auckland."

The mention of his father's name dampened the fire between Keegan's legs. "I guess, but that would be pretty fucking awkward to bowl on up and live with a guy I hardly know."

Damon blinked. His mouth opened and closed in a dreary line. "True. But if you came up then you would get a chance to know him better and you'll see why he is such a good sort. Honestly, your dad is one of the best people going and he would help you out as much as he could."

Keegan narrowed his eyes, casting a suspicious glare. Damon always talked his father up to him—when his mother wasn't around—but he had never tried to convince him to move up there. A part of Keegan wanted to get shitty and tell Damon to tell his father to fuck off.

Why would I want to live with a guy who never bothered to come and see me more than a small handful of times.

The pacifist in Keegan won out and he smiled. "That

would be nice but I'm not too sure." He thought how best to word his disinterest in someone who for years obviously had no interest in him. "It's not that I hate the man or anything or feel annoyed at him not being around but I think it's a bit unfair to suddenly want to get to know me now I'm all grown up."

Damon nodded like he wanted Keegan to continue.

"Mum and my grandparents raised me. They did the hard yards. Not him." Keegan felt almost rebellious for saying things that could ruffle feathers. He knew Damon would not enjoy hearing negative things said about his best mate.

Damon leant forward in the chair, resting his elbows on his knees, looking at ease for the first time. "I completely understand where you're coming from, K dog." He nodded. "Honestly, I do. But sometimes there is more to a story than we may know."

"What does that mean? Is there more to the story?"

"That really is a conversation for you and Matty to have," Damon said. He saw the way Keegan was staring back suspiciously. "I'm not saying there is anything, but it is something you should ask him ya know. Find out his reasons. He won't mind you asking. You deserve to ask whatever you like and he owes you the truth."

"I don't think I could stay with him though. That would be a bit weird. Don't you agree?"

Damon bit down on his lip thinking it over. "Hmm."

"It's you I know, Damon," Keegan said in a sweet voice. "Not my father." He could see Damon thinking over the seed he had deliberately planted.

"You're more than welcome to stay with me if you came up." Damon clasped his hands together, nodding. "You can go spend as much time with Matty as you like and if it gets too much then you are always welcome back at mine."

The idea of staying with Damon brought on all sorts of horny possibilities. Ones Damon would no doubt cringe at. "What I don't understand though, is why are you so keen on me seeing my dad after all these years. You've never tried to get me up to meet him before now."

Damon paused. His eyes spun with ideas of what to reply with. "Look. He has always wanted to see you, K dog. I was going to bring this all up my last visit but..." Damon didn't need to finish the sentence. Keegan knew what had made him trail off. "Anyway. The reason I am pushing for it so much right now is that he isn't too happy. Things are a bit sad for him, ya know."

"How come?" Keegan asked, concern slipping into his voice. "Is something wrong with him?"

"No. no. Nothing like that," Damon said. "It's just that him and Karina have split up. She moved back to London with her kids six months ago, and he's been moping about all lonely. I just think it would do him—do both of you—some good to hang out and get to know one another properly."

Keegan felt bad for his father. But not enough to commit to living with the man.

Damon continued, "I wondered if you would be keen to come back with me. Just a few days. Like I said you can stay with me if you like. Tell your mum you're coming up for New Year's Eve. It will be a rocking New Year's up there. I promise you'll have fun."

The word *fun* rolled off Damon's tongue with frisky enthusiasm. Keegan discretely locked his eyes in on Damon's bunched crotch. It was what was between Damon's legs that was the only fun Keegan had in mind. He felt like he was violating a sincere moment between them with the filthy thoughts he was brewing. "You really want me to come up?"

"Yeah, K dog. It would make Matty's fucking day."

"Okay," Keegan mumbled.

"Is that a yes?" Damon's eyes lit up excitedly. "You'll come up and visit your old man?"

"I'll think about it."

Damon smiled and quite innocently asked, "Is there anything I can do to help you decide?"

Keegan knew what he wanted to say. *Yeah. You can let me fuck you again. Fuck you a thousand times.* His inner sensible streak kept the dangerous words trapped in his mouth. All he managed was a feeble, "No. I don't think so."

"Okay. Let me know. It would be fucking primo if you do decide to come back with me." Damon stood up and proceeded to take his top off. Keegan was dumbstruck by the spontaneity Damon was showing. He admired the dark hair matted to Damon's perspiring chest. Keegan swallowed a lump of wanting in his throat. "Anyway, K dog. I am gonna go have myself a shower. Chat some more later, yeah?" He flicked his chin up and threw his damp shirt on Keegan's lap. He gave Keegan a sly look that was friendly in nature but beneath the surface said *don't fuck with me*. Damon tuned his back and walked away like he had all the control in the world.

How the fuck did that happen?

Somehow a shift of power had just happened and Keegan hadn't even seen it coming. In the blink of an eye arrogant Damon was back. He fingered Damon's damp shirt in his hands, desperate for them to make another mistake together. Last time he had been bold, driven by anger. Now the anger was gone and all he had was desire but he lacked the bravery to back it up.

Keegan heard the water pipe thrust to life. It was intoxicating knowing that only a few metres away Damon was getting undressed, about to step naked under the shower. He closed his eyes conjuring up the image. An image he knew the finer details of. The beautiful sight, musky smell and sexy taste that was Damon's manly body. He contemplated barging in and asking Damon if he could join him. Soap each other down. But he couldn't bring himself to do it. The fear of how Damon would react overcame him. Keegan groaned aloud, annoyed by his cowardice. New battle lines had been drawn and Damon was the superpower.

.

CHAPTER SIX

Matt couldn't believe what his eyes were seeing. Standing in his doorway was a bright blast from his past that he hadn't seen for far too long. Nearly ten years in fact. Jason marched inside like a storm of colour, dressed in a tight yellow shirt and lemon-coloured pants.

"Wow. You sure did well for yourself, Matty Pie," Jason said, swivelling his head and admiring the fancy home. "All that is missing is the Lamborghini you promised me."

"I promised you no such thing. You just always assumed that you would get one."

Jason eyed the clothes Matt was wearing; a plain white shirt and sleek grey pants. "It's good to see you ditched the wearing-nothing-but-black phase for good."

"Yes. And I see you ditched the PVC outfits to become the yellow wiggle."

Jason laughed and whacked Matt on the shoulder. "Good to see your wit is still as tragic as ever."

Matt motioned with his hand for Jason to follow him into the lounge. "Fancy a Christmas drink?"

"Sure. What are my options?"

"Normally I have quite a selection but I think my father has raided the liquor cabinet again so it's just beer I'm afraid."

Jason screwed his face up as he took a seat in the lounge. "If that's all you have then I'll just have to suck it up and be butch for a bit."

"Okay. Coming right up." He left Jason sitting while he quickly fetched two beers from the fridge.

"I still can't believe how you wound up living on Beaumont Boulevard." Jason shook his head. "You always said you would. I'm so proud of you."

"Said like a mother." Matt shot Jason a wink and

gulped down on the cold beer in his hand.

"Speaking of mothers. How are your parents?"

"They're both good. Mum is still with Stephanie and is living in Mt Albert. Dad lives around here just a few blocks from my place so he pops in way too much. Hence the emptied liquor cabinet."

"I see," Jason said, smiling. "Did he ever settle down again after your mother?"

"Nope. He's like a bloody tom cat though the amount he gets around."

"Oh god," Jason muttered. "At his age?"

Matt nodded. "I think his entire diet consists solely of booze and Viagra."

"I guess the man's gotta eat something," Jason said. "Even if it is lady bits."

"Nice one, Jason," Matt groaned.

"Sorry, I thought you were partial to a slice of fish pie?"

"I'm straight if that's what you mean," Matt said almost defensively. "But I don't want to think about my old man crouched down on his busted knees dining out."

Jason snorted. "Sorry. Probably not an image you want."

"Are you just back for Christmas with your Mum?"

"That was the plan originally but I am back for a little bit longer now."

"Oh, how come?" Matt frowned.

"This is my BIG news I have to tell you." Jason grinned ecstatically. "Will finally popped the question. And I said YES!" Jason stuck out his hand showing off a fancy ring on his finger.

"Wow. That's awesome news. Congratulations!"

"Thanks, girl."

"Boy," Matt corrected.

"Out of the blue he popped the question two weeks ago and since Australia is still stuck in the dark ages with the whole gay marriage thing we decided why not come back home and do the deed."

"You're talking about the wedding and not sex I hope."

"I was talking about the wedding but we will probably do the other a few times too while we're here."

Matt chuckled. "The bed is alive and well I see after so long together."

"We had quite a big interim of not being together," Jason said. He looked across at Matt who nodded to be filled in with the details. "We stayed together for about three years after I left here before splitting up. We got back together a few years later and split again and then just last year we mended the bridge—once and for all—and got back together for a third time."

"You two sound like a pin ball machine."

"Ha. I know right. I told Will he can't get rid of me that easily. I'm his boomerang for life. I'll always come back."

"Yeah, bad smells tend to do that." Matt laughed as Jason picked up a cushion he pretended to hurl at him.

"You're lucky you're in a rich house or I would throw this, but I'm too scared I'll break something I can't afford to replace."

Matt smiled at his friend. It felt good that the two of them could fit straight back into how they had always been. As he went to take a sip on his drink he was caught off guard when Jason threw the pillow anyway. It landed straight in Matt's face making him spill beer down his top and over the couch.

Jason squealed with laughter. "I'm still a good shot, Matty Pie."

Matt wiped his hands down his top, mopping up the beer stains. "Oi, dick. I thought you were worried if you broke something you couldn't afford."

"Well it hit you and you always were a cheap bitch so I don't imagine you would cost much to replace," Jason teased. "Besides, even if I did break something I'm engaged to a man who can afford to replace it."

"Well done on becoming a gold digger."

Jason waved his hand in the air. "I prefer the term

trophy wife. Well, I will be one as soon as the wedding takes place."

"When is it?"

"We haven't decided. I know its short notice but Will is coming over next week and we will have a look around and see if we can find a venue at such short notice. We both have work off till February so we can have a look around."

"I guess you could always do it poverty peak styles and have it under a tarpaulin in the backyard."

Jason laughed. "Oh god. That's what my saddo of a sister—love her to pieces—did." He smiled at Matt. "But to be honest I wouldn't care even if we did do that. As long as I'm with Will I don't care where it takes place."

Matt felt jealous at hearing this. He envied his pal being so settled.

"I'll let you know when we finalise the details. I expect you to be there, Matty Pie."

"Of course. I wouldn't miss it for the world."

"Good I want you looked all dashing and turning heads to make our Sydney friends drool over the kiwi talent."

Matt blushed at the compliment. "I don't think I'll be turning many heads."

"Probably not because all eyes will be on me," Jason said. He winked at Matt. "But after they are done with me and Will they won't stop looking at you." He looked at Matt's reluctance to accept the compliment. "You look great Matty. You almost look as young as me." Jason smirked. "You still have that gorgeous complexion and against all odds you haven't ended up a tubby monster like your dad."

"Yeah, I managed to dodge that bullet and keep all my hair so far," Matt said, pulling at his black hair.

"Anyway, enough with the flattery. Based on my Facebook stalking I gather you have a family so where's the wife and kids?"

"Gone," Matt said bluntly.

"Gone?"

"Yep. Gone. And Mason and Lance weren't my kids." Matt sculled back on his beer. He saw Jason looking at him wanting a further explanation. "Karina and I met while I was in London and she followed me over with her two boys. We were together about eight years but split up in June."

"Sorry to hear about that." Jason shot him a sympathetic smile.

"It's okay. We are better off apart but I still miss them all like crazy."

"What about Keegan. That's your son's name, isn't it?"

"Sure is," Matt said. He sat up excitedly in his chair. "He's eighteen now can you believe it? Damon is down there at the moment visiting him and Marie and Keegan might come back for a holiday with him."

"Damon," Jason said in a dreamy voice. "Does he still look like sex on legs?"

Matt laughed. "I don't know."

"Well, does he? You're the one who had sex with him. You should know."

Matt cringed. Him and Damon had never ventured down that path again since that sultry summer of 1997. It was a topic they had never even spoke of and until Jason blurted it out loud Matt had all but forgotten it. "He still looks good if that's what you mean."

Jason narrowed his eyes and looked over like he was enjoying a scandalous topic. "Did you two ever do *it* again."

"Nope. Never," Matt said flatly.

"Really? Not even once? Not even a drunken brojob?"

Matt laughed out of nerves. "Nope. Nothing. We just stayed mates and moved on."

"Interesting," Jason said. He chewed down on his bottom lip. "So it was just a little phase you were going through, was it?"

"I guess so," Matt said. He wished they could change the topic but he knew that Jason would only grab hold of it even more if he told Jason to drop it.

"Okay don't bust my nuts about this but I just thought you were soooo into him that you were bisexual at least and would have done more." Jason looked across like he was interviewing a murder suspect. "If not with Damon then at least with another dude."

Matt coughed up a smile and sculled back on his beer, wishing he could hide from the shameful topic. "Nope. When it comes to that sort of thing I was a bit of a one hit wonder you could say."

Jason laughed. "Better to have one hit than none at all. And even better to have that one hit with Damon Harris."

"Fancy another beer?" Matt quickly asked, steering the conversation to safer territory.

"Not just yet. I've barely dented this one." Jason lifted his bottle up expecting how much he had left. "But I could be up for another five or six yet. We have a lot of catching up to do."

"Do we now?" Matt laughed.

"Flat the fuck out we do." Jason tipped the beer up and downed a hearty mouthful before letting rip a loud burp. "The night is young and so are we."

CHAPTER SEVEN

Damon lay down on the bed in Marie's guestroom. The small room with white painted walls was tidy enough and came with a comfortable double bed. The walls had a couple pieces of abstract art painted by Marie, hanging from them, crazy dashes of colour to brighten the sterile room. Marie was good with colours and had renovated the inside of her home brilliantly, Damon thought.

Creativity was a passion they both shared but in different veins of the beating heart of what art was. While Marie had a passion for painting, Damon's passion was for photography. He had always felt bad for Marie not being able to finish her studies like he and Matt had. Still, Marie had managed to make enough of a name for herself to sell her artwork locally and help fund her comfortable lifestyle, which was supplemented by her wealthy parents.

So far the trip had not been as difficult as he had first imagined. He had already raised the topic of Keegan coming back up with him for a trip. The boy didn't seem sold on the idea, but Damon would continue to try and convince him. Matt needed something to look forward to. Something to take his mind off of his lonely and empty life. And if Keegan coming to stay helped offer Damon's best mate a bit of sunshine in his dreary day then Damon would do all he could to make that happen. It wouldn't have been quite so difficult had the small problem of the night in the cabin hadn't happened.

Not small at all actually.

No, nothing about Keegan was small. Discovering Keegan's same-sex desires had been a surprise. A fucking awkward one that dropped like a bomb. He had never once suspected the boy to be gay. Keegan had always talked about girls and for two years had dated the pretty Tess.

Damon covered his face and groaned when he thought about how he betrayed Keegan by sleeping with his girlfriend. It was a cruel move. Cruel to anyone but especially to someone so young, he thought. Damon didn't know why he did it. He knew better. But in that moment when Tess had batted her eyelids under the dim glow of the bonfire, stroking his shoulder seductively, Damon gave in to the desire in his pants and let his cock do the thinking for him. He had felt rotten as hell for what he had done, not that Keegan would believe him.

Fate though had intended Damon be caught and pay for his sin. Keegan Andrews may have been a virgin but he had fucked Damon like some sort of crazed porn star, drawing the submission out and reducing him to a pathetic mess.

Little fucking prick really got the better of me.

Damon had been so fucking nervous about coming down for Christmas. He had worried Keegan might pull another stunt like he had at the cabin. Blackmail his way back inside Damon's arse. When Marie had gone out leaving the two alone, Damon almost exploded from the awkward fear bubbling in his veins. This fear proved to be unfounded. Within a minute, he knew he was safe from Keegan trying anything. He had noticed the way Keegan looked at him, hopeful, not forceful. His eyes discretely dropping to perve at Damon's legs and crotch.

Probably wishing I'd flop my cock out so he could have another gobble on it.

Knowing he was in the driver's seat was comforting. Had Keegan not been his best mate's son then there was every chance Damon would use his regained authority and bend the little punk over, giving him a taste of his own twisted medicine.

So fucking tempting. But I can't.

Still, Damon found the new dynamic a wonderful one. He would be able to talk to Keegan like nothing had ever happened, simultaneously enjoying the lad wanting him. That kind of power was what Damon lived for. The power of being wanted. It didn't matter who wanted him as long as they did. It was strange to think Matt's eighteen-year-old son was one of his admirers but provided nothing happened again—and no one found out about the cabin incident—then that was fine. He would milk the admiration for all it was worth.

It wasn't going to be easy to get Keegan to agree to meet his father. Preaching the importance of family or how much his father could help him out with getting a job wasn't going to work on Keegan. Such practical advice was wasted on someone so young. But what would work was dangling flirts as bait.

Ditching his shirt and throwing it on the boy's lap was the first move. *I wonder if he sniffed it while I was in the shower?* Damon smiled at the thought. He was going to enjoy this. Keegan may have got one up on him in the cabin but not this trip. Damon was going to leave that boy with balls so blue they would look like two swollen smurfs. He would make sure Matt got to know his son while getting some harmless revenge on the boy who had reduced Damon to little more than a cum dump.

You are gonna be so desperate for a piece of this you'll follow me up in a fucking heartbeat.

The trick was to keep it as close to a sexual line without crossing it. A line that Keegan would follow and one that Damon could walk like a trapeze artist.

A knock at the bedroom door snapped Damon back to reality. "Yes."

Marie poked her head in the door. "Just me. I'm about to dish up dinner. Did you want some?"

Damon nodded. "Sounds good."

"Okay. It'll be ready in five minutes."

"Are we eating outside?" Damon asked.

"I wasn't planning on it but we can if you want."

"Yeah. It's still pretty warm out." Damon smiled. " It'll give me a chance to work on my tan."

Marie rolled her eyes. "Still vain as ever I see." She laughed and closed the door.

Damon got to his feet and peeled the clean shirt off his body that he had put on after his shower. He flexed his biceps, admiring his own strength. *It's show time!*

.

CHAPTER EIGHT

Boxing Day

Keegan wiped the steam from the bathroom mirror, inspecting how he looked for his horny visit to go see Liam. He had just finished showering and put on new clothes he had gotten for Christmas. Dirty denim jeans from his mother and a stylish orange slim-fitting top from Damon. Normally he preferred to go buy his own clothes—not trusting anyone over thirty to have any fashion sense—but he had to give it to his mum and Damon, they had both done well and picked out some decent threads. He dabbed a splash of cologne on his neck to give him an extra sexy scent. He wanted to look and smell his best for Liam and anyone who might be watching.

"Looking good," Keegan said to himself, winking at the mirror. He felt like a tosser saying such ego-stroking out loud but fuck it—he did look good. With the past two days being an abundance of the festive season and being surrounded by family it was going to be nice to get out of the house and enjoy some time with his mate. Especially the type of fun Liam had planned.

Actually… what does he have planned?

It probably didn't matter what it was just as long as Keegan would be getting a free perve at his best mate's body. He may finally be able to see what Liam's cock looked like fully erect. Maybe—just maybe—even get to touch it. The thought was enough to make Keegan lick his lips. The past two days had been hideous in how horny he had been, waiting for this moment. Matters were not helped by Damon who had sauntered about half-naked his entire visit, sending Keegan's loins into fiery overdrive. If Damon wasn't lounging seductively in just his briefs on the couch, then he would be outside on the deck working on his tan. He had even asked Keegan to put sunblock on his back for him, moaning lightly as Keegan blended the gooey cold liquid into his skin.

Christmas morning was the most challenging. Keegan, his mum and Damon all got up early to swap presents before spending the day at his grandparent's farm. Sitting on the floor, Keegan dished the presents out between them and while his mum was busy gushing over a bracelet Damon had gotten her, he let his eyes wander to Damon sat on the sofa, his legs spread wide enough for Keegan to peek up the leg hole of his shorts. To Keegan's shock—and delight—he spotted Damon's hairy sac dangling. The bastard had woken up and decided to celebrate Christmas by going commando.

For the rest of the day, Keegan found himself trying to get in line with Damon's open legs any chance he could get. That meant for the entire afternoon at his grandparents, Keegan had swum in the pool. Not because he loved swimming but from the water he was able to get sneaky peeks at the man's big sexy balls. Damon had shifted his deck chair right beside the pool's edge, his legs conveniently open whenever Keegan floated in line with them. It was almost like he wanted Keegan to see, daring him to look. Keegan got so fucking horny that he had started to rub himself under the water and without meaning to, he spoofed inside his togs. His face burned bright and his stomach knotted before rushing inside to dry off. For the remainder of the day he hoped like hell no one spotted any milky cum floating in the water.

Keegan gave himself one last look in the mirror. Today wasn't about Damon. It was about Liam. He chased away the shameful memory of jizzing in his grandparents' pool and made his way to the lounge where—sure enough—Damon was sprawled out in just his underwear again.

Keegan had been relieved to see his mum was out and wasn't going to grill him about his overly snazzy appearance. However, Damon noticed.

"Look at you," Damon said, propping his head up. "Somebody has a hot date by the looks."

"No," Keegan returned. "I'm just off to visit Liam."

"Liam, aye." Damon grinned. "So that who gets to see you looking like a movie star."

"We might be going to town," Keegan said, trying to come up with a plausible excuse for being so dressed up.

"Okay." Damon nodded. "You look really good in that top. I knew it would suit you."

Keegan smiled. "Thank you. You have good taste."

"I like to think so." Damon suddenly bucked his hips up, shamelessly groping at his bulge. "Its bloody hot today isn't it."

"Yeah." Keegan looked over, spotting the outline of Damon's dick, which was now fully noticeable from the readjustment. When Damon caught him looking, Keegan quickly sputtered, "Where's Mum?"

"She has gone to town to have lunch with your grandmother," Damon answered.

Keegan already knew this. He nodded. "Okay. I'll catch ya later."

"Hey, K dog," Damon called out before Keegan could leave.

"Yeah?"

"Have you had a think about coming up to see your dad?"

"Umm, not really. I'm still thinking about it."

"Oh k. Well let me know if you decide to come back with me, aye." Damon fidgeted with his bulge again. "Be good to have some company for the ride back."

"Will do," Keegan said. He scuttled away before he gave in to the voice in his head begging him to go jump atop of Damon. He wasn't sure if it was real or imagined, but he swore he could hear Damon chuckling as he made his way out the front door.

∞

When Keegan pulled up outside Liam's house, he sat quietly in the car for a moment, gathering his confidence to walk inside and act like the whole thing wasn't a huge deal.

After a few deep breaths to compose himself, Keegan opened his car door to make his way inside. Immediately the summer heat swallowed him whole like a wet blanket. The muggy weather was a pain how it made you start sweating the moment you left the coolness of air-conditioning or shade. He found the front door to Liam's house open so he made his way down the hall towards Liam's bedroom where he found his mate sat at his computer, typing away.

"Hey," Keegan greeted.

"Hey, man. Come in," Liam said without taking his eyes off the computer screen. "I am just sending out an email to my followers that I'll be posting a video shortly."

Keegan went and sat on the bed, waiting for Liam to finish typing. He took the opportunity to perve at his best mate while his back was turned. It became apparent that Keegan was overdressed. Liam was barefoot, wearing baggy shorts and a t-shirt—looking about as casual as he could. Keegan tugged at the neck of his shirt feeling like a dick for going overboard.

Liam swung 'round in his chair. "All done." He looked over at Keegan and honed his eyes like he was dissecting his appearance. "You certainly dressed up for the occasion."

"Sorry. I didn't know what to wear. I've not exactly done this sort of thing before."

"That's okay. As long as they like what's underneath then we're all good," Liam sniggered.

"What do you mean," Keegan said, the hairs on his neck prickling.

"Don't worry. I don't expect you to get fully naked," Liam said. "Unless you want to."

"Unless I want to?"

"I'm joking, Keegan." Liam stood up and lifted his shirt to wipe his face, exposing his toned stomach and the strip of hair below his belly button. That strip of hair Keegan had grown to love, he admired it as much as he envied it for the direction it headed. Liam dropped his shirt back down and locked his eyes on Keegan. To Keegan's relief Liam didn't seem to notice the sexual intent behind his stare and went and sat beside him on the bed like nothing was out of the ordinary. "So, what I was thinking was like just give you a massage or something. Start off with a bit of an introduction before I get you to lay down on the bed."

"Oh," Keegan said, thinking how dull that sounded. "Is that all?"

Liam laughed. "What did you think we were going to do? Fuck each other or something?"

"No," Keegan snapped. "I just didn't realise you would have people pay to watch you give someone a shoulder rub."

"It will be a little bit more than a shoulder rub." Liam smiled. "I was thinking more like you laying down in just your underwear and I'll start at your legs and work my way up."

Keegan felt movement in his pants. The idea of Liam's hands exploring his body was mind numbing. He cleared his throat. "Okay. I can handle that." Keegan suddenly wished he had jacked off in the shower to get rid of any potential erection giving his secret feelings away.

"Of course you can. It's just a massage and it's only me doing it."

Only you. If only Liam knew the truth of what he meant to Keegan.

When Keegan didn't respond, Liam added, "You are cool with this, right?"

Keegan nodded a little too enthusiastically. "Yeah. I'm all good with it." He patted his hands on his knees. "Like you say, this could be a good way to make some extra money."

Liam searched Keegan's eyes, scanning for truth. "You sure? Because you sound a little jumpy. I don't wanna make you do anything you don't want to do?"

"I'm not jumpy."

Liam rolled his eyes. "Really?"

"Okay, maybe I am a little jumpy but its only 'cos I haven't made a porno video before."

"This isn't a porn video." Liam laughed.

"I know." Keegan calmed his posture. "Liam. I'm

fine. I wouldn't do this if I didn't want to."

"Sweet. I'll go turn the camera on then," Liam stood up, catching Keegan by surprise at how quick they were getting into it. He walked over to his computer, switched the web cam on and went and sat back down beside Keegan. Liam looked straight at the screen and started talking, "Hey everyone. Kurt here. I know some of you guys have been following me for a while now and been big fans of my videos and I've had emails from some of you that you'd like to see something a little different. So today I have my best mate Regan with me to help make a sexy little video for you."

Regan! How fucking original, Keegan thought. He waved nervously at the camera, blinking profusely without a clue what to say or do.

Liam tapped him on the shoulder. "Say Hi, Regan."

"Uh, hi everyone."

"I've known Regan for years. He's the one I was telling you all about. The one about to join the army and who I had the three-way with the night we met the backpacker from Brazil."

For fuck sake! Keegan had to use all his strength not to cringe at the bullshit coming out of Liam's mouth. He was taken aback by how calm Liam was at spouting off utter lies. The guy was so convincing he should work in sales. Once Liam was finished with his introduction, he stood up, motioning for Keegan to get to his feet as well. While continually looking back at the camera, Liam rested a hand on Keegan's shoulder, rubbing soothingly through the material.

"He's not as muscly as me but I can vouch that he is a tough nut." Liam squinted sideways at him. He stepped behind Keegan and pressed his body into Keegan's back as his hands snuck around rubbing Keegan's chest for the camera. "I bet you're all wondering what my mate looks like with his top off."

Keegan felt his skin twinge and his flesh crawl into goose bumps. Liam was touching him in a way he had only imagined. It may have been all for show and come across corny as hell to anybody watching but it felt fucking fantastic.

Keegan focused on the tingles in his tummy of how wonderful Liam's hands felt while trying to keep any erection at bay. It was a tightrope of epic proportions.

"I guess it's time I show you what he looks like with his shirt off," Liam said in a gravelly voice, purposely sexy for his fans. He rested his head on Keegan's shoulder and looked over as he began using his fingers to unpop the buttons on Keegan's shirt. Liam whispered in Keegan's ear, "Ya ready, buddy?"

Fuck his voice sounded hot. It flowed like tiny orgasms walking straight into Keegan's eardrums. Keegan looked down at his body like it wasn't his own, watching as his flat stomach and smooth chest became more visible with each button being undone. When Liam unhooked the last button he pulled the shirt back, removing it from Keegan's body and dropped it to the floor. Keegan stood there shirtless, quivering. Liam proceeded to tell the camera about what he was seeing and touching. "My mate has got a good body don't you think?" Liam ran a hand over Keegan's bare chest. "See how nice his tan is. Regan has the nicest smooth skin." Liam then circled a finger around one of Keegan's nipples before giving it a light pinch. "He's also got nice nipples don't you think? Not too big, not too small." Liam chuckled in the flirtiest way he could. Keegan couldn't believe what he was hearing. He wanted to believe that Liam thought these things for real but he knew that his mate was playing up for the camera. Without warning Liam licked his neck and inhaled loudly. "And you wouldn't believe how fucking nice he smells. I think he put on special cologne just for me today."

Keegan's tummy somersaulted.

"Between you and me, one of my favourite parts of Regan is his stomach." Liam placed his hand to the faint outline of abs that Keegan had. He tapped his fingers atop of his belly button. "Nice and firm. I kinda wanna kiss his stomach."

Please do!

"He's also got pretty nice legs for a dude so I should

probably show you." Liam's hands lowered and began fiddling with the button on Keegan's jeans.

Keegan took a deep breath that he held in for what felt like an eternity, only letting it out when Liam had unzipped his fly. He felt Liam tug at the side of his pants and crouch down as he lowered Keegan's pants to the floor.

Keegan shuddered when he felt Liam's lips kiss the back of his thigh. Liam grabbed his ankle and slowly slid his hand up the inside of Keegan's leg.

Oh my god. Is he going to touch my balls?

His heart thundered in his chest. Keegan was torn between ecstasy and fright as Liam rested his grip firm in his inner thigh.

Think of dead puppies. Think of dead puppies.

Keegan closed his eyes and conjured up any gross image he could so his dick would stay in a flaccid state. With his eyes closed his ears pricked up at the sound of Liam getting back to his feet. He felt Liam press his crotch into his buttocks, almost grinding into him as his hands returned to Keegan's stomach.

It's like he wants to fuck me.

Keegan lost focus on the dead puppies the more Liam pressed his crotch into his behind, imagining what it would feel like skin to skin.

Liam chuckled over his shoulder. "Regan put on his best underwear by the looks too." He tugged at the elastic band of Keegan's underwear letting go of it so it made a loud *snapping* noise. "Yep. Definitely sexy underwear."

You're too bloody good at this Liam!

Keegan still had his eyes shut. He bit down on his lip so hard he thought it might bleed. It was all he could do to try and block out the wishful thoughts in his head that this was real. This was all so very fucking real.

"You know, if I was ever to go gay for someone, I think it would have to be with Regan." Liam's hand was resting dangerously close to Keegan's privates now as his fingers circled seductively just above the rim of his briefs. "Yeah. I think if I was to ever stick my dick in a guy's arse then it would definitely be my best mate here." He grabbed hold of Keegan's rump and squeezed.

Keegan winced. *Please don't say that. Do not fucking say that!* Keegan felt himself losing the battle to keep his calm. His dick twitched and he knew he couldn't fight off his need to express his pleasure much longer. *Just fucking hurry up and tell me to lay down for the massage so they don't see me get a stiffy!*

Liam didn't obey the subliminal message Keegan was screaming in his mind. Instead, Liam slipped his fingers under the waistband of Keegan's underwear, tickling the tip of his untrimmed pubes.

Holy fuck!!! What are you fucking doing?

Liam let out a soft and adorable laugh. "Wow. My mate hasn't manscaped in a while."

Keegan cringed in embarrassment. He didn't need the fucking world to know that he was yet to ever hack his pubes with a razor.

"It's all good though. He's still making me wanna try stuff," Liam said, still twirling his fingers amongst the nest of hairs.

Keegan's cock throbbed again, stiffening well into semi-erect territory.

"But today I just wanna give my buddy here a massage. I don't wanna freak him out too much." Liam kissed Keegan's neck so tenderly it made him want to melt. "Are you ready for your massage, Regan?"

Keegan finally opened his eyes and nodded, he stood in place, his legs wobbly like jelly. *Thank god!* He started to calm down after coming so dangerously close to being exposed for having a boner.

"You better lay down then big guy." Liam finished his sentence by slipping his hand right in Keegan's underwear and gripping his cock, giving it a firm tug.

"Fuck," Keegan yelped.

Liam let go of him and ran and turned the camera off. "Are you okay?"

Keegan shook his head. "I wasn't expecting that."

"Expecting what?"

"You to grab my cock."

Liam ran a hand through his hair. "Sorry, man. I guess I just got carried away. Playing up for the camera and all."

Keegan sat down on the bed and hugged his knees. He didn't want Liam to see the bulge of what he had already felt. Liam sat beside him and put a hand on his shoulder. "Honestly, Keegan, I'm really sorry. I just thought it would look hotter for the video if I did that."

"You could have given me some warning first," Keegan said in a pissy tone.

"That would have killed the vibe though."

"I don't fucking care."

Liam poked his shoulder. "Come on, Keegan, what's the big deal? Aside from the one in your pants."

Keegan blushed. "Excuse me?"

"Are you angry 'cos I didn't give you any warning or are you angry because I gave you a stiffy?"

"I don't have a fucking stiffy!"

"You had a bit of growth going on down there, don't lie." Liam grinned.

Keegan refused to answer.

"Look, man," Liam continued. "It's okay if you did. I was feeling you up all sexy like. I probably would have had one too if you were feeling me up like that."

Keegan slowly began to let his guard down. "You would?"

"Yeah, fully. Dicks have minds of their own. They don't know who's doing the touching." Liam nodded, his eyes glossed over with apology.

Keegan felt bad. "I'm sorry if I ruined the video."

"You didn't ruin it. If anything, it will probably make it better."

"How?"

"Well, it means when we do another one they'll be on the edge of their seats to see what happens."

Another one? Keegan wasn't sure if he were relieved or happy at the prospect. "You'd want to do another one?"

"Yeah. If you wanted to?"

Keegan let a few seconds of silence drape the air before answering. He didn't want to appear too keen. "Yeah, I could do another one."

"Brilliant. And next time I promise not to go off script like that."

Keegan laughed. "How about actually telling me the script next time so I know what I am in for."

"No worries. In future, I shall let you know every dirty detail of what I plan to do to you and your sexy body that could turn me queer." Liam winked. He opened his arms wide and hovered forward. "Shall we hug and make up?"

Keegan laughed and pushed his mate away. "You already had your hands in my pants, so we've probably had enough contact for one day." He said all this with a jovial smile but it pained him to turn down the hug and deny his truth. He wished he could have hugged it out. He wished they could lay on the bed and hug all day. But what Keegan wanted from his best mate probably wasn't in the script of Liam's life.

CHAPTER NINE

The night had just turned dark and Keegan was rearing to go. He sat in the passenger seat of his mum's car being driven to Liam's older brother's birthday party. Although it was a celebration for Joel—a world-class tosser— it didn't mean Keegan couldn't have a good night.

When Liam had called to invite him, Keegan assumed it was to plan another video. When Liam said it was to come to the party, he was slightly disappointed it wasn't to book their next session for the camera. It had been two days since Liam's hands and words gave him a hard on, and Keegan had been using the erotic memory as lusty fodder for whenever he was alone in his room or having a shower. Basically, any chance Keegan had in the past forty-eight hours to touch his dick, his mind clutched the moment Liam had touched it.

It made a change from relying on sneaking looks at Damon who was still staying with them and trying to talk him into going up to Auckland. Keegan figured maybe he should give it a chance, go back up with his father's best mate. Like Damon said, it would be a hell of a lot more exciting to have New Year's Eve in the city than be stuck at home in his small home town. Fuck staying with his father though. He would much rather stay with Damon who lived in the centre of Auckland, right at the doorstep of all the nightlife.

Keegan thought he could ask Liam to join him. They could go up and stay for a few weeks and have some fun checking out the city. They had talked about going to see Green Day who were coming to play in Auckland in just a few weeks time. Maybe they could go up a bit early, stay with Damon 'till Skippy and Tony came up and they could all go to the concert together. Of course, Damon may not be a fan of being used like a hotel for nearly a month but then if Keegan promised to go spend some of the time with his dad, maybe Damon would be more obliging.

The prospect of father-son bonding was hideous. Keegan had a niggly suspicion his father would use the time to try and patch up a damaged past. At least if Liam were with him, it may be more bearable and less awkward, Keegan thought. The other good thing about Liam coming was it might just stop Keegan trying anything foolish if he were alone with Damon. Being alone with the guy in his apartment would be too fucking torturous not to make a move. Especially if Damon waltzed about with his body on show like he had done so far this Christmas holiday.

"It's just along here, isn't it?" His mother asked.

"Yep, not too much farther now." He was too broke for a taxi to get to the party and rather than walk the hour it would take to get there he had accepted his mother's offer of being driven.

"I see it now," she said, forgetting the specific instruction not to drop him off right outside the party.

"Okay, just a bit further along please," Keegan mumbled, covering the side of his face with his hand.

His mother let the car roll past a few more houses before braking to a stop. She laughed to herself as she stared across at him. "Gee. It's so nice to know that my one and only child is so ashamed of me."

"I'm not ashamed of you, Mum," Keegan exhaled. "I just don't want anyone seeing me near you."

His mother laughed. "Wow. Thank you for clearing that up for me. Are you sure you don't want me to escort you to the door, darling."

"Don't you dare."

"Oh, go on. I could give you a big kiss goodbye so all your friends think your cool."

"Obviously our definition of what constitutes being *cool* is quite different," Keegan groaned.

His mother rolled her eyes. "I was joking, Keegan. I'm not that bloody old to know turning up with your mother isn't the done thing." She stroked her hair as she looked in the rear vision mirror at a car about to go past. "And for the record I was probably much more popular at your age than you are."

"Oh really?" Keegan smirked. She was probably right.

"Yep. I didn't need nana or grandad to drive me to parties."

"So you drove drunk did you?"

"Don't be stupid. I had boyfriends as chauffeurs. I didn't have to drive myself anywhere for years," she said, sounding very proud of the fact.

"Okay, Mum. Thanks for the lift and I'll call you later when I need to be picked up."

Keegan shot her a quick glance. "Picked up from here. Not outside the party."

"Okay, love. I will be sure to follow your very rigid instructions. And if its Damon who picks you up then I'll be sure to pass it on to him too."

"Damon," Keegan said shrilly. "I thought you were picking me up?"

"I probably will but if I get too tired he has agreed to come get you."

"Won't he be ditching you and going to town?" Keegan gave his mother a questioning look. "That's what he normally does when he visits."

"Apparently he is not up for a night out so we are both staying in to watch movies." His mother shook her head. "God that sounds old."

"You are old."

"I am forty-three Keegan not one-hundred."

"Well you probably are in dog years. Actually, you'd be more like a thousand." Keegan laughed as his mother flicked his shoulder.

"Okay, darling child, get out of the car now so I can run you over."

Keegan chuckled and slid out the car and waved goodbye to his mother as she drove off. He didn't have to walk far before he heard the noise of the party polluting the night sky. The clanging of rock music mingled with drunken yahooing so loudly that Keegan knew the neighbours would be having a grumpy, sleepless night.

When he got to the driveway he found the place littered with cars parked in disorderly fashion like a dyslexic car yard. A group of girls sat outside the front door smoking and drinking, eyeing him subtly as he walked past. He only managed to get two feet inside the house when a stern voice attacked him. "Outside please. Follow the signs with the arrows. The party is in the backyard."

Keegan looked up and saw that it was Liam's mother, Collette, standing in the hallway. "Sorry Mrs Corrigan. I'll go round the side."

"Oh, I am sorry, Keegan. I didn't realise it was you," she said. "I thought you were one of Joel's nameless guests." She motioned for him to come forward. "Cut through the lounge and go out that way. We know you, so you get a free pass."

"Thank you." Keegan smiled at Liam's mum and made his way through the nice home towards the ranch slider that would take him out to a deck and then down some steps to the backyard. When he stepped outside, he saw teams of people mingling in huddled masses. Keegan could hear now that the music was coming from the garden shed at the very back of the large property. To his left at the edge of the deck he saw two portaloos standing side by side. It was like Liam's parents had planned for a festival rather than a birthday, he thought.

Keegan looked down at the crowd of people that he estimated numbered about fifty. It was just after 9 o'clock so he figured more guests would be arriving yet. As he looked down at the sea of bodies and nameless faces he felt lost. These were all Joel's friends who would be around the same age as the birthday boy—twenty-four.

Keegan scanned desperately for Liam. Beautiful Liam. It was stupid but he had been looking forward all day to see what Liam would be wearing. He assumed his pal might be snazzed up for his brother's party more than normal. Not that it mattered. Liam could wear a rubbish bag and still be the hottest guy at the party. Right away Keegan began imagining Liam in the garbage attire and then naked. Anytime Liam entered his thoughts the poor guy wound up naked.

It was a strange thing this whole secret crush business. When he was younger and thought he was straight, Keegan could talk to Liam, Skippy, Tony or anyone about the girls he fancied. It was fun to discuss who you liked or have your mates tease you about it. But this crush. This *gay* crush. It was different. He didn't have anyone he could talk to about it. He had no choice but to bottle it up and let his feelings bubble like boiling water.

Keegan stared out, trying to catch a glimpse of his pals. Near the back of the garden he saw someone wearing a white baseball cap who stood taller than everyone else. *Skippy!* Keegan was glad his Aussie mate was so damned tall. It made him easy to spot. Keegan lowered his gaze to the people beside Skippy. He saw flaming ginger hair; Tony and beside him; dashing dark hair which belonged to Liam.

He ushered his way through the sea of limbs, knocking into arses and elbows until he managed to reach his pals. Liam was first to spot him and shot him a generous smile. Keegan admired Liam's outfit. Slim fitting black pants and a white ruffled shirt that made Liam look like he was an updated version of a hero from the Victorian era.

"Finally!" Liam bellowed over the music. "We were beginning to think you weren't coming."

"I'm here now." Keegan nodded hello at Skippy and Tony. "I had to wait for Mum to be ready to drop me off."

"How is your mum," Skippy asked eagerly like he was pouncing on prey.

"She's fine," Keegan answered.

"Seriously, bro. If she was my mum I would never leave the house. I'd much rather stay home with her if you know what I mean." Skippy arched his curved eyebrows, insinuating his devious intentions.

"Sadly, I do know what you mean. And gross." Keegan pulled a revolted face.

"What's gross about it? Your mum's hot as fuck, man." Skippy slipped a drunken smile. He was obviously well ahead on the drinks tonight, Keegan thought. It didn't help that even when the guy was sober he was dumb as he was tall.

Liam laughed. "So you're saying that if Keegan's mum was your mum then you would fuck your own mother?"

Skippy blinked a few times. "Yes. That is what I'm saying."

They all burst out laughing.

"You're fucking grim, Skippy," Tony said, slapping him on the back.

"Nothing grim about Keegan's mum." Skippy grinned.

Keegan groaned internally. He was used to comments like this about his mum but not from his inner circle. They usually kept any comments to themselves but Skippy's slurred speech told Keegan that his mate had lost all control of appropriateness.

Skippy suddenly turned to his side and let out a loud burp that erupted down to the face of a girl standing near them. She flicked them a disgusted look. "You pig," She huffed.

"Ignore the cave man here, he's just had a few too many beersies," Tony apologised on behalf of his friend.

Skippy smiled at the disapproving girl and burped again. This time she walked off leaving Skippy in hysterics at his ability to revolt. "I think she wants to hump me."

"I'm thinking probably not." Tony chuckled.

"Tony's right," Liam said. "The only thing you'll be humping is the ground when you fall into it from passing out."

"Whatever, bro." Skippy shook off the joke. "I'm wearing my lucky undies. I always score when I have these fellas on." He lifted his shirt, exposing his flat tummy before tugging his jeans down a smidgen to show he was wearing green silk boxers. "They're my mean greens."

Liam snorted. "Fuckin hell. The only thing mean n green about down there is the gonorrhoea you never got cleared up."

Skippy frowned, unaware Liam was only joking. "I've

never had that. I swear." He took his cap off running his hand through his short brown hair, looking worried that they might not believe him. "Honest, Liam, I ain't never been in any huckery boxes."

They all began to laugh at Skippy's inability to sense a joke. The tall numbskull only made it funnier by trying to defend his cock's honour.

Keegan nearly jumped when a hand landed on his shoulder. He spun around surprised to be greeted by a familiar face he did not expect to see at this party. "Tess," Keegan coughed out. "What-what are you doing here?"

"My brother is friends with Joel," she said, pointing to a group of guys behind her where her geeky brother, Jamie, stood. While Tess was naturally good-looking with her blonde hair and slim frame, Jamie who had the same features as his little sister managed to make blonde and slim appear geeky with a nest of fluffy hair and his thick-rimmed glasses.

They hadn't seen each other since he broke up with her after the trip away with Damon. The trip away that had seen him seduce Damon in dubious fashion and realise that Tess had been a cover up for where his true feelings lie. He had felt bad about what he had done but not as bad as he could have. The weirdness of who he had slept with only got weirder when you factor in that the only reason he pounced on Damon in the first place was out of revenge for Damon sleeping with Tess the night of his birthday. Tess didn't know that he knew. He hadn't mentioned anything, partly out of respect for her, but also it didn't seem fair to expose her secret if he wouldn't divulge his own.

Keegan swallowed hard. "So umm… how have you been?"

"I've been good." Tess nodded. "And you?"

"Yeah, I've been great."

"We're gonna go grab ourselves some more drinks," Liam cut in. He shot Keegan a knowing glance to let him know that they would give him and Tess some privacy.

"Okay. I'll come find you guys soon," Keegan said before turning back to face Tess.

"It's weird being here and not being your date," she said.

"True." Keegan tilted his head to try and look thoughtful about the observation. He supposed it was weird. They had dated for two years and had been each other's plus one to any social event going. This was his first time truly solo and hers too probably.

"How was your Christmas?" Tess asked, fiddling with the shoulder strap of her dress.

"It was okay. Same old really. Ate way too much and then sat around my grandparent's pool feeling bloated."

Tess laughed. "Sounds like mine was... but without the pool."

Keegan nodded. *What do I say?* For someone he knew so well he had no idea what to talk to her about.

"Have you decided what you're doing next year with university?" Tess asked.

"I think I've left the whole uni thing a bit late to be going now. I was thinking I'll get a job round here and have a gap year. Have a think about what it is I wanna do."

"Sounds sensible." Tess smiled. "Which is totally you."

"It is?"

"Yes. You always have been sensible. Always the one to make good decisions."

"Well, I chose to date you, so I must do."

Tess rolled her eyes. "Yes, and you also chose to end the relationship, which was even more sensible."

Keegan was surprised to hear her say this. Sure, she hadn't been upset when they broke up. They even hugged afterwards but it was odd to hear Tess almost thank him for it. "You liked that decision?"

Tess nodded. "I did. It was the right thing to do."

"Don't look too happy about it. I thought you would be at home pining for me for years."

Tess laughed. "Sorry. Would it help if I lie and say I cried for days?"

"It would help a little." Keegan grinned.

"If I'm being honest, I was thinking about breaking up with you too, so it's kind of weird you did it first but I mean it doesn't matter. It's all for the best."

"I agree." Keegan began to think maybe they could be friends. They could still attend the same parties together.

"Is your uncle staying with you?" Tess asked. Her voice came out brittle but hopeful. This instantly killed any idea of a budding friendship.

Keegan hesitated and ran a hand through his hair. "Uh, yeah. He is. He's been down here for Christmas but I think he is going home tomorrow."

"Okay." Tess nibbled on her lip. "Well it was nice seeing you. Have a nice night."

"You too." Keegan watched her walk away and join her brother. He shook his head, amazed how ballsy she was to come and snoop for info about Damon. Keegan didn't feel mad, he sort of felt sorry for her. He knew what it was like to fancy someone who was unattainable and although Damon had slept with her he was never going to date her. The guy stayed single so much you would think he was allergic to commitment. Damon had a very long trail of broken hearted girls. Tess would just become another to add to the list if she pursued the vain bastard.

Keegan waded through the crowd to go find his mates. He put Tess and Damon to the back of his mind. Tonight wasn't about them. Tonight was about having fun. When he found Liam and the others by the deck he was pleased to see Liam holding a spare bottle of bourbon for him. Keegan snatched the drink with greedy speed and wasted no time in downing its contents.

Had he only known the shit storm the night ahead would bring—thanks to getting so pissed—he wouldn't have touched a drop of it.

CHAPTER TEN

Keegan slammed the drinks back like they were going out of fashion. Each time he got near the bottom of a bottle Liam would go fetch him another one. The more he drank, the more he found himself losing subtlety, spilling his gaze over Liam.

He knew he should have told Liam to stop fetching him round after round, but Keegan loved how his best mate was doting on him, handing the drinks over so their fingers touched, carrying a caring glint in his eye. A small sober segment in Keegan's brain told him that this was all imagined but his wishful thinking kept pushing it aside.

"Are you alright?" Tony asked, piercing Keegan's concentration. "You look about as fucked as Skippy is."

"I ain't farrked," Skippy slurred loudly.

"You're fine aren't you, Keegan?" Liam stated as much as he asked.

"Yeah, man. I'm fine." Keegan swallowed down another mouthful of booze. His vision wasn't blurry yet so he knew he wasn't too far gone. "I gotta go take a slash though," he declared, putting his empty bottle on the ground. He staggered away, making his way in the direction of the portaloos. If it wasn't so crowded he would have just gone and pissed in the garden but he didn't fancy being shrieked at by someone who disapproved of sprinkling flowers with urine.

When he got to the toilets he was annoyed to find them both in use. He stood tapping his foot impatiently, waiting for one of them to open up. Finally, before his bladder burst, one of the doors opened and he raced inside, sighing in relief as he quickly flopped his cock out and let flow a steady stream of piss.

When he was done, he zipped up and stepped out to

go find his way back to Liam but before he could take two steps someone grabbed his shoulder. He whirled around expecting to see Tess. "Hey, Tess," he started before realising his mistake.

Garth!

"Hey, blondie," Garth said, smiling like a loon.

"You know my name is Keegan. Not blondie."

"I know." Garth grinned, displaying his cute dimples. He took a swig on the bottle of beer in his hand, keeping his eyes locked on Keegan while he gulped down his drink.

Keegan had only met Garth a few weeks earlier and although their meeting was brief, the rakish Garth had left quite the impression. Garth had attended Keegan's birthday party with Liam's older brother—one of many strangers who had turned up to take advantage of someone else's party— and while there, Garth had tripped along the edge of the bon fire, setting his jeans leg alight. Damon had rushed to the rescue and whisked in, whacking the fire out with someone's jacket. After Damon had saved the day, he had sent Keegan up to the house to help Garth tend to his burn. Luckily the damage had been minimal but the short time they spent together had been pleasant. Keegan had been a bundle of raging hormones that night and while Garth's back was turned as he stripped out of his jeans to wash his singed leg, Keegan had taken advantage of the situation and quite freely checked Garth out.

To Keegan's horror, Garth had picked up on his rear end's visual violation, but instead of being angry he had found it amusing and flattering. Keegan had denied checking him out, insisting he was straight and that Garth was dreaming.

Since that night Garth had text him a few times, telling him to come and have a drink at the bar where he worked in town but Keegan had yet to take him up on the offer. As much as he liked Garth—based on the little he knew about the guy—he didn't want his sexuality scrutinized any further by someone who seemed hellbent on proving Keegan had a crush on him.

"So… Keegan. What brings you here tonight?"

"I'm friends with Joel's brother, Liam."

"Oh true." Garth nodded. "Good looking guys both of them."

Keegan rolled his eyes at what he knew was Garth testing the waters again. "I hadn't noticed," he lied.

"Really?" Garth shrugged. "How could you not. Those guys could be models." He shot Keegan a flirty wink. "But so could you."

"For a supposedly straight guy you seem hung up on dudes," Keegan said.

"It's more for your benefit really. I was taught it is good manners to talk to people about things they are interested in." Garth let his eyes glow. "And since I know you like cock then I know it's a good topic." He attempted a seductive pose that was more comical than sexy.

Keegan laughed. "Nice try." The pose may have failed but it didn't hide the fact that Garth had a certain charm. He wasn't model material like Liam but something about the way he looked was appealing. Keegan couldn't decide what it was. Was it the boy's messy brown hair that looked in a constant state of rebellion like he had just rolled out of bed? Was it his jagged smile of sharp teeth? Or was it the way he oozed strength despite his skinny body? It was probably all those things wrapped together, gifting him a casual masculinity that was oh so fucking sexy.

"Fancy joining me for a smoke?" Garth arched his eyebrows up, encouraging Keegan to join him.

"I don't smoke."

"No. I mean the green."

"Again. I don't smoke."

"Wow. You really are as innocent as you look."

"I'm not that innocent," Keegan snapped back with a portion of aggression in his voice.

"Calm your farm. I was only joking." Garth flicked his eyes across to a quiet area by some bushes. "If you ain't that innocent then you can come sit and talk some shit with me while I spark up." Keegan didn't want to seem rude but he wanted to get back to Liam and the others. Garth spotted his hesitation and added, "If you come I'll make it worth your while." He groped his crotch.

Keegan laughed. "You have issues."

"I know right. That's why you wanna come hang with me." Garth started to walk away then turned 'round waving his arm. "Come on, man."

Keegan sighed, giving in to the pushy invite and followed the nutty smoker into the shadows.

Garth led them over to a sheltered spot in a hidden corner of the garden where they were conveniently alone. Garth sat down on the grass and pulled out a fat joint that he wasted no time in sparking to life. He inhaled deeply, holding it in before letting it out like a dragon. "Fuck, I needed that," he said, letting out a satisfied breath.

Keegan nodded, watching Garth drag back on the spliff. He felt twitchy, wondering what the hell they could talk about. He settled with the generic topic of work. "So how's the bar?"

"It had been super busy with all these functions leading up to Christmas but I quit last week."

"You did. Why?"

"Got over it." Garth laughed without smiling. "I needed a change."

"Did you get sick of working two jobs?" Keegan asked, remembering that Garth's main source of employment was as a grease monkey working alongside Liam's older brother, Joel.

"Nar, bro. I had already lost that job."

"You quit that too?"

"Nar. I didn't quit the workshop. They fired me."

Keegan frowned but hid it quickly. "How come?"

Garth turned his head and smiled. "I lost my shit on a poxy arse Mitsi that wasn't cooperating so I attacked it with a hammer."

"You fucking what?"

"Attacked it with a hammer. Smashed the bonnet up real good."

Keegan laughed. "For real?"

"Yeah." Garth grinned at him. "I just lost my fucking rag with it and yeah... apparently you don't keep ya job for long when you pull stunts like that."

"I imagine not." Keegan chuckled. "I hope you don't do that to people when they annoy you."

"Nar, man. I'm a lover, not a fighter."

Keegan rolled his eyes. "Good to know." He looked at Garth's long fringe dangling forward. "So now you need a haircut and a job."

Garth laughed and ruffled his hair. "Nothing wrong with my hair, bro. And yep I am officially one of the unemployed."

"What will you do for work?"

"I can find another job a piece of piss," Garth said. "Might be a bit hard landing a mechanics role down here after the stunt I pulled but I can easily find other hospo work 'till I know what I'm doing."

"I hope you find something soon," Keegan said sympathetically.

"Bugger that. I don't wanna work New Year's. That's half the reason I quite the bar job."

"What about money?"

"I'm just using my savings account at the moment. That should see me through a bit before I need to look for work."

"Cool," Keegan muttered.

"Maybe I could sell my body," Garth said. He patted his chest, grinning at Keegan. "Whataya think?"

"I think... good luck." Keegan sniggered.

"Aww, come on, blondie, I bet you'd pay for a piece of this premium meat."

"In your dreams."

Garth winked at him. "You need to be inside my head before you make such claims."

Keegan couldn't tell if that was a real flirt or a joke. He chose to ignore it and let Garth ramble on about how glad he was to not be working two jobs anymore. He watched

Garth's lips move but paid little attention to the words coming out. He began wondering if Garth had brought them over here for a reason.

He seemed pretty keen for us to be alone.

When Keegan saw Garth was getting to the end of his joint, he felt a strange panic grip his feelings.

Maybe he wants to do something but he needs me to make the move?

Keegan looked towards the noise of the party. No one was anywhere near their secluded spot. No one would see if they fooled around. Keegan felt butterflies flutter in his stomach, prompting him to do something. The frisky feeling felt like he was falling. He tried ignoring the hunger growing inside him but it wasn't working and Keegan found his dick stiffening.

He brought me here for a reason. I just have to try and let him know I am keen.

The idea of just blurting out "let's hook up" seemed too risky. Too blunt despite the determination growing in his pants. Keegan wracked his brain to think of how best to bring about the right circumstances.

"Has your leg healed up okay?" Keegan asked. The randomness of the question caught Garth unaware.

"What?" Garth stared at him blankly.

"Your leg. From where you fell in the fire at my birthday."

"Oh that," Garth said, nodding. "Yeah healed up fine, but there wasn't any damage really if you remember."

Keegan licked his lips. "Can I see?"

Garth chuckled by the random request. "Sure." He bent forward and rolled his ripped jeans up to his knee. He ran his hand along the thick crop of brown hairs running down his leg. "See. No scar. Nothing."

"You must be a Targaryen after all," Keegan joked.

"Ha. That's me, man. If only I had a dragon."

Garth was about to roll his jeans leg back down but Keegan jerked his hand forward latching onto Garth's arm. "Do you mind if I touch it."

Garth's lips turned into a crooked smile. He didn't say anything. He just stared back with a goofy look on his face. Keegan chose to be bold. He lowered his hand to Garth's ankle and ever so gently ran his fingers up Garth's leg, groping at the firmness of his calf muscle. "Yeah. Healed up fine by the looks," Keegan murmured, continuing to let his hand roam the hairy terrain.

Garth cleared his throat with a soft laugh. "Are you enjoying yourself?"

Keegan realised that Garth wasn't as clueless about his intentions as he had thought. He pulled his hand away and straightened his posture. He took a deep breath and said, "I was 'till you said that."

Garth leant back resting on his elbows, stretching his leg out. "I didn't say you had to stop."

No, you didn't.

Keegan chewed his lip. It seemed pointless skirting around the horny issue. He took a deep breath, bracing himself. "Is it alright if I kissed you?"

Garth threw his head back with a laugh. "I fucking knew it!"

Keegan flinched. Unprepared for the response.

"I knew you fancied me," Garth said. He shook his head, looking pleased with himself. "I knew you digged guys. Fucking knew it." He kept smiling like he had won a prize.

"You're… you're not gay?"

"Nar, man. I told you. I'm straight as."

"But-but you keep flirting with me," Keegan stammered.

"Yeah, but it's just for a laugh." Garth sniggered. "I ain't gay. I just like kidding around."

Keegan's stomach tightened; he felt dizzy, bombarded by the moment. He wanted to get up and run away but he fought the urge to flee, worried it would make a scene. A scene where Garth could tell everyone what he was running from. *A rejected gay kiss.* Keegan curled his fingers into a fist, trying to figure out what his next move should be.

"I gotta say, bro, that was a seriously smooth move

trying to feel up my leg like that," Garth lifted his leg off the ground, admiring his exposed hairy limb. "I guess I do have nice legs though, aye."

Keegan heard the words but they weren't registering. He began to sink into his own world of gloom. *What have I done.* He felt his eyes sting and his cheeks slowly become wet with tears.

"You're not crying are you?" Garth asked.

Keegan raised his hands, covering his face.

"I'm real sorry. I didn't mean to make fun of you," Garth sounded remorseful. He placed a hand to Keegan's shoulder.

Keegan ignored the comforting touch. He kept snivelling under his hands, too scared to show his face.

"Oh, come on, man. I'm sorry. I really am," Garth kept rubbing his shoulder. "I won't tell anyone if that's what you're worried about. Promise. I won't say a fucking word." He lowered his hand to stroke Keegan's back affectionately. "You can kiss me if it'll make you feel better?"

Keegan rubbed his eyes and removed his hands, sniffing back tears. "Just leave me alone."

"Come on, Keegan. Stop being such a sad arse and just stick ya fucking tongue in my mouth." He tugged on Keegan's shirt trying to bring their faces together. "You can do anything you like above the waist," he whispered. "That's all good by me."

Keegan pushed him away. "You don't have to keep making fun of me." He got to his feet and saw Garth looking up shocked.

"Settle down, man. We can still talk, can't we?"

"I'm really sorry I made a move on you." Keegan rubbed his eyes dry. "Please don't tell anyone." He stormed off, leaving Garth sitting alone.

"Come back, bro," Garth called out but Keegan strode ahead refusing to look back.

He couldn't handle this. He hadn't been ready to spill his truth. He needed to get away from Garth and away from any potential fall out for being so incredibly fucking stupid.

He snuck around to the quiet side of the house, stomping his way through fluffy flower beds to access the front yard. He was about to cross the lawn and barge onto the street when he saw a group of partygoers sitting on the fence.

Fuck my life!

He realised that he was still crying. *Fucking pull yourself together, Keegan,* he told himself. He didn't want to walk past them while he looked so upset. Instead of going onto the street he snuck along the front of the house and crouched down below Liam's bedroom window. He wrestled his phone from his pocket and with shaky fingers, dialled his mum's number. He sucked back his sobby breaths, trying to settle the emotion constricting his throat.

"K dog," said Damon's voice.

"Damon," Keegan answered back surprised. "Where's mum?"

"Your mum's fallen asleep. She left me her phone in case you needed a lift home."

"Oh." Keegan wondered if maybe it was a good thing it was Damon picking him up. His mother knew him too well and would have picked up if he sounded even the tiniest bit upset. "Are you able to pick me up?"

"Yeah buddy. Not a problem." Damon said.

"Thanks," Keegan mumbled.

"Where am I picking you up from?"

"Liam's place please. It's on Caldwell Street. Seventy-five."

"Righto. See you soon. I'll call you when I am parked up outside."

"Cheers." Keegan hung up and waited in the shadows, wishing the darkness could swallow him whole.

CHAPTER ELEVEN

It didn't take long for Damon to arrive. Keegan stayed low, hiding beneath Liam's window. He wasn't risking waiting on the road in case Garth or anyone else turned up and sprung him looking distressed. His plan was to run straight to the car and tell Damon to just fucking go!

When Damon did call saying he was parked out the front, Keegan felt like his army of protection had arrived. He crept from the safety of the shadows and made his way onto the street, relieved to see that the partygoers on the fence had disappeared. He spotted Damon's black sports car two houses down. He traipsed along ready to jump straight in, but before he could, Damon hopped out of the car.

"Hey, K dog. Sorry but I am busting for a piss. You don't suppose Liam's folks would mind if I use their bathroom."

It was the first time in days Keegan had seen the guy with a t-shirt on covering his chest.

"Umm," Keegan began to say, wanting to tell Damon to just hold it in, but he saw the way Damon appeared to be squirming as he stood.

"Quickly," Damon snapped. "I'll piss my pants if I don't go soon."

"Yeah sure. Follow me," Keegan said reluctantly.

He took Damon back towards the house, the front door was still open so he bowled right in. He half-expected Liam's mum to have a go at them both for wandering into the house but the coast was clear.

"This way," Keegan whispered. He led Damon down the long hallway to the bathroom situated right at the end. Damon shoved past him and raced inside, shutting the door. Keegan stood outside waiting. He heard the splash of the toilet bowl followed by Damon erupting with a sigh of relief similar to the one Keegan had unleashed earlier.

Just hurry the fuck up so I can get home!

Keegan felt like he would spontaneously combust, scared of being spotted by Garth and an army of followers to mock him. Keegan's ears pricked up at the sound of the toilet flushing.

Thank god. Now come on!

Just as Damon walked out of the bathroom, Keegan saw a figure approaching the front door. It was Garth. Keegan's stomach squirmed. He hauled Damon by the hand and dragged him into the nearest bedroom to hide—which just happened to be Liam's.

Damon appeared amused to be led so gruffly. "Who are you hiding from?"

Keegan raised a finger to his lips. "Be quiet," he whispered. He heard Garth's footsteps getting closer to the room. He flashed a look at Damon, willing him to remain silent. Damon glared back with a curious expression on his face.

Just as Garth was about to pass the room a voice thundered down the hall. "Can I help you." It was Liam's mum.

"Oh sorry, Miss. I was just looking for a friend of mine," Garth answered.

"Well, he won't be in here. Sorry for sounding rude but we are trying to keep everyone outside... so if you don't mind."

"Yeah, sure. No worries." Garth sounded happy to follow the rules, which surprised Keegan. He expected Garth to have been a bit ruder. "Anyway. If you do see a sad - looking blond guy wandering about called Keegan, can you tell him Garth is looking for him."

Keegan's stomach dropped. *Don't you fucking dare tell Liam's mum about what I did!*

"Keegan?" Liam's mother said, sounding concerned. "Is he okay?"

"Uh yeah, he's okay. He was just feeling a bit sick and disappeared so I was just trying to make sure he didn't wander in here throwing up all over the place," Garth answered.

Great! Now she will probably tell Mum about how drunk I imaginarily got at the party.

"Okay. If I see him I will be sure to give him a bucket or direct him to the toilet," Liam's mum said pleasantly. She chuckled softly. "It isn't like Keegan to be irresponsible. He is usually the good influence amongst his friends."

Keegan grimaced hearing him being outed for being such a boring sod. At least he wasn't being outed for other reasons though. Keegan kept listening till the voices dissipated and the coast was clear. He turned and looked at Damon, urging him with his eyes to leave.

"Not so fast, K dog." Damon walked over and sat on Liam's unmade bed, which was a tangling mess of white sheets. "Come sit and tell me what's wrong."

"Nothing. I am fine." Keegan refused to budge from where he stood by the door. When he saw Damon frowning sternly he gave up. He pushed the door to and went and sat beside him.

"I just wanna know what's happened," Damon said, his voice soft like a melody.

"Nothing has really happened."

"We both know that boy was lying about you being sick cos you look fine to me."

Keegan lolled his head back and stared at the ceiling. Maybe Damon was the one person he could tell. Until Garth, Damon was the only one who knew Keegan's secret side existed.

"You can tell me, K dog." He tapped Keegan on the shoulder. "Do I need to go give some fucker a hiding for giving you a hard time?"

Keegan laughed at Damon's protective instinct. "It's nothing like that." He looked Damon in the eyes. His father's best friend looked back with nothing but concern. No judgement lingering. Keegan swallowed. "That guy who was looking for me. Well... I hit on him cos I thought he was interested and it turned out he's straight. I asked if I could kiss him and when he said no, I panicked and ran away." Keegan saw Damon's face flinch at the confession.

"I see," Damon said. "And your worried he might say something?"

"Pretty much." Keegan let out a pitiful laugh. "Until tonight you were the only one who knew about me but after the stunt I pulled fuck knows who Garth might tell."

Damon didn't say anything. He sat rigidly, his hands clutching his knees. Keegan assumed Damon must be regretting provoking such a heart to heart. The silence was only broken when Damon came out with, "Maybe he won't say anything. He didn't tell that woman about what you did."

"Yeah, but that was Liam's mum and I can't see him telling her but what about everyone else at the party?"

"Nar. I don't think the guy will say anything. He has a trustworthy voice."

"A what?"

"He had a trustworthy voice. He sounds like someone who will keep things to himself."

Keegan knew Damon grasping at straws to try and make him feel better. It didn't work. "I would fucking die if everybody found out."

Damon kept staring at the floor as he nodded along. "So this isn't some phase? This is what you are?"

Keegan felt like cringing at the question. He couldn't say the answer out loud so he just nodded slightly.

"Cool. Ain't nothing wrong with that," Damon said confidently. "And it's nobody's business but yours, so if the guy was a dick and opened his mouth spouting off to his mates then you just tell them it's none of their fucking business. Lie if you want to. It isn't like they have proof, do they?"

"I guess not." Keegan started to feel a bit better. Damon was right. He didn't have to admit anything he didn't want to. It was his truth and up to him when he parted the words of it to anyone.

"I actually thought you and Liam had something going on," Damon said, a coy smile slipped across his lips.

Keegan frowned. "Why would you think that?"

"Because of the way you dressed up for him the other day and I have noticed the way you look at him for a while now."

"What do you mean *the way I look at him?*"

"Like he is the only person in the world that matters."

"Do I really do that?"

Damon smiled. "A little. At first I thought it was just because he's your best mate and you just enjoyed his company but—" Damon's sentence hit an invisible wall, it was only when he finished it that Keegan realised why he struggled to complete it. "But after the night at the cabin I realised there was more to it than that. You like him."

Keegan nodded. "Guilty as charged. I have like the biggest fucking crush on him. He is just so… so perfect." It felt so freeing to say this out loud and share his affection for the boy who was always on repeat in his mind. "I like him so fucking much it hurts. I know he doesn't feel the same way but it doesn't make me stop wanting him."

"Sorry to hear that, K dog." Damon rubbed his back. "Love can be a real bitch like that."

Keegan chuckled. "Maybe you're more observant than I give you credit for."

"Yeah, I'm not quite as self-centred as I like to make out I am. I do pay attention to the people I care about."

Keegan felt warmed by Damon's words. Outside Liam's bedroom there was potentially a scandal unfolding with his name written all over it. But in here he was safe. Damon was an army of one designed to protect Keegan from harm. "Thanks, Damon." Keegan leaned forward and planted a kiss on Damon's cheek.

Damon flinched.

Keegan lurched back when he realised what he had done. "Sorry I didn't mean to do that." He covered his face and groaned aloud. "Sorry. Sorry. Sorry."

Damon said nothing. He stood up and walked towards the door.

Keegan panicked. "I'm Sorry Damon, I didn't mean

to do that. I don't know what I was thinking." To Keegan's relief, and then utter surprise, Damon didn't leave. He pushed the door to and twisted the lock on the handle. He slowly turned around and showed a face that was a wild mess of emotions. He bit down on his lip nervously, nodding his head.

"What's going on?" Keegan asked. The words limped out his mouth.

Damon stepped in front of him and looked down with a determination brimming in his green eyes. "Whatever you want to go on."

"What do you mean?"

Damon darted his eyes to the side, smiling. He groped his crotch with a firm grip, giving that as his answer.

The room became draped in a vibe Keegan could only describe as *potential*. But the potential for what? He flicked his teeth with his tongue, thinking over what Damon was doing. Last time at the cabin Damon had been reluctant to take part but now he seemed to be the one instigating something. He cleared his throat. "Are you saying you want me to fuck you?"

"I am saying I want to help make you feel better any way I can."

"So you do want me to fuck you?"

Damon grinned. "If that'll make you feel better."

Keegan scanned the length of Damon's body. "Take your shirt off."

Damon smiled. "Sure thing."

Keegan felt the burn of an erection coming on fast. Damon was offering exactly what he had hoped for.

He is giving me himself.

Damon peeled the shirt from his body, tossing it on the floor. His tanned chest with its crop of chest hair glowed under the dim light in the room.

Keegan rose to his feet, extending a hand to Damon's chiselled-chest, raking his fingers through the manly feature. It felt just as inviting as he remembered. An untamed coarseness overtly sexual in every way.

Damon stood there unperturbed by Keegan's hand going lower, sliding south over his midriff, stroking down his hard abs 'till finally his palm landed on the warm firm mound jutting Damon's shorts.

"Would you like me to play with this again?" Keegan asked in a slight drawl.

"You're the boss, K dog." Damon's voice came out a crazy level of sexy.

Keegan felt the darkness coming, stinging his blood as it began to fill his veins. The same darkness that had hurled him to a sadistic state that night in the cabin. His teeth lightly chattered with the frisson of anticipation for its vicious arrival. He rubbed Damon's growing erection, licking his lips. He stared Damon in the eyes and squeezed his cock. The darkness had arrived. "Did you like having my young dick in your arse?"

Damon swallowed.

Keegan squeezed his cock harder. "Did you like it, I asked you."

"I think so," Damon whispered.

Keegan licked Damon's bristly cheek then whispered in his ear, "Should I fuck you like I did last time?" He let go of Damon's dick, refilling his hand with Damon's jiggly balls.

Damon took a breath and shuddered when Keegan squeezed them. "Yes. Fuck me just like you did last time."

Keegan ignored the risk attached to fucking in his best mate's room while a party raged outside. Damon was a stunning specimen and giving himself freely. The risk seemed worth it. "Good answer," Keegan replied. "Now get naked cos I am gonna go even fucking harder on you than last time."

"Is that a threat or a—"

Keegan raised a finger, signalling Damon to be silent. "Just get naked and start lubing my cock up with your mouth."

Damon simpered, returning with a challenge, "Maybe I should fuck you. Show you how it's really done."

Keegan didn't know where it came from but instinct

told him to act and wrestle control of the moment; he slurped up a ball of saliva and spat it right in Damon's face. "I don't take it up the arse," he snarled. "That's your job, remember?"

Damon looked horrified, he hadn't expected that. He dropped his gaze to the floor like he was suddenly embarrassed about someone half his age defiling him. Very slowly he raised a hand and wiped the spit from his face, flinging it on to the carpet. His stare returned but this time the smirk was gone and was replaced with a reluctant glint of acceptance.

Keegan grinned, pleased to see the older man knew his place. "Now get naked."

"Yes, boss," Damon said in an almost shitty tone. He stepped back, scuffed off his shoes and began to remove every stitch of clothing from his body 'till he stood before Keegan nothing more than an offering of the flesh.

Keegan smiled salaciously, he tapped the denim crotch of his jeans with his finger.

Damon followed the direction being given, he dropped to his knees and shuffled forward. With a shaky hand, Damon pulled the zipper down, freeing Keegan's cock. He gripped the swelling prick between his fingers, squeezing, casting a pathetic look up at Keegan before surrounding the young hot knob with his sticky lips.

Keegan gasped at the feel of such a warm obedient mouth. Dubious or not, he loved having control.

I fucking love being the boss.

CHAPTER TWELVE

Why did I fucking do it? Why did he have to go and fuck his best mate's son? *Again.*

Damon had asked himself that question all week since he had returned from visiting Keegan and Marie. He sat on the patchwork couch in his apartment looking aimlessly out the window at his view of Waitemata Harbour. No amount of scenic beauty could take his mind away from the question though. It was mid-afternoon but Damon still hadn't gotten dressed. He sat in just his underwear, eating a bowl of cereal, tapping his foot nervously as he ate the bland cornflakes.

It wasn't like Keegan had forced him or cornered him into doing it like last time. No. This time Damon had given himself away more than willingly. So fucking willingly that he had been the one to make the move. Been the one to bend over the bed and take every inch of pent up aggression Keegan had to offer.

Keegan's cock had hurt every bit as much as last time but it also had felt unbelievably hot. The hurt was a turn on in how fucking intimate it all was. How fucking thrilling and wrong it all was. And it didn't get more wrong than being fucked by a guy half your age who happened to be your best mate's son. Someone you had known their whole life, someone you'd watched grow from a boy to a young man.

Matt will fucking kill me if he finds out.

The moment he had seen how vulnerable Keegan looked, worried about people finding out about him being gay, Damon had felt compelled to make him feel better. His words hadn't felt enough. He had wanted to give the boy more. Replace any fear with a sense of lustful adventure.

But I enjoyed it too. I really fucking enjoyed it. Damon couldn't deny this. Yes, as much as locking the door and letting Keegan take control was a way to make the boy feel better, it was also a way for Damon to get his rocks off too. And he certainly had gotten his rocks off, ejaculating a tonne of cum all through Liam's sheets.

At first he had nearly backed out, annoyed to have Keegan spit in his face. But in a weird way he enjoyed that too. He was being told what he was, that he had no power in this sexual exchange. If he wanted the younger buck, then he had to agree to Keegan's sadistic terms. And, so he did. But Damon hadn't realised that by agreeing to the terms he wasn't just surrendering power of the moment, he was losing it altogether and making Keegan the boss for good.

This submissive side to Damon was queer in more than just the sexual meaning. It didn't seem to fit with his sexual personality. But maybe that was why he did it. After so many years of being in the driving seat with his partners, it was fun to be letting go and allow someone else to take charge.

He had fucked up big time and there was no way he could have Keegan come stay with him now, no matter how much he wanted to help Matt reconnect with his son. Not now that the connection Damon had made with the boy was so fucking warped. He loved Keegan, he really did. But not in the physical way they had been expressing. Damon grimaced as some of the milk from his cereal dribbled down his chin, making him remember some of the dirty details of his permanent fall from grace. A fall that had left him *used goods*.

∞

After the shock of being spat on Damon surrendered to the dominance Keegan was exuding. He wanted to submit. He needed to be conquered. Keegan had made him take all his clothes off then get on his knees and suck his cock 'till he was ready to put Damon's arse to work. While Damon opened up and began sucking him, Keegan grabbed tufts of Damon's hair, guiding him lower on to his cock, demanding he take more. Damon gagged on the generous size being fed to him while trying to service his young master. Last time at the cabin having a man's cock in his mouth had felt strange, this time it felt more natural, a warm fulfilling sensation that he couldn't get enough of.

Damon's jaw was aching by the time Keegan pulled him by the hair, ripping his lips away from the young cock jabbing the insides of his mouth.

Keegan snapped, "Get on the bed. Get on your hands and knees."

Damon swallowed a lump of horny fear when he realised the position Keegan wanted him in. It was one that left Damon feeling vulnerable and a position that meant Keegan intended to fuck him hard. Fuck him hard and deep.

As Damon scrambled onto the bed, naked and waiting on all fours to be entered, Keegan rummaged through Liam's drawers looking for a condom. When he was done searching, he came and stood behind Damon's arse, which pointed out like an open invitation.

Keegan didn't appear to be in any hurry. He just stood there, observing Damon's submissive stance as sexy breaths transpired between them. Keegan stepped forward, roaming his hands all over Damon's body like he was inspecting him for quality. When he slapped Damon's arse, Damon knew he had passed the test.

Keegan then dropped his pants, letting loose his huge dick that seemed overly large for such a gentle-looking creature. He rubbed his bare cock around Damon's buttocks, slipping into his hairy crack, prodding Damon's quivering hole. Keegan was so fucking horny that Damon could feel the slippery precum sliding up and down his crevice.

"I couldn't find a rubber so it looks like you'll have to just take me bare," Keegan said.

Damon squirmed at the thought, feeling both blessed and doomed.

"Do you want me to cum in you?" Keegan asked, offering a dubious choice.

Damon hesitated for a stiff moment. He reached around and clutched his fuzzy butt cheeks, parting them for a bare invasion. *Fill me.*

Keegan slapped his rump, slowly slipping a finger inside to tickle his hole. "I can't hear you. Is that a yes?"

Damon felt his face go red in embarrassment when he realised how desperate he was to be filled with young hot spunk. "Fuck me, boss. Give me your load. I wanna feel you squirt inside me." Suddenly, Damon heard the sound of teeth ripping into something. He craned his neck, looking back to see Keegan unrolling a freshly opened condom over his thick penis.

The little shit had lied.

Keegan grinned back at him. "Sorry to get ya hopes up." He took his shirt off, joining Damon in the naked stakes. His tanned smooth chest was more than appealing. Damon's lips were dry but his cock sure wasn't, his dick slit leaked streams of precum as he found himself wanting nothing more than to worship Keegan's youthful body, to kiss and lick the boy from head to toe. There wasn't a piece of him Damon was too scared to touch. He didn't care how hairy or male certain parts were, he wanted to lick them all. "Can I kiss you," Damon blurted.

Keegan frowned, surprised to hear Damon speak. "What?"

"Can I kiss you, boss."

Keegan narrowed his eyes and shook his head. "I don't kiss sluts. I just fuck them."

Damon's feelings sloshed inside him. "Please, K dog. Let me kiss you."

Keegan reached down between Damon's legs, yanking his balls viciously. Damon yelped, his gut churning with a sick heat as his eyes began to water.

"You don't get to call me that anymore," Keegan said in a slight drawl.

"Sorry, boss."

"That's more like it." Keegan tickled his injured balls affectionately.

"Is there any place on your body you would let me kiss, boss?" Damon asked cautiously. "Anywhere you want. I need to kiss you somewhere. I wanna show you how much I need this."

Keegan looked amused, he cocked his head to the side. He may have been playing tough but he now seemed to realise how real the control was that he possessed. "Anywhere I want?"

"Yes, boss. Anywhere you want."

Keegan's answer was simple. He merely turned around, displaying his tight arse.

Damon shuffled 'round on the bed, staying on his hands and knees, he pressed his face against Keegan's buttocks, pecking a gentle kiss on his unblemished flesh. He kissed again. And again. And again. He finally gave in to his need to taste the boy and licked his tongue all over, grazing his stubble against Keegan's smooth arse.

Fuck you taste good!

He grabbed hold of Keegan's cheeks, opening him up like a book. Damon started at the tip of the boy's crack, running his tongue up and down the sparse hairs buried deep within Keegan's crevice. He flicked his tongue against the tiny muscle in the centre, desperate to get a thorough taste of this strict top with a virgin hole.

Keegan writhed, his body swaying in pleasure from Damon's anal slobbering. A series of mumbled groans escaped his lips. He may be the boss and the one about to do all the fucking but it was clear as day he enjoyed being eaten out. "Fuck that's good," he gasped.

Hearing the praised spurred Damon on. He licked more ferociously and reached around to tug on Keegan's condom-covered cock.

Keegan ripped his hand away. "Nope." He stepped away from Damon's mouth and turned to face him. A smiled danced on his face. "You're too fucking good at that."

"Thank you, boss."

"It's time I take care of your arse," Keegan said firmly. "Last time was good but tonight I am going harder. Tonight you get no mercy. You take it how I give it. Got it?"

Damon nodded. He wanted to smile but he didn't want his sheer admiration to be confused as being mockful.

Keegan clicked his fingers. "Get in position, slut."

Damon swivelled his body 'round, shuffling forward to give Keegan room. The bed sank a little further with the added weight of Keegan joining him on the mattress, positioning himself directly behind Damon. He grabbed Damon by the hips, spat into the palm of his hand, slathering it over his member then steered his cock straight towards Damon's less-than-experienced hole.

Damon buried his face into the mattress, silencing his yelp of pain that came when the head of Keegan's cock breached his entrance. The boy didn't seem to care or notice Damon's suffering, he pushed his cock again, slipping the fat meat in another inch. Damon gritted his teeth, sweat began to pour down his forehead. He breathed heavily through his nostrils.

"Don't be such a bitch. You haven't even got half of me in yet," Keegan taunted. He locked his feet over Damon's ankles then rammed ahead, attacking Damon's arse like it was target practise.

Pain seized Damon's limbs, making him shiver and tighten. Keegan's cock burned roughly as it slid farther inside him, not stopping 'till the boy's balls pressed against his arse cheeks. Damon couldn't stop panting hectically. It was all he could do to stop himself from screaming and running away.

Keegan dragged his blunt nails down Damon's back and sides, the scraggy touch hovering somewhere between sensual and animalistic. Keegan kept pressing, maintaining his balls-deep position, he slipped his hand underneath, running his fingers over Damon's raised abdominal muscles.

Damon continued to bite down on his teeth 'till the pain too-fucking-slowly began to mellow and fade in its intensity. He felt his sphincter loosening, adapting to the hefty girth impaling him. Damon swallowed hard, accepting this fate. He had succumbed.... He had submitted.

Keegan stay still, the only movement came from his cock throbbing like a beating heart.

Damon blinked away the tears and sweat poisoning his eyes. This was more than pain. This was motherfucking intimacy. A special closeness that came from the eight inches of young cock wildly tunnelling him, breaking him open. Damon ached for more as he accepted that this dismissive aggression was all he deserved. "Fuck me, boss. Fuck me," he whimpered, lifting his head from the sheets.

Keegan sniggered at the pathetic pleas. After making Damon wait just a moment, he dished out a magnificently wicked debut thrust.

The way Keegan's cock withdrew nearly all the way out and slammed back in with brutal aggression told Damon this was not going to be a marathon. It was going to be a sprint. A fast and furious fuck that would leave Damon out of breath, stretched and sore.

Keegan harpooned his hole, zapping him like a magic wand.

In and out.

Empty. Full. Empty. Full.

Fast and hard.

Deep and sharp.

Side to side.

Keegan was doing everything he could to obliterate the friction stubbornly clinging to Damon's butthole. It didn't take long before Keegan's effortless stabs gave way to puffed pants, he draped his chest over Damon's broad back, drenching him with his brewing sweat. Keegan grunted and growled as he continued to chip away at the remaining tightness Damon had left. Once Damon's arse had given up the fight and become slack, Keegan slowed his rhythm and started adding insults to Damon's slavish predicament. "Do you like being fucked like this? Like a cheap cum dump?"

"Yes, boss," Damon panted back, embracing the sexual slander designed to push him down some invisible sex-chain.

"You know, once I'm done with you, you'll be nothing but used goods," Keegan said, firing a spiteful pump of his hips.

"Ye-yes, boss." Damon lapped up the ruthless words, embracing his degrading ordeal like somehow it was freeing him. He didn't know how the fuck a nice lad like Keegan had learned to be so cold-blooded but he figured he probably had a porn addiction of some kind to thank for this incredibly sexy session.

"You like my *young* cock don't you, slut," Keegan taunted.

"I do, boss. I fucking love it," Damon heaved, praising the young buck for the way he was pummelling his anal canal.

"Good," Keegan huffed, slamming his pelvic bone into Damon's rump. "You know. After tonight. No matter who you fuck. No matter how many women you score, tryna be the big man. You will still be mine. My bitch." He laughed callously. "I used to think you were the man. Not now."

Holy fuck. The darkness in Keegan's words spurred a light within Damon. "Yes, boss. My arse will always be yours."

"That's right. You belong to me now." Keegan whacked his arse again, then shoved Damon's head down 'till his face was smooshed into the mattress, forcing him to sniff Liam's whiffy sheets. "You know the best thing about all of this?"

"What's that," Damon mumbled through mashed lips.

"Fucking you in Liam's bed. At least he's got some pride. Unlike you."

Damon knew they were only words but he could feel them reverberating through his body. Their meaning being blasted into his battered hole. He breathed in the naked male scent glued to Liam's bitter sheets while Keegan ploughed his arse from behind. His senses were under siege by youthfulness, penetrating him at either end. Reminding him, he no longer wore the crown. Keegan was taking it from him with every thrust his cock gave. Casting Damon forever in a submissive role between them. He knew Keegan would probably go on to fuck loads of other guys like this, and aside from being the first, he would be nothing special. Just some *slut* that was part of an ever-growing sadistic collection.

Finally, Keegan gave one last hard thrust that hit

Damon deeper than ever before. Keegan let out a muffled cry and his cock shook about, twitching forcefully as it emptied into the end of the rubber buried eight inches deep inside Damon's arse. To add salt to the wounds, Keegan kissed Damon's shoulder and whispered in his ear, "Consider yourself used."

The twisted gratitude nudged Damon towards climax, he gripped hold of his cock and only managed to give himself two quick tugs before he let out a humiliating squeal, showering the sheets with an abundance of creamy semen.

Damon gasped again when Keegan retrieved his cock, it felt like a vacuum sucking his insides out. He stayed still, transfixed in his conquered position. He could hear Keegan unravelling the soiled condom, a sloppy thud followed when it dropped to the floor. Damon slowly lifted his face, he stared down at Liam's twisted, sticky sheets. It resembled a blood-stained spot of sacrifice. A soft alter where Damon's pride and self-worth had just been slaughtered.

"Quick. We better go," Keegan urged, snapping Damon out of his trance.

Damon pushed himself up and started to get dressed. He went and unlocked Liam's door but rather than risk being snapped walking back through the house they opened Liam's window and lowered themselves onto the ground, creeping through the front yard towards the safety of Damon's car parked on the road.

The whole way home neither said anything. The eerie silence that had plagued them the night of the cabin incident seemed to have returned. It didn't carry the same guilt-laced flavour though, Damon thought, but it was still very heavy in mood. A mood that had an unspoken danger in its misty feel.

Once they were back at Marie's, Damon immediately felt safer. He nodded goodnight to Keegan in the hallway and made his way to the guest room. He knew he would have to get up early to avoid any repeat of what they had done. As hot as it was to be made feel small and worthless, he had no desire to feel insignificant around the breakfast table in front of the lad's mother.

He crawled into bed, stinking of sex and Keegan's sweat staining his back. He could feel how his hole gaped open, he couldn't believe he had endured such an annihilation. As he drifted to sleep, Damon knew that he had failed in his supposed mission of trying to convince Keegan to come back to Auckland with him. How could he? Not now they shared a dangerous secret. Damon's submissive secret.

∞

Damon finished off his cereal and went and put the empty bowl in the sink. He glanced at the bench where his cell phone sat flashing with a message. He picked it up and saw that it was a text from Matt. A simple message saying **call me**.

He still hadn't gone to see Matt since he got home. He had broken the news about failing to bring Keegan up via text. Normally Damon would see Matt most days but he had avoided his mate's visits, too ashamed to look him in the eyes just yet. It wasn't just Matt who Damon had been avoiding, it was everyone. He had hardly left the apartment since he got back. He hadn't even gone out and had a wild night for his New Years. Just stayed at home and drank himself to sleep.

He was in hibernation mode. A rare thing for him. But then the whole Keegan thing had been a rare event. A curious experiment that had backfired. Hiding away seemed the best option for now 'till he felt less shit about the immoral act he had committed. Last time he had come back and trawled bars for women, trying to fuck the gay deed out of his system. Such tactics seemed pointless this time. He had given far too much of himself away to ever claim it all back. He may have lost some of his male pride forever but Damon was still sure he was straight. *Pretty sure.*

He took a deep breath and dialled Matt's number. His mate answered after the second ring. "Hey, Matty. How ya feeling, brother?" Damon tried to sound as confident as possible.

"I'm good, aye." Matt's voice came back chirpy.

"Hey, I am sorry I haven't been able to visit since I got home. I've been bogged down with photo shoots the moment I got back," Damon lied. "And I'm sorry about not being able to convince Keegan to come up with me."

"That's not your fault," Matt sighed. "At least you tried."

"No worries. Anything for you, man."

"Did you have yourself a reckless New Years?" Matt asked. "I kept ringing you to come out but couldn't get hold of you."

"I know. I kept missing your calls. I must have had my phone on mute." Damon swore he could feel his nose growing like Pinocchio.

"Bugger. It would have been good for you to join us. We had a pretty big night," Matt said, excitement dripped off his voice.

"We?" Damon spluttered. "Have you met someone?"

"No. I wish." Matt laughed. "My friend Jason Tuki is visiting from Sydney."

"Jason Tuki? The funny gay dude from Port Jackson High?"

"Yeah. That's who you're thinking of, but he was way more than just that. He was such a fucking blast," Matt said. "He still is."

Damon immediately tensed up. A slither of jealousy gripping him. He hadn't seen the camp boy since their school days together in Port Jackson so in Damon's mind Jason was still a teenager walking around looking like a cheap version of cat woman crossed with Julian Clary.

"He is here organising his wedding. Him and Will are getting married," Matt said.

"You mean William Jenkins, don't you?"

William Jenkins was the older brother of Todd Jenkins; Damon's best mate growing up. They had forged a friendship based on the shallow traits they shared. Port Jackson boys with cash, good looks and egos the size of the fancy homes they lived in. Damon hadn't thought of Todd for years. He had pushed him to the back of his mind like the bad memory he was.

"Yup. Can you believe it. After all these years, they are still together. Or back together I should say. I'm kind of excited 'cos Jason has asked me to help plan the whole thing."

"Crikey." Damon laughed. "Matty Andrews, gay wedding planner extraordinaire."

"That's me."

"How will you find the time?" Damon asked seriously.

"I've taken the month off work."

"A whole fucking month?" Matt may have been his own boss—running his own accounting firm specializing in tax obligations for the creative industries—but he rarely took days off. Desperate to set a good example for his staff.

"Yeah. I figured why not. I haven't had a decent break in ages. After the wedding, I can kick back and relax. Maybe go away somewhere for some r n r."

"Sounds good. Where are you taking me?" Damon teased.

Matt laughed. "I was thinking Cairns for seven days at the end of the month. You wanna come with?"

"If I have a break in my schedule, then yeah, sure." A week in Cairns would be great but Damon wasn't in a hurry to be alone in a resort getting drunk with Matt just yet. He didn't trust himself not getting too pissed and slipping out any incriminating tales about Keegan's sexuality or how he had got tangled up with it.

"Anyway, I have a favour to ask," Matt said. "I was wondering if you would mind being the photographer for the wedding."

Damon groaned. He hated doing wedding shoots. He preferred his current line of *art* because it paid more. He had ditched wedding gigs for good after sleeping with a bride on her big day—leaving him laid but not paid after one of the groomsmen caught them fucking in the bathroom. "I dunno, Matty. I ain't too big on the whole wedding shoot thing."

"Come on. Can you do it for me?" Matt pleaded. "I

want Jason and Will to have the best. And you are the best."

"Well… I am the best at glamour photographs—nude models, Matty—not wedding parties."

"I imagine Jason would be up for posing nude if you asked him. Probably more so if you offered to show some skin too." Matt laughed.

"I bet he would," Damon mumbled.

"Jason's like family to me and I sort of already promised him you would do it," Matt's voice trailed off in a shamed tone.

Damon didn't like hearing Matt refer to Jason as family. *I'm your friend who is like family. Not that fucking looney tune.* He sighed into the phone.

"Oh, C'mon. Please. I will pay double what you would normally charge."

"You're only saying that because you know I wouldn't expect you to pay."

"Will you do it?" Matt asked again.

"Okay. I will do it. But only because it's you and because I fancy seeing what a gay wedding looks like."

"I think you'll find it will be a lot like a normal wedding."

"Boring you mean."

"I don't think Jason knows the meaning of that word," Matt said. "Anyway, he's coming round for some drinks this evening. Did you fancy coming over? It would be great if the three of us could hang out. My shout for you being such a good mate."

"I can't make it today sorry. The car has a flat tyre—absolutely shredded—and I haven't gone to buy a new one yet." Damon lied.

"Just put the spare tyre on. That's what they are for."

"That's fucked too. Didn't even realise that I hadn't replaced it from the last flat I had." Damon wiped his brow, worried if he was going to trip over his own lies.

"That's a shame. I haven't seen you since you got back. I haven't done something to annoy you have I? You can just tell me. I know I can be a pain and sometimes I don't even know I am doing it."

This was typical Matty. He always worried if he had somehow unintentionally offended or upset people. Truth was, he was as far from being a pain as anyone could be. "No, Matty. You haven't done anything. I just can't get out to Port Jackson tonight. That's all."

"Are you sure? It feels like you're hiding."

Damon cringed. Keegan's face flooded his mind as his body twitched in private places the boy had been. "I'm not hiding."

"If you feel bad about Keegan not coming up then please don't." Matt let out a sad sigh. "If he doesn't want to come see me then that isn't your fault. You can't force someone to do something they don't want to do."

Tell that to your son.

"I know. I just can't get there 'cos of the car. Otherwise I would. It would be great to have a drink tonight but I just can't make it."

The phone went quiet before Matt finally replied, "That's okay then, I'll bring Jason with me to yours."

"You'll what?" Damon rolled his eyes.

"Come to yours. At least we can hit town if we want afterwards. Ain't much to see out here in Port Jackson and I think Jason would be keen on seeing the city. He hasn't been out since he got back."

Damon knew there was no avoiding this bullet. Matt's voice carried excitement and it was obvious he wanted Jason and him to get to know each other. "Okay. Matty. That sounds great." Damon didn't like to say no to Matt. Some people deserve only yes's in life. "What time should I expect you both?"

"Say... just after nine?"

"Sounds good, my friend. See you then." Damon hung up and lay back into the couch. "Fucks sake," he muttered.

He wasn't in the mood for this. He just hoped that Matt wouldn't ask too many questions about the trip. Damon looked around his apartment at the mess of dishes on the bench and clothes strewn across the polished wooden floors. He sighed in annoyance to himself that he would have to now get dressed and start cleaning up.

But first I better go let the air out of these supposedly flat tyres in case they see my car.

CHAPTER THIRTEEN

Damon couldn't decide what was brighter; the city's thousand lights sparkling outside his window or the petite Maori man sitting on his couch looking like a fluorescent peacock. Jason didn't look too different to how Damon remembered. He was still a tiny wee thing with a lively face that never stopped performing dramatic expressions. His hair was black with a flaming red dyed streak along the fringe— which of course clashed hideously with his green glittery top and mustard-coloured skinny jeans.

"You have such a beautiful place, Damon." Jason nodded his head, gazing around the spacious apartment. "I know they say size doesn't matter but I beg to differ."

Damon coughed up a smile while Matt laughed a little too loudly. Since they had arrived that was all Matt had done. Sat beside Jason, laughing at everything coming out the guy's mouth. Begrudgingly, Damon accepted, that yes, Jason was good company, but he didn't like how he seemed to hog Matt's attention.

"I still can't believe I am sitting here with old school chums," Jason said. "It must be like heaven for you Damon to finally be sitting with the cool kids."

Damon chuckled. "I think we may remember the school hierarchy a little differently, Jason."

"Okay, I will admit, Matty may not have been too cool." Jason waggled his eyebrows at Damon.

"That's a slight understatement," Damon said, holding in a laugh.

"Oi, what's with all this picking on me," Matt said. "I was cool in my own way."

"Of course you were, girl." Jason pat Matt on the shoulder.

"Boy," Matt grumbled.

It was funny watching Jason call Matt girl. Every time Matt would correct him and Jason would ignore it.

"Remember how Matt used to wear nothing but hideous black baggy clothes," Damon said.

"Yes!" Jason grabbed his side and cackled. "Port Jackson's very own wannabe goth."

Matt rolled his eyes so hard he looked like a gambling machine about to win free spins. "Gee, don't hold back you two."

Jason smiled mockingly. "I never do, Matty Pie. Don't worry."

"So I wasn't the most popular guy at school. Shoot me," Matt moaned. "But just remember it was you who sat with me, Jason, so that can't say much for your reputation back then."

"I was more of a floater if I remember correctly," Jason said, a tickle of humour in his voice.

"Yeah in the toilet bowl." Matt jerked away as Jason slapped his arm.

"Nar. I remember you two used to be together all the time." Damon nodded. "Usually sat on the rugby field with all the rebel smokers."

"I'm amazed that you even noticed us," Jason said thoughtfully.

"How could anyone not?" Damon sniggered. "You both stuck out like infected dog's balls."

Jason whacked Matt again.

"Ough!" Matt laughed. "Why'd ya hit me. Damon said it."

"Because I am in Damon's house and trying to make a good impression. I know you better so you can take all the hits for both of you."

Matt rubbed his shoulder. "I swear by the time you go back to Sydney I'll be black and blue."

"If you're lucky." Jason giggled to himself as he took another sip of his drink.

Damon could see why Matt liked Jason. He was good company and never without a quick comeback. He imagined the pair must have had quite a lot of fun the way they bonded together at school. In a way, Damon envied them. They had been the down-trodden. The underdogs. The perfect characters to play unlikely heroes.

Damon focused his attention to Jason. "How is Will? What does he do with himself?"

"Will is fine. He still works in IT but is self-employed now taking on short-term contracts. Stuff like that." Jason knitted his brow. "Not that I have a bloody clue what *stuff like that* involves.

Damon chuckled. "Being your own boss is the way to be."

"For sure." Jason looked around at Damon's photography hanging on the wall. "And these are all your works?"

"Yep. All mine," Damon said proudly, resting back in his seat.

"Some of them are truly exquisite." Jason's eyes floated around the room inspecting each picture. "I just wish there were more men hanging up there. There's more tits out than a Boobs on Bikes parade."

Damon laughed. "Well, *exquisite* women are who help pay the bills more."

"Hmm." Jason looked back at Damon, regarding him with frisky eyes, tasting his lower lip. "I imagine you'd sell just as much if it were you in the photos."

"Shit, you're embarrassing," Matt sounded, blushing wildly

"What?" Jason exclaimed. "What did I do?"

"Maybe you can try marrying your fiancé before you start hitting on Damon."

"Calm down, Matty pie. I was merely pointing out the truth." Jason flicked his eyes back to Damon. "Your friend here is a gorgeous-looking man and he probably could make money with his body splashed on a canvas."

"Thank you, Jason." Damon smiled, laughing at Matt who looked like he wanted to melt into a puddle of shame. "If I ever stop making money from my talents behind the camera I'll be sure to whip my clothes off and make money from my talents hidden elsewhere."

"Oh god," Matt whined. "You're as bad as each other. Should I leave the room for a moment."

Jason laughed. "Sorry Damon. As stunning as you are, I am afraid I am taken. Will is all the man I need."

"Thank you for letting me down gently." Damon winked.

"Your most welcome. Besides, I don't want Matty's sloppy seconds anyway." As soon as Jason said it he looked like wanted to kill the words that had tumbled out of his mouth.

Matt sat upright and looked nervously across at Damon.

Damon cleared his throat. "What do you mean?"

"Nothing," Jason coughed on a laugh. "It was just a joke. One that apparently isn't funny." He quickly sculled back the last few drops in his wine. "Okay time for a refill." Jason reached over to the wine bottle and filled his glass up as quick as he could, probably in a rush to be drunk to forget his faux pas.

While Jason's attention was busy with pouring the bottle, Damon glared across at Matt accusingly. Matt held his gaze for all of a second before guiltily looking down at his fidgety feet.

What the fuck have you told him? Damon shouted in his mind. Yes, they had hooked up a couple times when they first became friends but that was nearly twenty years ago when they had both been horny teens trying things out. Innocent exploring. Damon never thought for a second that Matt would have told anyone what they had done. How fucking embarrassing. Damon's stomach twisted in knots as he hypothesised if loose lips were genetic. Keegan had inherited his father's big cock, did that mean he would inherit his big mouth as well?

Damon's fear was interrupted by a buzzing in his pocket. He fished his hand in and retrieved his cell phone. As if the universe were punishing him, it delivered a new issue to worry about. A phone call coming from Keegan.

What do I do?

Seeing Keegan's name brought on one hell of a dilemma. What if it was the young gun calling up to demand a sexy chat. He hadn't pulled a stunt like that but there was always a first time. *He's the boss,* Damon reminded himself. He gets what he wants. He couldn't seem to shake this bizarre subservient attitude hardwired in his brain; that from now on he must obey the blond teen.

But his father is right fucking there!

Damon's heart skipped in fear.

"Are you going to answer it?" Matt gave him a questioning look.

Damon shook his head. "Nar. It's one of my model clients. She can leave a message." He shoved his phone back in his pocket, burying it like a lie. He felt bad, like he had failed in some unwritten contract. Before he could even take a breath to try and relax, his phone fired off again.

"Maybe you should answer it. They are obviously desperate to talk," Matt said.

"Yeah. It could be important," Jason added.

Damon slouched his shoulders in defeat. "Yep. It might be important. Can you just excuse me for a moment?" Damon got up and walked to the balcony and shut the door firmly behind him. The symphony of the city screamed around him with its sirens and cacophony of crowd noise below. He took a deep breath and answered the phone. "Hey, boss. What's up?"

Keegan didn't say anything. He didn't have to. The sound of tears told Damon something was very wrong. This was not a phone call to demand sexual gratification. Damon drew a cautious breath. "Keegan. What's happened?"

"I've fucked up, Damon. I have really fucked up," Keegan sobbed into the phone.

"Tell me what's happened. Whatever it is it can't be that bad."

"It really is," Keegan said. "Bad for both of us."

Damon felt like he had been shot. "Tell me," he said

bluntly.

He stayed outside on the balcony and listened to the story. The city continued to scream around him but it petered out like a windy whisper compared to what Damon was being told. All his ears listened to was the nightmare Keegan was describing down the phone. It was *that* bad. It really fucking was.

.

CHAPTER FOURTEEN

He thought I was so nice he let me tap him twice, Keegan sung inside his head as he walked along the street on his way to Tony's house. His sneakers scuffed the concrete pavement in a happy rhythm matching the joyful tone in Keegan's mind. It was a warm afternoon and smelled of summer with the salty ocean air mingling with the fragrance of garden flowers. Keegan walked with a spring in his step the whole way as he thought about his second rendezvous with Damon.

The entire hook up had been unplanned. One moment he was upset, worried about what Garth may be telling people outside at the party, the next moment he had Damon locking Liam's bedroom door and initiate what felt like a ceremony. The sex had been sticky and hot. It was rough and mean, just like the porn he liked to watch on his computer.

In the cabin, Damon had been so reluctant and apprehensive to touch him, only at the end did he let slip moans of joy. Not in Liam's bedroom. In Liam's bedroom, Damon begged for it—lapping up spiteful words like the cum-soaked sponge Keegan used him as.

The handsome city slicker had been the one to offer himself, asking to be fucked. Keegan happily obliged, giving Damon the hardest fuck he could muster. Damon had gasped and groaned through the intrusion, burying his face into Liam's sheets muffling his sharp gasps. He had sounded torn between bliss and hurt but never once did he ask Keegan to stop.

To begin with Keegan had thought it was a game. Some sort of role play where afterwards they would return to normal and carry on like nothing had ever happened. But it didn't go like that. Damon's broken body language as he had lay on the bed afterwards, covered in spit, mesmerised by the sight of his own mess, reeked of something else. The older man had lost his usual cocky shine. He now glowed in a different way. A way that was pitiful and defeated. A glow that Keegan felt like he had created and now owned. Damon was no longer his elder, worthy of respect. He had become a possession, not a person.

When Keegan awoke the next morning to discover Damon had gone without saying goodbye, he knew that he hadn't imagined this shift in power. His father's best friend had run away before his mind and body could be put to the test again.

He really did make me the boss.

It was flattering but peculiar at the same time. Whenever Keegan tossed off daydreaming about kinky domineering fantasies, all that would happen was that his dick would spunk a hot mess that he would then have to clean up with tissues. Damon's broken pride felt like it came with a responsibility, not some quick easy mess he could wipe clean. Keegan didn't want that. He just wanted to get his end away.

Fuck he takes it up the arse good though. Sexy fucker.

Keegan had to do his best to only let the memory swell his ego and not his cock as he got closer to Tony's house for a day of board games. Tony was a board game fanatic and every Sunday he would try and get Skippy, Liam and Keegan around to play a round of the strategy game Risk. The game was sort of fun but the best part was the petty jokes slung at each other while they killed one another's armies off and took great delight in flinging the pieces off the board.

The other highlight of today's geeky play was that it would be the first time Keegan had seen Liam since the night of Joel's party. He had tried to get hold of Liam all week but his best mate had been missing in action. The only contact Liam had made was a couple of stingy texts text messages apologising for being so busy. Keegan wondered what could be keeping Liam so preoccupied.

There was only one answer; *A girl.*

The dark-haired stud was never short of female

attention and Keegan figured maybe Liam had finally met someone he liked for more than just one night. Someone he was hiding and keeping all to himself.

Still, it was strange that New Year's Eve had been and gone and Liam had been a complete no show. He was supposed to have joined Keegan and the gang for a night in town but text Skippy to cancel. Tony too had cancelled, saying he was unwell, which left Keegan and Skippy to face the celebration as a twosome. When they realises it was just the two of them they quickly ditched the idea of town, replacing it for a night of online gaming at Keegan's house.

The ditching of town was probably a good thing, Keegan thought. He couldn't guarantee that they wouldn't bump into the scraggly Garth who could quite easily bring up Keegan's failed gay flirt. Damon was right though, if Garth ever told anyone, all Keegan ad to do was deny it. There was no proof he had asked for a kiss.

Why did I even want to kiss him anyway? It's Liam I like. And maybe Damon?

Liam was the object of his desire, but Damon was a different sort of desire. The vain thirty-something was basically Liam in twenty years—which was a good thing for Liam because Damon still looked smokin' hot. Both men were similar in height and physique, nudging six feet with muscular and lean bodies. Sure, Liam had black hair and blue eyes while Damon's hair was brown and his eyes green but they both shared cocky attitudes and looks that demanded attention. Keegan imagined that they were like yummy dishes on a cooking show. Liam was the spicy ingredients needed to begin the recipe and Damon would be the finished product where the host would point and say, "Here's one I prepared earlier."

Keegan looked up and could see the road sign for Tony's street. He picked up his feet's pace and excitedly made his way to join his mates. When Tony's house came into view and Keegan saw Liam's car parked on the road, he let his Damon daydreams get replaced with his lust for Liam.

Keegan walked up the concrete path to the entrance

of Tony's home but before he knocked he heard Skippy's voice bellow, "He's here." Keegan dropped his hand from knocking, opened the door and walked inside. He found his friends all lazing about in the lounge. Tony and Skippy sat on the floor in front of the boxed game waiting to be opened while Liam appeared sat at the end of the couch, slouched over the arm rest. His muscly pale arms conveniently on full display in the blue singlet hanging loose from his body.

"Hey guys," Keegan greeted. He went and sat beside Liam.

"What a surprise he went to sit there," Skippy said.

Keegan shook his head. "What?"

"Nothing," Skippy said. "It's just funny that you chose to sit beside Liam."

Keegan narrowed his eyes and tilted his head in confusion. "Umm, I sat here because it's a couch. You floor dwellers may not know this but couches were built to be sat on."

Tony laughed and whacked Skippy's shoulder. "He sure told you, didn't he?"

"Yep. Keegan's the one in charge," Skippy said.

Liam groaned aloud and appeared to lean farther away from him.

Keegan stared at his best mate wondering what was up. "Is everything okay?"

"Yep," Liam said frostily.

"Okay," Keegan mumbled.

Liam stood up and looked down at Tony. "Is it okay if I grab a drink?"

"Help yourself," Tony answered.

"Quick keep your arse to the wall now that Keegan's here," Skippy blurted.

Liam dismissed the comment by pulling the finger at the tall Australian and walked off to get a drink.

"That's a fucking random thing to say," Keegan muttered. The room carried a weird vibe. He felt like he had walked in on a secret meeting.

"Sorry, bro, I don't mean to be rude," Skippy said

loudly. "We just know that you're an arse man."

Keegan laughed more out of nervous politeness than finding the comment funny. "Actually, I'm more a legs man than anything."

"I bet," Skippy snorted. "Me personally. Tits and pussy."

Keegan darted his eyes to the side, smiling. "Good to know."

"What about my legs, Keegan?" Skippy stretched out his long legs, rubbing them with his hands. "Do they pass the test?"

"What the fuck are you on, dipshit." Keegan laughed. "No Skippy. They don't." Secretly Keegan did think his tall friend had nice legs but he wasn't about to state that fact.

Tony chuckled. "Anyway, Keegan, what colour did you want to be?"

"Pink," Skippy blurted. "Poofs love pink." He gave Keegan a wicked glare.

"What the fuck is your problem, Skippy?" Keegan's eyes shifted uneasily.

"No problem," Skippy replied, blinking. "I think Liam's the one who has the problem. Not us." He burst out laughing again.

"Okay does one of you want to tell me what is so funny cos the joke is flying over my head like a fucking fighter jet at the moment." Keegan stared them down, demanding an answer.

"We're only teasing, Keegan," Tony said, catching his breath. "Honestly we don't mind that you're gay. It's all good."

Keegan shot his back straight. "I'm not gay!"

"Uh, yes you are," Skippy said patronisingly. "You like to skewer dudes arses like a kebab stick."

"Piss off," Keegan gruffed.

"Videos don't lie." Skippy beamed a foul smile.

Keegan rolled his eyes once he realised what they were going on about. "Don't be giving me shit about that. That video was Liam's idea."

Liam's deep voice startled him, "They aren't talking about that video, Keegan."

Keegan turned to find Liam standing behind him. "Wh-what video are you talking about?" He asked, trickling out an innocent tone. "We only made one."

"Look it isn't a big deal. You're still our mate. We don't care what you do," Tony said, sounding diplomatic.

"Yeah, bro. We don't care if you're a fag," Skippy added cruelly.

"Just tell me what video your talking about," Keegan snarled. He felt his skin begin to crawl.

"The video of you fucking your uncle," Skippy said, sounding almost gleeful.

"Damon isn't his uncle," Liam corrected.

"Damon?" Keegan shivered. "What the hell are you talking about. I haven't made a video with Damon. That's just gross!"

Liam pulled his phone out his pocket and fiddled with the screen before showing Keegan. "This video."

It was hard to see at first under the dim light in the video but slowly he made out what it was. The single worst fucking thing imaginable. On camera was him and Damon both buck naked, fucking wildly atop of Liam's bed. Damon's voice pleading, "Harder, boss, harder."

Skippy burst into hysterics. "Fuck man that is the funniest shit ever." He shook his head in disbelief. "You got some good moves there, *Boss*." He stared blatantly at Keegan's crotch. "And a huge fucking cock apparently." He fell into fits of laughter again.

Keegan couldn't move. His palms started sweating and it felt like the entire world had collapsed in his gut. He placed a hand to his mouth and raced out of the room 'till he found the bathroom. He crashed on to his knees and retched into the toilet bowl. He heaved up again and again as he felt dizzy from the social Armageddon unfolding around him. He spat out the last drops of vomit, huffing and puffing. "Fuck, fuck, fuck," he muttered to himself.

Tap, tap.

"Keegan. You okay?" It was Liam.

"Go away," Keegan mumbled.

"I'm coming in," Liam said.

"I don't want to see you." Keegan punched the floor. "Why would you do that to me."

Liam pushed the door open and poked his head in. He looked down at Keegan as if he were viewing a diseased lab rat. "Keegan, I didn't film you on purpose. I had the webcam on 'cos I had been live streaming earlier that day. I just forgot to turn it off."

Keegan's vision misted with rage. "You're telling me that that video is on the world wide fucking web?"

Liam dropped his eyes to the floor. "Yeah…sorry."

Keegan slapped his face and groaned. "You've fucking ruined my life, Liam. How could you?"

"It's not my fault," Liam said defensively. "No one told you to fuck Damon and leave cum all through my sheets."

Keegan's lip quivered as an avalanche of stress bulldozed his body.

"Sorry," Liam mumbled. "I'm not mad at you about it. I'm just—" Liam stopped.

"Just what, Liam?" Keegan glared up at his best mate who appeared reluctant to give an answer. Suddenly Tony and Skippy both appeared behind him. All three staring down like they were viewing a zoo animal.

"I'm just sort of creeped out that you have this huge crush on me and never said anything," Liam said. "It's kinda deceitful ya know. Like all the times we hung out I thought it was innocent, but you just wanted to get off with me."

Keegan shook his head. "I'm not some rapist, Liam."

"You raped that dude's arse by the looks," Skippy said, grinning.

"Fuck up, Skippy," Liam muttered, elbowing his tall friend. He looked back down at Keegan. "And I ain't saying you're a rapist. I just… ." He paused. "Don't know if I can trust you at the moment."

Keegan couldn't believe what he was hearing. He

scrambled to his feet. "Fuck this." He shoved his way through his mates and marched towards the lounge and front door. He needed air and he needed to be as far away from them all as possible.

Tony chased after him, catching up in the front yard and grabbed his shoulder. "Keegan. Don't go. It's not that big of a deal. We don't care if your gay. I know I don't."

Keegan flicked Tony's hand away and stared back at the flushed freckle-faced boy. "What do you mean it isn't a big deal?" He looked up at the sky as if the answers were painted in the clouds. "There is a fucking video of me porking my father's best mate all over the internet and you all think it's a big fucking joke."

Tony's face softened. "We don't think it's a joke. Come inside. Skippy is just being Skippy and Liam will calm down. He is just in shock."

Keegan blinked away tears and shook his head. "Nope. No fucking way. I have to go." He turned around and bolted. Running for his life. He didn't stop running till he ran out of breath. He hunched over gasping for air and clutched his side that ached with stitch. With a trembling hand, he pulled his phone out and dialled the only person he could speak to for help.

Damon.

.

CHAPTER FIFTEEN

The café was packed. Every table was taken and it was flooded with noise. Any other occasion Damon would be annoyed to see his favourite lunch spot so filled but today he was relieved to see it teeming with people. He was about to have lunch with the only woman who scared him as much as inspired him. The only person who might be able to help him.

Jenna. His mum.

Jenna didn't suffer fools and she didn't mince her words if you were brave—or stupid—enough to ask for her opinion. Normally Damon would know better than to ask the feisty baby boomer for her take on his personal life but with what Keegan had told him on the phone last night, he didn't have a choice. He didn't know what to do and he hoped like hell Jenna did.

Jenna wasn't like most mothers. For starters, she didn't let Damon call her mum. She was *Jenna* and had been since he was a teenager when she decided she didn't like the sound of being referred to as mum 'cos she thought it made her sound terribly old. Even now in her early sixties the rule applied. A plus side to her age denial was she never hounded him for not having any children yet. Most childless bachelors his age would be hounded relentlessly by pesky parents desperate for grandchildren. Not Jenna.

One thing most people didn't realise about his haughty mother was she knew she had her faults. She may have made a point of convincing people she was inwardly perfect whilst trying to look like a woman half her age—a vanity he had inherited—but underneath her shiny shell, Jenna was real and she knew how to protect that side of herself so no one would ever see her cracks. Her vulnerability. She was ferociously brilliant, Damon thought.

Jenna had made her own share of mistakes in her past—including one similar to the issue Damon was now facing—but had fought hard to correct them. After divorcing his father, Jenna had moved back to her home town in the Bay of Islands where she had fallen into a career in real estate and became what she had always wanted. A success. She had used her sharp wit and attractive looks to her advantage and before long became the top residential agent in the region, amassing a more than comfortable lifestyle without the aid of Damon's wealthy father.

During her time up north Jenna had met a new man, Keith Dunbar. He was completely different in every way to Damon's gawky professional father. Keith was a foul mouthed, rum swigging, car painter who thought the world of Jenna and treated her like a queen. Damon liked seeing this. His mother deserved nothing less and it was obvious she expected nothing less. After Keith sold his business, the pair—just last year—relocated to Auckland where Jenna worked part-time for a real estate firm on the North Shore while Keith enjoyed his retirement playing at home like a big kid building model planes that he would take out and fly at the park on weekends.

Damon flicked his eyes towards the entrance awaiting Jenna's arrival, tapping his foot uncontrollable under the table. He wiped his brow, telling himself to *remain calm*. He just had to go through the motions of asking how she was. How was Keith? How was work going? She would then ask similar mindless questions. It was then that he could approach the subject of Keegan.

A light gust of wind flew inside the café, Damon looked over to view his impeccably dressed mother walking in with dark sunglasses covering half her face. It was sunny outside but Damon suspected the tinted eye shields were designed to hide wrinkles more than block out the sun. Jenna soon spotted him and offered a light friendly flick of her wrist as a wave. She sauntered over as if the café were her runway and sat down to join him.

"How are you, Damon," she asked curtly, removing

her eyewear, placing them in her leather handbag. Her elegant perfume swirled across the table, digging its way into his nostrils.

"Really well. And you?" Damon looked around for a staff member to come take their order.

"I'm good as can be expected for a woman married to a ten-year-old boy trapped in the body of a pensioner." Jenna sighed dramatically. "You wouldn't believe what your idiot step-father has gone and done."

Damon shrugged.

"He went and adopted a bloody dog."

Damon curled his lips into a grin. "Okay. Why is that a problem? Surely you would love to walk around with a little fluff ball in your handbag like all the other ritzy ladies."

Jenna rolled her eyes. "Why on earth would you think I would want to carry something around that would just crap everywhere in my handbag." Jenna shook her head. "Women like that have issues, I tell you." She narrowed her eyes and whispered, "And for the record this beast wouldn't fit in my hand bag. It's a bloody Doberman!"

"A Doberman. Why did he get a big breed like that?"

"Apparently, it is a suitably manly dog for a manly man," Jenna said with a smearing of sarcasm.

"Oh boy."

"Yes. *Oh boy* alright. I told him he won't be so manly once we chop his nuts off."

Damon laughed. "You're gonna chop Keith's nuts off?"

Jenna shook her head. "No, the dogs. I chopped Keith's off years ago." She chortled. "That's what I carry around in my handbag."

Damon nodded, smiling.

Jenna drummed her manicured nails across the table. She squinted her eyes, honing her gaze on Damon. "When are you going to tell me what's wrong."

Damon flinched. "What do you mean what's wrong?"

"Well, you never ring me up for lunch and since I sat down you haven't stopped tapping your foot or twitching around like you've been tasered." She gave a clipped nod. "Now spill."

"Okay firstly, I do invite you out for lunch."

Jenna's stare became harder.

"Okay. I don't invite you out for lunch as often as I would like," Damon sputtered. "And maybe I am just tapping and twitching cos I'm excited to see my mum."

"Don't try that one." She dropped her angry face, replacing it with a softer look and very cautiously asked, "Am I about to become a grandmother?"

Damon shook his head. "No."

Her body loosened. "Thank god for that. I was worried how well I could feign excitement."

"Gee, Jenna. Don't overdose on your maternal instinct."

"I can assure you that has never been a problem." She touched his arm. "If something's wrong, you can tell me what it is."

Damon knew this. He looked around at the crowded establishment and lowered his voice. "Okay before I tell you, please remember that we are in the middle of a very busy café so people will hear you if you flip your lid."

Jenna gave him a pointed stare. "This is sounding ominous."

"Yeah. It's kinda bad I guess you could say." Damon scratched his neck, flicking his eyes to the menu on the table. He was scared to look at her while he told her his dilemma.

"For god sake, Damon, tell me before I'm dead and buried will you."

"You know Matty has a son, right?"

"Karina's boys? I thought they had moved back to London."

"They have. I mean his other son. His *real* son."

"Oh, yes. Kieran."

"Keegan," Damon corrected.

"That's the one. I've only met him once when he was about twelve or thirteen when you had him and his mother visiting on holiday. But gosh what a handsome wee thing."

"He isn't so wee anymore," Damon said. "He's eighteen."

"Breaking hearts all over town I imagine."

Damon shook his head trying to remain focused. "Anyway, I umm did something stupid. Like really fucking stupid."

Jenna leant back in her chair. Damon could see her mind at work trying to connect invisible dots to try and work out where this was going. He knew damn well she wouldn't get the correct answer. "Go on," she said lightly.

Damon clasped his hands together. He felt like he was going to burst open. Any notions Jenna may have had of him being a good person were about to be dismantled. He looked at his mother as her mouth gaped open, urging him to hurry up. "I had sex with Keegan while I was down visiting him and Marie for Christmas."

Jenna blinked. She looked like a mime stuck in a glass box. She blinked again. "You what!" Her voice came out far too loud. "You had sex with little Keegan!"

Damon groaned in embarrassment when a table of women next to them all looked over at him and his mother. He waved his hand at the nosey table and said, "Sorry my mother is a bit doolally and just misheard a story." He circled a finger at his temple to try and lighten the mood.

"Sorry my son is just embarrassed by you all listening to our private conversation, so if you wouldn't mind," Jenna said, casting a venomous glare at the nosy patrons.

The table of women soon turned away and resumed their own conversation.

"Now you were saying," Jenna said warmly, luring him into a false sense of security.

"I had sex with Keegan while I was visiting for Christmas."

Jenna muttered something indecipherable under her breath.

"And it wasn't the first time. We spent a night together when I was visiting for his birthday."

"Dear god, Damon. This just keeps getting better."

She rubbed her face like it was about to fall off. "Please tell me there isn't anything else." Jenna narrowed her eyes. "There is, isn't there?" She shook her head ruefully.

"It turns out that when we were... together this last time, it was accidentally recorded on someone's computer and has somehow wound up online."

Jenna's forehead creased with shock. "You're saying there is a sex tape of you having sex with a young boy on the internet."

"He's eighteen, Jenna. Not a young boy. You're making it sound really bad."

"It is really bad, Damon!"

"Gee, says the woman who pashed my best friend Todd Jenkins when he was the same age."

Jenna looked like smoke was about to float out her nostrils. She lowered her voice to its most ruthless and scorching tone. "That is quite a different story and you know it. That Todd Jenkins was crazy and took advantage of me in a moment of weakness and then wouldn't leave me alone. What happened with him was one kiss that went too far... not... not whatever it is that you have done."

"Sorry, okay." Damon heaved out a frustrated sigh, running a hand through his hair. "I am only telling you this because I need your help. Keegan rang me in tears last night telling me all about it and now I am worried that he might tell his parents. He is talking about coming up to stay with me to try and get away from the drama down there."

"Drama?" Jenna asked. "Does his mum already know?"

"No. But all his friends do and you can imagine the kind of crap their giving him."

Jenna nodded sympathetically. "Poor boy." She tapped Damon on the arm. "The first thing you have to do is tell that kid everything will be alright. Tell him that it isn't a big deal." She saw the way Damon looked at her. "Lie if you have to. The main thing is to keep him calm so he doesn't do anything stupid."

"I know. I did all that on the phone. I told him that

we can sort it out. That it isn't the end of the world."

"Now. Did you tell him he can come stay?"

Damon shook his head. "I told him that you were staying with me so if he came up he would have to stay with Matty." Damon felt his mother's disapproving look. "I can't have him stay with me. What if it happens again. He's a great kid—I mean man—and I care for him lots but not in a romantic way. It was just a stupid thing I did. Really fucking stupid."

"Yes. You were doing what all men do. Thinking with the wrong brain."

"I know, Jenna. I know. But what do I do?" Damon bit down on his tongue. "I-I am so fucking scared that he will tell Marie or Matty about what we did. Matty would never forgive me if he found out."

"Yes. I don't imagine he would be too thrilled to find out you slept with his son."

"So please. I'm asking you. Tell me how do I fix this?"

Jenna stroked her long dyed brown hair. "Okay. As your mother, I am obliged to tell you that honesty is the best policy and that you can't be sure that Matthew wont forgive you. Maybe he will forgive you. He is a sweet man and he does treat you like a part of his family."

Damon saw a glint in her eye that told him she wasn't believing her own spiel. He asked, "So that is the mother response out of the way. What about the *Jenna* response?"

She smiled. "I am glad you know there is a difference." She bowed her head, leaning in closer to tell him quietly. "You don't say a word. You pray to god that no one finds out. If there is a way to get rid of the video then do it. In the meantime, you need to think long and hard about anything—and I mean *anything*—that you have on Matthew. Anything that can be used as some sort of leverage."

"That sounds intense."

"It is. But you don't have much choice Damon. You need Matt to be in a position so that if he does find out that he will never ever in a million years want to speak of it to anyone. You both move in similar circles. If he breathes a word of this then you could find your career and reputation in tatters." Jenna looked almost sad at what she was telling him. "Now I like Matthew, I really do. He is a lovely, lovely man but he's not my son, Damon. You are. So, you need to have his heart in your hand and be ready to squeeze it if you have to."

CHAPTER SIXTEEN

Keegan lay on his bed, staring at the pale ceiling as he pondered how the end of the world never happened how he had imagined it. End times was meant to be ushered in with fiery meteors crashing into the earth, a nuclear holocaust, or maybe even flesh-eating zombies rising from graves. No such gory catastrophe brought about the end. Instead, the end of Keegan's world had come in the form of a fuck caught on film. A film hovering about on the internet, exposing Keegan for what he was. *Gay*.

Since he had stormed off from Tony's house—three days earlier—Keegan had endless amounts of text messages. All of them asking about this mystery video of him fucking another man. He didn't respond to most of them. He didn't want to encourage people to go looking for the video. The few he did respond to, he just replied. **Yes. It's true.** It wasn't like he could deny it.

Skippy had text a couple times, sending images of nude men, asking Keegan if he found them hot. Keegan's sexuality was just a big fucking joke to the retard. It was infuriating.

Tony had been to visit him, wanting to make sure he was okay. Keegan hated what felt like pity being spoon fed to him. He put on a brave face and told Tony he was fine, he cut his friend's visit short when he lied and said he had to go out.

Keegan felt bad for pushing Tony away but it was all so fucking embarrassing. They didn't just know he was gay. They had seen him naked... *and fucking*. They had witnessed his most private of moments. It was hideous. He hated knowing that from now on whenever he walked into a room where his mates were, they could look at him and know exactly what he looked like under his clothes. Even his heart's secrets had been undressed. They all knew he was head over feet for Liam—his best bloody mate.

Liam, however, was the one friend who hadn't messaged or tried to see him. He had remained hidden from the drama. Probably worried Keegan would hit on him or try grabbing his cock or something stupid. Keegan knew he should be upset by the very real fear of losing his best mate but with the horror of the whole situation, his sad heart didn't have the energy to break. He was too consumed with fear to think about love or any lack of it.

Keegan couldn't bring himself to try and find the video to watch it. He didn't want to see how bad it was. He had been there. He knew exactly what him and Damon had done together. How bizarre, filthy and scandalous it all was. He had deleted all his social media accounts. He didn't want anybody posting clips to his profiles where his mum or grandparents could see. They didn't deserve to find out about him like that. Still, he wasn't brave enough yet to tell them.

It felt like every hour a text would roll in from someone new finding out about the scandal. Even Tess had called saying that she had heard about it. "I don't want to pry but there's a rumour going around that you're gay and that there's a video of you online having sex with a guy."

He wanted to hang up. Ignore it all. But he worried if he did that then she would try and seek the video out herself and discover who was in the video with him.

"Yep. It's true," he had mumbled in a soft laugh. "I'm gay."

"And the video?"

"Yeah. Apparently so."

"I'm so sorry, Keegan," she had sounded genuine. She assured him she had no intention of trying to find the video and that whoever had uploaded it was a disgusting human being. Keegan wished he knew who had been so menacing to record Liam's live feed and then repost the video. If he ever found the person he would throttle them. But then it could have been anyone anywhere in the bloody world.

The past four days, Keegan had stayed in his room

trying to get lost in his online gaming but even that was a struggle when in the middle of a battle he would remember he was on the internet and using a technology that had betrayed him. As a last-ditch attempt to keep his mind busy he had started to read books instead. Trying to get lost in fictitious worlds. Safe worlds where no one knew him.

"Keegan," his mother called out, breaking his ceiling-staring pity party.

He sat up. "Yeah?"

"You have a visitor, darling."

Keegan wanted to tell her to pass on to whoever it was to just piss right off. He didn't want to see anyone.

His mother came into his room. "Did you not hear me?" His mother pointed towards the front of the house. "There's someone here to see you."

"Is it Liam?"

"No. Some boy whose name I don't know."

Keegan wondered who the hell it could be. He scraped himself begrudgingly from the bed to go find out who it was. As he got closer he saw the *whoever it was* had their back turned, wearing raggedy jeans and a baggy black shirt.

"Hello," Keegan said, causing the boy to spin 'round and reveal their identity.

"Hey, bro," Garth greeted, smiling. "You're a hard man to track down, Keegan Plummer-Butt."

"That's my Mum's last name. My surname's Andrews." Keegan hated his mother's maiden name that he had carried around with him till he turned thirteen and demanded he change it to his fathers. "How do you even know that name?"

"Your grandparents told me." Garth chuckled.

"My grandparents told you?" The look on Keegan's face must have given away his confusion.

"Yeah. I went by their place to see if you were there. That's where your birthday party was, so I figured that's where you lived." Garth nodded along as he spoke. "Turned out I was wrong but your grandmother invited me in for a cup of tea and we had a nice chat about you."

"Oh god. You had tea with my grandmother and talked about me."

"Nothing bad, bro. Only nice stuff. I told her I was an old school friend and was trying to get hold of you so she invited me in."

"Umm you're like six years older than me. How did she buy that?"

"Guess I must still have a baby face, aye?" Garth waggled his eyebrows. He didn't have what Keegan would call a baby face but then he probably didn't look 24 either. "Anyway, I wanted to come by and see how you are and apologise for the other night."

Keegan looked over his shoulder to make sure his mother wasn't nearby. He stepped forward onto the front steps and closed the door behind him. "You didn't have to come say sorry, Garth. It's okay. I'm sorry for being creepy and making you uncomfortable."

"You weren't creepy at all. Horny and awkward maybe. But not creepy."

"Thanks." Keegan smiled. "So yeah. No need for apologies and thanks for stopping by."

"Hold up, blondie," Garth blurted. "Are you trying to get rid of me already? After I spent all day looking for you and telling your grandmother imaginary stories about our school days."

"You told her imaginary stories?"

"Yeah, man. Like the time you got jealous of me when I beat you in the school cross country race and how much of a big crush you used to have on Suzie Macdonald."

"Who the heck is Suzie Macdonald?"

"Not a clue. Like I said; imaginary tales."

Keegan laughed. His first laughter in days. It felt good.

"So can I come in and hang out?" Garth pouted his lips, trying to look adorable.

"Why are you so determined to hang out with me?"

"Dunno," Garth said casually. "You seem a cool sort and I like the vibe I get from you. You're really chilled and polite. I like that."

"Really? A cool sort so chilled that he tried to kiss you then ran off crying?"

"Okay. The crying and running off was a bit dramatic but the way you pulled your smooth moves was pretty chilled." Garth smiled, giving him a wink. "I told you I would have kissed you. It was just a bloody kiss. It wasn't like you asked to fuck me." Garth pointed with both hands to his hips. "Anything above the waist is fine by me."

Keegan shook his head, smiling. "You're a bit different aren't you."

"I am wrong in all the right ways my mother tells me." Garth's long brown fringe fell across his eyes, blocking his vision, he quickly huffed back into place. "She also tells me I need a haircut and a job."

"Your mother's right." Keegan saw the way Garth was looking at him. Waiting to be invited in. "Come on then. You can come in. But I am warning you I'm boring as hell and just sitting in my room."

"Fine by me. We can be bored in your room together." Garth grinned excitedly and followed Keegan inside.

∞

For the next hour, they sat on Keegan's bed talking mindless drivel. It was surprisingly nice to have Garth with him. Someone to help break the monotony of his self-imposed social exile. Garth spoke about his passion for music, cars and girls—generic things most guys Keegan knew talked about. Yet, the shaggy-haired lover of ripped jeans seemed anything but generic, he had a coolness that Keegan couldn't quite put his finger on. A sort of *I don't give a shit* attitude that gave him a rebel streak, Keegan admired.

Garth flitted from one topic to the next like a bird jumping branches, his voice and body language always lively. While he was excited to share his own stories, he seemed even more interested in Keegan's. He sat listening while his face oozed a warmness, giving up his full concentration.

After Keegan had finished telling him about his failed plans for university, the room fell quiet for just a moment. Garth looked at him with concern in his hazel eyes.

"Is there something on my face," Keegan joked.

"No." Garth kept staring.

"Then why are you looking at me all weird?"

"Trying to see if you're okay."

"Umm, that's random. Of course I'm okay."

"Glad to hear that." Garth nodded. "So you're definitely okay?"

Keegan knew something was up. "You didn't come here about me hitting on you, did you?"

"No," he mumbled. "I heard some stuff about you and I wanted to see you're alright."

"You know about the video, huh?" Keegan shook his head. "Fuck sake."

"Joel told me about it." Garth gave him a sad smile. "I'm really sorry, blondie."

Keegan felt his stomach squirm. He swallowed and in a flaky voice asked, "Have you seen it?"

"Nar, man. I would never watch that." His body twitched like he had done something wrong. "Not 'cos its two guys or nothing but out of respect for you, ya know."

Keegan stared at the floor. "Cheers."

Garth leaned over and rubbed his arm. "Now tell me. Are you okay?"

The touch of Garth's warm fingers made Keegan crumble. His eyes stung and he choked on a sob. He shook his head. "Not really." He sucked in a breath to stop himself from blubbering. "I- I am so scared to go out anywhere in case I see anyone I know. Like what if they've seen it?"

Garth scooted closer, wrapping an arm around Keegan's back, rubbing affectionately. "Don't worry about what they think. It's none of their business."

"Easy for you to say. It's not you in the video." He scrunched his face up, wringing tears from his eyes. "It's not fucking fair."

Garth squeezed him tight. "Hey. Hey. I'm telling you.

It isn't the end of the world. And yes, you're right, I'm not the one in the video. But I'll tell you this. You're a good-looking dude. Who cares who sees you naked. They're all just gonna be jealous they don't look as hot as you."

Keegan sniffled on a laugh. "Thanks, but I know you're just talking shit."

"I'm being serious. I might be straight but I know a handsome bloke when I see one. I wish I looked half as good as you. I'd be dripping in sex."

Keegan rubbed his wet cheeks, smiling. He appreciated the effort Garth was making. "Thank you," he whispered.

"Don't thank me. Thank your mother for passing her genes on." He cocked an eyebrow. "And if it makes you feel better; word on the street is you're packing some major d in your pants."

"Oh god. That's embarrassing."

Garth removed his arm and bounced on the bed excitedly. "How is that embarrassing? If I had a monster cock like people are saying you do then I'd be whipping it out all the time to show it off." He stood up and pretended to unzip his pants and swing his dick about.

Keegan laughed at Garth's comical impression of flashing. "I'd believe that."

"I know I have a nice arse and I flashed you that at your birthday remember?" Garth patted his bum.

"Yep. You did." Keegan chuckled. His tears were beginning to dry.

"I can show you again if you think it'll make you feel better."

"I think I'm alright," Keegan smiled at his new friend who stared back with a crazy grin. "Thanks for the offer though."

"No worries, blondie." Garth's grin faded and a more serious expression covered his face. "Now is there anything that I can do to help?"

Keegan thought about this. There wasn't anything Garth could do. What he wanted was to escape to Auckland

and hide away for a while but as nice as Damon had been on the phone he hadn't been able to offer a room, saying his mum Jenna was staying with him.

Garth leaned forward and tickled Keegan's knee. "Anything at all?"

"You could build me a time machine so I can go back and stop myself from being so fucking stupid."

Garth looked down at his hands, pretending to jot it down on an imaginary pad. "Note to self. Build blondie a time machine." He glanced back at Keegan. "Cool. Anything else?"

"Nope." He flopped backwards, laying on his bed. "What I wanted to do was go away for a while and stay with a friend in Auckland but he has his mum staying with him and doesn't have room for me."

Garth plonked down and lay beside him. "Just tell him what's happened. I'm sure he would understand and make room for you."

Keegan shook his head. "He does understand. It's the guy who's in the video with me."

"Oh..."

"Yeah. And its hella awkward because he's actually a good friend of my family—my father's best fucking mate!"

"Your dad's best mate is gay?"

"I don't think so. He's fucked more women than anyone I know. I think fooling around with me was just him trying something new."

"I see." Garth exhaled. "If he's your dad's best mate does that mean your dad lives up there too?"

"Yeah, just north of Auckland."

"Then why not go stay with him?"

"I barely know the guy. I haven't seen him for nearly five years."

"Then you're overdue a visit, aren't you?"

"That's what he would say." Keegan lolled his head to the side and met Garth's eyes staring back at him. "Do you really think I could just turn up there and he'd be cool with it?"

Garth shrugged. "I dunno. He's your dad. But the way I look at it, I think he should. If you need to get away from the bullshit then you need to just go. Don't let the fuckwits around here get you down that you're too scared to leave your house. You should be out and about sharing yaself with the world."

Keegan couldn't help but laugh. "You should be a preacher."

"Maybe that's my next career move." He laughed. "Anyway. you should go up and see your dad."

"I couldn't even if I wanted to. My car's a piece of shit that will probably break down and I can't afford the gas or a bus ticket."

Garth leaned up, resting himself on his elbow. "Then I'll take you."

"What?" Keegan sat up. "You can't take me there."

"Sure I can. I have a full tank of gas and all the free time in the world without a job now." Garth's eyes fogged over with a possibility. "Shit. If your dad wouldn't mind, maybe I could stay a couple days and look around up there for a new job. I fancy being a city stud for a bit."

Keegan laughed. "Are you serious?"

"Serious as syphilis." Garth leapt up from the bed and spun around excitedly. "Pack your shit, blondie. It's time for a road trip!"

CHAPTER SEVENTEEN

Matt had spent the past two days with Jason hunting around the local area for wedding venues. They had tried everywhere from churches, halls, historic cottages and private garden estates but nowhere was available at such short notice. Jason was staring down the barrel of a backyard shindig. Jason didn't seem bothered by the scenario. If anything the idea of marrying in his mother's backyard was amusing to him. He thought Will's pretentious family would die at the prospect.

Secretly Matt also found the idea of upsetting the snooty Jenkins entertaining, but he still wanted Jason to have the best day possible. As a last resort, Matt offered Jason and Will the opportunity to use his own home's sprawling gardens for the ceremony. It was easily three times the size of what Jason's mum's section was and thanks to the efforts of the elderly Mr Bishop who Matt paid to do gardening, the backyard was a leafy oasis filled with exotic sub-tropical plants and rock pools. Provided Matt didn't have to tend to the maintenance of such beautiful work he was happy to have the garden look like it did and had let the old man design it how he liked.

Jason had squealed when Matt offered him the chance to use his home. "Are you really sure, Matty?" Matt insisted he was and so it had been decided that the wedding would be held at his home. It seemed nice that the oversized place—which had been so sad and lonely the past six months—would finally get some attention and make good memories.

Matt sat in his lounge going over Jason's long and bizarre list of things he would like incorporated into the ceremony. Matt had insisted he would take care of it, adamant to strive and deliver the type of wedding his zany pal dreamed of. As his eyes floated over the mental list, he wished he hadn't.

"Matty it's your old man," bellowed Matt's father as he stomped through the hallway. He didn't have to yell and say it was him. Matt always knew. The heavy footfall of chunky steps always gave away who it was approaching. It would have been safe to assume his father would make a terrible burglar.

He had given his father a key several years earlier for him to come feed the cat while Matt had been on holiday with Karina and the boys. His father conveniently never returned it and often would drop by most days and let himself in even if the door was locked. To most people— including Matt—this was an intrusion on privacy but to his father it was what family was for. Unexpected visits whenever they chose. The truth was his father found having unlimited access to Matt's liquor cabinets an added incentive.

His father appeared in the lounge dressed scruffy as usual. He plopped his chubby creaking body down on one of the arm chairs across from where Matt was sitting. He yawned like a lion as he patted his jelly belly. "I tell ya, Matty. That walk here leaves me knackered these days."

"You live two blocks away, Dad. It's hardly a marathon."

"Ha! I'd like to hear you tell me that when you're my age."

"I would, but I'd probably need a medium to contact you because you'll be dead."

His father gasped on a half-laugh. "Cheeky shit." He looked over at Matt fussing with the wedding list on his lap. "Whatcha got there?"

"I'm just going through Jason's wish list for the wedding." He kept his eyes glued to the paper. "Anyone would think I'm arranging a child's birthday party."

"How come?"

Matt cleared his throat and then began to read from the list, "A yellow carpet so it looks like I am walking to Oz. A life-sized My Little Pony. A copy of the Spice Girls greatest hits to be given to each guest." Matt looked over at his father.

"I don't think he wants anyone to ever forget his special day."

His father grinned. "Considering it's two blokes standing up there, I know I sure as hell won't forget it."

Matt shifted in his chair. "Who said you were even going?"

"Why wouldn't I be going? I've known the boy since you two were making mud pies together at kindergarten." His father chuckled. "Even back then wee Jason was a fan of mud ponds."

"Nice one, Dad," Matt groaned. "If you do come then maybe go easy on the gay jokes cos us straightys will be outnumbered I think."

"Does that mean your mother is coming?"

Matt couldn't tell if this was a cheap shot or a genuine question. *Probably a cheap shot.* His father and mother played nice on the rare occasions they came into contact but Matt sensed his father had never really gotten over the fact his wife spurned him by leaving him for a woman.

"No. She is in Hawaii competing with Stephanie in an over sixties triathlon. Not the kind that is two blocks long."

"Triathlon," his father muttered. "The woman's mad if you ask me. Who in their right mind in their sixties does that sort of codswallop for fun. It isn't fun at any bloody age, so I can't see how being brittle boned with saggy tits makes it any more enjoyable."

Matt had to hold in a laugh at the ridiculous image his father was painting and try to remain diplomatic. "You know, dad, you might find if you did some exercise yourself you'd be out doing more like mum does."

"Piss off. I'm too buggered for all of that nonsense at the end of the week." His father blurted. "Besides, I do all the exercise I need."

Matt frowned. "Which is?"

"I get my cardio by walking to the fridge and I do my weights when I lift a nice refreshing cold beer to my lips."

Matt laughed. He did like how his father had simple pleasures. "You got me there, Dad."

"Anyway. Find out from Jason if I can attend. I'd be

quite keen to see how one of these gay weddings work."

"Going by Jason's wish list I don't think this is a typical wedding for anyone on earth."

"Is there anything I can help you with for the wedding?"

Matt looked down at the list again going through the items. "Hmm. Not unless you have a wand to turn my backyard into a Disney theme park." Matt handed the piece of paper over to his father. "Have a look and see if there is anything you can find."

"Hmm." Matt's father scratched his balding head as he scoped out the scribbled items. "Crikey. The boy is fucking dreaming." His father chuckled. "Is this a wedding or a circus?"

"I know, right?" Matt sighed. "I guess if it's what he wants, it's what he wants."

Matt's father looked lost in the list 'till finally he put his hand up. "Got one," he said. "I can get the birds he wants."

"Are you sure?"

"Yeah, shouldn't be a problem."

"You'll need to get them a gold cage too. I think it's on the list."

"Excuse me?"

"The cage," Matt repeated. "Jason wants them in a gold or bronze coloured cage before their released." He shrugged his shoulders. "Just buy any fucking cage and we can spray paint it. But make sure it's quite big otherwise its cruel."

"That boy doesn't ask for much does he," Matt's father said sarcastically before giggling.

"I can do it if it's too much hassle," Matt said.

"No, no. I would like to do my bit." Matt's father's eyes twinkled in cheeky fashion. "If I ain't the one paying. They don't come free."

Matt groaned. "Would you like to use my card?"

"That would be mighty generous of you, Matty." His father shot him an overbearing grin. "Have I told you you're the best son in the world."

"Yeah, yeah," Matt said dismissively. He pulled his wallet out and flicked his card across to his father. "Don't go crazy with it."

"Does crazy include shouting myself a couple rounds at the tavern later?"

"Yeah, that's fine. Just as long as you drop it back round tomorrow."

"Good man." His father eyed up the card like he was about to take it on a date. "I am so glad I passed my smarts on to you so you'd wind up so financially secure."

"Ha!" Matt couldn't hold in the laugh. "From you? Mum's the one who passed on the brains."

"Ya mother." He shook his head. "That woman isn't bright enough to attract a moth."

"Come to think of it, my moneys on me being adopted."

"Nope. You're definitely mine. I remember the night we made you. It was one of the only times ya mother got creative in the sack."

Matt cringed.

"Yep. Good night that was." His father said, nodding. "We nearly called you wheelbarrow in honour of the conception."

Matt closed his eyes briefly, trying to block out the hideous image. "Okay, old man. I don't want to know any more." He stood up from his chair and pointed towards the kitchen. "Did you want a coffee, Dad?"

His father shot back a ginormous grin. "I thought you'd never ask."

Matt went to go to the kitchen but a clamour of knocks echoed from the front of the house.

"Are you expecting company? A new lady friend, perhaps?" His father's voice sounded hopeful.

Matt shook his head. "No such luck. It's probably Mormons." He left his father sitting in the lounge and went to see who it was. When he saw the outline of two figures through the frosted glass panes of the door he groaned to himself assuming it was a religious house call. He rehearsed a quick polite decline in his head then opened the door. "Sorry but we already have a faith in this—" The words instantly hit a wall of shock at the sight of the two young men standing with packed bags at their feet.

"Hi, Dad," Keegan said with a feeble wave. "Got room for two?"

CHAPTER EIGHTEEN

Port Jackson's beach was so different to what Keegan was used to. Back home the west coast sea was rough and crashed angrily on black iron sand littered with chunky rocks and driftwood. Here though was quite the opposite with smooth golden sand and a sheltered harbour cradling calm waters. Yachts floated in the sea while people swam, families picnicked and beautiful bodies played volley ball. The beach was buzzing and quite packed for a week day but with such muggy weather it wasn't surprising that him and Garth weren't alone in wanting to cool off via a dip in the Pacific Ocean.

He stretched his legs out and dug his toes in the sand, letting the warm sunshine dry his wet skin. He looked out at the sea where Garth was still splashing about like a manic toddler. Garth kept pulling faces at him in-between a huge grin he had planted on his face. It was nice to see him happy. Garth always looked happy though. He suited happy.

Keegan also found himself happier being up here. It had been three days since they arrived unannounced at his father's doorstep and the break away had been therapeutic for sure. His father's home was awesome and Port Jackson was a nice place for sure. The house was far too big for just one person, Keegan thought. He felt bad for his father, knowing that not too many months ago it had been a family home with a wife and kids.

Saying that, it wasn't like the house was void of activity. Keegan's grandfather stopped in everyday by the looks, making his way straight to the fridge in search of a beer. The old man was just how his mother and her parents had warned. *An uncouth individual with his mind always in the gutter.* He was these things but in the most entertaining and goodhearted way. He was always cracking dirty jokes and asking Keegan and Garth about helping him pick up young birds. Garth humoured him and said that they could be a trio hitting on chicks down at the beach. Keegan though, would just sit there nervous that his family didn't know his preference for guys.

The other visitor to the house was his father's good friend, Jason, visiting from Sydney. The quirky man was a walking piñata of campness. Each time Jason walked in the room he made Keegan want to smile with his exuberant personality and whacky take on fashion. While Keegan's grandfather and Jason were constantly dropping in, the one person noticeably absent was Damon.

Keegan had hoped to see Damon. Maybe his co-star in the shameful sex tape would know what he should do. How to try and fix the problem. But so far Damon had not been around to his father's house despite Keegan texting and telling him he was there. His father had even called Damon and told him the news so it wasn't like he hadn't got the message and was unaware.

Is he avoiding me?

Keegan hoped not. He would feel better if he knew Damon was supporting him and sharing the ride of shame. Share the hurt and embarrassment with him a bit. Keegan still hadn't gone near a computer since discovering he had become an internet sensation but the change of scenery was proving to be good for the soul. Knowing he was hundreds of kilometres away from the scene of his biggest mistake had a calming influence. No worrying about running into any of his friends who could mock him and tell him how they had seen the video. No need to stress about his mother finding out. Here in Port Jackson he could just relax and unwind while he figured things out.

There were some big choices to make. Before the video incident he had been lazy, putting off finding a job or enrolling to study. He knew he could have spent all year at home with his mum not paying any board and just be a slob. She was soft on him and wouldn't have pushed too hard to get him out of the house. But life wasn't soft. Life was hard and had snuck up on him with its nasty gnashing teeth and its cold bite of reality.

Still, he didn't have to decide what his plans were right away. He didn't have a job or school to go back to and it was obvious from how stupidly generous his father was being that he could stay for as long as he liked. The man was giving cash out like a money machine and nothing at all seemed too much trouble.

The day they arrived and knocked on the door, his father had reached out and grabbed Keegan in for a hug like he was afraid to lose him. When his father had finally let him go, he looked embarrassed for coming across too eager. It was almost funny the way his father's pale skin glowed so bright, giving away even the slightest feeling of shame.

Thank god, I have Mum's olive skin.

It had been weird standing there, having not seen each other for four years. He was now an inch taller than his father. When they had last lay eyes on one another Keegan's voice was still breaking and coming out in squeaks and he had still been a year away from shaving.

The awkward family reunion only went up a notch when they had gone into the lounge and Keegan had found his grandfather sitting there. The man looked the same how Keegan had remembered. Old, chubby and jolly.

Thankfully after his father had gone and grabbed them each a drink, Keegan began to feel more at ease. They started off with how great it was to see him, asked how his mother was, how long was he in town for? After the polite formalities were out of the way, they talked for hours, going over the lost years they had not seen each other. *Lost years.* Keegan felt a tad guilty from all the hospitality being offered and that he hadn't bothered to come up any sooner. But then it wasn't like his father had ever bothered to come see him either.

"Oi, blondini!" Garth yelled from the water's edge. He began trudging forward, holding up his baggy black shorts that kept drooping. In a sloppy thud, he crashed his butt down on the towel beside Keegan. He dipped his head forward and started to shake his hair like a mangy dog, sending drips of water torpedoing all over Keegan.

"Cheers for the shower, motley. Now I'm wet again!" Keegan laughed and shoved Garth's shoulder.

"Aww don't you want my body's juices."

"You can keep your juices to yourself."

Garth leaned forward, running his hands down his legs. "That's not what you thought the night of Joel's party," he teased.

"Okay, let's not forget I was so pissed I was probably seeing two of you."

"You must have been in heaven having two of me," Garth smirked.

"You know, I just love how down to earth and not-vain-at-all you are."

"That's me," Garth said, flashing a sly wink. He looked down at his wet body, inspecting himself. "Are you serious that I ain't your type?"

"Yes, Garth. I can assure you that you're safe from me ever trying to hit on you again. If the sun was my type, then you would be Pluto."

"Ouch," Garth rubbed his chest dramatically like his heart was broken. "Way to let a fella down gently."

"I am sure you'll live."

"What's wrong with me then?" Garth asked in an accusing tone.

Keegan laughed. "Nothing."

"Nar, come on," Garth leered across at him. "What's so wrong with me that I ain't on your list?"

Keegan nibbled on his lip. "I guess I prefer guys with muscles."

"Ha! What do you call these?" Garth sat up straight and flexed his bicep.

"I would call those baby muscles that are waiting to grow up."

"Ooosh." Garth laughed. "Their bigger than your muscles."

"You asked what I like in other guys, not what I look

like."

"True," Garth said. "What else?" His eyes daring Keegan to divulge more.

"Well…" Keegan stared his friend up and down. "I prefer guys who know what something called a haircut is."

Garth ran a hand through his wet hair that was beyond shaggy. "Nothing wrong with my hair. You make it sound like it's long or something."

"I just mean I prefer guys with shorter…tidier hair."

"How short are we talking?" Garth tugged on his hazardous fringe. "Like bald?"

"No. Not solar panels."

"Right. Anything else about me you want to pull to pieces and give me a complex about?"

Keegan rolled his eyes. "Oh god. You asked me to tell you, don't get shitty."

"I'm not shitty." Garth shook his head. "I am just amazed that you can't see how fucking stunning I am." Garth bent his legs up to rest his elbows on his knees. "Now I know you like my arse. Don't even try to deny you checked it out the first night we met."

Keegan chuckled. "Okay, Garth. I admit. You have a nice arse for a weakling with a Woodstock hair doo." He patted Garth on the shoulder. "Feel better?"

"Pfft. Keegan, you need—" Garth's mouth dried up of words as his sight was hijacked by a dark-haired beauty running past in a bikini. His eyes looked like they wanted to pop out and run after her.

"You look like you have moved on already," Keegan said, nudging him with his elbow.

"Ha. Sorry. But that deserved my undivided attention." He turned and faced Keegan. "I bet she would appreciate this hot body even if you don't." He patted his flat stomach, which was pale and smooth aside from a wide trail of hair that fed down below his belly button. Keegan flicked his eyes down at the self-confessed *hot body*. It wasn't unattractive. Garth's almost skinny appearance was probably fine to most people but it wasn't Liam or Damon fine. Garth pointed a finger out at the crowd of people on the beach. "So then, Mr fussy, if I ain't your type, which one of them are?"

"Do we really need to find out what my type is? I don't even know if I know yet."

"Yes we do," Garth said quickly back. "You have had a rough arse fucking week and we need to find you the man of your dreams to take your mind off of things. So tell me... which one of them fine gents would you like to be bent to take it up the rear vent."

"Wow... your poetry is amaaazing," Keegan mocked.

"What can I say. I have a way with words."

Keegan nodded. "Mrs Palmer must get weak at the knuckles when she hears such romance."

Garth laughed. He held his hand out, wiggling his slender fingers. "Yep. One lucky lady I have here and she always puts out." He finally laughed before launching back into Keegan about what his type was, "So... which guy here do you like?"

"I dunno." He scanned the beach, his eyes hopping from shirtless guy to shirtless guy. "I don't know if any of them are *my type*."

Garth scoffed. "Oh, come on. You're telling me you wouldn't sleep with any of them?"

Keegan shrugged.

"Well, is there anyone back home that you like?" Garth asked.

The fact Garth didn't know the answer to this told him he hadn't seen the video. "I suppose I have a bit of a crush on Liam."

"Joel's little brother? Isn't that one of your best mates?"

"Was," Keegan sighed. "I don't think he has handled the finding out about me too well."

"Have you spoken to him?"

"Not really." Keegan shuffled uncomfortably on the towel. "I... I haven't called him cos I don't know what to say. In the video there is a part where I talk about how much I like him and so that has made shit more awkward."

"I see," Garth said softly.

"Like if it wasn't bad enough seeing me fuck another guy it's made weirder cos he knows how I feel about him." Keegan cringed thinking about it. "I really screwed shit up."

"He could always contact you." Garth nodded, backing up his claim. "It doesn't have to be all up to you to be ringing and mending bridges."

"You reckon?"

"Yes. Shit, Keegan, all you did was have sex and say you like someone. It's hardly the crime of the fucking century. If it hadn't been recorded then none of this would be a big deal. And if Liam with his *big muscles* and *short tidy hair*," Garth said in a pissy voice, "is freaked out about it then that just makes him a fuckwit in my books." The words came out with an angry edge. "I haven't known you that long but I think you're a decent guy and if Liam and you have been best mates for however many years then he should get over himself and fucking ring you already and find out how you are."

"You really think that?" Keegan asked, feeling better from hearing Garth's perspective.

"Fucking oath I do. I don't *think* it. I *know* it." Garth slowly nodded, a look of concentration on his face. "So guys like Liam are your type, aye?"

"Apparently."

"How about you and me go out clubbing tonight and find you a Liam replacement."

"Clubbing?"

"Yes, Keegan. Clubbing. We can go to a gay bar and see if we can find you some mindless gym bunny who doesn't mind if you call him Liam number two."

He had never had a night out in Auckland before. The idea of it sounded fun but he wasn't sure about hooking up with anyone. "I don't think I am in the mood to be doing anything with anybody just yet."

"Don't be silly. You need to get back out there and find yaself a new stallion to ride." Garth's lips curled up mischievously. "Unless of course you want to be the one getting ridden."

"Let's not go there." Keegan shook his head.

"Why not?"

"Would you like it if I asked you how you like to fuck?"

"Fuck. I don't care. I'll do any position the girl wants if she will have me."

Keegan sniffed loudly.

"What are you doing?" Garth asked, frowning.

"Just smelling that cologne, you got on. I think it's called desperation by desperado."

Garth laughed, elbowing Keegan in the side. "I'll give you desperate." He looked out at the sea, lost in thought. "Yep, before I head back home I wanna make sure you have met someone awesome who can keep an eye on you while I'm not around."

Keegan's stomach somersaulted hearing Garth mention he would be leaving. He didn't want Garth to go. Having a friend with him was making staying with his father less awkward. "I thought you were gonna find a job and hang around."

Garth shrugged. "I was but... I haven't even started looking. It could take a while to find something and then I'd have to try and find a flat and that would take ages. I can hardly stay with your dad much longer and wear out my welcome."

"You aren't wearing out your welcome."

"Aww, will you miss me?" He eyed Keegan for a moment. "I know I'll miss you."

Keegan smiled. "I'll miss you too." It felt like a sweet moment.

Then Garth blew the moment to shards. "Yep. Tonight we hit town and find you some butt love."

CHAPTER NINETEEN

Damon stood out on his balcony admiring the beautiful sunset while his mind mulled over ugly deeds. Matt had phoned him earlier and said he would stop in for a drink of water after his jog around the domain. Normally Damon liked that Matt would bother driving all the way to the city to get his cardio workout and then come see him, but now it was a painful inconvenience.

Matt would be here any moment, completely unaware of the dirty game Damon was about to begin. A game he never thought he would do again. He brushed his sweaty palms down the front of his shirt. Damon didn't do nervous as a rule. His natural disposition was one of confidence like most other good-looking people. An air of ease people like him took for granted. He didn't take it for granted anymore. Not with how he had felt the past month with so much guilt and fear worming through his body.

Jenna's words of warning and how he go about solving his problem had been haunting in their cruelty. He knew Jenna adored Matt and that she was only giving Damon this advice to protect himself, but it was ruthless. Extremely ruthless.

He may never even find out about me and Keegan.

Damon had tried to comfort himself with this thought all week, hoping he wouldn't have to resort to such duplicity. The internet was a universe and the video with Keegan was only one tiny spec in its vast ocean of stars. The chances of it surfacing were slim, surely.

Weren't they?

It felt like being locked in a cold war, perched on a knife edge, waiting to fire the ghastliest weapon he possessed if Matt ever stumbled across the truth. The problem was he didn't have a weapon. He didn't have the kind of leverage

Jenna said he needed. Matt was a nice guy and was void of scandal. A regular guy who had made himself wealthy through hard work and a bit of luck. As far as Damon knew not a cent of it was dirty money. This is why he was left to play the *dirty game* he had planned. It was the only chance he had to protect himself against an angry father's backlash if the video were discovered.

Damon let his mind wander through twenty years of friendship. Twenty awesome years. Even while Matt had lived overseas they had been in touch via email and Damon jetting over to holiday in London and catch up once every year. When Matt had returned to New Zealand, Damon became a regular guest at his waterfront home and was warmly welcomed by Matt's new wife Karina. They had had some wonderful evenings and now Damon was on the verge of losing ever sharing another one with his best mate. He wished he had a remote control that could flick a switch inside Matt, making him obey, make him not get angry for Damon sleeping with his son.

Damon's trip down memory lane ended at the beginning. The summer they became friends. When anybody asked how they got to know each other they would both give the same bullshit answer. *We knew each other growing up in Port Jackson.* That wasn't the whole story. Damon had never given Matt the time of day back in high school. Back then, Matthew—*Fatty Matty*—Andrews, was a lonely teen who was as uncool as you could get, dressed head to toe in shitty black outfits and who hung out by himself after his only friend Jason had left school. It was only once Matt took a job as a house cleaner for Jenna that Damon and Matt got to know each other. And it wasn't the type of introduction to friendship you shared with others.

Matt had been so enamoured by the popular kid Damon was back then that he would do *anything* for him. Absolutely anything. Damon had taken advantage of this and had got the young Matt to do him favours of a sexual nature. It had started off with just getting Matt to suck him off. Quick messy blowies. Matt wasn't keen on the idea at first and had tried talking his way out of it. The dorky guy was straight but he was so fucking desperate to impress and be liked that he eventually relented and sucked Damon's dick anyway.

But then the strangest thing happened. Matt became attached. Needy and clingy like he was in love or some crazy shit. It had been a weird thing to have to deal with but rather than deal with it sensibly and explain to Matt it was just harmless fun, Damon took advantage of the boy's emotions by stepping up the favours to full blown sex; bending Matt over and using him as a convenient place to stick his cock. *Any hole's a goal* had been the philosophy and Damon followed it so brutally that Matt took more than one load inside him just to please the selfish horny teen Damon had been.

In the end though Damon had regretted his actions. The way he had treated Matt was fucking ghastly and he succumb to a guilt so severe that he did everything he could to apologise. He had gone to Matt's house where he said sorry for all the bad things he had done, all the selfish shit he had pulled and he made a promise to Matt that he would never ever hurt him again. *Ever!* After that promise was made they had gone to Matt's bedroom and made love. Not fucked. It had been love. The weirdest kind of lovemaking though. The type that said goodbye and hello at the same time. It was a farewell to the sexual side of their dynamic but a big warm welcome to them becoming friends. Equals.

After that last night spent intimately together, fusing their bodies in a mess of sticky limbs, they never mentioned any of it again. Damon didn't know about Matt but he himself had done his best to never give it any thought. He threw the memory away like a piece of litter. As far as he was concerned they had both been young horny kids, exploring their sexuality and pushing some boundaries. That was all. Nothing more. And most definitely not something they would ever do again.

'*Till now.*

Damon swallowed hard. The only time he had ever

had control over Matt was those early days. Those dark dubious days where he had ruled Matt's heart. It was a fucking long shot but Damon needed to have Matt back to that dynamic. One where they weren't equals. The one where Damon was ruler. Things had changed so fucking much though and it wasn't high school anymore but Damon knew that even at thirty-seven he was still one of life's cool kids and somewhere deep down Matt was still the unpopular loner desperate to be liked and given approval.

This is so fucking bad, Damon thought.

He may have let Keegan become his boss, but Damon needed to regain his sexual authority. He needed to copy Keegan's ruthless approach and exert control over Matt. Damon felt his tummy squirm and his face burn with a shame that wasn't entirely unpleasant. It was fucking crazy but he knew if Keegan walked in the door right now, he would probably do whatever the little punk wanted. Probably even beg him to degrade him… use him again… punish him.

Until Keegan had buried his dick inside him like he had erected a flagpole and conquered him, Damon had always done what Damon wanted. Nobody got shit from him unless he thought he was getting something out of it. He was selfish and he liked being selfish. But now he found himself under a spell where he had to give someone else what they asked for, no matter how destructive the request was. Keegan wasn't even someone he was romantically interested in. He was only eighteen and had a fucking cock!

None of this makes sense.

Damon's attention was swiftly brought back to Matt when he heard heavy footfall echoing up the stairs outside his apartment. He took a series of deep breaths, slapped his cheeks and said to himself, "Calm down, Damon. You got this." He quickly stripped his shirt off, wanting his body to help do some of the work. He ignored his inner voice telling him how bad this all was.

I'm sorry Matty, but this is the only way I know.

CHAPTER TWENTY

Matt clutched his side that burned with stitch as he used his free hand to knock on Damon's door. He felt woozy from all the running and when his mate opened the door it was a relief to go inside and collapse on the couch.

"You look knackered, Matty," Damon said, standing with his arms akimbo. He had no shirt on and showed off the type of body Matt wished he had.

"Knackered," Matt wheezed, "would be an understatement." He pulled the bottom of his shirt up and wiped his sweaty face. "You know what they say, though. No pain, no gain."

Damon smiled. "That is true." He walked over to the open plan kitchen, fossicking through his yellow Smeg fridge 'till he emerged with a jug of icy chilled water, which he poured into a glass and brought back over. "Here you go. Nice n cold to cool you down."

"Cheers." Matt grabbed the glass from Damon and down the whole thing in three thirsty mouthfuls.

"Another?"

"Yes please." Matt handed the glass back and greedily accepted the second round when Damon returned.

Damon put his thumbs in the waistband of his pants. "You know, Matty, you don't need to be going so hard with all this training. You're already in pretty good shape."

"You think?" He pulled forward his shirt and looked down at his torso. "I' still nowhere near what you look like."

Damon laughed and took a seat beside him on the long couch. "Yeah, but I have been working out for years and eating the dullest diet imaginable. You don't need to look like me. You look great as you are."

Matt raised his eyebrows and pulled a face. "Bullshit."

"Nope. Not bullshit." Damon shook his head. "Take

it from me. You're a good-looking dude."

"Thank you. I hope others think so when I finally venture out next."

"Trust me, Matty, I won't be the only one who thinks you're a good catch." Damon rested into the back of the couch, spreading his legs wide and dropped a hand to his crotch, blatantly adjusting himself. He cast Matt a sneaky smile.

Damon seemed in a stupidly good mood the way he sat there showing off his perfect teeth. Another feature Matt wish he had.

"So what is K dog up to tonight?" Damon asked.

"Him and his friend Garth are going out clubbing."

"I see," Damon said, nodding. "Who is this Garth character?"

"Just one of his friends from down home. Do you not know him?"

Damon shook his head. "I know the usual suspects. Liam, Skippy, Tony. Not a clue who Garth is though."

"Yeah. I wondered if maybe he has a new group of mates 'cos he hasn't mentioned the others the whole time he's been here. Normally when I speak to him on the phone he usually goes on about Liam a bit. But nope. Nudda."

Damon clawed at the hairs on his chest, then flicked his eyes down to Matt's bare legs. "How's the calf muscles?" He lurched over grabbing hold of Matt's leg, groping greedily.

Matt was taken aback by the sudden move. "Umm they're good."

Damon groped harder. "Good work. Feeling firm." He sat back and patted his lap. "Chuck your leg up here."

"Sorry?" Matt frowned.

"Put your leg on my lap. I am gonna massage the muscles for you. It's good to have a rub down after all your running."

"Is it?" Matt asked surprised.

Damon patted his lap again. "Come on."

Matt swivelled round, leaning in to the end of the couch and raised his leg to rest over Damon's knees.

Damon's hands started at his ankle and began rubbing under his leg, stroking smoothly along Matt's tired calf muscle. "Sorry if I'm a bit clammy." Matt laughed nervously. "I just hope I don't stink."

"No worries," He pulled his hands back and sniffed his fingers. "You don't smell bad. Good people like you never do." He dropped his hands and continued rubbing, his thumbs pressing deftly into Matt's sleek skin. "You've actually got pretty nice legs." Damon flashed him a grin. "For a guy, I mean."

"Aww shucks." Matt chuckled. He felt awkward laid back with his leg being rubbed down. The affection was great though. He hadn't been touched like this in such a long time, it just felt weird that it was his best mate's hands gifting his body such tenderness. Damon rolled the leg of Matt's shorts up, then rubbed deeply into the tissue of his thigh. *That feels so bloody good.* Matt groaned in pleasure from the feel of Damon's strong fingers kneading him in a way that verged on sensual.

"I can tell you're enjoying yourself." Damon cleared his throat and spoke up, "These hands like to give pleasure."

"Yeah. You're definitely good at this."

"Thanks. I picked a few pointers up from Sandra if you remember her? The massage therapist I dated briefly."

Matt nodded like he knew who Damon was talking about. He didn't really have a clue. Damon had "dated" so many bloody women that they had all became a blur of different faces. And what Damon considered dating most people would call fucked-more-than-once. The guy could have opened a museum of past lovers. Matt's lids shuddered as he began to feel swoony from the touch of his mate's fingers tickling behind his knee. He could have fallen asleep if it wasn't for Damon's next move; sliding his hand high up into the leg hole of Matt's shorts, getting dangerously close to restricted areas. Matt widened his eyes, glaring at his friend. "Umm, if you're going up that high, isn't it policy to buy the person a drink first."

Damon laughed. "Settle down. It's part of the rub

down." He lifted his chin and held Matt's stare. "I'll grab you a drink afterwards if you like though?"

Matt grinned. "Sounds good. Rub away then." He lolled his head back and let Damon keep going. But he couldn't relax as much now when he noticed Damon's fingers edging ever closer to his underwear. Matt swallowed hard when he felt Damon's fingertips gently brush the fabric of his briefs.

"Sorry," Damon mumbled. He kept the rubbing going for a while longer then out of nowhere cupped Matt's balls. "Massage over, big fella," he let go of Matt's scrotum and laughed.

Matt pulled his leg off and looked over at Damon suspiciously. "Thanks for the massage and free molestation."

"No worries, mate. Anytime." Damon seemed unfazed.

Despite the awkward joke of groping him, Matt still enjoyed the massage. "What about the other leg?"

"I'll leave you to do that one yourself. I showed you how it's done."

"Yeah like I am gonna be able to massage my own leg like that."

Damon shrugged and changed the topic. "Did you fancy joining me for a movie?"

"What in town?"

"Nar, here with me on the couch." Damon pointed across the room to the television. "There's a thriller on Netflix I wouldn't mind watching."

Matt looked over at Damon's television, which was so large it could have been perceived as looking stupid if it weren't for the snobby spacious apartment to help balance it out. Arrogance suited arrogance in this regard. He looked down at what he was wearing, his damp sweaty clothes clinging to his body. "I would stay but I think I oughta head home n get showered."

"Just have a shower here," Damon suggested. "I can lend you some clothes."

Matt nibbled on his lip, thinking the offer over. He

didn't have anything special planned at home. Keegan and Garth would do what young people do and probably be out all hours of the night. "Sure. Beats me sitting at home on my own like some sad git."

"Good shit." Damon pointed towards the bathroom. "Should be a fresh towel on the rail and I'll bring you in some clothes when you're ready."

"Okay."

"It'll be good to have you all to myself after Jason's hogged you all week," Damon said curtly.

"Sorry about that. I guess I have been a little unavailable." Even though Matt willingly took blame for the lack of recent contact, it wasn't as if he hadn't tried getting Damon involved with the wedding or to come visit. If anything, Damon was the one who had been doing the avoiding. Matt got to his feet and shuffled towards the bathroom.

"Nar, it'll be good us hanging out," Damon said. "We need to have good a chat."

Matt spun 'round. "We do?" He hovered in the doorway of the bathroom. Damon's gaze burned across at him. "What about?"

"Nothing too major," Damon answered. "I just wanted to ask why Jason seems to know about what we used to do together." The words came out laced with a hidden depth.

Matt felt exposed and motionless. It was the first time in twenty years that either of them had spoken of *it* aloud. Matt choked on his response, "I-I don't know—"

"Nar, I ain't angry. I'm just curious. That's all." Damon softened his tone with a disarming smile. "Go have your shower and when you come back we can talk about how I used to fuck you."

∞

Matt used the shower as much to get clean as he did to hide from the unravelling of history waiting for him in the next room. He wasn't looking forward to this conversation about how Damon used to fuck him. The way Damon slung the words across the room had left Matt feeling dirty and vulnerable. As he stood naked in the shower, he couldn't look at his penis without imagining it gripped in Damon's vice-like grip.

When Jason had let slip his knowledge of Damon and Matt's secret it had felt like a bomb being dropped—one that didn't detonate. *Too bad it's about to explode right fucking now!* As stupid as Jason was to make the comment, it wasn't done vindictively. It was merely an innocent slip of the tongue.

Tongue.

I put my tongue everywhere on him back then. Everywhere!

Matt shuddered as he remembered how raw their past was. They hadn't just fooled around like a couple of horny school boys discovering the joys of mutual masturbation.

They had fucked... They had fucked hard...

I was crazy back then. This was true. Matt had behaved like a pre-teen obsessed with a boy band. His feelings had been intense to the extreme, controlling his mind and striking faster than a lightning bolt. But how real were those feelings? He never dwelled on this question because he wasn't sure he really wanted to know the answer.

Fucking Jason! Matt screamed internally. He reluctantly turned the nozzle of the shower off, shutting down the warm water falling like rain from the large ceiling shower square. He stepped out, treading carefully over dark tiles 'till he reached for a towel and wrapped it around his waist. He took a breath of courage and opened the door, poking his head out. "Hey, Damon. Can you grab me those clothes now, please?"

"Coming right up, matey," Damon said chirpily. He jumped off the couch and raced to his room. He returned with the clothes tucked under his arm and handed them over. "There you go."

"Cheers." Matt gave a smile of thanks and closed the door. He dried his body and sifted through the clothes he had been given. A baggy navy-blue top and a pair of jeans. To Matt's surprise there was also a clean pair of boxers for him to wear. Matt had assumed he would be sitting around commando. If it were any other guy, he would have thrown them to the side and not worn them.

Once dressed, he opened the door and dawdled across the lounge on his bare feet, settling back on the couch where Damon was sitting. The television was all lit up, waiting for the movie to play. Damon had a Vodka RTD in his hand, another sat on the coffee table for Matt to drink.

Damon gave him a coy look, his lips creaking apart. He looked ready to begin his questioning.

Matt beat him to the chase.

"Look, I am sorry about what happened the other night here with Jason mentioning... us. I- I didn't think he would be stupid enough to say anything. I don't think he even realised he said it and he certainly didn't mean any harm by it. And it isn't like I had just told him. I told him about us years ago when we were... doing what we were doing." Matt ran a hand through his wet hair. "I'm really sorry, Damon, if it upset you in anyway but that was never my intention and like I said, I told him about that stuff like twenty fucking years ago and..." Matt looked down and saw Damon grinning, holding in laughter. "What's so funny?"

"You, ya gabby chicken neck." Damon smiled. "I didn't mean for you to get so stressed out about it, Matty. I told you it isn't a big deal, I was just curious to know how he knew." He pat the coffee table. "Now chill the fuck out and drink your drink before you have a heart attack."

"Oh," Matt mumbled, suddenly feeling stupid for annihilating the room with an onslaught of messy words. He picked his drink up and slurped back on the chilled vodka drink.

Damon shuffled 'round to face him. "I know you just said you told Jason about us way back then, but can I ask why you even bothered telling him?"

A silence fell between them as Matt searched for an answer. He laced his fingers tightly around his drink and began nodding. "Okay," he started, "I think—if I remember correctly—Jason actually put two and two together, because if you recall, we weren't exactly mates at school. And yet here you were, coming and hanging out at my house."

"But why would you own up to it? Why didn't you just deny it like any other guy would."

"Do you really want to know?"

"I wouldn't ask if I didn't."

"I know," Matt sighed, tilting his head. "But is it something that you need to know?"

"Come on, Matty, just bloody tell me. What are you scared of? It isn't like I'm going to disown you." He squeezed Matt's knee. "You have me for life regardless of the answer."

Matt felt a wave of kindness wash over him, relieving some of his fear. "Okay, I told Jason because I needed to tell somebody what I was feeling. Share with them how happy I was." Matt felt his cheeks redden. "I had had such a rough year that year with Jason leaving school and leaving me an utter loner, Mum walking out on me and dad. Life was shit. It really was." Matt let out a sad laugh before grinning. "But then you came along. Damon Harris. The coolest guy in town. The guy everybody wanted to be friends with. The guy all the girls threw themselves at."

Damon laughed. "C'mon, Matty, I was just a regular guy. Not a fucking rock star."

"I don't think you get it."

"Get what?"

"You were a rock star! Well, you were to me." He didn't know if he should continue but he did anyway. "When we started fooling around, I felt so honoured in a way because you could have had anybody you wanted, but you chose me." Matt dropped his gaze to the floor and uttered in a whisper, "You *wanted* me."

"Do you really mean that?"

Without looking up, Matt said, "I know it sounds silly but I sort of fell in love with you that summer."

Damon touched Matt's chin and raised his face, forcing him to look him in the eyes. "Thank you," he whispered and let go to take a swig on his drink. "That was quite the heart to heart."

"It sure was," Matt responded. It was sort of freeing to let the caged confession out in the open. "And just so you know, you don't have to worry about me going all gay on you. I sorted those feelings out long ago." He laughed to break the tension. "Like I still love you but just as a mate, ya know?"

"I know," Damon agreed. "I love you too, bro." He raised his drink gesturing for Matt to do the same. "Cheers," they said in unison, clinking their bottle together.

"Shall we watch this movie now?" Matt asked, motioning at the television.

"I just want to ask one more thing."

"Fire away."

"What was it about me or the stuff that we did that made you like me so much?" Damon narrowed his eyes, striking an almost seductive pose. "Was it the way I fucked you?"

Matt tugged the collar of his t-shirt and laughed nervously.

"Sorry, I probably didn't word that as good as I could," Damon said, chuckling. "What I mean is; what was your favourite part of what we used to do?"

That doesn't make the question any less fucking strange Damon! Matt took a deep breath. He knew the answer but was reluctant to share. "I don't know if I could pick one thing."

"So out of all of it? Not one thing stood out?"

"Oh god," Matt mumbled into his hand. "If I had to say my favourite part then it was the way you kissed and hugged me afterwards."

"Really?" Damon looked shocked.

"Yes. Really."

"Why that?"

"I dunno." Matt shrugged. "I guess you made me feel safe. I liked feeling that."

"Aww," Damon said.

Matt flipped him the finger. "Don't make fun of me. Keep in mind I was only eighteen and a bit messed up."

"I am not making fun of you, Matty. I honestly think

that's really fucking sweet."

"You do?"

"Fucking oath." Damon nodded. "So sweet that it makes me wanna hug and kiss you right now."

"Okay. Now I definitely know you are making fun of me." Matt laughed.

"I'm not." Damon put his drink down. "Come here," he said with his arms wide open.

"What are you doing?"

"I want to hug you. I want to make you feel safe while we watch the scary movie."

"It's okay, Damon, I think I'll manage to get through the movie without pissing my pants."

"Come on, Matty." He kept his arms open, pleading with his pretty green eyes.

Matt inhaled loudly. "The things I do for our friendship." He placed his drink down and went to go join Damon in the waiting embrace.

As Matt leaned in for the hug, Damon grabbed his shoulders and said, "Lay down. We can spoon."

"What?"

"Go on. That way we can both watch the movie. Me big spoon, you the little spoon."

Matt pulled a funny face. "You're acting weird tonight."

"Yeah it must be you rubbing off on me." Damon smiled and mouthed *come on.*

Matt slumped his shoulders and gave in to his mate's suggestion. He found it odd but it wasn't like anyone was here to see them acting like cuddly idiots. He stretched out and lay down on his side in front of Damon who placed an arm under Matt's head to act as a pillow. Damon reached over top of him and grabbed the remote to start the movie then draped that arm over Matt's waist, reeling him in close.

"This is nice," Damon said before kissing Matt on the top of his head.

Aside from the initial awkwardness of it all, Matt tended to agree. It was nice. He relaxed his body and nestled into his best mate's warm embrace, feeling every bit as safe and protected as the last time he were wrapped up in these strong arms.

CHAPTER TWENTY-ONE

The club was cramped with a jumble of arses and elbows inconveniently blocking the way to the bar and the shirtless bartenders behind it. Keegan followed Garth through the crowd, letting his pushy friend spearhead the way towards their dash for another round of drinks. Once they finally reached the glorious smooth wooden surface of the bar, Keegan ordered them a bourbon each. With their bottles in hand, Garth took charge again, drilling his way through the crowd 'till they were sat outside in the smoking area.

They had been here for two hours and so far it had been more trouble than it was worth. If his father hadn't been so stupidly generous—again—giving him two hundred in cash for the night out, he might have suggested they head home. While it wasn't enough money to go crazy with, it was enough to cover him and Garth for the evening. Or so he hoped.

The cool air of outside licked Keegan's skin, while the stench of tobacco swirled all around him as countless lungs puffed out the toxic fumes. Keegan didn't care though. He preferred the stench of smoke to the inferno of bodies grinding inside to the catastrophically loud music.

"This place is fucking manic, bro," Garth said, watching as a new line of people past them to enter the club.

"It's manically something," Keegan grumbled.

"What's wrong?" Garth stared at him with concern. "Aren't you having fun?"

"I suppose I am."

"You could lie a little more convincingly."

"I am having a fan-fucking-tastic time!" Keegan grinned facetiously.

"That's better." Garth stuck his tongue out. "You should be having fun considering how many guys keep checking you out."

"I wouldn't go that far," Keegan said, downplaying the level of attention he knew he had been getting. Attention that had come in a wave of eyeballs following him and Garth the moment they walked in the door. One guy wearing a red shirt seemed overly enchanted with him and had been throwing sultry looks Keegan's way all night. The guy had black hair with a bleach-blond stripe down the middle, which unintentionally made him resemble a skunk. And considering his eyeballing persistence, Keegan had nicknamed him Pepé Le Pew.

"Are you fucking blind?" Garth suddenly pointed into the crowd of people. "All those guys have been looking at you. Him. Him. The tall bald dude. And especially that fucker in the red shirt."

"Shut up," Keegan hissed, yanking Garth's arm down.

Garth smiled, finding Keegan's embarrassment funny. "I was just showing you who they were."

I didn't need help with that.

Keegan's stomach rumbled in shame. He turned around to see the mentioned men all flick their attention away after being so crudely snapped out. Except Pepé Le Pew. He braved the outing and kept staring, not the slightest bit bothered. Keegan turned to face Garth again. "They won't be looking as much now they probably think I am out with my crazy jealous boyfriend."

Garth smiled, looking pleased with himself. "Ha. They'll all envy me thinking I'm the one that's shoving my cock in you tonight."

"You wish. If anything, it would be me shoving my cock in you."

"Ooo, I love it when you get all aggro, baby," Garth said in a girly voice. "Are you gonna take me home and take it out on my sweet virgin ass?"

"Please refer to my previous response. You. Fucking. Wish."

Garth arched his eyebrows. "Do I now?"

Keegan turned around again to see if there was

anyone outside that might be his type. He perused the crowd like he was looking for a shirt to wear. One that was the perfect fit and that looked just like Liam. There weren't any Liam lookalikes here though. He hadn't seen any inside either. It wasn't that the bar was void of talent. It was just that none of the talent stood out. No one had an x factor. If he were going to do something stupid like hook up with a complete stranger, then the least they would have to do was make him go *wow*.

Even if fate smiled down on him and a long-lost twin of Liam walked in the door, Keegan would still be screwed because it wasn't like he could bring a guy back to his father's house for sex. Aside from the rudeness of it, it ran too greater risk of being busted with another guy. The alternative would be to go back to the other guy's place but that brought a whole different set of problems like not being able to find his way back to Port Jackson. At least with Garth he would feel safe if they did lose their way.

"I can tell you're looking for a root," Garth said bluntly.

Keegan spun back 'round. "You're the one who told me I should be."

"Yeah, but that was before I found out I was your crazy jealous boyfriend," Garth teased. "You don't want to make me look bad in front of all these guys now that we're officially a pretend couple."

"Ha. Maybe we can tell them we have an open relationship?"

"Oh great, so now I'm dating a slut." Garth grimaced. "Is that the kind of thing you would be into?"

"No, dick. I was joking," Keegan snapped back. Keegan noticed Garth looking over his shoulder with a snotty look on his face. "Why do you look like someone just killed your puppy?" Keegan asked.

"That dude in the red shirt keeps staring at you." Garth sculled back on his drink, his eyes remaining fixed on the adamant admirer behind Keegan. "That's just rude."

"Well, you can chill out pretend boyfriend because I

ain't planning on hooking up with him."

"That ain't the point. He doesn't know we aren't a couple." Garth shook his head. "He's encroaching on my man and making me look like a weak one."

"You really get into role playing don't you," Keegan teased. "It isn't like we have a sign saying we are together, is it?"

"Good point, blondie." Garth waggled his eyebrows. "We should make one."

"What are you talking about?"

Garth suddenly got off his chair, walked around the table and grabbed Keegan by the collar of his shirt, bringing their mouths together for a kiss.

Keegan flinched at first but then relaxed as Garth slipped his tongue inside his mouth, locking their lips together. Keegan could taste the sweetness of bourbon on Garth's taste buds, topped off with a slight hint of cigarette smoke.

Garth lowered his hands; his fingers dragging like blunt claws down Keegan's spine before resting at the seat of his arse crack. A group of people began cheering as the steamy kiss lingered past casual territory.

Just as Keegan was about to run out of air, Garth retrieved his tongue, nipping gently on Keegan's bottom lip on the way out. Their breath mingled, faces hovering only inches apart.

Garth smiled, staring into Keegan's eyes, "Now he should get the message."

"Fuck, you're a good kisser," Keegan whispered without meaning to.

Garth looked amused but before he could question Keegan about the compliment a high-pitched voice squealed in delight, "Is that who I think it is?"

Keegan lurched away from Garth's face, spinning 'round to see a life-ruining moment mincing towards them in yellow skinny jeans and a black top that said *it won't suck itself*.

Keegan wanted to run but it was too late. They had already been spotted and were trapped.

Jason smiled, waving erratically as he toddled over to their table. "Well, well, well," Jason purred. "You two boys sure know how to put on a good show."

CHAPTER TWENTY-TWO

The movie was okay. Not great but okay, Matt thought. Okay, if he were being honest, he hadn't paid all that much attention to the young woman alone in her house being stalked by a menacing intruder. Matt's attention had been lost in the moment of being wrapped up in the safety of Damon's arms, snuggled against his mate's bare chest.

They were halfway through the movie when Matt suddenly felt Damon's hand slip from being perched on his hip across to his stomach. Instead of just resting it there, Damon's hand disappeared under the hem of the t-shirt. Matt squirmed from the ticklish feel of Damon's fingers twiddling around his tummy.

"Sorry," Damon said. "Did I hurt you?"

"No. It just tickles."

"Do you want me to stop?" Damon's hand stilled. "Or can I keep doing it?"

Matt swallowed hard. The inbuilt part of him that loathed being rude or saying no to people kicked in. "I don't mind."

Damon kissed the back of his head. "Thank you." He started stroking in circles around Matt's belly button. "I like your stomach. It feels nice. Not too soft but not too hard either."

"Thanks," Matt whispered, bewildered by the compliment as much as the scene unfolding above his waist. He flicked his eyes back to the television set. He was torn between watching the movie and wanting to keep an eye on Damon's shifting hand. After a couple minutes Damon's palm started gliding higher, clawing his fingers over Matt's chest. The size and roughness of Damon's palm was odd at first, not slender and petite like Karina's hands had been. She had been the last person to touch Matt this way. The more

Damon rubbed, the more it felt like any lingering traces of her love were being wiped away.

Damon's lips slipped a light groan. He wriggled, pressing harder into Matt's back as his fingers kept traversing Matt's torso, creating a sandpapery sound as they dragged across the dark hair on his chest.

What are you doing?

Matt wondered if he should sit up and tell Damon to stop messing around. This wasn't funny. *Was it?*

"Fuck you have a hairy chest, Matty." Damon chuckled.

Matt let out a nervous cough. "Ha. Just a little."

Damon raised his leg and hooked it over the top of Matt's, entwining their bodies together even more so. The restricting manoeuvre only reinforced that Damon was the alpha male in this interaction; his biceps oozed strength and his athletic legs exuded power.

With his lower body pinned down and Damon's hot hand roaming under his shirt, Matt knew any notion that this was some jovial couch-cuddle was misguided. The line of friendship was beginning to blur as Damon's frisky fingers drew over his skin, writing a steamy story.

Damon's hand began to recede, resting at the waistline of the jeans Matt had on. Very delicately his fingertips slipped beneath the waistband and scratched gently against the tip of Matt's wiry pubes.

A shudder rippled through Matt's body. He held his breath like he was about to go under water.

Damon's body was burning with heat, his lips slipped out a faint groan as he started to grind his crotch against Matt's arse, revealing a questionable firmness. Matt released his trapped breath when he realised the firmness he felt was an erection.

He's fucking hard!

The room felt like it was spinning, hurling around like a time warp that was taking them back to 1997. Matt opened his mouth to speak but all that came out was a muted croak.

Damon nuzzled into his neck, groaning hungrily,

kissing his way up. He began tracing the outer rim of Matt's ear with his tongue, sinking his teeth into his earlobe. His hand began to fiddle with the zipper on Matt's jeans, ripping it down to grant himself access. He dug his hand in the open space and grabbed hold.

"Damon…" Matt said in a voice as brittle as an autumn leaf.

"Yes?"

"What are you doing?"

"Being nice to my mate." Damon breathed deeply, his fingers tickling Matt's balls through the borrowed boxers. "Don't you want me to be nice to you, Matty?"

A frazzled panic surged through Matt's body, stabbing his abdomen and tightening his chest. His tongue dried up, rendering him speechless.

"Let me make you feel good." Damon kissed his neck again. "Go on, babe," he dropped in a breathy whisper.

Babe. A magical word in Matt's world. A word that made him melt like butter in a pan. All apprehension from what Damon was doing was exterminated. He didn't want to fight off such romantic affection. He may not have considered a physical encounter with Damon in all this time but now all these forgotten feelings were flooding his veins, buzzing his crotch and heart simultaneously. His dick twitching to life did not go unnoticed.

"I'll take that as a yes." Damon groped him. "Fuck I have missed this." His sexy voice dripped inside Matt's ear. He reached inside Matt's underwear and grabbed hold of his stiffening cock.

Matt gasped. He squirmed and pushed his back deeper into Damon's chest.

Damon pulled Matt's cock out from the pesky underwear. He rest his head on Matt's shoulder and glanced down at the manhood seized between his furled fingers. "I wish I had a cock as big as this," he murmured, stroking the complimented tool.

"From what I can remember, you're plenty big enough." Matt craned his neck around and found Damon's lips waiting for him. They kissed deeply, swapping spit and feelings. Matt poured groans into Damon's mouth as his cock grew rock hard in his best mate's grip.

Once Matt was fully erect Damon pulled away from the kiss and let go of his meat. He tugged Matt's pants down impatiently, exposing his pale behind. Damon's voice seeped a low grumble as he ran his index finger through Matt's freshly-showered crack. "I can't wait to be inside you," he said in a way that was void of asking.

Matt wasn't sure if he were ready for this. He hadn't been fucked ever since Damon broke him in all those years ago. For twenty years now, his arse had been dick free. He knew that if Damon put his cock inside him it would be like the first time all over again; a thick blunt knife capable of making him bleed. But he didn't want to deny someone who seemed so intent on being his lover. The fleshly want radiating from Damon's heaving body was electric, and it wasn't a want you deny. Such want was rare and Matt knew not to ignore it. How could he? He bit his tongue and shot his fear in the face, refusing to roll away.

Damon's finger removed itself from Matt's rift.

Plip, plip, plip

Damon spat into the palm of his hand, brewing his saliva into lube. He placed his wet fingers to Matt's arsehole, lubing him up for his impending arrival. After three more rounds of spit being applied Damon rolled Matt forward— just a little—to have the angle he wanted. He placed the tip of his bare cock to Matt's hole. "Are you ready? Damon asked.

"Shouldn't we use a condom," Matt said. He had been waiting for Damon to dig into a pocket and present a wrapped rubber for them to use. It appeared Damon had other ideas.

"I can grab one if you want." Damon kissed his shoulder. "But I would love to fill you up, babe. Please?"

Babe!

That magic word quelled the inner voice of sensible reason. Matt didn't even put up a fight. His pathetic need to impress had taken over. He grabbed Damon's hand and laced their fingers together, giving it a kiss. Giving his full permission.

Damon wasted no time. He pushed ahead, breaching the entrance of Matt's hole.

"Ough, fuck!" Matt clenched his jaw. He breathed fast and erratically. His eyes stung shut.

Damon pecked his neck, soothing him with pacifying kisses. "I'll go easy, babe. Promise." He squeezed Matt's hand as he continued to push his way inside, ever so slowly, gaining hard-fought inch after hard-fought inch. Matt couldn't stop groaning from the hurt but he didn't want Damon to stop either. He wanted his mate inside him; he needed to show Damon that he cared enough to put up with this initial pain.

"Fuck yeah," Damon finally grunted, expressing his pride at being all the way in.

"Fuck. I forgot how good this feels," Matt lied through gritted teeth.

"Does it really? You sound more like I'm hurting you," Damon said with concern.

"It hurts... but it's a good hurt."

"Are you sure? I don't wanna break you."

"You won't break me," Matt said. "I want your breakfast of champions."

"Okay." Damon chuckled. "Breakfast of champions coming right up." He squeezed Matt's hand and started to fuck him. His voice whimpered softly as he maintained a steady and tender tempo. "I swear your tighter than last time."

"Then best you go harder," Matt encouraged. He knew Damon was holding back from fucking the way he really wanted to. Matt knew from experience that his mate could thrash his burning hole.

"Are you serious? You want me to go harder?"

"I want you to cum," Matt said. He kissed Damon's arm. "I want you to have fun."

"I am having fun, babe." Damon stroked his bristly cheek. "I always have fun when I am with you." He tugged on Matt's hair. "But if you want me to cum then I better go harder and give you this breakfast of champions."

Matt erupted with a moan as Damon did exactly what he said. *Go harder.*

Damon propelled himself forward, pounding his cock in heavy thrusts, burning Matt's hole whilst smashing him open. Apparently age hadn't diminished his mate's appetite for rough pleasure. It had only heightened it.

Matt's head bobbed around spilling noise out of his open mouth like an upturned bottle. He rode the wave of jabs, grateful for what felt like an honour. He could smell Damon's tangy breath puffing over him, whisking over his face like smoke. "Fuck me, babe," he spluttered, egging his mate on. Through half-lidded eyes the room appeared fuzzy and vast while his rock star fucked his arse like planets crashing into dust.

Damon's dick's strategic twists and gyrating penetration were testimony to a man with more sex experience than the last time they'd been together. Their laced fingers slipped apart and Damon grabbed hold of Matt's pubes, tugging on them like he was picking weeds. Just when Matt thought things were running at full volume, Damon let go of his pubes and grabbed hold of his cock instead, squeezing, shifting gears. Suddenly his best mate was fucking like a war machine, blasting heavier and harder than before, hitting spots buried so deep they were being unearthed for the very first time.

Damon's light whimpers were replaced with beastly groans mingled with the thumping of his pelvis crashing into Matt's arse. The sweat from his naked chest began dampening Matt's back. The feeling of being one was intoxicating and the perfect remedy to overcome this price of pain. Damon was deep inside him, feeding him every solid inch he had. He could feel Damon's muscles tightening, his feet digging into his ankles.

The finish line was in sight...

"I'm getting close, babe. I'm getting real fucking close." Damon fired one huge thrust, impaling Matt's hole with passionate force as he collapsed atop of him. "Ohhh fuck!" he yelped.

Matt dug his nails into Damon's hip, keeping him deep inside to absorb every drop of cum that was spilling out of his mate's twitching cock. *Fuck that feels amazing.* Damon's cock spasmed hard, shooting out a load that Matt knew was huge. The warm seed piled in, filling him up like a pond. Matt clutched Damon's arm, giving it a kiss. "Thank you for sharing that with me."

Damon's body trembled and shook. He bit Matt on the neck, giving him a slick lick. "Thank you for letting me share it."

Matt looked down at his own cock, which was still rock hard, begging to be pleased.

"Did you want me to finish you off," Damon asked, trying to pull his arm away to grab hold of Matt's dick.

Matt fetched Damon's arm back, wanting to stay in the hug. "I'm fine. I just wanted to make sure you were sorted."

"You're such a fucking thoughtful bugger, aren't you?" Damon kissed him again.

"I try." Matt turned his face up to look at Damon without breaking the fusion of their bodies. "Is it okay if we stay like this a while?" He didn't want to leave this couch anytime soon. He just wanted to lay there with Damon still inside him.

"If that's what you want?" Maybe after the movie we can have another round?" Damon raised his eyebrows. "My stocks should be replenished by then."

Matt giggled like a school boy and rest his head on Damon's arm. "Sounds good to me."

"I think for round two though we should go to my room so we can have even more fun."

"More fun?" Matt smiled. "I don't know if that is possible."

"Oh, I have more tricks up my sleeve than what I just showed you, Matty."

"Such as?"

"You'll have to wait and see. But I can tell you I'd

love to make use of my photography skills with you," Damon said with a glitch of cheek to his voice.

"You what?"

"I reckon it would be hot if you let me take pics of you."

"Oh god, no. I don't think so." Matt laughed.

"Oh, come on. Live a little. Maybe I would like something sexy just for myself to remind me how fucking hot my best mate is?" Damon blew a kiss. "I'll make it worth your while, babe."

"We'll see," Matt sighed, playing coy. Truth was Damon could ask for anything he wanted if he kept using the magic word. Besides, if he were to do something foolish like nude pics then why not take them with the person he trusted most in the world.

Damon tightened his embrace, his arms surrounding Matt like a solicitous circle. "Fuck you're beautiful."

"Ditto." Matt's cock was still hard but that didn't matter. It was his heart feeling the most pleasure in this moment. That was better than any orgasm. He lay there in bliss, absorbing Damon's spunk and the love humming heavily in the room.

Damon really cared about him. He really did.

CHAPTER TWENTY-THREE

Keegan wished for the power of invisibility as he sat on the bar stool watching Jason watch him. Garth wasn't any fucking help the way he stood there rubbing his lips, smiling like a fool.

"Hi. How's your night going Jason," Keegan fuddled.

"My night's fine," Jason cooed. "Not quite as good as yours though judging by how bloody steamy that kiss looked." He walked around the table and sat down across from Keegan. He patted Garth on the shoulder. "You look like you were about to swallow Keegan whole."

"Nar, that'll come later wont it, boyfriend." Garth patted Keegan on the back, winking salaciously.

Keegan thrusted Garth's hand away. "No it won't because you're not my boyfriend."

Jason giggled. "Oh, so you're not a couple?" he narrowed his eyes as he looked at them both. "Sure looks like you're a couple."

"Does it?" Garth said excitedly. He nodded, looking pleased with himself. "I didn't do too bad then for a straight guy."

Jason waved his arms in the air. "Okay. What? Your straight?" He looked at Keegan suspiciously. "I thought you were both straight before I stumbled across your intense round of tonsil tennis, now Garth is saying otherwise. Can one of youse please get this queen up to speed?"

Garth looked at Keegan as if asking for permission to explain. Keegan groaned affirmatively. It seemed pointless denying it but he wasn't in the mood to do the explaining. Garth pointed across at red shirt who still looked over. "That dude kept checking Keegan out so I decided to put on a wee show so he thought we were a couple."

"Okaaaay," Jason slurred, still not following.

"In a nutshell. I love the V and Keegan loves the D," Garth blurted. "Don't ya buddy?"

"I wouldn't put it quite like that," Keegan mumbled.

"Are you attracted to men?" Jason asked.

Keegan reluctantly nodded.

"Then yes, I would say Garth said it perfectly." He chuckled. "Oh god, I wish Matty was here. That would be classic."

"No way! That would be a fucking nightmare." Keegan shook his head. "I don't want dad knowing."

"Cool your heels, kitten. I didn't say I would tell him." Jason gave a warm smile. "I just mean it would have been funny if he found out like this. Well... not funny for you but you know what I mean." Jason screwed his face up. "Sorry, I really am not making much sense."

"Nar, you are," Garth said. "It would have been fucking hilarious."

"Gee, thanks," Keegan said. "I am so glad my potential misery brings a smile to you both."

"Sorry, toots. It's all in good spirit." Jason eyeballed Garth. "Pity you aren't gay too. I think you would make an adorable couple."

Garth nudged Keegan with his elbow. "Hear that, blondie. You and me would make an adorable couple."

Keegan rolled his eyes. "Don't encourage him, Jason. He already likes to be the world's biggest tease."

"I ain't a tease, bro. I just pashed you so hard I almost tasted your breakfast."

"Kissing is one thing but will you follow through?" Jason giggled.

Garth picked his drink up, swigging back a mouthful to avoid answering.

Jason tapped Keegan's shoulder. "And I promise I won't say a word to Matty about any of this."

"Thank you," Keegan replied.

"You do know that he wouldn't care though." Jason pursed his lips. "You probably couldn't ask for a better dad when it comes to accepting you."

"Really?" Keegan questioned.

"Umm hello!" Jason waved a hand in Keegan's face. "You do know he has been friends with me forever and not to mention your grandmother's gay." Jason nodded. "Yes. Matty is more than equipped to handle the joy of knowing he has a gay son."

"See, Keegan," Garth said. "You should just tell him already."

Keegan shook his head. "It's kind of awkward enough being back here without adding to it." He looked at Jason and Garth who both appeared to disagree with his sentiment. "I can hardly be like 'oh I know I haven't had anything to do with you my whole life but by the way I'm gay.'"

"You can be exactly like that," Jason said adamantly. "Your father wouldn't care who you choose to sleep with."

"Oh, I can think of *one* person he might." Garth snickered.

Fuck up idiot! Keegan glared at Garth, knowing exactly who he meant.

Jason may have been drunk but his senses were still sharp enough to sniff out the scent of scandal. "What do you mean?"

Garth went rigid, realising he had dropped the ball on a secret. "Oh, nothing. I just meant he wouldn't be happy if Keegan brought home an animal." He laughed awkwardly.

Great let's add bestiality to the table. Keegan wanted to hit his pal but he didn't want Jason to have more evidence.

"Pleeeease, Garth. That is the weakest cover up line ever." Jason rolled his eyes. "I wasn't born last pride parade, sweet cheeks." He flicked his back eyes to Keegan. "What was the cock tease talking about?"

"I ain't a cock tease and I was honestly talking about sweet fluffy animals," Garth said pointlessly.

Jason didn't take his eyes off Keegan. He was staring him down waiting for an honest answer.

Keegan took a sip of his drink, steadying his nerves. "Can you keep a secret?"

Jason's lips twitched trying to hold in a smile. "Of

course." He struck a more serious expression. "Look, Keegan, I love gossip as much as the next person but if this is something you don't want me to know then you don't have to tell me."

"Okay." Keegan nibbled on his lip. The fact Jason didn't hound for the gossip made him want to share it. Maybe he could help? "But if I tell you, you have to promise me that you will never tell my dad. Ever!"

"You have my word."

Keegan took a deep breath. "The reason I am here in Auckland is because I did something really dumb down home." He paused, gathering his thoughts. "I hooked up with someone at a party and we didn't know that the room we were fooling around in had a camera on recording us."

"Oh dear…" Jason clasped a hand over his mouth before crossing his chest like he was at church. "You poor thing."

Garth remained silent, staring at the ground.

"It's online and some of my friends have seen it and I just…" Keegan sighed. "I couldn't hang around waiting for who else might end up seeing it."

"That's understandable." Jason tapped his fingers on the table. "Is there any way you can get it removed? Surely websites can be contacted and be told that it must be taken down."

"I don't know. I don't really have the energy for all that at the moment. Fuck knows how many sites it's on or how many people have a copy."

"Fucking internet," Jason said heatedly. "Is that what you're worried about? Matty finding out? Cos I really don't think he would be angry with you, Keegan. I think he would do everything he could to help you get it removed."

"That's not the reason," Garth said ominously.

Jason's forehead crinkled. "It' not?"

"Nope." Keegan let out a pitiful laugh. "It's about who is in the video with me."

Jason pursed his lips. "Who?"

Keegan looked around at the other tables to make

sure no one was watching their discussion. "It's Damon," Keegan admitted. "I had sex with Damon."

Jason's mouth dropped open and a scratchy gasp came out. "Damon, Damon? As in Damon Harris? As in Matty's close friend Damon? As in Damon—"

"Yes," Keegan hissed. "That Damon."

"Holy fuckaroony." Jason fanned his face with his hands. "Hooooo, girl. That is some heavy shit. Like wowsa. Super bad."

"I know, I know," Keegan said, regretting to confide in a drama queen.

"Like wow, Keegan. That is just… wow." Jason took a deep breath. "Like not bad for you, but oooo bad for Damon. Very fucking bad for Damon indeed."

"I think it's bad for both of us," Keegan said.

"No, Keegan. No." Jason fluttered his lashes. "You are the innocent party and its bad for you that there is a video but what I mean is Matty will want to kill Damon for this. Hands to his throat and throttle him."

"I'm not a little kid, it isn't like some old man took advantage of me," Keegan spat out defensively. It felt like Damon was being cast in the role of villain unfairly.

"That's not what I mean at all. Damon is the same age as me so I can assure you I would never refer to him as *old*." Jason gave him a worried smile. "But Damon and Matt are tight. Best mates—if you don't count me of course—and that is a big big BIG betrayal. I mean, that is just something you don't do. What was Damon thinking?"

It felt like Keegan's insides were being ripped out the more Jason went into detail about how greater the betrayal was. *I was the one who started it. I made Damon do it.* The night at the cabin was what had started the whole illicit affair thanks to his anger and thinly veiled blackmail.

"I can't believe that Damon did it," Jason said, scanning Keegan head to toe. "Not that you're not attractive, because yes you are. I just assumed he was straight."

"What's this Damon look like?" Garth asked.

"Hot!" Jason said directly. "Incredibly hot."

Garth laughed. "I might have to watch this video to be the judge of that."

"No, you won't," Keegan snapped. "You are never watching that video."

"Calm down, Keegan. I was only joking." Garth touched his arm soothingly. "I wouldn't do that to you."

Keegan looked back at Jason. "Now you promise that you won't say a word about this to dad?"

"Cross my gay heart and hope to die." Jason gave him a reassuring smile. "As far as I am concerned my queer ears heard nothing."

"Thanks," said Keegan.

"Don't worry about it. The only thing I am going to have trouble with is not asking you for all the dirty details about what Damon was like." Jason sniffed and frowned. "I mean I'm dying to know but that would be entirely inappropriate."

"Exactly. And what goes on tour stays on tour," Keegan said smugly.

"Bollocks," Garth laughed. "I think this is the perfect kind of story to be sharing with friends."

"I second that," Jason quipped.

Keegan glared at his father's friend. "I thought you said it would be inappropriate."

"Umm, hello!" Jason tugged on his shirt with its humorous line. "Do I look like someone who knows how to behave appropriately." He chuckled to himself. "And anyway, Damon's the one who slept with you, Lolita. Not me! Talking to you about sex is kind of a non-event in comparison."

Garth egged Keegan on, "Go on, tell us what you did together. Who put what where?"

"For a supposedly straight boy you sure have an intriguing interest of the ins and outs of gay sex life," Jason teased.

"I am just being a good friend," Garth said smiling. "I wanna make sure that my mate's cock is going in the right places."

"And that his tongue is going in your mouth," Jason

shot back.

"Yeah, Garth, you sure you don't have anything to share with the group?" Keegan squeezed Garth's hand mockingly. "You're with friends remember?"

Garth shook his head. "Nope. Mock me all you like but I am comfortable in my sexuality. And as for the kissing, you know I am fine with—"

"Anything above the waist. Yeah, yeah." Keegan laughed.

"Is he one of those boys, is he?" Jason winked.

"What's that supposed to mean?" Garth huffed.

"Nothing." Jason smirked. "But just be careful, Garth. One too many kisses with boys and you may find you start to enjoy it."

Garth grinned and wrapped an arm around Keegan's shoulders. "Who says I didn't like it already." He gave Keegan a sloppy kiss on the cheek. "Ain't that right, pretend boyfriend."

Keegan smiled, wiping his face free of Garth's slobber.

"Watch out for that one, Keegan," Jason chirped. "She's a cock tease to the bone. Your bone."

CHAPTER TWENTY-FOUR

Keegan tried turning the key in the door as softly as possible. He was drunk and struggling to make it click open. Garth giggled behind him at how long it was taking Keegan to open the door. He spun 'round and put a finger to his lips, urging Garth to be quiet. It was a little after four in the morning and he didn't want to wake his father up at this crazy hour to find him and Garth shitfaced and only just returning home from town. He knew he was probably worrying for nothing since his father seemed too passive to ever get mad. Keegan suspected he could have thrown a wild house party and his father would be too scared to react negatively, worried that any disproval would send Keegan running back home.

After the fifth attempt of trying the key, Garth laughed loudly. "Fuck, Keegan. Let me do it." He tried pushing Keegan out of the way to take over.

"Keep your voice down," Keegan harked in a throaty whisper. "Dad's in bed."

"Not his bed," Garth replied.

"What are you on about."

"His car. It's gone."

Keegan looked over Garth's shoulder towards the garage. The side door was open. There was no sign of his father's car inside at all. "That's weird. I wonder where he is."

"Probably out getting some nookie."

"Gross." Keegan mumbled, trying the key in the lock again.

"Nothing gross about it," Garth said. "If it was one of my parents it would be gross but your dad's good-looking."

"No he's not." Keegan managed to flip the lock. He pushed the door open and let them inside.

Garth walked past him and switched the light on.

"And yes, your dad is good-looking. I bet he gets loads of action."

"Well yeah, he isn't ugly but I doubt he gets *loads* of action." Keegan screwed his face up. "I don't even want to think about it."

"Just saying." Garth smiled at him. "But it makes sense he'd look good. He would have to be to have scored your mum."

"Gee, thanks for bringing her into this too." Keegan laughed and walked ahead, he led the way upstairs to the bedrooms with Garth following behind.

"Yeah, I'd bring your mum into anything if I could."

Keegan sighed internally and ignored the comment. Once at the top of the stairs he turned around to face Garth. "Thanks for dragging me out tonight. I actually had a lot of fun."

"See. I told you it'd be good to get out and have fun, didn't I?"

"Yeah you did," Keegan admitted. He started to smile to himself as he remembered their evening. "Jason is a fucking crack up. I can see why Dad enjoys hanging out with him so much."

"For sure."

"What about when he started doing rolly pollys on the dance floor and crashed into those girls dancing." Keegan laughed. "Fuck, I swear that was probably my favourite part of the night."

Garth gave a half-nod. "Yeah. That was good."

"What about you? What was your favourite?"

"I think it was probably when you told me I was a good kisser."

Keegan gulped. He had forgotten all about that. The words had just slipped out without meaning to. "Oh yeah, that."

"So you liked me kissing you?" Garth grinned.

"Why do I get the feeling you are never going to let me forget saying that."

"More like you will never forget how good it was."

Garth gave him a self-satisfied look.

"There's that modesty of yours we all know and love."

"You know it." Garth pointed his finger up, pretending to blow smoke from a gun. "But you didn't answer my question. Did you like kissing me?"

"Isn't that the same thing as saying you're a good kisser?"

Garth shook his head. "Not always."

Keegan bugged his eyes and stared back with a silly look on his face. "Yes, Garth. You're a good kisser and I also enjoyed kissing you."

Garth almost looked like he was about to blush. He turned his head slightly and began to nod. "That's fucking awesome."

"Okay, weirdo." Keegan looked at his friend stood there with a goofy grin on his face. "I need to crash so I'll see you in the morning or more likely afternoon." He walked away to go to the bedroom he was staying in.

"Hey, Keegan."

"Yeah?" Keegan spun back 'round.

"I lied," Garth looked at the floor, rubbing his heels together. "that wasn't my favourite part of the evening."

"Oh." Keegan didn't know why Garth had to correct himself.

"My favourite part was actually kissing you. Not you complimenting me."

Keegan tugged at his shirt, feeling nervous by the way Garth was looking at him. The guy seemed to enjoy playing these games. "Thanks man. Night." Keegan smiled and walked away again. He opened the door to his room and switched the bedside lamp on. He stripped his shirt off and sat down on the bed to take his shoes off. As he stripped his socks off his feet a light knock flew its way through the room. He looked up and saw Garth standing in the doorway. "Did you need something?"

Garth shrugged. "I dunno."

"Okay. You're the one standing there so only you know why you're here." Keegan laughed and stood up, unbuttoning his jeans. He shimmied them down his legs and stepped out of them so he was only in his underwear.

"Would it be okay if I joined you?" Garth asked in a soft voice.

"Excuse me?"

"Can I join you?"

Keegan threw his head back and groaned. "Garth, it isn't funny anymore. There is a time and place for cock teasing, and it isn't here and now." He pulled back the duvet and slipped into bed. He waved at Garth who still stood in the doorway. "Maybe tomorrow, Valentino."

"I'm not cock teasing. I just want to sleep beside you."

"Dude, come on. I'm tired and this joke is old."

"I'm not joking," Garth said. His cheeks speckled with a light blush. "I would like to share the bed. Maybe we can kiss some more? If you wanted to that is."

Keegan sat up, resting on his elbows. "You're serous? You wanna share a bed with me?"

Garth nodded.

Keegan narrowed his eyes analysing the way Garth stood there with slouched shoulder. *Is he for real?* "Are you wanting sex?"

Garth's eyes bulged. "No. not sex. Just... kissing, cuddling."

"I thought you were straight and all about *above the bloody waist.*"

Garth ran a hand through his hair looking flustered. "I'm not saying I want to do stuff below my waist."

"So basically you are cock teasing. But in the politest way possible."

"Nar, man. I just don't want to commit to something I may not be able to follow through with."

Keegan's pulse quickened. This felt like a step towards something new. "What are you saying?"

"I am saying that if I were to let a guy go below the waist then it would be a guy a lot like yourself." Garth chewed on his lip. His voice lowered, "It would be you."

"Okay then. If you are being serious and aren't

making fun of me, then sure, you can sleep in the bed with me."

Garth's eyes lit up. "Yeah?"

"Yes. But on one condition."

"Which is?"

"You sleep with no clothes on." Keegan waited for Garth to laugh and run away. This game of chicken cock tease was being exposed one way or another.

Garth laughed. "Naked?"

"That's what no clothes means doesn't it?"

"But you have your briefs on. That doesn't seem fair."

Keegan sighed. "Okay, Garth. Good night."

"Hold up, moody arse," Garth chuckled. "I know you think I'm teasing but I ain't." He pulled his shirt up over his body and dropped it to the floor. He flung his shoes off then whipped his pants off. He stood there in just a pair of red boxer briefs as he hoisted one foot up at a time to remove his socks. Keegan was speechless, he couldn't believe what Garth was doing. Garth may not have a gym-toned body like Damon or Liam but under the dim light of the lamp he still radiated sex appeal. The soft bulge prodding Garth's underwear was enticing and Keegan hungered to see it. "Scoot over," Garth said as he stood at the edge of the bed.

Keegan slid over and held the blanket up for his mate who promptly lay down beside him. "I didn't expect you to do that."

"I know you didn't," Garth said, lifting his bum up. His hands disappeared under the blanket as he hunched forward and returned holding his underwear. He swung his briefs around like a lasso, flinging them across the room. "Now I am naked as requested." He rolled onto his side and stared Keegan in the eyes.

Keegan looked at Garth's face, admiring the way his lip curled up in a sexy sneer. "You know how I said you weren't my type?"

Garth nodded.

"Well… I may have been exaggerating that a little bit."

"Really?" Garth narrowed his eyes. "As soon as I'm

naked in your bed you say you fancy me?"

"Ha. Let's not go too far."

"Admit it, blondie." Garth rubbed Keegan's leg with his foot. "You want me."

"Says the one who asked to hop in bed with me and is feeling my leg up."

Garth stopped touching him with his foot and laughed without smiling.

"And yes. I fancy you." Keegan reached out and brushed Garth's fringe down to cover his eyes. "But I still think you need a haircut."

Garth huffed his fringe back in place. "I will do if you keep pulling that vision blocking move."

Keegan dropped his gaze to Garth's pale chest, admiring the few stray wispy hairs that lived there.

"Typical male," Garth said. "Looking at my tits."

Keegan smiled "Is it that obvious."

"Yep. Just a little." Garth stroked Keegan's face. "It's okay though." His breath poured across Keegan's nostrils. The smell of liquor was undeniable. It probably explained Garth's stupidity for wanting to join him in bed.

Does he not know he's feeding himself to a lion?

Keegan's chest hitched with a hot breath. Garth was there wanting cuddles and kisses. Keegan didn't want that. He wanted more. Much, much more. Desire flared between his legs. The rush of blood to his cock was happening so fast he felt dizzy. He had had enough to drink to lose inhibitions and certainly enough to make some bad decisions. He wandered how far this could go.

"Did you wanna keep kissing?" Garth asked.

Keegan shook his head.

"Oh," Garth said, sounding disappointed.

Keegan's heart hammered as he said what he knew he shouldn't. "I want to touch you. I wanna see your body."

Garth laughed. "You can see me."

"No. I want to see *all* of you."

"Is that so, blondie?" Garth's voice came out in an adorable fashion but Keegan wasn't interested in adorable.

"Maybe another time, yeah?"

"Show me," Keegan said. "I want to see."

Garth didn't react. He stayed on his side, staring at Keegan with disapproval in his eyes

"Show me," Keegan repeated, wanting him to concede. "Let me see your cock."

Garth sighed. He pushed the blanket back, exposing his nakedness. Keegan's eyes trailed the length of Garth's slender body. He honed his sight on his mate's cock, which was surrounded by a nest of trimmed brown pubes. Garth wasn't hard but he suspected he had a semi. Keegan smiled fiendishly, approving of what he saw. "How big does it get when your fully hard?" Garth hesitated to respond so Keegan pushed again. "How big?"

"6 inches," Garth replied. "Just an average sized cock I'm afraid. Nothing porn star about me." He laughed softly but sounded more nervous more than anything.

"That's okay." Keegan smirked. "You're in bed with a porn star, remember?"

"True, I didn't think of that."

"Which means you're one too." Keegan placed a hand to Garth's shoulder, slowly dragging his fingers down to his chest where he gently squeezed his nipple. "You have nice nipples."

"Thanks, man." Garth ran a hand through his hair. "This is a little bit intense."

"It is, but intense in a good way." Keegan's own cock was raging with a hard on hidden beneath the blanket, safely tucked away inside his briefs. He glided his hand over the spattering of brown hair on Garth's chest, gradually sliding south, stopping at his waist. "Can I go lower?" He grinned at Garth hopefully.

Garth's chest heaved and he nodded affirmatively.

"Good," Keegan whispered. He ran his fingers across his mate's trimmed pubes and wasted no time in seizing Garth's cock between his fingers. Garth's whole body shuddered, his torso twisting. Keegan squeezed the squishy manhood. Garth's cock instantly pulsed, becoming fatter and harder the more he squeezed. Keegan was pleased to see the result. He let go and then ran his hand over to Garth's thigh. He swooped down the masculine terrain, enjoying the roughness under his palm. Keegan ran his hand back up to Garth's cock, which was now jutting out fully erect. "I think you might fancy me a bit judging by this." He grabbed hold of the hot cock, tugging gently while he glanced back to see the look on Garth's face.

Garth's face shone with a strange sort of innocence. Keegan smiled at what he was seeing; he lowered his face and started to lick Garth's chest, trailing down to his abdomen on a speedy collision with Garth's cock.

Just before Keegan was about to seize the curious guy's dick in his mouth, Garth spoke up, "I really like you, Keegan."

The words came out barely above a whisper but they stopped Keegan going any further. "Really?"

"Yes, really," Garth said. "I wouldn't be letting you do this if I didn't."

"You're not really straight, are you?" Keegan gripped hold of Garth's cock again while his sight remained fixed on Garth's hazel eyes.

"I'm…" Garth shivered, giving into the dick-tugging bliss. "I'm not sure what I am," he managed. "I've kissed guys before but never this. Never been touched like that."

Keegan found it funny that for someone who prided themselves on filthy humour, Garth seemed incapable of saying what it was being done to him. "You mean you've never let a guy tug on your cock." He tugged harder sending Garth's eyelids fluttering.

"Mmm hmm," Garth moaned.

"I feel honoured." Keegan let go of him and went back to staring up and down the length of Garth's naked body. A body that was still virginal in certain ways. A body he could claim. "Will you give me the honour of fucking you?"

"What?" Garth's eyes popped open. "Fuck me? In the arse?"

"Yes. In the arse," Keegan laughed. "That's how us

boys do it together you know."

"I don't know if I am up for that. I can't believe I'm even letting you do this."

Keegan snorted derisively. "Yep. Back to being a cock tease." He flopped onto his back, annoyed.

Garth put his hand out and rubbed Keegan's chest. "Don't be like that, blondie. I just told you that I like you."

"What does that even mean coming from you?" Keegan said snottily.

Garth shuffled closer and kissed Keegan's closed mouth. "It means I think you're an awesome and lovely guy who I wanna get to know better."

"Lucky me," Keegan said sarcastically. He knew he was sounding like a dick but he didn't care. His cock was about to explode and he felt like he was in bed with a frigid little bitch.

"Not just that. I also happen to think you're the hottest guy I have ever met. No other guy has ever made me want to try these things."

Keegan knew he should be flattered but it was all so frustrating. "Okay," he grumbled.

Garth placed his lips to Keegan's and forced his tongue inside. Keegan obliged and rolled onto his side to follow the kiss. Their legs banged together and he felt the hot tip of Garth's cock prod his thigh. Keegan was so wrapped up with Garth licking inside his mouth that he got a slight fright when the shaggy-haired stud groped his bulge by surprise.

Garth promptly slipped his hand inside Keegan's underwear and squeezed his fuzzy balls. He tugged on Keegan's restricting underwear, ripping them down low enough so Keegan's cock was freed. His slender fingers enveloped Keegan's hot hardness with a firm grip. He groaned inside Keegan's mouth in sweet surprise from its large size. He pulled his mouth free. "You are a fucking porn star," Garth exclaimed. He threw the blanket away to have a look at what was in his hand. "Whoa. That is quite the disco stick you got there, bro."

"Thanks," Keegan reached around and squeezed Garth's arse cheek. "So does that mean I can fuck you?"

"Crikey, someone is a little bit pushy, isn't he?"

Keegan's cock throbbed impatiently, needing its desire drained. "No offense Garth but don't start something you can't finish."

Garth looked at him with wounded eyes. "Don't be mean, blondie." He ran his fingers through Keegan's hair. "Let's just kiss a bit, yeah?"

Keegan's mind danced in dark places thanks to the alcohol coursing through his veins. "If I'm that special, prove it. Show me how much you like me."

Garth's swallowed, his Adams apple rising in his throat. Keegan expected him to bolt out of bed any moment. "Okay," Garth said flatly. He wriggled down the bed and wrestled Keegan's underwear down his legs and over his feet, chucking them on the floor.

"What the hell are you doing?" Keegan asked.

"Showing someone how much I like them." Garth spread Keegan's legs apart with gruff purpose, hoisted himself over and sat between the v shape of Keegan's opened legs. He ran his hands up Keegan's hairy limbs, raking his fingers all the way up 'till he found Keegan's cock. He squeezed it at first, then gave it a couple light slaps. His face was illuminated with intrigue like he was discovering a new culture. "Are you ready?" Garth said bluntly.

"Ready for—"

Garth suddenly bobbed his head down and placed Keegan's cock inside his mouth.

Fuuuuuuuck! Keegan gasped in response to the wetness soaking his pole.

Garth sucked eagerly, slobbering up and down the big cock. He dug his blunt nails into Keegan's hips as he forced his mouth to take as many inches as he could. The sound of Garth slurping and gagging was hot as fuck. Keegan could tell how hard he was trying. It was obvious it wasn't something he had done before but it was just as obvious how keen he was to please Keegan and make a good impression. He pulled his mouth off and began licking the skin of Keegan's ball sac. Garth then sucked down on his balls—one at a time—wetting them thoroughly.

Keegan covered his face with his hands, giving into the pleasure being down to him. *You really do fucking like me!* Garth continued sucking on his balls while wanking his cock at the same time. The combination sprung what Keegan had wanted so badly. To cum. To blow a big messy fucking load. A bleary tingle buzzed his taint and he panted, "I'm gonna cum, I'm gonna cum."

Garth wanked him off faster and just before Keegan roared with a grunt, Garth shoved his mouth down over the head of his cock, capturing the forceful load firing out.

Keegan gripped locks of Garth's hair in his hands and pushed his mouth lower, desperate to feed him every single drop.

"Take it all," Keegan whispered, still emptying his seed. When he finally felt his cock splurge out the final drips of juice, he let go of Garth's hair and sighed exhaustedly.

Garth flicked his head up showing a mouth that was still full, cum was seeping from the corner of his lips and dribbling down his chin. He gulped, swallowing everything in his mouth. He grimaced at first then smiled. "I got the lot like you told me to, blondie." He opened his mouth wide like he was visiting the dentist.

"You did too," Keegan said through ragged breaths. He shivered uncontrollably when Garth bent down and kissed the sticky tip of his cock.

Garth collapsed down on the bed beside Keegan. "I told you I liked you." He latched his arm over Keegan's chest protectively and hitched a leg over, reeling him in so they were skin on skin. "Is that proof enough for you?"

"Yes, you proved your point." Keegan held Garth's draped arm.

"Good. Can we kiss now?"

"I think so," Keegan answered.

"I hope you like the taste of your own cum cos there may or may not be some still stuck inside my mouth."

"Gross," Keegan chuckled.

"It's your jizz, bro. What are you complaining about." Garth hugged him closer.

"Absolutely nothing," Keegan said with a smile. He pressed his lips against Garth's and melted into his arms, where for the first time since his life unravelled, he felt truly happy. "Thank you," Keegan whispered.

"That's okay. It didn't taste as bad as I thought. It's kinda tasty... in a weird sex-eating way."

"Not that." Keegan nuzzled into Garth's shoulder. "For making me feel safe."

Garth kissed the top of his head. "No worries, blondie. That's what I'm here for."

CHAPTER TWENTY-FIVE

The sun streamed through the window toasting Keegan's skin. He still had his eyes closed, refusing to let go of full sleep. But the more the sun burned, the less choice he had in the matter. As he lay locked between the land of dreams and reality he started to hear a light rumbling sound. That sound made him aware he wasn't alone, he started to realise that the heat he was feeling wasn't only from the sun—but another body. With his eyes still closed he focused on the friction rubbing against his legs and side. *Garth!* He forced his eyes open and immediately saw Garth's arm draped over him and his face mashed into the pillow as he snored away.

Oh fuck! Keegan suddenly remembered the blurry patches of his night out and what had happened when they got home.

Garth was so fucking drunk he hopped into bed with me. He sucked my cock. He even fucking swallowed!

Keegan started to panic. What if Garth woke up and freaked out? Sure he was open minded and flirted, but he had always insisted it was one big piss take. Never anything serious. *What if last night was something he didn't mean?* The thought of being accused of taking advantage of a friend was sickening. Keegan groaned as he recalled how rude he had been, how he had railroaded Garth into sucking his cock. *Well technically I was trying to railroad him into being fucked. He chose to suck my dick.* Keegan's inner voice fired off excuses that didn't seem to help make him come across any better.

Garth's body was glued to his. He couldn't risk rolling away and waking him up. Their pressed bodies felt sticky, sweating up a storm under a clammy blanket. He wondered if Garth might not remember anything, maybe he would be off the hook. But as he looked under the sheet and saw his own morning wood as well as Garth's, it seemed pretty safe to say that their nakedness would give away what they had done together. *Maybe if I just lay here very fucking still I can wait for him to let go and roll over. I can chuck my pants on at least and play innocent.* This seemed a good plan until his ears pricked up at a shuffling noise coming down the hallway.

Dad's home!

Keegan's stomach dropped when he remembered that Garth's bedroom door was open and it would be clear to see he wasn't in there. As the footsteps got closer, Keegan could hear some sort of clanging. It was only when the footsteps stopped right outside his door and a voice called out, "Matty? Are you home?" that Keegan realised it was his grandfather.

Keegan watched in horror as the door knob began to turn.

As the door creaked forward, Garth rustled under the sheets and groaned with a yawn, "What's going on."

Before Keegan could respond door swung open and his grandfather stepped inside carrying two bottles of whiskey. "Oh shit! Sorry lads. Didn't mean to interrupt anything." His face looked shocked but soon grew into a smile and he began to laugh. "Looks like you two got up to some mischief last night."

Keegan choked on silence. No noise was willing to come out and join his embarrassment.

Garth buried his face into the pillow and began to laugh. Instead of freaking out he just held his arm over Keegan's waist even tighter.

"It's not what you think, granddad," Keegan finally blurted.

His grandfather tilted his head, looking at the clothes on the floor. "If you're about to tell me you boys are playing scrabble then it ain't what I think." He cleared his throat. "But if you tell me you been playing hide the sausage then it is what I think."

Garth raised a hand and gave a thumbs up. "That's the one, Glen."

"Don't tell him that," Keegan whispered.

"Keegan, son. I might be old as the hills but I know there's only one way a room ever ends up smelling as funky this." He flicked his eyes across the floor. "Especially when everyone's clothes are on the carpet."

Keegan wanted to bury his face under the blanket but politely laughed instead. "Yep. I guess you're right." He tried to force a laugh. "Sorry."

"Don't worry about it son. It seems to be quite fucking normal in this family. I stumbled in on your father in bed with another bloke when he was about your age." He scratched his beard like he was thinking about how to tell the story.

"Oh god," Keegan groaned under his breath. "Okay, Granddad. I don't need to hear about that."

Garth finally raised his face from the pillow and smiled. "He's lying, Glen. Keegan would love to hear all about how his dad was caught playing hide the sausage."

Keegan discretely elbowed Garth. "Nope. I really don't." He smiled politely at his grandfather. "Sorry Granddad, I don't mean to be rude but can me and Garth be alone for a moment?"

"I think that's Keegan's way of telling you to piss off," Garth said, giggling.

"Sorry, sorry," His grandfather said. "I'll leave you boys to it." He went to walk away but popped his head back and said, "If you don't tell your dad that I snuck out with two of his whiskeys I won't say a word about you two dipping ya wick in each other."

Garth laughed.

Keegan thought his head would explode. "Nobody dipped anything anywhere."

"I'm just pulling ya tits, son. Calm down." He smiled sincerely. "I'll see you boys later when I pop round in the afternoon."

Keegan smiled and waved as his grandfather shut the door. He lay back down and covered his face with his hands and groaned loudly. "Fucking hell! How many times do I have to be busted having sex?"

Garth wriggled into his side kissing Keegan's chest. "It wasn't that bad. Glen will just think it's funny."

"For someone who I thought was straight till last night you're sure taking things well for being busted in a not-so-straight act."

"Why would I be embarrassed?" Garth frowned.

"Umm, he thinks I fucked you."

"To be fair, he didn't specify who did who," Garth said sounding diplomatic, "and even if he did, it wouldn't bother me. Why would anyone be ashamed of waking up next to you?"

Keegan's heart galloped. "You are like the sweetest person in the mornings."

"And you are like the sexiest." Garth licked his tongue along Keegan's flank, nuzzling into his armpit. He pulled his face back and grinned. "I always wanted to try that."

Keegan laughed. "Be a pit licker?"

Garth curled his lip. "To lick yours." He leaned in and kissed Keegan on the lips. "What do you fancy for breakfast?"

Keegan scratched his head, thinking it over. "I can go make us some toast if you like?"

Garth shook his head. "You're not going anywhere, blondie. I will go make us breakfast."

Keegan grinned back at him. "Will you now?"

"Yep. So what do you want? My pretend boyfriend has a rich father who has a fridge loaded with delicious shit. Bacon, eggs, hash browns?"

"Hotcakes with syrup?"

"Don't push your luck." Garth smirked back.

"Bacon and eggs and the biggest glass of orange juice you can find, please."

"Coming right up." Garth threw the blanket back then got up on his hands and knees, leaning in for one last sticky kiss. "See you soon." He jumped off the bed with zest-like energy. He stood in the centre of the room gathering his clothes. Before he put his undies on he wiggled his arse in Keegan's direction. "I know you'd rather have this for breakfast."

"You ain't wrong about that."

Garth glanced over his shoulder, grinning like a tease. "I can't give you all the goods right away. That would make me easy."

"Maybe your pretend boyfriend would like you easy."

Garth put his shirt on then with a very serious face said, "Maybe. But I don't think *he* knows how scared I am of doing it." He quickly replaced his gloom with a smile. "Breakfast coming up in a jiffy." He turned on his heels and marched out of the room, whistling a happy tune.

Keegan could feel the happiness flowing off Garth. He could feel it within himself too. Everything he had said the night before was real. He had meant it when he said he liked him. He loved how Garth dropped the word *pretend boyfriend* like he was flirting with the real thing. Keegan rolled the word *boyfriend* on his tongue. It sounded nice. It felt a good fit. He leaned down and sniffed the pillow where Garth had slept. It instantly registered as belonging to his *pretend boyfriend*, a faintly musky scent that smelt rebellious and was entirely Garth. Keegan tried to contain romantic notions before they run amok.

Before Keegan could get any more lost in his sweet fantasy his cell phone flared to life in the middle of the room buried deep in his jeans pockets. *Bling Bling. Bling Bling.* He ignored the call. He was too hung over to speak to anyone and if it was important he figured they would leave a message. A minute later when his phone dingled with the sound of a text he realised maybe it was important. Whoever it was had left a voicemail. The blue light from his phone's screen flashed through the material of his jeans, demanding to be noticed. Reluctantly Keegan scraped himself out of bed and stumbled over to his pants and pulled his phone out. He rubbed sleep grit from his eyes and sat on the edge of the bed. It was only with half-hearted interest that he checked the call log to see who it was from but when he saw the name displayed his entire attention was hijacked.

Liam!

Keegan looked at the name again just to make sure. He hadn't heard from Liam at all since that day at Tony's. Not once. Why would he be calling now? He felt his hand become jittery as he pressed the voice mail button and put the phone to his ear. Liam's deep voice sighed down the phone like he was about to launch into a long story. But he didn't. The call just ended without him saying anything. No apology. No rant. No nothing. Just a thoughtful sigh.

CHAPTER TWENTY-SIX

Damon sat on his couch, wearing nothing but a pair of black socks. The only other thing covering his naked body was a tingling sadness for what he had done. With what he had become. Outside the Auckland afternoon looked as dreary as his situation. The blue sky had clouded over with the colour of concrete, cementing the city in gloomy darkness. It was the height of the New Zealand summer but it wasn't unusual to experience all seasons in one day, even as far north as Auckland.

Despite having fucked Matt more than once overnight, the note Damon held in his hand told him he was not yet in control. He may have had the dirt he needed—in the form of filthy photographs they had taken in the bedroom—but he was still missing Matt's complete adulation. Damon stared down at the scribbled note Matt had left behind on the breakfast bench.

Thanks for letting me crash. Talk soon. Matty.

"What the fuck," Damon muttered. He screwed the paper up and biffed it against the wall. It didn't make sense. He thought the challenge would have been to get Matt to surrender his body. But that had been surprisingly easy. With wandering hands, gentle neck kisses and mutterings of *babe*— a word he knew that made Matt weak—Damon had climaxed inside Matt's arse well before the movie's climax.

It wasn't the most beautiful or steamy fuck of all time, but it had been enough to make Matt's pensive blue eyes stare at him longingly. *Hadn't it?* It was supposed to be like last time. Fuck the guy, tell him sweet things, and voila, Matt would be head over feet for Damon and everything about him. Apparently not. If that had been the case then Matt wouldn't have woken up early and slip out without saying goodbye.

Damon stared down at his dick and balls squashed into the seat of the couch. He knew his cock wasn't impressive when flaccid but when hard it became a meaty weapon—one that Matt seemed to enjoy. *Then why did he disappear?*

After the movie, Damon invited Matt to the bedroom "for a bit of fun." Matt had nodded dutifully and shadowed Damon's footsteps into the bedroom. Damon didn't say anymore. He stripped his clothes off, then ripped Matt out of his clothes too, and began ravishing his mate's body. He instructed Matt to pose in a variety of positions. Damon clicked away on his camera, making sure he got as many filthy shots as possible; Matt sprawled out on the bed, sucking Damon's cock, his arse cheeks spread and being fucked raw. The dirt was so thorough that if it rained it would become a mud slide.

It may have been part of a mission but Damon couldn't deny he had enjoyed the body he explored through touching, licking, kissing… fucking. He was used to the smooth supple bodies of women not the rough coarseness of men. The two times with Keegan may have provided male features but the young lad came in a smooth package in comparison to his much hairier father. Despite the ruggedness of Matt's body the sex carried a sweet softness. Damon thought he had been in control but the truth was he hadn't been. Sure, he had been the one barking orders and doing the fucking but Matt's energy morphed the deed from beastly to something romantic… something loving.

We made love last night. Not fucked.

Damon's stomach knotted and a sting of sadness rippled through him, zapping the soles of his feet. "Fucking hell," he muttered. He was missing Matt already. He felt robbed of something by Matt not being here, not being able to wake up and play some more.

He had always been confident with his sexuality. Both women and men found him attractive. He liked that women and men found him attractive. He just loved the ego thrill of being wanted. He didn't care who wanted him. But he had never pursued attention from men like he had with women.

He nibbled on a finger nail, wondering why he was suddenly more than capable of fucking men.

You were always able to do it. You just chose not to.

His inner voice was right. It wasn't that he didn't find certain men attractive. His years of photography had taught him he appreciated beauty in many forms. Not just the mainstream and accepted. Beauty was beauty. He knew most men would disagree that sexuality could be fluid but he also knew that every single guy in a group situation was subliminally aware of where they stood in the male pecking order; which men were their competition and who the weak were. It was primal and instinctive.

It was in those rare situations—usually on a night out in a club—where Damon would find someone on par with him—or arguably better-looking—that he would envy them. He would *want* them. He wouldn't just stop at comparing their physique and face, he would sometimes imagine how the guy would size-up with no clothes on. How that guy would *perform*. Damon wondered if this is where he tipped the scales of heterosexuality and was a slider along some invisible spectrum.

At eighteen he wasn't aware these shades of grey existed. You were one thing or another. In his twenties, he was far too worried about being accepted and popular to ever step across a line society would mock him for and label him something he wasn't entirely. But now... now he probably could cross the line and walk for miles past it.

That is what he had done with Keegan. *Crossed the line.*

Damon ran a hand up his toned legs, darted it inside his thighs and cupped his cock and balls. Keegan had owned these. He had owned all of him. The young guy's cock penetrating him had felt like some sort of transaction leaving Damon feeling like a possession. It was different to any sex he had ever had before. Not the dubious controlling aspect but the sense of purpose it had given him. He may have hated being made feel worthless but he had enjoyed feeling like he was part of something greater than just his own cock's enjoyment.

He knew Keegan was in town and he knew he should go see him but that was dangerous. If Damon were around the boy who he had crowned his boss then he would crumble and give Keegan whatever he wanted. He was invested. And he finally knew why.

Damon let go of himself and coughed out a pitiful laugh. "How fucking lonely am I?"

Saying it aloud felt good. He may have an enviable lifestyle with all his nice things, money, trips away and endless lovers but after so long living such a selfish life he was growing tired of it. It was empty. It had little purpose. What he had done with Keegan was rich in other ways. It helped dull the loneliness.

Not anymore.

In his mind, Damon tore up the receipt Keegan had of him. The damaging arrangement was over. The little shit no longer had control. Yes, the lad had helped open his eyes in some way to what was missing in Damon's life but the blond teen was not the person to fill it. It was his father.

Matty…

Last night with Matt was beautiful. It wasn't a one-sided ordeal. Tucked up beside his best mate and calling him *babe* wasn't an act. Damon had meant all the kind things he had said. He had felt them. They were real.

Damon stood up to get dressed. He raced through his apartment like a man about to cash in a winning lotto ticket. He didn't care if he run in to Keegan. He wasn't his fucking boss. The dark hold the boy had on him was gone. All Damon cared about was going to see Matt. He needed to see him. Hold him. Kiss him. He needed to be with his new-found purpose.

CHAPTER TWENTY-SEVEN

Matt went to make himself a coffee, walking over the sunshine draped across the tiles of his kitchen floor. His mood felt as bright as the shimmering light he was treading on. Nothing was bringing him down today; not even the hideous mess of piled dishes splattered over the sink bench, which he assumed was from Keegan and Garth's messy attempt at a cooked breakfast.

Since waking up he had worn a silly grin smeared all over his face, his mind dancing in happiness from what him and Damon had done together. *The love we made.* Twenty years of denying and suppressing feelings had come to an end last night when Damon entered him, roaring Matt's heart to life from a self-induced slumber.

He had woken early that morning while Damon still slept. Side by side, he had laid there spending far too long admiring his beautiful mate asleep that it began to border on creepy. When it became apparent Damon wasn't waking up anytime soon, Matt made the decision to get up and go home. He wished he could have stayed in bed and spend the day with Damon, but Matt knew if he wanted to experience sizzling passion again then he best not come across too clingy. The last time they shared a sexual journey, Matt had scared Damon off with his enthusiasm.

In delicate motion, he had rolled away from Damon's arms, got dressed back into his running gear, left a note for him and went home. As soon as he was in his car Matt played the radio as loud as it could go, blaring some cheesy pop track. Even once he got home happy songs jingled in his head like a juke box.

Matt sat down at the table with his hot cup of coffee and contemplated how to spend what was left of his Saturday. He figured he should probably go see Jason and go over some of the stuff on his *wish list* for the wedding. As he sat sipping away, rowdy footsteps burst into the room and he looked up to find Keegan and Garth appear in the kitchen wearing togs and towels draped over their wet shoulders.

"Good to see you had enough energy to go for a swim today," Matt said pointing at them. "I thought you'd both spend the day with your heads in a bucket."

"Nar, Dad. We didn't get that hammered."

"Yes we did," Garth blurted. "But we had a wicked breakfast to cure any hangover."

"I can see that," Matt murmured.

"Sorry, we'll clean the mess up." Keegan glared at his friend, accusingly.

"Sorry, Mr Andrews, I'll do that now," Garth said like he was following the orders of Keegan's disapproving frown.

"You don't have to do it right this instant," Matt said. "I am sure the mess isn't going to kill anyone."

"Cheers, Mr Andrews," Garth replied.

Matt grinned. "I've told you Garth, you can just call me Matt."

"Sorry… Matt." Garth smiled.

"Would you mind if we go out again tonight?" Keegan asked.

"No worries. You can come and go as you please." He wished secretly Keegan would stay in more but he didn't want to be *that* parent. He knew that at eighteen you lived for nights out, not spending an evening in to get to know your father better. Just as both the boys went to leave to get changed, Matt called out, "Keegan, is it okay if I speak with you for a moment?"

Keegan stopped in his tracks. "Yeah." He looked at Garth, nodding to his friend to go on without him.

"Take a seat," Matt said. He waited for the sound of Garth's footsteps upstairs before he started. "I have been wanting to tell you something for a while now." Matt took a deep breath, forcing himself to continue. He had been wanting to come clean for years but only now did it feel right. "I know you must wonder why I never came and saw you as much as I could have."

"Oh no, you're about to have the conversation, aren't you?"

"What do you mean *the conversation*?" Matt asked.

"The one where you tell me why you never came to visit and how sorry you are."

Matt gulped. "Umm."

Keegan buried his face with his hands. "It's okay, Dad, we really don't need to have *that* conversation."

"But I feel like I owe you an explanation... an apology."

Keegan lowered is hands to the table. "I really don't need one. It's okay."

"I don't think it is okay," Matt said

"Dad, I don't need a heart to heart just so you can make yourself feel better."

The words stung Matt like a bee.

Keegan's eyes widened like he hadn't meant to say what he did. "Sorry I didn't mean—"

"No. don't apologise. Maybe it is selfish of me to apologise for being selfish." Matt sighed. "I just wanted you to know that it wasn't because I didn't care about you or anything like that it was just..."

The room drifted into silence. "Just?" Keegan asked reluctantly.

Matt scratched at his chest, taking his time to answer, thinking of the answer. "When I left your mum, we weren't happy. We really weren't." Matt laughed to himself thinking about Marie and how they had gone from loved-up to loathing in a heartbeat. "Your mum couldn't stand me. Nothing I did was ever right—which is probably true cos I didn't have a clue how to raise a baby."

"I don't think she did either but she did a good job," Keegan said, defending Marie.

"I know she did. She has done an awesome job." Matt smiled at his son, hoping to fend off any more angst. "Look I was young and stupid. Stupid and selfish. Selfish and... I thought I had things to prove to other people. That I had unfinished business back here. I don't know why, but I felt like I had to come back and study, work hard and make something of myself."

"It looks like you did," Keegan said coolly.

"Yeah, but I regret not doing it while being closer with you. I should have tried harder."

"Maybe," Keegan mumbled. "Why didn't you come down once you had made something of yourself." The words came out laced in snotty sarcasm. This was the closest to angry Keegan was probably going to get. In a way, Matt wished Keegan would scream at him, throw a punch, do something that would help clear the debt of eighteen years of neglect.

"I don't know," Matt answered. "I think I was scared. I always seemed too busy to make the time those early years and by the time you were at school, I was too embarrassed to come down and show my face. Then I moved overseas and spent even more time away... farther away. By then, I was worried what your mum and grandparents would say to me. And they would have been entitled to say anything."

"Yep. They have plenty to say. Mum not so much but definitely Nana and Pop." Keegan nodded. "They really don't like you."

"I can imagine." Matt flicked his eyes down at the floor and chuckled. "They weren't big fans of me even when I was with your mum."

"How come?"

"They thought your mum could do better." Matt stared back at Keegan. "Between you and me I tend to agree with them."

"Yeah, Mum says she was out of your league."

"She still is, I bet."

Keegan's young face gave into a smile and small laughter that made Matt feel better.

"Anyway, Keegan, I want you to know I am sorry for the past. I regret not giving you my time and you missing out on having a father around."

Keegan bit down on his lip like he was contemplating

what he was about to say. "I don't mean to be rude, Dad, but I don't feel like I missed out on anything by you not being around."

Matt wasn't sure to be hurt or relieved. "You don't?"

Keegan shook his head. "Like you said, Mum did an awesome job."

Matt rolled his eyes over Keegan. The boy looked so much like Marie it wasn't funny but underneath the golden locks and handsome features was a quieter personality, one that reminded Matt of himself. He kept staring, lost in the moment of seeing a piece of himself in his son.

"You're looking at me weird," Keegan said.

"Sorry. I'm just so happy you're here." Matt rubbed his eyes, trying to hold back his happiness that threatened to leak down his face.

"All good," Keegan mumbled, breaking the intense gaze.

"I was just so worried that you'd be angry with me and—"

"Dad, lets drop it. This heart to heart is bordering on child abuse," Keegan joked.

Matt smiled. He stood up from his chair and walked around to where Keegan was sitting. "Stand up," he asked.

"Why?"

"So I can inflict one last bit of child abuse with a hug."

Keegan grimaced. "Do we really have to?"

Matt hitched his eyebrows up.

"Fine," Keegan groaned with a heave of his shoulders, slowly getting to his feet.

Matt wrapped his arms around his son. "I love you." As he said it, Matt realised he had never told his son this.

Keegan was stiff in the embrace at first before capitulating and hugging back. "I love you too, Dad."

Hearing those words was like a shot of adrenalin, Matt squeezed Keegan tighter. "Thank you." He closed his eyes and kept hugging, reluctant to let go.

"Uh, you can let go now, Dad," Keegan whispered,

patting his father's back.

Matt let him go and stepped backwards, smiling. Keegan's face returned an awkward grin. He quickly darted out of the room, disappearing upstairs to get changed. Matt sat back down with his coffee. He didn't think he could be any happier after his night at Damon's but here he was, feeling even better than before. Nothing was going to break this wave of happiness.

Absolutely nothing.

CHAPTER TWENTY-EIGHT

The chat with his father was cringeworthy. The kind of mush that should be kept to the confines of cheesy sitcoms. Keegan had worried his father would pounce on the opportunity to have this sort of talk. He raced out of the kitchen leaving the cringeworthy moment and his smiling father behind. Keegan wasted no time in hauling his arse upstairs to use the ensuite attached to his bedroom and wash off the stubborn sand still clinging to his body.

As Keegan let the warm water pour over him, he let his mind mull over the day spent with Garth at the beach. Their dunk in the sea had cooled their bodies of heat but also cooled the connection that had burned between them in the bedroom. After being snapped by Keegan's grandfather, Garth had gone downstairs and made them both a delicious breakfast. Together they had sat on the bed, devouring the tonne of food on their plates. Garth dropped sprinklings of compliments Keegan's way throughout the meal, constantly telling him how sexy he looked.

Secretly, Keegan wanted his pal to continue pumping his ego up the rest of the day—saying sweet complimentary things—but as soon as they'd finished breakfast and got dressed for a day out at the beach, Garth changed. The cocky laid back dude was still confident and laidback, but he didn't mention a thing about what had happened in the bedroom. *Not one bloody thing.* If anything, Garth had gone out of his way to reinforce his hetero side by perving at every bikini-clad babe who happened to pass them on the beach.

It pissed Keegan off that the compliments dried up, but he refused to say anything. If Garth knew it bothered Keegan then that would feel like he wasn't in control. Keegan needed control.

He lathered up some body wash, scrubbing his

ZANE MENZY

armpits and between his legs. Touching his dick made him
think of Garth's mouth sucking him. A familiar horny ripple
splashed Keegan's loins. He looked down at his skinny feet,
grazing his eyes up his dripping legs till he focused on his
drenched, stiffening cock. He laced his fingers around his
tool and began to pull, closing his eyes as he imagined having
his wicked way with Garth. It didn't take long for him to get
fully erect, he placed a hand against the wall and bowed his
head, grunting as he tugged at a furious pace. Keegan was
about to gasp and shoot his load when the squeak of the door
opening made him loose his focus, he let go of himself and
spun 'round to see Garth walk inside the bathroom.

"You gave me a fucking heart attack," Keegan panted,
holding his chest.

"Are you sure it was me and not playing with your
cock that did that?" Garth smirked.

"I wasn't playing with my cock… I was washing
myself," Keegan lied.

Garth leant against the bathroom wall. He pointed
towards Keegan's crotch, which was visible through the glass
shower door. "Really? So it just got big and hard from the
feel of the water, did it?"

"Whatever," Keegan muttered, dropping his hands to
try and cover his erection.

"Settle down, blondie, we all play with ourselves."

"Yeah but we don't all like being busted while we do
it."

"I know what you mean. My parents busted me all
the time growing up. I was never too wise at listening out for
footsteps." Garth laughed. "The worst time was when Mum
busted me on my bed trying to bend down and suck my own
cock."

"Why doesn't that story surprise me."

"Oh, come on. Don't tell me you never tried." Garth
hitched his eyebrows up. "I bet with a dick as big as yours
you probably could suck yourself.

Well not suck but I can lick the tip. Keegan wasn't going
to share that detail though. "As much as I'd love to stand

214

here naked and talk to you about your wanking history, I'd appreciate it if I could finish having a shower in peace."

"Why are you worried about me seeing you naked?"

"Because I am naked."

"Considering I sucked your cock last night I thought I'd maybe earnt shower watching privileges."

Hearing Garth say that was weirdly flattering. "Watching me shower is a privilege?"

"It sure is." Garth scratched the back of his neck then lowered his voice, "I wouldn't mind if you wanted to keep jacking off."

"I didn't think you'd be interested."

"Why wouldn't I be?"

Keegan shrugged. "Dunno. Just thought you'd be too busy fantasising about all the chicks you raped with your eyes at the beach today." As soon as Keegan said it he knew how jealous he sounded. "Not that I care."

"Aww, I think somebody does care just a little bit," Garth said in a cutesy voice. He stepped forward 'till he was standing right at the shower door. "Did someone get an incy wincy bit jealous?"

"No," Keegan scoffed, looking away.

Garth tapped on the glass, trying to get Keegan's attention. "Tell me the truth and I'll tell you something true in return."

Keegan flicked his eyes back to Garth. "What's something true that you'll tell me?"

"Nope. You tell me first—honestly—did you get jealous when I was looking at the girls down at the beach?"

Keegan bit down on his lip. *Don't tell him.*

"You're hesitating," Garth said, smiling.

"Fine. I confess. I was jealous. Shoot me." Keegan let out a shy laugh. "Happy now?"

Garth's smile was immediate. "I am. Very happy. I knew one night with me and you'd be hooked." He raised his shirt, rubbing his tummy. "You just can't get enough of this hotness."

Keegan rolled his eyes. "What were you going to tell

me in return?"

"Okay so my truth is..." Garth dropped his shirt back down, pausing like he waited for a drum roll. "I may have been perving at all those chicks on purpose. Like a couple of them were hot, but I was only doing it to see if you'd react." He grinned, looking pleased with himself. "And looks like it worked."

"What worked? How is making me jealous a good thing?"

"Because, blondie, it means that you like me. Like *Really* like me." Garth pressed his face to the glass door and licked his tongue up it.

Keegan laughed at the ridiculous manoeuvre and splashed water against the door. "So you think I *really like* you?"

"Yep. People only get jealous if they have feelings for the person."

Keegan looked down at Garth's pants and a bulge that was beginning to grow. "Is it safe for me to assume that he likes me too."

Garth groped himself and nodded. "This fella really likes you."

"Okay then. What about you?" Keegan pointed at Garth's face.

"I think you're a bit of alright," Garth downplayed. "I tend to agree with my cock on most things. He's the one with all the brains."

Keegan snorted. "You're such a dork."

"But I'm *your* dork."

Keegan smiled and continued to scrub his body. The room went quiet. The only noise came from the rushing water of the shower. It drowned out anything too serious lurking between them in the misty space.

Garth finally said, "Why didn't you say anything at the beach if you were getting annoyed."

"I wasn't getting annoyed."

Garth shot him a condescending look. "Sorry. Let me rephrase it then; why didn't you say anything if you were feeling jealous. You could have said something and I would have stopped."

"You're not my boyfriend. You're free to do what you like."

"I am your *pretend boyfriend* though," Garth said. "That gives you some rights."

"Does it now?"

Garth narrowed his eyes in an approving glare.

"So I could have made a big scene and packed a wobbly in front of other people and outed you?" Keegan laughed.

"What do you mean outed?" Garth said derisively. "Out. In. Fuck that shit. If I like someone, I like someone."

Keegan decided to test Garth's beliefs. "You'd hold hands with a guy in public?"

"Yep," Garth fired back. "Especially if it was you."

"Bullshit," Keegan scoffed. "You'd be too scared."

"Scared of what?"

"Reactions. What people say or do when they saw us?"

"No I wouldn't. I told you this morning. I'd never be ashamed to be seen with someone like you," Garth's words danced around the room, romancing the hell out of Keegan. "I kissed you in the bar, remember?"

"Yeah. A gay bar. Not a straight bar."

"I'd kiss you in a straight bar too."

"You would?" Keegan spluttered.

"I'd kiss you in front of anyone, anywhere. No fucks would take flight and no shits would be given."

"Bullshit."

"Do you not believe me?"

"I didn't say that."

"I'll prove it tonight. You tell me when and where and I'll grab your face and shove my tongue down your sexy throat." Garth's eyes widened, egging Keegan on. "We can go down and do it in front of your dad right now if you like?"

"Nope. It's quite alright." Keegan cringed at the scenario of making out with Garth in front of his father. "I'll take your word for it."

Garth sniggered. "Chicken."

"You just want an excuse to kiss me again."

"And what?" Garth wasn't denying anything. "I like kissing you and I like to do things I like."

Keegan admired the way his *pretend boyfriend* stood so relaxed, he focused on Garth's lips. "So if I say, 'kiss me,' you'll kiss me wherever?"

"You have to use the magic word."

"Which is?"

Garth scratched his chin, thinking up an answer. "Cactus balls."

"Cactus balls? That's two words."

"Not if you say it fast enough."

"I guess I won't forget it in a hurry."

"I think you're clean enough now," Garth said, changing the topic suddenly. "Turn the shower off so I can dry you."

Keegan liked the idea of being towelled down but he didn't like the idea of his father snapping them out. "What about my dad? What if he walks in?"

"Settle down. I checked before coming in. He's on the phone to someone about having them round for dinner tonight."

"Who?"

"I dunno. Maybe it's your former lover," Garth said, wagging his head.

"Huh?"

"Damon. That old guy you fucked?"

"Damon isn't old," Keegan said defensively. "He's actually quite hot."

"Ouch," Garth said, rubbing his arm. "I might need some ice for that burn you just gave me."

"You brought him up, not me."

"True." Garth chuckled, warm and breathily. "Does he have a bigger cock than me?"

Keegan flinched. Where the fuck did that question come from? "Umm no," he lied. "You're about the same size."

"Cool," Garth sighed. "Was he a better fuck than me?"

"Okay, someone is beginning to sound a tad insecure."

"I'm not insecure," Garth insisted. "I just wanna know who you enjoyed more. Me or the pensioner with saggy grey balls."

Keegan held in a laugh. "For starters, Damon doesn't have *grey saggy balls*. And also, I can't really compare you both. You know... considering you haven't let me fuck you yet."

"Well played, Mr Andrews. Turning it around to try and get what you want."

"How about you turn around and give me what I want then."

Garth smiled like something had just clicked into place. "You really want to fuck me, don't you?"

"Like you wouldn't believe," Keegan said in a growly tone. He switched the water off and stepped out of the shower.

Garth grabbed a towel from the rail. He stepped over, dropping to his knees and began to dry Keegan off starting at his feet. "So how would you feel about me fucking you instead?" Garth glanced up with a hopeful look.

"I'd rather do you."

Garth dabbed the towel up Keegan's legs. "Why does it have to be me taking it?" He wrapped the towel over Keegan's cock, then tucked it under and gently dried his balls. "Your cock is fucking huge. At least I'd be a more comfortable fit."

"I would rather be the one in control."

"Is that what you call it?" Garth flicked him a smile as he got to his feet, placing the towel to Keegan's chest.

"You're the one with a cute arse," Keegan said in smarmy fashion. "You were born to be a bottom."

The corner of Garth's mouth drew up, he reached around grabbing Keegan's bum cheek. "You have a pretty nice arse too, though."

Keegan looked at him defiantly, shaking his head.

Garth grabbed Keegan's hips, grinding their crotches together. "It sounds like I don't have much choice in the matter," he whispered sexily.

"I'm afraid not."

"I guess you better be nice to me in town tonight. No sneaking peaks at other men."

Keegan's heart skipped a beat. "Is that a yes?"

Garth rolled his eyes back, toying with the question. He lifted Keegan's knuckles to his lips for a caring kiss. "Yes, blondie. That's a yes."

Keegan smiled. Sometime tonight, his darkness could finally come out to play.

CHAPTER TWENTY-NINE

Damon smoothed his sweaty palms down the legs of his pants as he stood on the front porch of Matt's house. He had been standing there for well over a minute, waiting for the courage to knock on the door.

You come here all the time. Don't be such a fucking pussy.

Damon couldn't work out why he was so nervous or why he was clutching a bottle of expensive red wine under his arm. He didn't even drink the stuff but it *felt* more appropriate for some crazy reason than his usual alcoholic poisons of choice.

Damon was decked out in some of his finest threads. Clothes he usually reserved for trendy functions he attended as part of his photo exhibitions. The meticulous presentation hadn't stopped there; he had even shaved and showered before coming around, dabbing his neck and wrists with his most expensive cologne.

I only ever go to this much bloody trouble for a date!

Is that what this was? A date?

The only thing he knew for sure was that waking up and finding Matt gone had left him jilted. Driving all the way out here was insane but Matt had left Damon's heart feeling tethered and chained. He wanted more of Matt, if Matt would have him. His mate's vanishing act was a confidence killer. Damon had never had a lover get up and leave like that. It pissed him off as much as it worried him.

"Bloody hell," Damon muttered under his breath. *I'm a fucking catch, Matthew Andrews! You couldn't get enough of me twenty years ago.* Damon shook his head, trying to dislodge his insecurities about feeling unwanted. This was not an emotion he was accustomed to at all. He always got what he wanted and *who* he wanted.

Finally, he cleared his throat, raising his curled-up

hand and knocked on the door. No one approached. The only noise piercing the early evening sky was the song of cicadas screeching like fingernails down a blackboard.

Damon turned on the balls of his feet, looking around, admiring the pristine yard. All the houses and gardens along here were well-kept though. It was Beaumont boulevard. The best street in Port Jackson. Damon had grown up in a waterfront home only four blocks down the road. He had a lot of good memories from his time growing up in the affluent seaside suburb, but not enough to ever want to live here again.

Click. The door swung open, catching Damon by surprise. He spun back 'round and saw Jason standing there.

"Jason," Damon spluttered.

"The one and only." Jason clicked his fingers.

"Sorry I didn't know you were here. If you and Matty are busy I can come back another—"

"Fooey. Don't be so silly. Come in. We're making Matt dinner to say thank you for all his help with the wedding"

We? Damon wanted to bolt but before he could step away, Jason grabbed him by the hand and dragged him inside. "Come on. There will be plenty for everyone." Jason said, letting go of Damon's hand.

"Oh nice," Damon mumbled. He wasn't hungry for food. He was hungry to be alone with Matt. When they walked into the lounge, Damon saw who the *we* were. Will Jenkins. Jason's fiancé. Damon hadn't seen Will since the 90s. He was the older brother of Todd—Damon's best mate before Matt. Damon and the younger Jenkins brother had been tight until Todd had become obsessed with Jenna in a school boy crush that turned psycho, damaging their friendship beyond repair.

"Look who I found outside," Jason said. He waved his hands like a magician's assistant, motioning towards Damon who stood there with a feeble smile.

Will stood up and strolled across, shaking Damon's hand with warm enthusiasm. "Wow. It's good to see you,

Damon."

"Same," Damon replied, he smiled at the friendly Will who still had that unmistakable Jenkins family blond hair, albeit a little thinner. "How's your mum and dad doing?"

"They're good." Will grinned. "Considering their son is about to marry another man."

"I can only imagine." Damon chuckled. "Congratulations by the way."

"Thanks, man." Will darted a look across at Jason who was nestled in one of the lounge chairs, watching the two catch up. "But you've seen who it is I am getting hitched too, right? Wishing me luck may be more appropriate." Will laughed at his own joke.

"Pfft." Jason rolled his eyes. "William Jenkins, you will have sore knees for the rest of your life because of me."

Will's face became flustered by the comment, "I don't know if that's appropriate talk in front of others."

Jason screwed his face up. "What? No, not sex, fool. I mean sore knees from being on the ground praising the lord for being so lucky to have me."

"Oh right," Will said, tugging at the collar of his shirt like the room had nearly became too hot for a prude. He cast his eyes back at Damon. "I can't believe it. You still look the same. I Wish I knew your secret."

Damon ran a hand through his hair. He loved running into people from days gone by, they all paid him this compliment. Not everyone had stayed quite so young or so in-shape as he had. "Thank you. Jenna passed on some good genes." *Not to mention my rigorous gym routine and an unhealthy fixation on moisturising day and night.*

"Or maybe it's the blood of virgins you go around collecting," Jason snickered.

Damon shot him a questioning look. "I can't say that I have resorted to such tactics just yet."

Jason sent back a smug smile that looked almost rude in its intent.

Damon returned his attention to Will. "Where's Matty?"

"Here," said Matt's voice.

Damon twirled 'round and saw Matt walking in from the hallway, wearing a baggy jersey and blue shorts. Damon gave him the biggest smile he could muster. "Hey, man."

"Hi...," Matt's voice drawled at an uncomfortable pace.

"Sorry for just turning up, I didn't know you had plans." Damon raised the bottle of wine in his hand. "Thought it would be a good night for a drink."

"Oh, sure," Matt mumbled. His face tinged ever so slightly red.

"I can come back another time. It's no problem."

"I've already told Damon there is more than enough for all of us. The more the merrier." Jason got up from his seat and crossed the room towards Damon. "Let's open this baby up. I don't know about youse but I fancy myself a wine."

Damon reluctantly handed the bottle across to the presumptuous Jason. He had wanted to save the expensive bottle to share alone with Matt.

"I'll go find us some glasses," Jason said, disappearing into the kitchen like he owned the place. Will followed quickly behind his fiancé, saying he was checking on the dinner cooking.

Damon made sure they were out of sight before he spoke. "You disappeared this morning."

"Uh, yeah." Matt looked nervous. "I had heaps to do today with helping Jason with the wedding." His eyes looked around the room like they were scared to meet Damon's face.

"Did you want me to go?" Damon asked, sounding wounded.

"No. God no," Matt answered quickly. "You can stay for dinner."

"I can come back another day. I don't mind. You don't get to see these guys much." He went to step past Matt and leave.

Matt clutched Damon's tanned arm. "Don't go. I want you to stay."

"Only if you're sure?"

"I am sure. Please stay." Matt's blue eyes shone convincingly as he still held on to Damon's arm.

"I had fun last night," Damon said, glancing over his shoulder to make sure there was nobody prying.

"Me too," Matt whispered.

The sound of clinking glasses began to rattle behind them, Matt quickly let go of his arm. They shot their attention to the dining room and saw Jason holding three wine glasses. "Okay, bitches. Who wants one."

Matt laughed. "Yes please."

"And me." Damon nodded.

"Did you wanna drink in here or at the dining table so we can make fun of my husband-to-be as he tries not to burn your house down while cooking?"

"I heard that," called Will's voice. "And don't worry, Matt, I know what I'm doing."

"I trust you Will," Matt called back. He gave Damon a thoughtful glance. "Dining room?"

"Sure." Damon followed Matt and Jason into the dining room where they sat at a large oblong table. Jason poured them each a drink and took a seat at the end closest to the kitchen—bitching distance to Will—while Damon sat right beside Matt at the other end like a loyal dog. "Where's Keegan tonight?" Damon asked.

"He's in town with his friend Garth," Matt said.

Damon mulled over the name Garth. It had a familiarity to it, but he couldn't summon the face. "It's good that he is out having fun." Damon took a sip of the wine. "He probably needs to go out and get his mind off everything." As soon as Damon said it he wished he could rewind time and shut his mouth.

"What do you mean *get his mind off everything*." Matt frowned. "What's he got to get his mind off?"

Damon hesitated. "I mean it's good for him to get out of the house and go out and be with real people. Not stuck inside on a computer, playing games."

"I guess." Matt swished the wine around in his glass, a

pondering look on his face. "But to be fair he hasn't been on a computer the whole time he's been here."

"That seems weird for, K dog. He usually lives on the bloody things." Damon's chest tightened. He knew the reason why Keegan wouldn't have been anywhere near a computer.

Jason leaned forward, placing his elbows on the table. "You know Keegan quite well, do you?" The question was asked politely but felt loaded with other emotions.

Matt answered for Damon, "Yeah, Damon knows him better than me. Isn't that bad of me?"

"I wouldn't say that," Damon fended.

"I would. You and Keegan are really close." Matt let out a soft laugh. "I get a bit jealous."

"Interesting," Jason purred.

"He's here now though, isn't he?" Damon said, patting Matt on the back. "You can get to know him as well as you like."

"That's true," Matt mumbled, quickly downing a mouthful of wine.

"Not trying to stir up Matty's misery, but is it safe to say you're sort of like a father figure to Keegan?" Jason eyes twinkled at Damon mischievously.

"I wouldn't go that far," Damon retorted.

"Nar, you probably are," Matt conceded. "I was never there like I should have been, but you always were." Matt smiled, nodding towards Jason. "Damon has been super awesome with standing in where I couldn't."

"True." Jason nibbled on his lip. "It's good someone was there to fill the gap."

Damon found Jason's wording curious but chose to ignore it.

"Parents friends are the best," Jason said. "Growing up, I was very close to my mother's best friend, Mihi." He giggled to himself. "I used to tell her all my antics and secrets."

"If you were telling her the same things you used to tell me," Matt said, "then I hope she never told your mother what you were up to."

Jason laughed. "Yeah. I was quite naughty back then. Dressing up as a woman and going off to meet strange men off the dating lines."

"Oi. I was one of those strange men you met, remember?" Will blurted from the kitchen.

Jason twirled around in his chair, laughing. "Sorry, honey. You were my favourite of the strange... and the strangest."

"Aww, thank you." Will blew him a kiss then dropped his face, concentrating on what he was cooking.

Jason turned back to face Matt and Damon "Yep. I was definitely up to a lot of no good. Meeting up with people I shouldn't." He lowered his voice to a throaty whisper "Doing things that probably weren't good for me."

Damon's tummy turned. He smiled at Jason and said, "We learn good things from our mistakes though, don't we?"

"Sometimes. But I do wonder if some of the men I was with back then were old enough to know better and not help me make those sorts of mistakes."

"Crikey. Don't go getting all Oprah Winfrey on me, Jason," Matt teased.

"My bad." Jason glanced over at Damon. "So, Damon. Does Keegan confide in you like I used to with my mum's best friend?"

"Sorry to disappoint, but I can't say he does."

"Pity," Jason said, smiling. "Would have been one hell of a party to watch Matty freak out hearing about Keegan's sex life."

Matt placed his hands to his ears. "I don't want to hear about my son's sex life. That's if he even has one." He lowered his hands and began to laugh. "And I'm so glad you're here, Jason. I can always rely on you to lower the tone."

"That's what I do; lower tones." Jason sighed thoughtfully, discretely locking his honey-brown eyes on Damon. "Better to lower tones than cross lines we shouldn't."

Damon held in a snarl. The skinny little cunt knew something. Something he fucking shouldn't. Damon kept his cool, politely smiling back and answered, "That's right. We have to be careful not to trip over other's lines."

∞

The dinner Will served up was superb. A chicken dish he had flavoured with a sweet Mango sauce. It wasn't the usual taste Damon liked but it had gone down a treat and the bonus of food being on the table was that it meant it kept Jason's big mouth full.

Luckily, Matt's camp guest didn't mention anything else about what he may or may not know. It was moments like these Damon was glad for Jenna being his mother. She had taught him to never lose your cool, remain charming and smile through the poison being thrown at you. Damon didn't do it with quite the same level of finesse as his mother managed, but he had enough skill to avoid any more dangerous dancing around the topic of Keegan.

After they had polished off a second bottle of wine following dinner, Jason and Will declared that they were heading home. Home being Jason's mother's house where they were staying. Once friendly handshakes and goodbyes were exchanged at the door, Damon and Matt were finally alone. It was a little after ten o'clock so he knew that he would have plenty of time to enjoy Matt's company undisturbed.

When they wandered back into the lounge Matt asked if Damon fancied another drink.

"I wouldn't say no." Damon plonked his butt down on the couch and stretched his legs out. He unbuttoned the top two buttons of his shirt and flicked his shoes off. He lay back into the couch wanting to look sexually appealing to relax with.

"Here you go," Matt said, extending a freshly poured glass of wine across to Damon. He went and sat on his own chair on the other side of the lounge.

Damon chuckled. "What are you doing all the way over there?"

"Just sitting." Matt's eyes flickered.

"I can see that, but why don't you come sit here...with me." Damon patted a free space of couch in front of his crotch.

Matt hesitated before climbing out of the seat and crossing the lounge to join him. He sat nearer Damon's feet, looking rigid.

Damon brought his legs up and swung his feet to the floor to sit up right. He reached over and grabbed Matt's shoulder, rubbing him affectionately. "How come you're so nervous?"

"I'm not nervous," Matt muttered into his glass.

Damon grinned, giving Matt a look that said he didn't believe him.

"Okay, I'm nervous," Matt confessed.

Damon kept rubbing Matt's shoulder. "Loosen up, Matty. You don't have to be nervous with me." He lowered his hand down Matt's back, slipping a finger into the tip of Matt's arse crack. "I think we are well past *nervous*."

"I guess so." Matt forced a smile. "It's just kind of weird."

"What's weird is waking up and finding your best mate has done a cum n run."

Matt laughed. "I wouldn't put it quite like that."

"Well, you weren't there when I woke up." Damon pulled his hand from Matt's pants and placed it on his mate's bare knee. "I call that a cum n run."

"I can assure you it wasn't that." Matt placed his drink down beside Damon's. "I just had heaps to do today."

Damon rubbed his fingers further up Matt's leg, slipping them under the hem of his shorts. "I see." He could feel how tense Matt was; his muscles stiff and locked. "Do you not like me touching you?"

"No. it's nice."

"Just nice?" Damon arched his brows, grinning.

"It's more than nice."

"Then how come it feels like I'm making your skin crawl?"

Matt heaved a sigh and dropped his shoulders. "I'm scared, Damon. Really fucking scared."

"You don't have to be scared of me."

"I do though, Damon. I don't think you understand." Matt flicked him a sad stare. "I really enjoyed last night. I never thought we would ever go down that path again ya know."

"I know what you mean," Damon agreed. "It just sort of happened. I didn't plan it," he lied. "But I'm glad it did happen."

"Are you?"

Damon nodded. "Of course."

"It's just that," Matt started, "last time we fooled around like this, I got a little attached if you recall?" Matt laughed to himself. "I don't wanna do that again. I know for you it's just fun and I agree it is good fun but I have to be careful with fun like that... fun like that seems to come with feelings for me."

Damon felt bad seeing his friend's vulnerability peel open like a skinned orange. "You know I'd never hurt you, Matty?"

"I know you would never hurt me on purpose but that doesn't stop it happening."

"Are you saying that you could—" The words suddenly got stuck as if his throat was made of mud. Damon coughed and tried again. "Are you saying that you could fall in love with me?"

It felt like a small forever waiting for Matt to answer. "Maybe."

"Wow," Damon whispered.

Matt ran a hand through his hair, avoiding Damon's eyes. "I already love you as a mate and I don't think it would take much to love as more than that."

"Are you saying that you could date a guy?" Damon asked, intrigued. "That you could be with a man the rest of your life? No pussy? Just cock?"

"Said like a real Casanova."

"No. I am genuinely curious."

Matt turned and looked him right in the eyes. "Yes, Damon. If I loved the person then I could quite easily only ever have sex with another man the rest of my life."

Yes! Yes! Yes! Damon felt like the cure for lonely was within his grasp.

Matt took a sip on his drink and elaborated on his admission, "Until last night I had always thought what we did at eighteen was just some phase. A fucked-up scenario that I got carried away with, but now I think maybe it wasn't." Matt took a deep breath. "When I woke up and saw you in my arms this morning it hurt just looking at you. I literally wanted you so bad I ached. I'd be kidding myself if I tried saying I didn't find you physically attractive. Because you are. You are perfect. Inside and out."

Damon blinked. Stunned.

Matt covered his face and groaned. "See, this is why I should keep my fucking mouth shut. I didn't mean to freak you out."

Damon clasped his hands either side of Matt's face and planted a kiss on his lips. "I'm not freaked out, Matty. I think all of that is pretty fucking awesome." He grinned ear to ear. "Seriously. That is one of the best things I have ever heard."

"It is?"

"Yes." Damon nodded. "You have my full permission to get attached as you like?"

"Are you saying that you could do this—you and me—more than just for fun?"

"All I know is that when I woke up and saw that you were gone this morning I felt like you'd ripped my heart out. I haven't been able to stop thinking about you all day. You've got me feeling things I've never felt before. And I fucking love it!"

Matt looked dizzy from Damon's confession. "I—I don't know what to say."

"Don't say anything," Damon breathed into Matt's

ear. "Just fucking kiss me."

Matt's body let go of its rigidness, surrendering to the emotion in the room. He poured himself atop of Damon, melting into his open arms.

Damon ripped at the back of Matt's t-shirt, hungry to force his mate's body into his own as hard as possible. Matt's stubble rubbed against his face but instead of being put off it made him want more of the manly body melting into him. He spread his legs apart so Matt could slip between them as they continued sucking each other's air.

Matt ripped his mouth away for a split second only to say, "Fuck you're hot."

"You too, babe," Damon sputtered, rewarding Matt's compliment with the word he adored.

They promptly locked lips again and returned to spitting groans in one another's mouths. They were so wrapped up in each other they didn't hear the front door open, they didn't hear the footsteps coming down the hall or even walk into the lounge. It was only when they heard a voice cry, "What the hell," that they knew they had been caught.

CHAPTER THIRTY

Keegan pushed the rattling trolley with its wonky wheel through the colourful confectionery aisle of the supermarket. The wheel had a fit, spinning the trolley out of control and nearly hitting a young girl stacking shelves.

"Sorry," he mumbled.

She shot him a customer-service smile weighed down from her menial drudgery. Keegan quickly rustled the menacing food wagon back into a straight line and continued on with his junk food jaunt.

He and Garth had grown tired of the swanky viaduct bar they had chosen as their Saturday night watering hole. When Keegan declared he was bored and wanted to go home, Garth hadn't questioned him. Keegan wondered if Garth would have been quite so keen to agree to culling the evening short had he known Keegan's motivation for bailing; to take Garth home and strip him of all his clothing and fuck him senseless.

After the bar, they had stumbled past the supermarket on their way to the bus station. It was Garth who had suggested they nip inside and buy some goodies. Keegan agreed. Garth would be needing some treats to keep his energy up with what Keegan had planned.

"What about these?" Garth said, pointing at a jumbo-sized bag of Maltesers.

"Throw them in." Keegan looked down at the growing pile of candy they had. Chocolate bars, sour lemon lollies, tubs of ice-cream, chips and dips. "Grab four bags."

Garth gave him a hesitant look.

"Go on," Keegan urged.

Garth frowned but quickly hid it. "We already have a tonne of crap in here."

"And?"

Garth fidgeted. "And, I don't know if I can afford to go halves if we put much more in."

"Who said you were even paying a cent?" Keegan saw Garth about to respond. "Nope. Don't worry about it. It's my treat."

"Are you sure?"

"Yep. I still have heaps of Dad's loan he gave me."

"I like how you say *loan*."

"I know right." Keegan grinned. "It's not like I'll ever be able to pay him back. Well, not anytime soon."

"I don't think he minds, though." Garth threw the Maltesers into the trolley.

Keegan eyed the expensive pile of food they had. "I'm guessing we have enough now. Anything else you wanted?"

"Just one more thing," Garth grabbed the end of the trolley, tugging just for a second to let Keegan know which direction he was headed. They went past all the food aisles 'till they got to the health and beauty section.

"I didn't realise you wanted to eat soap," Keegan joked.

Garth ignored him, scanning the aisle looking for whatever it was he was searching for. "Ahh, here we go." He reached out and grabbed a box of condoms from the shelf. Kegan felt embarrassed, wondering if anybody passing by would make the connection they were using them together. Garth read the label then glanced at Keegan's crotch. "Yep. Extra-large. These are the babies we need." He threw them in the trolley then grabbed a bottle of lubricant to go with the packet of shaft shielders.

They pushed the wonky trolley to the checkouts where a middle-aged woman scanned and packed their items at lightning speed. After coughing up nearly $130, Keegan went to grab the four bags she had filled.

Garth stepped in front of him, pushing his hand away. "Nope. I'll carry them." He swooped in and plucked the four bags up.

Keegan tapped Garth on the shoulder. "Come on, let me carry at least one. They look heavy."

Garth shook his head. "Me, strong man. You, sexy weakling." Garth flexed his biceps as he let out a masculine grunt for show.

Keegan laughed. "You idiot. Me not."

They made their way outside and footslogged to the bus stop. A sweet air of affection hummed between them. The connection they shared still felt light and innocent. But it wouldn't be for long. Garth was on a one-way ticket to Keegan's dark places, a state of mind that had no room for sweetness. Tonight, Garth would become his. Just like Damon had.

∞

The moon hung in the sky like a hard disc; its lunar rays shimmered across the calm waters of Port Jackson's sheltered harbour. In the distance, Keegan spotted the orange glow of Auckland City. It seemed strange to now be surrounded by such tranquillity, when an hour before they had been amongst the noisy mayhem going on under the source of the far-off lights.

He could see why his father liked living here. It was close enough to the city centre to be handy but far enough away to be peaceful. Keegan imagined himself staying here. It would be easier to find a job than back home and his father seemed laid back enough to live with.

I wonder if Garth would hang around if I wanted to stay?

The question seemed a bit rash to ask a guy who was still just a mate. A mate who may or may not be keen on something more. A mate who was yet to find out if he could handle the sex that came with anything *more*. Keegan's mind drifted ahead of him to the bedroom, wondering if Garth would love or hate what was about to be done to him.

Before they even were in front of the house, Keegan recognised Damon's car parked on the street. He found himself slightly apprehensive at running into the only notch under his sex belt. When he had driven up with Garth last week, Keegan had been desperate to see Damon, wanting to touch base with the person floating in the same doomed raft as he was. But things had changed. Changed quickly. Now he wasn't sure he even wanted to see Damon just to be reminded about the whole thing.

Garth could tell something was up. "Are you okay?"

"Uh yeah." Keegan flicked his eyes towards Damon's vehicle. "Damon is here by the looks."

"The guy you hooked up with?"

Keegan nodded.

"I can't wait to see what he looks like," Garth said cockily. "See who my competition is."

Keegan chuckled. "He isn't your competition. And for god sake don't say a word about it."

"Why you gotta spoil my fun?" Garth teased.

"I'm warning you. Don't say a single word."

"Settle down, blondie. I ain't gonna say anything in front of ya daddy about how his best mate porked his baby boy."

"Thank you for saying one of the creepiest sentences ever," Keegan grumbled. "And for the record, I porked him."

Garth sniggered. "Sorry, I forgot about you being the *man* in these things."

They climbed the steps. The rustling of the grocery bags in Garth's hands were louder than the fidgeting of the key. Keegan took a deep breath and pushed the door open, ready to pretend he was catching up with a family friend and not a former lover.

"Fuck, I can't wait to put these bitches down," Garth said, swinging the heavy bags. "I swear had we walked much further my fingers were gonna rip out."

"I offered to help carry one but nope you—" Keegan lost his words as he stepped into the lounge, barging in on a scene that could only be described as fucked-up-to-the-extreme. "What the hell," he cried, locking eyes on his father and Damon kissing on the couch.

His father leapt off of Damon, doing a full 360 spin and facing Keegan with the most frightened face he had ever seen. "Keegan. I-I wasn't expecting you home so soon."

"Evidently." Keegan flicked accusing eyes at Damon who brought his feet forward to sit on the edge of the couch.

"Hey, K dog," Damon said in a guilty voice.

"Look, Keegan. I am so sorry you had to see that," His father prattled. "But it isn't what it looks like."

"It looks like exactly what I saw," Keegan huffed. "You two were making out!"

His father's face was bright red. "Okay. Yes, we were kissing but…"

Damon got to his feet, standing beside Keegan's father in an almost protective stance. "I know seeing your old man make out with me probably isn't something you wanted to ever see, K dog, but we're all adults here." He made his eyes glow, encouraging Keegan to be calm. "You're cool with things like this, right?"

Keegan felt a rumbling of rage in the pit of his stomach. Instead of a man he had started to trust and confide in, he saw nothing but a fucking rat. A cunning, sexy rat that was up to no good. "When did you two being together start to become a thing?" Keegan asked, regarding Damon with suspicion.

"Nothing's started. We were just goofing around," his father pleaded. "One too many drinks." He pointed at empty wine bottles on the table. "I really am sorry."

Damon held Keegan's shitty gaze, touching his father's shoulder. "Don't be sorry Matty. We haven't done anything wrong here. Two grown men having *consensual* fun. Keegan knows that."

You fucker! Keegan bit the tail of the nasty words that wanted to fly out of his mouth and stab Damon in his handsome face. It was clear to see his father was only one insult away from breaking into nervous tears. He took a soothing breath and nodded. "Yeah, Dad. Don't stress. It's a free world."

"See Matty," Damon said. "Keegan doesn't care."

His father ignored the pacifying words being given. "Maybe you should go, Damon."

"No, Matty," Damon said hastily, "Keegan just told

you it's fine."

The room felt like it was spinning. Keegan knew he was losing control of an interaction that felt like a battle. He resorted to the only weapon he had. "Cactus balls," he whispered like he was casting a spell.

Garth dropped the groceries to the floor, causing a dull thud. He grabbed the back of Keegan's head and reeled him in for a hard, messy kiss.

When they finally plied their lips apart, Keegan turned to see his father and Damon with dropped jaws.

"What was that?" Damon stated more than asked.

"Are you two… together?" His father stammered.

Keegan wiped his face, which was wet from the slippery kiss. "Like I said, Dad. I'm cool with it."

His father's face went from panicked to softly curious. "Are you gay?"

"I am. That's why Damon knew I would be *cool with it*."

"You knew he was gay?" His father's voice warbled.

Damon scratched the back of his neck, his previous calm starting to unravel. "Umm yeah… like I knew maybe but…"

"I told Damon when me and him went away for my birthday weekend and stayed in a cabin up at the lakes." Keegan's throat burned from the recklessness of what he was saying, his words walking an edge of danger.

"So you did know!" His father's eyes remained fixed on Damon.

"Don't be annoyed, Dad. Damon was actually really cool about it. I wasn't even sure if I was gay or not, but he helped me understand that this is who I am." Keegan smiled facetiously, enjoying seeing Damon sweat. "Anyway, me and Garth are off to bed."

Garth had a silly smile on his face. He waved goodnight to the older men. "It looks like I've been given my orders. It was nice meeting you, Damon. And sorry about the interruption. Real blue balls material." He laughed and groped his crotch. "Night."

Keegan had to hold in a laugh at his mate's wacky version of goodnight. Garth picked up the grocery bags and followed him back into the hallway.

"Good to see you got yaself a real charmer there, K dog," Damon spat out bitterly.

As they got to the stairs, Keegan could faintly hear his father pleading for Damon to be quiet. He lapped up the snotty tone in Damon's voice. Normally he hated conflict and loathed drama, but it felt like drama and conflict stalked him these days. Rather than run scared he would meet it head-on.

As they climbed the stairs, Keegan found his cavalier attitude crumble fast though. He was horny as hell. Angry. Jealous. Upset.

But most of all he felt a worrying glitch nibble at him as he asked himself, *What the fuck is Damon playing at?*

CHAPTER THIRTY-ONE

Liam looked around the hotel room he was staying in. It was pretty nice for the relatively cheap price he had forked out for it. Two bedrooms on the twelfth floor of what really was just a matchbox apartment block. It may have been twelve floors up but there weren't any views out to sea or the harbour bridge that he had hoped for. Instead, it was a narrow view down the busy street, looking out on offices and other apartments. Still, it wasn't a view Liam was used to back home so it made it quite scenic in its own urban way.

He looked out at the skinny balcony, which clipped on to the side of the building like an afterthought. Not much scared Liam but heights were a weakness. He had tried standing out there with his morning coffee, but had only lasted two sips before giving up and heading back inside. From the safety of behind the window he looked out at his city view, imagining he could see through the buildings out towards the North Shore and farther on towards Port Jackson. That is where Keegan was.

He wondered if Keegan had been coming into the city at all. Had he been shopping along Queen Street? Lunching in Ponsonby? Clubbing at the viaduct? They were all things that made Liam's stomach twitch with a glitch of jealousy. It didn't seem fair that Keegan was up here living some city slicker lifestyle while Liam was locked in for a year-long course in electrical training back home at a provincial polytechnic. Admittedly, he could always move up to Auckland when he finished the course and find an apprenticeship.

Maybe then we can be mates again? Proper mates.

A bit of time and distance from the scene of the scintillating deed caught on camera in his bedroom was all their friendship needed. Liam missed his pal terribly. Not terribly enough to turn up at Keegan's father's doorstep. That would be too desperate. He had felt embarrassed enough going to visit Keegan last week when he turned up at his mate's house only to have Keegan's mum tell him that Keegan was in Auckland, staying with his father.

Liam had tried calling him but Keegan hadn't answered his bloody phone. Liam knew he should probably text and say he was up here but if he was going to make amends then he wanted to do it on his terms. His terms meant that Keegan would have to come into town and meet him. Alone. Then they can have a chat. Then things could be set straight.

Liam walked into the bedroom he was staying in and flopped down on the bed. He exhaled loudly, staring up at the pale white ceiling. He mulled over all the questions he had running around in his head. Questions about himself and questions for Keegan; not to mention all the questions Keegan would ask him when he told him the truth about what had really happened that night.

"I'm sorry, mate," Liam whispered to himself, hoping his quiet uttering of an apology would somehow take to the sky and find its way to Keegan. He knew that was impossible. He had no choice but to try calling his best mate again.

Are we still best mates though? After what I did?

Liam knew he had behaved like an arsehole the way he handled things. He should have been nicer to Keegan at Tony's that day. He should have offered a shoulder to lean on. But aside from being angry at the time, Liam hadn't felt right offering a shoulder to lean or cry on when it was himself who had caused the whole mess—not Keegan.

Fuck it, Liam thought. He had to try and make things right. Keegan had said on the video how much he cared for him. How fucking crazy and obsessed he was for him.

If he wants to fuck me so bad then he will accept my apology, surely.

There was more than just trying to mend broken bridges behind his reason to apologise. Much fucking more. Buried beneath the need to repair a frayed friendship, Liam's competitive streak had a dark desire to level the score between them. Liam had watched Keegan and Damon's video more than was heterosexually acceptable. But it wasn't the cocks, hairy bodies or strong limbs he was interested in. No. The male aspect of it was neither a turn on or a turn off. He knew that around mates like Skippy he would have to play up being grossed out about the fact two guys fucked on his bed, but the truth was he dint find it foul at all.

Two men together neither thrilled him or repulsed him. They were just two people getting it on. What had thrilled him about the video was the power radiating from it. The control Keegan had had, the sound and sight of Damon submitting to Keegan's big cock. *That* had done things to him, that had stirred Liam's own cock to life. Keegan had exuded a raw sexual energy that Liam envied and craved. The deviance of it all was hot as fuck.

Liam closed his eyes, replaying the video in his mind. He had watched it so many times to know every thrust, moan and groan. He focused on Keegan's hand slapping Damon's arse as his dick ploughed the mature guy with his face buried in the sheets. Liam reached down and fondled himself as the vision stiffened his prick.

Liam won every contest they'd ever had; running, gyming, swimming, losing his virginity, dating—admittedly that was a hollow victory now he knew Keegan liked guys. Liam was used to being the winner... the man, so it stung to see Keegan fucking like a porn star. Liam had never fucked anybody quite like that.

He wanted a shot at exuding the kind of power Keegan had in the video, he wanted that sort of control. He knew that he had the attitude to pull it off, he just needed help in finding the right partner for it. No girls down home would gift themselves quite so freely. Certainly none of the ones Liam knew.

Keegan was going to help him find that partner so Liam could have one more shot at winning another race between them. If Keegan liked him as much as he claimed then he would do anything he could to deliver the goods

Liam craved.

Liam threw his eyes open, glancing across to the bedside table where his phone was. He reached across, grabbing it with a clumsy grasp and nearly dropped it to the floor. He scrolled through his contacts 'till he came across Keegan's number. He knew it was time to try calling again. It was time to put his plan into action.

With anxious fingers, he pressed the call button and waited for his mate to answer. It rang and rang. Just before Liam was about to give up and hang up, Keegan's smooth voice trickled down the line with a friendly, "Hello."

.

CHAPTER THIRTY-TWO

Keegan lay on his bed, fully clothed with a morning wood so hard, it hurt. He imagined his cock screaming out "timber" to be cut down in size to reduce the throbbing pain. He looked beside him and saw Garth tucked up asleep on his side, his face squished into the pillow. If he were on his own, he would unzip and just sort himself out, cum into a sock and throw the sticky evidence under his bed. Too much jostling though would wake Garth up.

"Bastards," Keegan muttered under his morning breath, blaming Damon and his father for his hard-dicked predicament. Last night he was supposed to come back, hang out in the room for a bit, chillax, then pounce on Garth and ravish his body like there was no tomorrow. Now, tomorrow was here, and there had been no wild night of debauchery with his *pretend boyfriend* thanks to the toe-curling awkwardness they had barged in on.

As horny as Keegan had been last night, he wasn't in the mood to fuck after seeing his father tonguing the man who had popped his cherry. It felt like he had been part of involuntary incest. He wondered if the two had done more than just swap saliva. He grimaced at the thought. It didn't matter how supposedly good-looking your parents were, it was still gut churning.

He had come upstairs to his room with Garth and feasted his way through the junk food like he was eating his feelings. Garth had been brave enough to go down and grab spoons for the ice-cream, when he returned he informed Keegan that Damon had gone and that it was just his father down there. Hearing that Damon had gone was a small relief but it didn't change the fact that the condoms and lube sitting in the white plastic bag on the floor were not getting used that night.

They hadn't even kissed or hugged, just ate and ate 'till they fell asleep atop of the blankets at some ridiculous hour. It was like the universe was scheming against him, making sure him and Garth were always out of synch, never on the same page to actually get their rocks off together.

Keegan looked down at the burning bulge raging in his pants. He grazed his eyes across the bed 'till he found Garth's crotch jutting out in similar fashion. *He's hard too!* Keegan licked his lips at the appealing sight beside him. With shaky fingers, he carefully reached out, hovering his hand over the mound in Garth's jeans. He swallowed his apprehension and placed his hand down gently on the denim material, feeling the warmth of Garth's erection.

Fuck that feels good.

"Are you enjoying yourself," Garth mumbled.

Keegan ripped his hand away like he had been caught about to steal. His heart slammed against his ribs. "Fuck you gave me a fright," he hissed.

Garth wriggled onto his back, rubbing the sleep from his eyes. "I guess you get that when you get freaky and try to cop a feel."

"Sorry," Keegan whispered. "I shouldn't have done that."

"Don't apologise." He shot Keegan a grin. "I was looking forward to waking up with a blowie."

"Were you now?"

"Yup." Garth prodded his tongue against the side of his mouth, sticking his cheek out. "What ya waiting for?"

"Hate to burst your bubble, but I wasn't actually going to suck you off."

"You weren't?"

"Nope." Keegan shook his head. "I just wanted to touch you."

"Oh." Garth frowned, a mix of befuddlement and disappointment straining his voice.

Keegan smiled as he looked at Garth's messy bed hair. A lot of guys would spend ages in front of the mirror styling it to look like how Garth woke up naturally. For someone who had just stirred awake he sure looked fucking sexy. Garth's tired hazel eyes sparkled back and his lip curled into a half-sneer. Keegan didn't know what it was, but there was something about Garth's smile and sharp teeth which captivated him; a smile capable of making him look filthy and angelic at the same time. Keegan stared a little too long, his body wanting more than just a mere touch.

Garth coughed up a small laugh. "Are you okay? Anyone would think you got eyes for Christmas."

Keegan slipped his hand under Garth's shirt and began twirling his treasure trail. "I was just thinking how much I want to fuck you right now."

Garth's eyes looked up at the ceiling as his smirk slipped into a flustered smile. "I was sort of hoping you would take advantage of my offer last night."

"I think you could agree that last night was a bit ruined."

Garth put a hand to Keegan's arm, touching him affectionately. "Yeah. It was a bit of a mood killer, aye."

Keegan's eyes locked in on the plastic bag on the floor. "But we can do it now. The condoms are right there. Be a shame not to use them."

"Hold your horses, blondie. They don't expire for a few years. We don't need to use them all up today."

"You've changed your mind, have you?" Keegan grumbled, his face souring.

"I didn't say that." Garth sat up. "I just mean we don't have to do it right this moment."

"It's okay if you have," Keegan said, hoping to play the victim even though his cock was casting him in the role of villain. "Better I know now."

"Bro, I just woke up and I dunno if I'm in the mood." Garth rubbed his eyes again, playing up his statement.

"Your cock looks in the mood."

"He's in the mood every morning when I wake up. If I want it or not."

Keegan huffed a defeated breath and folded his arms.

"Are you packing a sad?" Garth said. "There's always

tonight?"

"Gee, I love how spontaneous you've become," Keegan said sarcastically.

Garth laughed, unfazed by the prickliness in Keegan's voice. He yawned loudly, stretching his arms out. "Mmph. Okay, moody arse. Let's do it."

Keegan wasn't sure if he'd heard right. "What?"

"I said let's do it." Garth narrowed his eyes. "I'm not having you think I'm some boring prick who doesn't know how to be spontaneous."

"That bothers you, does it?" Keegan asked. "People thinking you're not spontaneous and fun?"

"I couldn't give a fuck what people think of me," Garth threw back. He dropped his hand down and squeezed Keegan's thigh, he changed his volume to a whisper, "But I do care what you think."

Keegan felt special hearing this. "Thanks."

"Also, I know that if I don't put out I am gonna have to put up with you walking around with a face like a cats arsehole all day."

Keegan gagged on a laugh. "Fuck you, too."

"That's what you're about to do isn't it?" Garth waggled his eyebrows.

"Damn right."

Garth smiled at him. He scuffled up from the bed, stood up straight and pushed his shoulders back, cracking his back. "But before we do anything, I need to take a slash." He waddled towards the bathroom, stopping in the doorway. He turned around and looked back at Keegan. "I swear my arsehole is twitching in fear."

"You'll be fine," Keegan replied.

"Easy for you to say." Garth laughed. He ran a hand through his hair, looking muddled. "I can't believe I'm about to be fucked by a dude." The statement seemed a thought said out loud rather than directed at Keegan. Silence followed, a heavy mood draping the room that was matched by the poignant look dripping from Garth's face. Finally, he forced a smile. "YOLO," he blurted and trudged out the room, leaving Keegan alone.

Keegan stretched out, limbering up for what he hoped would be a sweaty workout. He could hear Garth sighing in relief as the sound of piss splattering the toilet bowl echoed from the ensuite. Keegan suddenly realised how nervous he was. The first time with Damon had been intense as fuck and scary with the newness of it all. The second time was decidedly easier. He had assumed that each time he fucked someone the sex would be easier, the feelings of fear diminishing. But he found himself rubbing sweaty palms down his pants, worried how he was going to approach this. Sure, he would put a condom on his cock and steer it towards Garth's virgin hole. But what else?

How do I play this? What do I make him do for me?

Keegan had been a porn fiend for years and the countless hours he had spent jacking off watching men and women use each other with next to little or no regard had taught him a thing or two. He liked to think he knew how to be a stud. He knew that to get what you wanted, you had to take charge. It had worked with Damon; degrading him, fucking him like a piece of meat. The smug womanizer had gagged for more dick. *He even came back for seconds!* It made sense it would work now too—one size fits all.

Or does it?

Somewhere in the back of Keegan's mind a tiny voice was doubting his urges. *Garth isn't Damon though.* He quickly buried his self-doubt when he heard the toilet flushing. He wasn't about to give away his power. If someone liked you then they'd do what they're told.

Garth strode into the room, appearing more relaxed than when he had left. "I'm back, blondie."

"I can see that."

"Yeah. I was gonna jump out the window and escape but I figured falling that high and breaking my leg would hurt more than your cock."

"The lesser of two evils, you reckon?" Keegan said light-heartedly. He fought off aggressive thoughts as he offered Garth a passive smile. "Are you all good?"

"Yeah, man. Just a little nervous."

Keegan shuffled to the edge of the bed, placing his socked-feet to the floor. He glanced over, motioning with his finger for Garth to come stand in front of him.

Garth appeared mesmerized, blinking heavily. He took a moment to move. In unsteady steps, he staggered over, coming to a shaky stop with his legs planted apart. His face emanated an innocent glow, an acknowledgement to the unknown of what was to come. He may have been fully clothed but his emotional essence was naked.

Keegan glanced up, meeting Garth's edgy stare. He shot the scared guy a horny grin then slipped his hands under the hem of Garth's shirt, rubbing erotically over his warm skin. Keegan fiddled with Garth's belt buckle, hooking it open with a jingling *clink*. He snaked the belt through the loop holes of his jeans, dropping it to the floor. Keegan licked his lips, knowing he was getting close to fully unwrapping his newest conquest. He popped open the pants button, tugging the zipper down speedily, then hauled Garth's jeans down to his ankles, exposing his soon-to-be-fucked pal's bulging black briefs.

Keegan focused on the white legs in front of him. Garth's thighs were deceptively muscly for someone with such a trim physique. He reached around, grabbing hold of one of his furry calf muscles.

"Tense it," Keegan whispered.

Garth obliged and flexed the muscle. Straight away the back of his leg went from soft to rock-hard. Keegan groped the strength he could feel burning beneath his palm. He manoeuvred his hand up behind Garth's knee, tickling him gently with his fingers. He took a breath and raked his fingers up the back of Garth's thighs, feeling the furry down of brown leg hair.

Keegan shifted his hands to Garth's inner thighs, which were smooth compared to the rest of his legs. Immediately, he noticed how Garth's skin felt much softer than Damon's had. Keegan pressed his fingertips up 'till they touched the fabric of Garth's briefs where his balls filled the material. Keegan stared up at Garth, their gazes met, exploring the other.

Garth's hazel eyes were glossed over like he had a secret to confess. He opened his mouth to say something, maybe something extraordinary? Instead, he just gave the slightest nod of the head.

It was okay to progress.

Keegan didn't fuck about. He slipped his thumbs over the black underwear, dragging them down to meet the bunched jeans already circling Garth's ankles. Garth's cock sprung out hard like a loaded weapon. The tip of his cock glistened with tiny specks of precum. Keegan locked his eyes on it, enamoured by the beautiful prick inches away from his face.

Somebody is more into this than he likes to let on.

Garth breathed heavily through his nose. "Do you like my dick?" he asked in a splintery whir.

"Very much." Keegan leaned forward, kissing the leaky tip.

"It-it's an okay size?" Garth's voice gave away his fear and worry. The vulnerability in his voice was both beautiful and endearing.

"It's perfect. I want you to take all your clothes off for me," Keegan said without bothering to look up at his mate. "I want you naked."

Garth obliged. He stripped his top off and then stepped out of his already-floundering briefs and jeans, casting them aside. He raised one leg up at a time, peeling his socks off. He resumed his standing position in front of Keegan, waiting for what was to follow.

Keegan surveyed Garth's cock some more, paying attention to its sleek shape and the manscaped testicles swinging below like a bell. His cock wasn't huge. Just an average size. But if there was such a thing as a pretty dick then Garth was the proud owner of one. Keegan cupped Garth's big smooth balls in his hand, outlining them with the pad of his thumb. Garth gave a low, throaty murmur as Keegan stroked them, gently rolling them between his fingers, weighing them. Inspecting them. Their heaviness was unbelievable. Keegan tugged on them. Gently at first. Then harder. Harder again.

Garth winced in pain.

"Sorry," Keegan murmured. He draped his open mouth over the head of Garth's penis, slowly sliding down, sucking away any hurt he had caused.

Garth's body jolted, gasping from the feel of frisky lips wetting his dick.

Keegan sucked down firmly, tasting a light sweat. He carefully cupped Garth's nuts in his hand again, this time caressing them in an almost nurturing manner.

Hushed words fell from Garth's lips, none that made sense but a mix of sounds and syllables that told Keegan his pretend boyfriend loved what was being done to him. As the taste of precum leaked over his busy tongue, he knew he had Garth's unwavering approval. He rammed his mouth down as far as he could, nearly deepthroating Garth's entire cock. The fullness of so much dick in his mouth made him gag, Keegan pulled his lips free and sucked in a breath of air.

"Fuck that felt awesome," Garth heaved, reduced to shivers.

Keegan lolled his head back, looking up. "I'm glad you're liking it 'cos I'm just getting started." He tapped Garth's hip. "Turn around," he instructed.

Garth shifted on his feet, turning around slowly 'till his sexy behind was looking Keegan right in the face.

Fuck I love this arse!

Garth had many nice features but his firm perky arse was definitely one of Keegan's favourites. His mounds reminded Keegan of beautiful white dunes. He grabbed hold of Garth's taut buttocks, resisting the urge to sink his teeth in. He stroked a finger down the crack, grazing over the fine hairs that lay within.

"Spread your cheeks," Keegan said, slapping Garth's arse dismissively.

Hands shaking, Garth reached around and spread his cheeks.

Keegan smiled when he saw Garth's dim hole, tight and scared. "Fuck yeah," he muttered. He crouched forward, blowing his hot breath over the virginal territory. Garth's entire body rolled with a shiver. Keegan could sense how vulnerable his lover was feeling by being examined so thoroughly. His hole looked so tasty, Keegan leaned forward and rolled his tongue over the quivering hole then kissed down on it, sucking it with all his might.

Garth began to leak pretty little noises. Almost girly in nature.

Keegan decided to lick deeper, thrusting his tongue like he would be using his cock very soon. He couldn't budge the seal of tightness blocking his path. He pulled his tongue out and slapped Garth's arse again. "I can't wait to get in there," he mumbled. He stuck a finger in his mouth, slobbering it with saliva then pressed it to Garth's entrance, swivelling around in slippery circles, gently prodding.

Garth continued to quiver, waiting for the intrusion. Keegan kept him hanging, massaging around the untarnished territory in the most sensual of strokes. Without warning, he pressed forward, burying the tip of his finger inside.

Garth groaned loudly as his sphincter retracted and strangled around the finger pushed inside him. He sounded uncomfortable, but he didn't say pull out.

Keegan wriggled his finger side to side, trying to stretch him open a little. He bit down on Garth's arse cheek as he pushed his finger in as deep as he could.

Garth's entire body went tense. "Fuck," he cried out.

Keegan pulled his finger out. "Sorry. Too much for you?"

Garth turned around to face him. "If that's what a finger feels like I dread how bad your cock will feel."

"You'll be fine."

"You think?" Garth laughed. He took a series of deep breaths and nodded. "Okay, blondie. Do what you gotta do. I trust you."

Keegan nodded. He looked down at the plastic bag by Garth's feet that had the lube and condoms. Seeing the instruments of sex made his stomach rumble with a twisted darkness. He tried hard to fight it off, quash it before he succumbed to its demands. But it was too late. He never stood a chance. He felt the words slip out of his mouth before he could rope them in, "Drop to the floor."

Garth's expression questioned the order.

"Get on the floor," Keegan barked. "On your hands and knees. I'm gonna fuck this hot arse of yours doggy style."

Garth's eyes widened.

"Come on," Keegan urged. "On the floor."

Garth swallowed and stood his ground. "I don't want my first time to be like that."

"You've had sex before with girls, haven't you?" Keegan scoffed, surprised by Garth's reluctance. "What's the big deal?"

"Yeah, but I've never been the one getting fucked! That's the *big deal*."

"I'll go gentle, if that's what you're worried about."

"It's not that." Garth said. "I don't want you fucking me in that position."

"Okaaaay," Keegan dragged out, looking around the room.

"This might sound strange but," Garth ran a hand through his hair, "I want to look you in the eyes while you're inside me," he whispered.

Keegan wasn't happy to have his selfish plans derailed.

Garth spotted the disappointment; he reached over and stroked the side of Keegan's face. "Being fucked—by a guy—is quite scary for me and I am hoping that if I can see your face then that might take away some of my fear."

Keegan felt a warm ripple in his chest. Its loving power obliterating his dark selfish thoughts. He swallowed, trying to down his guilt. With a smile he said, "Sure. We can do that." He grabbed Garth by the hips and leaned in, kissing his lower abdomen. "We can do it any way you like."

Garth brushed locks of Keegan's hair through his fingers. "Thanks, blondie."

"So how do you want me?" Keegan asked, raising his

eyebrows.

Garth took a deep breath, mulling over his options. "Laying on your back. That way I can try and take you at my own pace."

Keegan responded affirmatively by standing up and removing all his clothes. He lay down on the bed, lacing his hands together behind his head. "I believe this is what you ordered."

Garth laughed at the quickness of Keegan's cooperation. "I don't think I have ever seen anybody move so fast in my life."

"You never seen anybody so horny before probably."

"True." Garth smiled. "That might be it." He bent down and picked up the box of condoms, tearing into the packet and ripping one open. "Can I do the honours and put it on for you?"

"Go for gold." Keegan stay laid back, smiling; his cock at full attention, waiting to be wrapped up.

Garth's face ignited with fascination. He placed the rubber to the tip of Keegan's dick and rolled it down the long length of flesh. "I swear this thing is gonna split me in fucking two."

"You'll be fine." Keegan winked. "I'll keep my hands behind my head the whole time if that's what you want."

Garth didn't say anything, his eyes staring at the thick eight inches of dick throbbing to get inside him. He squirted dollops of lube into his hand and slapped it all over Keegan's shielded shaft, lathering it up into a sleek wetness. With the residue on his fingers, he darted his hand behind him, his face contorting as he lubed his hole up. He climbed onto the bed and hitched a leg over Keegan's waist like he was saddling up for a ride. He stay levitated, floating his arse above Keegan's aching cock.

Keegan knew it wasn't just the pain Garth was weary of. Once he sat down on that cock there was no going back. Garth could never undo what he had done. The moment he took even just one inch of Keegan inside him that meant he had been fucked by a guy. And there was no way he could ever be un-fucked. Keegan found the whole idea thrilling. He was about to welcome his *pretend boyfriend* to a different kind of club.

Garth grabbed hold of Keegan's cock, lining it up for his anal descent. He sucked in a breath of air like he was about to dive into a deep swimming pool. He squeezed Keegan's cock… and slowly lowered.

Keegan's whole body shuddered from the feel of Garth's scared hole touching the tip of his lubricated cock, hovering there, teasing him.

Time stood still. Their friendship locked in one final moment of innocence before it crossed an unchartered frontier.

Garth pushed down.

Keegan moaned.

Garth gasped.

The threshold had been crossed—Garth's arse had been breached.

Keegan's eyes rolled to the back of his head, pleasure flooding him like a dam being opened up. The first-time friction of Garth's arse burned his cock in the best way imaginable. He cast his eyes to Garth's face which was locked in teeth-gritting determination. He wriggled his butt down, trying to fit more of Keegan inside of him.

The ends of Garth's mouth curled up as he grizzled from the pain but it was clear to see by the fire in his eyes that he wanted Keegan all the way in. He lowered his hands, grabbing Keegan's chest and cast his eyes to Keegan's. "Fuck, man. I swear you got two inches bigger the second I sat down."

Keegan held in a laugh. He unlaced his hands and reached out to stroke Garth's trembling shoulders. He blew him a kiss. "You're doing great."

"Really?" Garth asked, grimacing after trying to push down further.

Keegan resisted the urge to force him down. "Yep. Doing great. And you look sexier the more you get in."

"I do?" Garth laughed. "I guess I better have the

whole beast in me then." Garth's eyes were half-lidded and he rammed himself down hard and fast over Keegan's cock. "Arrgh, fuck," he cried out, digging his fingernails into Keegan's flesh. He panted in rapid breaths, adjusting to the fullness impaling him.

Keegan's cock surged with a throb. "Fuck, you feel amazing." He dropped his hands from Garth's shoulders down to his hips, latching on with a firm grip. "Thank you so fucking much."

Garth winced. "You're. Very. Fucking. Welcome." He shifted his lips over his teeth. "Now what? I'm too scared to move."

Keegan laughed. "Just relax. I will do the work for us. Slow and steady and if I hurt you, just say, okay?"

"Okay, blondie." Garth circled a finger around one of Keegan's nipples, giving it a squeeze.

Keegan followed Garth's lead with the nipple play, placing his hands to Garth's chest. He tickled his fingers around, running over the stray hairs on his lover's pecs.

Garth leaned forward, dropping his face to gift Keegan a kiss. The kiss was fragile… like their lips were made of glass. Garth licked inside his mouth, sending a hotness zapping through Keegan right from the blond hairs on his head down to his toes. He oozed hot breath after hot breath into Garth's mouth, desperate to taste him. Craving his sex. Keegan reached around and touched the soles of Garth's feet before scratching his nails up and down his legs, eager to discover more of him.

"Fuck me," Garth echoed through the kiss. "Fuck me."

Keegan pulled his face back, sucking down a mouthful of spit. His eyes spoke for him. *Yes. I will fuck you.* He latched his hands over Garth's smooth back, reeling him in 'till their chests were pressed together. Garth slipped his tongue back in Keegan's mouth, and Keegan ignited his arse-fucking rhythm.

He started slowly, pulling out a couple inches before sending his cock back in with kind force. Garth's hot, hard prick pressed against his belly, leaking precum like a spilt drink. As each shove helped loosen Garth up, Keegan would pull out a little more, hitting back a little harder. He was firm but controlled.

Garth whimpered, pouring soggy breaths down Keegan's throat. He began feeding his butthole down harder, meeting Keegan's thrusts halfway. He mumbled through the kiss, "Harder, blondie, harder."

Keegan obliged. He bucked his hips and thrashed Garth's hole with wild shoves.

"Uh," Garth moaned. "Uh. Uh." He pulled his mouth away and pressed his face against Keegan's cheek.

Keegan waited for his lover to ask him to stop but he didn't. Garth just kept his face pressed to Keegan's skin, slipping out affirmative groans the more Keegan loosened him up. Keegan feasted on the butthole being served to him, his fuzzy sac jounced up and down beneath the mounds of Garth's rump, jostling the cum brewing in his balls.

It was too much, he was on the edge of an orgasm already. *Oh fuck!* He didn't want to be a two-minute man but the whole experience was too fucking much. "I'm about to blow, I'm gonna cum." He was about to say sorry but the words escaped him as his orgasm hijacked his senses. A sparkling tingle fired off from his anus, travelling along his taint then up into his balls and shot straight up out his cock. "Fuuuck!" Keegan cried. His cock spurted so hard he thought he would break the rubber. As his body jolted, he let out a tonne of cum in three rupturing bursts followed by a series of smaller tremors. Keegan shivered from his release, his body weakened. He wiped the sweat from his brow and gave Garth an embarrassed look. "Sorry," he mumbled. "That's kind of shameful."

"What's shameful?" Garth asked, a smile beaming from his lips.

"I just lost my lollies in record time. Turns out I'm not much of a porn star." Keegan offered a feeble laugh.

"Don't be silly, blondie. You were hot as fuck!"

"I was?"

Garth nodded enthusiastically. "Look at my cock. Can you see how much jizz I'm leaking?" He laughed. "I never do that. Never!"

Keegan looked down at the streams of precum oozing over his stomach courtesy of Garth's leaky dick. "There's quite a bit."

"The best part was feeling you cum." Garth's eyes danced excitedly, matching the hyperness of his voice. "I literally could feel you spurting. Every fucking twitch of your cock I could feel."

"So you'd be ke-ke-keen to do it again?" Keegan asked; his teeth chattering as another post-cum shiver rolled through his body.

"Do I have a cock in my arse right now?" Garth waggled his eyebrows.

Keegan mumbled a faint laugh. He raised himself up and kissed Garth's shoulder. "Thank you." He gently pushed Garth back so he could pull his cock out.

"What do you think you're doing?" Garth said with a wry smile.

"I thought you might want your arse back now."

"In a minute." Garth pushed Keegan to lay back down. He gripped his dick in his hand and started jerking off.

Keegan watched as Garth's face screwed up, his mouth slipping grunts.

After one particularly load moan, Garth's dick slit opened up, firing dashes of thick cum streaking out in a frenzy of heavy white dollops.

Keegan felt Garth's swimmers splatter against his chest.

Garth collapsed on top of him, cementing his wet seed between their bodies. He lay panting, riding Keegan's breaths like a wave. "I can be a one-minute-wonder too when I need to be."

Keegan rubbed Garth's back affectionately. "Thank you for this."

"And thank you." Garth had a cheeky glint appear in his eye. "I don't know about you, blondie, but I feel completely buggered after that."

Keegan laughed. "You look buggered."

"Buggered by the best." Garth licked Keegan's chest, sucking up his pools of cum. He then opened his mouth and gave Keegan a kiss, gifting him his semen so they could snowball the taste. Keegan swivelled his tongue around, licking up as much of Garth's sweet spunk as he could. They pulled their faces apart, both gulping down the creamy mouthfuls they each had.

Keegan grinned back, impressed by the mutual swallow.

Garth mashed his lips together, making sticky noises with his tongue. "I must say I think I preferred swallowing yours."

"Nar. Yours tastes way better, I reckon."

Garth smiled. He gently pulled Keegan's cock out of his arse then rolled over to lay beside him. They wrapped their arms around one another, bathing in the mess of sex they had created. Neither spoke for a while. Just laid together, sharing in the specialness circling their damp, exhausted bodies.

This hadn't been a fuck, Keegan thought. *This* was something else. Something Keegan hadn't felt with Damon. His heart soared in his chest, flying on the hopeful air Garth had blown inside him. He could feel his pulse still throbbing in his ears from the euphoria.

I want more of this.

Finally, Garth broke the silence. "Fancy joining me for a shower?"

Keegan kissed his forehead. "Sounds perfect."

Garth leapt over him, racing towards the bathroom. Before Keegan could catch up, his jeans pocket lit up from the screen of his cell phone humming with an incoming call.

"Aren't you gonna answer that?" Garth asked.

"It'll probably just be Mum being nosey." Keegan went to walk past his crumpled jeans that housed the ringing phone.

"Don't be so mean. She probably misses you," Garth

said. "I know I would."

The phone kept buzzing. He didn't want to answer it; he just wanted to stand next to Garth naked under the hot shower.

"Answer it, blondie. Talk to your mum. I'll get the shower warmed up for us." He gave a flirty wink and left the room.

Keegan sighed. He knelt down, fished through his jeans pocket and answered the call, "Hello."

A slight pause drifted down the line until a deep voice spoke, "Keegan, buddy. Fuck, I've missed your voice."

Keegan froze, the phone nearly slipping through his fingers. "Liam?"

"Yeah, man," said Keegan's estranged mate. "Is now a good time to talk? Or are you busy?"

Keegan looked towards the ensuite where he could faintly hear Garth singing—horrendously—in the shower. He grimaced, hating himself for what he was about to say. "Now's fine. I'm not busy."

CHAPTER THIRTY-THREE

Liam had said it was important he be there at 12.30 p.m. on the dot.

"Yeah, really important we catch up," Liam had said. "I have a few things to ask you that I can't say over the phone." The fact he needed to meet to ask questions felt ominous.

The hotel Liam was staying at was a dull white building on a skinny steep street that walking up was not dissimilar to climbing ladder-like stairs. The burn of the walk on already tired legs took a backseat to the conundrum of what the hell do you say to the person whose bed you soiled with cum and scandal. Looking the guy in the eyes was going to be hard, but it had to be done. You can't run away from life's problems, eventually they will catch up with you and sometimes it was better to meet them head-on sooner rather than later.

The glass doors of the complex opened and suddenly the cool summer breeze brushing his body vanished and was replaced with the artificial coolness of air-conditioning. In the centre of the lobby were two shiny elevators leading to the rooms above. On the left-hand side was a small reception desk, whoever was manning it was missing in action. Directly across from the reception were two green couches either side of a tall fish tank. Liam said that he would be waiting by the fish tank to let him in.

But surprise, surprise. There was no Liam. *Fuck sake!*

As if this whole "catch up" wasn't bad enough, being stood up was just adding salt to the wounds. For someone who had been so fucking adamant you be there by 12.30 on the dot, then surely, Liam himself would make sure he was there at the exact time.

Sitting, waiting on the couch like a loitering dropkick

was embarrassing and in a way degrading. It felt like Liam had control of the situation by running late. Almost like he had done this on purpose. But then he did have control, he could afford to be degrading because he knew secrets—he knew about the video.

He was on the verge of screaming after ten minutes of waiting and watching the fish swim in dizzy circles appearing just as bored as he was. Finally, the elevator made a buzzing sound.

Someone's coming down!

The doors opened and there was Liam, looking summery in a red singlet and white shorts. His face erupted with a smile and he crossed the lobby over to the green couches.

"Sorry man, I totally forgot about the time." Liam put his hand out for a friendly shake. "It's good to see you again." He nodded like he was unsure of what else to say. "Come with me." Liam motioned towards the lift. They walked over and Liam pushed the button, letting them inside the small metal box. The lift hummed its way up twelve floors before they got out and walked to the end of a well-lit hallway.

Liam stopped outside the room numbered 1221. He slotted his room card in the lock and pushed the door open. They were only two steps inside when it felt like the twilight zone had swallowed them.

What the fuck is Liam playing at?

Already sat at a kitchen table in the tiny apartment, sipping on a can of coke was Keegan.

"Damon!" Keegan said, frowning. He put his drink down, scrambling to his feet. "Wh-What are you doing here?"

Damon turned to Liam and scowled. "I want to ask Liam the same question." He could tell by the shock radiating from Keegan's face that the boy had no idea what was going on, but Damon was old enough to know the shit-eating grin on Liam's face had a menacing quality. Whatever the reason was for luring them both here, it was not innocent.

CHAPTER THIRTY-FOUR

Sunday mornings were meant to be about resting and sleeping in. Not this Sunday morning. Jason's wedding was to take place next weekend and Matt still had a long list of things to do before the backyard was transformed into the crazy dream wedding Jason had envisioned.

Matt had woken early and come down stairs where he had hidden in the kitchen, reading the news on his laptop. He had been sitting on a stool by the kitchen bench, closest to the back door, just in case he had to make an emergency exit at the sound of Keegan and Garth coming into the room. He knew this was ridiculous, feeling unwelcome in your own home, but he wasn't ready to face the music.

Last night had been humiliating. Utterly humiliating. Any inroads he had made with his son were surely broken and ruined after being busted ramming his tongue down Damon's throat.

What were we thinking?

Matt knew they should have been more careful, less reckless.

Damon had been so warm, so inviting with the kiss. It felt like they were sealing a future together. A future where they were more than *just* friends. What had seemed crazy and unthinkable suddenly felt entirely possible. Matt had loved Damon for years. They were best mates. Loving him or any close friend was inevitable. But this love transcended mere friendship, it carried a sexual energy that was only now being unleashed and realised. He didn't just love his best mate, he was *in* love with his best mate.

Matt also found himself accepting that this wasn't just a case of *gay for you*. Damon was the one he loved but in the back of his mind he secretly knew that he had always had a thing for guys. Especially guys like Damon Harris. Men who carried a natural confidence with them wherever they went; men who could walk into a room and own it with their mere presence. Matt was turned on by this strength especially when it came with equally strong arms and legs, and chiselled chests he could lay into and feel protected by.

He found himself wondering why he had never ventured down the same-sex path again since his teens. Dating women was easier, he guessed. He was attracted to them and nobody asked questions. Life was easier when people didn't question you. Dating a guy would have been problematic— just like being caught kissing one by your own son.

"What am I going to do," Matt groaned to himself. He got up from his seat and wandered to the espresso machine to make his second coffee of the day. He panicked when he heard a scramble of feet yomping down the stairs, he was about to dart out the door and hide in the garden but the sound of the front door swinging open and shutting calmed him down.

They've gone out!

Matt wiped his brow, relief settling him.

It wasn't just questions coming from Keegan that Matt was trying to avoid, it was his own questions he had for his son. Finding out Keegan was gay had been a twist he had not seen coming. Matt had always assumed his boy was straight. A good-looking lad who chased after girls. That wasn't the case of the chase. Instead, Keegan was a good-looking lad who pursued other guys and was dating—Matt assumed—a shaggy-haired unemployed mechanic. Not the catch of the century in Matt's books. He felt bad for thinking this. Garth seemed a nice enough guy but he had a roughness to him that made Matt feel his son could do better.

Matt promised himself that he would have a talk with his son when he and Garth got back home. He would let Keegan ask any questions he may have about Matt being with Damon, and in turn, Matt would assure Keegan he loved him no matter what. It seemed cheesy but he felt it needed to be said.

He finished making his coffee then went and sat at the

kitchen table, bringing up a fresh web page on his lap top and typed in *my son has just come out*. He hoped he could find some pointers to help guide him. Matt knew that his own way of approaching things would be fuddled.

He had barely finished his cup of coffee when the front door swung open again.

Damn it! You were meant to be gone longer than that.

Matt clasped his hands together, trying to brace himself for the uncomfortable father-son moment that was fast approaching the kitchen.

Here they come...

Matt took a quick breath and looked up with a friendly smile about to greet his son. "Oh… it's only you."

"Gee. Nice to see you too, Matty Pie," Jason said. He went and took a seat beside Matt.

"Sorry. I was just expecting you to be Keegan." Matt offered a friendly smile. "Fancy a coffee?"

Jason waved his hand, shaking his head. "Not for me, girl."

"Boy," Matt said pointlessly. "What do I owe this Sunday morning pleasure?"

"Will and my shit-dribbling sister—love her to pieces—wanted to go to the museum so I fibbed and said I had already made plans with you."

"Why would you not go with them? I've heard they have great exhibits on at the moment."

"If I wanted to go see old shit dug up from archaeological dig sites, I'd call up some of my exes." Jason smirked. "And also, Will is a fucking nightmare in anything like a museum or art gallery. He just goes on and on and on about what it is he knows about whatever is on display."

"Bit painful, is he?"

"Like a fist without lube." Jason laughed, his eyes flicked over at the lap top and the search results on the screen.

Matt quickly slammed the laptop shut. "Not for your eyes I'm afraid."

"Still a big porn fan I see," Jason teased.

"Nope" Matt rolled his tongue in his mouth. He tried to

come up with a believable lie. "I was just looking up stuff to do with your wedding. Gift ideas." He nodded, pleased with such a good fib.

"Aww, that's so nice of you Matty," Jason purred. "I've always wanted a gay son."

Matt threw his head back and groaned. "So you saw it."

"Gotta be quicker than that to stop my beady little eyes." Jason saw the filthy look Matt was giving him. "And don't worry. I already knew."

"You what? You know Keegan is gay?"

"Well, I do now."

Matt gasped, his heart booming, worried he had just outed his son by accident.

Jason turned with a titter and said, "I'm just pulling your tits, Matty. Yes, I already knew."

"But how?" He narrowed his eyes suspiciously. "Is your gaydar that good?"

Jason extended his hand out admiring his painted nails. "Whilst I do claim to have the most finely tuned gaydar in the greater Sydney area, it failed to detect Keegan's thirst for..." He dropped his hand down and looked across at Matt. "I only know because I bumped into him and Garth at the gay bar... kissing."

"You did!" Matt shook his head and lowered his voice, "Like I'm not against Keegan being gay—obviously—but I'm not too keen on him and Garth together." He cleared his throat. "Does that make me a bad person?"

"Not at all. It makes you an arsehole, not a bad person. Besides, you're just being a dad, looking out for your little girl."

"Boy," Matt groaned again.

"Anyway, I wouldn't worry. Garth and Keegan aren't together. They're just friends."

"But they kissed in front of me last night."

"Did they?" Jason's eyes became playful. "Interesting."

"Yep. Me and Damon were... were sitting having a drink in the lounge and they walked in and just started kissing. And I'm not talking about some little kiss. This was full-on tonsil-tennis stuff."

"Hmm. At the bar, Keegan admitted to being gay, but Garth insisted he was straight. I did wonder if the shaggy-haired stud wasn't quite as unbendable as he claimed to be." Jason rested into the back of his chair. "But he's pretty cute, though. In his own weird way."

"I don't care what he looks like, I just think Keegan needs someone who has more direction. Not a mechanic turned bartender turned jobless twenty-something who doesn't seem to own a single pair of pants without rips in them."

Jason laughed. "Have you listened to yourself?"

"What?" Matt said defensively.

"You are sounding like a complete bloody snob."

"I can't help that. I just want what's best for Keegan."

"Yes, but no need to forget where you came from, Matty Pie. You may have this gorgeous house, a great job and more money than sense, but it doesn't change the fact that you and me are still poverty peak trash—and I say that with pride."

"Meaning?"

"Do you remember how much you hated the way people judged you around here back then? How they made assumptions based on how you dressed and which street you lived on."

"That's a bit different."

"It's not really. You're jumping to a conclusion without giving him a chance. Garth may not be working now—and yes he would benefit from buying some new clothes—but that doesn't mean he will always be without a job."

"True," Matt mumbled.

"Anyway, you should be more worried about Keegan not having a job. I saw how much cash he had on him the other night. You can't keep giving him so much money like that."

"He's hard up."

"Yeah, so give him twenty bucks. Not hundreds," Jason replied. "If you wanna be giving out that kind of cash then you should be giving it to some cracked out bitch on a street corner working hard for her money."

"You, you mean."

"Touché, Matty pie, touché."

Matt went back to Jason's original point. "I feel bad for Keegan though. I was never around when he was growing up and it feels good to give him money. Sort of like payback for being such a shit father."

"You aren't doing him any favours by doing that. You need to sit down with him and help him decide what he wants to do. With everything he has going on right now, I think he needs someone to help him find his way."

"What do you mean, *everything he has going on*"

Jason looked away briefly. "Nothing. I just mean it isn't easy at that age. You remember what it was like."

Matt sighed. "I suppose you're right."

"I'm always right." Jason smiled.

"Right about what?" Fired a voice.

Matt glanced over Jason's shoulder and saw his father walking in. "Nothing, Dad. We're just talking about Keegan."

"Did ya just find out he's a fan of the pole?" His father smirked.

"You knew too?" Matt cried. "How the hell did you know?"

"I dropped by the other day and I couldn't find you anywhere down here so I went looking upstairs and I came across Keegan and his pal having… an intimate moment shall we say."

Matt rolled his eyes. "That explains why I have two bottles missing from the liquor cabinet upstairs."

His father shot back a guilty grin.

"You need to stop barging into people's rooms. You did that enough to me as a kid."

"Don't get angry at me," his father responded. "You should have been smarter and learnt not to get caught playing with yaself so bloody much."

Jason laughed. "Was Matty bad for that?"

"Was he what! Couldn't leave his bloody pecker alone after he knew how to use it. Mind you, I think the worst time was when I walked in on him in bed with Damon."

Jason covered his mouth and giggled. "That is priceless."

Matt began to blush.

"My heart broke a little that day," His father said in a contemplative sigh.

Jason's shoulders pricked up, getting defensive. "Because your son was in bed with another boy?"

"No. Not that. I don't care where he dips his wick," His father said honestly. "It was the way they were laying together. It was obvious poor Damon had been the one doing all the work while Matthew laid there like a log." His father burst out in laughter. "Yep. Couldn't believe I'd raised such a dud root."

Jason flicked Matt on the shoulder and joined in with the laughter. "Yeah, I'd be ashamed of that too, Glen."

"Okay, thanks for dragging up some of the finer moments of my past, Dad." Matt rubbed his face that was burning with blush. "Before I ask you to leave, why are you here?"

His father smiled hopefully. "I was wondering if I could borrow your car for the day. I've got a date with Aroha and I wanted to impress her."

"Whose Aroha?" Jason asked.

"A fine-looking wahine who's just started working down at the tavern. She has invited me and some of the other punters around to her place for afternoon tea."

"It isn't exactly a date then is it," Matt said.

"I am sort of hoping if I turn up in your car she might think I have money and then it might become one."

"Okay. Keys are hanging up by the door. Just don't be gone all day and night."

His father walked over and patted him on the back. "Thanks, son. I promise not to break her." He began to walk off. "And I won't break the car either." He roared with laughter at his own joke and disappeared.

"I love your dad," Jason said, smiling.

"Yeah. Embarrassing as, but he's pretty cool."

Jason's smile turned into a questioning grin. "You never told me that he busted you and Damon together."

"Didn't I?" Matt answered, knowing damn well he hadn't.

"I still find it funny how you and him fooled around together."

"Yeah." Matt smiled.

"You two would have made such a hot couple."

"Do you think so?"

"Definitely." Jason's eyes looked foggy with a fantasy. "Damon would make a hot couple with whoever he was with."

"Gee, thanks," Matt grumbled.

"I'm joking. You were about as hot as each other, so it would have been a match made in gay heaven."

Matt liked hearing this. He decided to test the waters of hope. "What about now? Do you think we would still make a hot couple?"

"Okay, random." Jason wrinkled his forehead. "But I'm guessing that ain't happening."

Matt felt a rush of elation wanting to escape him. A need to share his joy with someone. He took a deep breath. "What would you say if it was happening?"

Jason went to laugh but stopped himself. He adjusted his posture and stared Matt in the eyes. "Is there something you want to tell me?"

Matt couldn't stop the grin spreading on his face.

"Oh my god," Jason whispered. "Are you…"

Matt nodded, his grin now a goofy smile.

"Shiver me gay timbers," Jason gasped. "When did this happen?"

"Just the other night. I was at his place and I don't know how it happened but one thing led to another and we ended up." Matt hitched his eyebrows up. "You know. Doing *it*."

"You didn't!"

"Yep. more than once." He looked at Jason whose mouth gaped open in shock. "I still can't believe it. I never thought it would happen again. But I'm so glad it has."

"This is for real? Not like last time?"

"What do you mean last time?" Matt asked, knowing full

well what Jason meant.

"Last time he used you, Matty. I know youse are great friends now, but are you sure this isn't just Damon being... Damon?"

"No. This is for real. After you and Will left last night, he told me he couldn't stop thinking about me. He has feelings for me." Matt nodded. "I really think this time me and him could be something special. Something long-term."

Jason blinked. "Wow."

"You don't look pleased."

"No, of course I am pleased. Anything that makes my Matty Pie happy pleases me." Jason's eyes gave him a sweet look. "I'm really stoked for you."

"Thank you." Matt felt relieved that he could finally tell somebody. It wasn't fair to have such happy feelings and have no one to share them with.

"I just didn't think you two were *that way*," Jason said.

"I think I always have had this side to me, I just chose to ignore it. But I can't anymore. Not after the other night."

Jason grinned. "Was he good, was he?"

Matt was reluctant to get into details but Jason glared back demanding secrets. "Yeah. He was. He was amazing. Just like he was when we were young. Actually, it was even fucking better."

"Like a fine wine they get better with age," Jason said. "I must be crap at sex though cos I never aged past 21."

Matt laughed. "You wish."

"So did the old dog teach you some new tricks?" Jason winked.

Matt's heart fluttered remembering all the stuff they did. He wasn't going to tell Jason everything but he figured he could share one dirty detail. "I did end up doing one thing I'd never done before."

Jason leaned forward, eager to hear. "Ooo, do tell. I love me some juicy sex stories."

Matt bit his lip, looking around the room as if worried someone might overhear. "He took pictures of us. Of me mostly. I can't believe I let him. That's so out there for me."

Jason's happy face dissolved to a worrying frown. "You let him take pictures of you?"

"Yeah. Of both us. Together. He said it would be hot to have a reminder of our night together."

"Did he now," Jason mumbled.

"Have you never done that?" Matt asked, catching Jason's cynical glance.

"I've done heaps of silly shit like that. Me and Will have our own bloody home movie collection. But the difference is, I trust him."

"I trust Damon, too," Matt said protectively. "I've known him as long as you've known Will."

"That shifty motherfucker," Jason hissed.

"Damon?" Matt wanted to laugh at his friend who looked angry. "Damon isn't shifty."

Jason's eyes looked almost sad. He slumped his shoulders and sighed. "Matty, I think there's something you should know."

As Jason began his story it didn't take long for Matt to realise that this was something he wished he had known already. It wasn't photos Damon had been snapping that night. It was Matt's heart.

CHAPTER THIRTY-FIVE

Keegan stood in a trance. Why the hell was Damon walking into the scene. Liam had told him he was just going downstairs to check with the receptionist if his wallet had been found. Keegan was taking a stab in the dark that there was no missing wallet. Something funny was going on here.

Liam had been edgy the whole time since Keegan had arrived just twenty minutes before Damon. The room had been filled with pointless small talk. Not the way two guys who had been best mates for years would normally talk. Neither of them breathed a word about the video or Keegan's sexuality. Now with Damon standing metres away it seemed obvious that both topics were up for discussion.

"Would you like to tell me, Liam, why you interrupted my gym session just to bring me here?" Damon asked in a growly tone.

"Look, I know this must be weird but I needed to talk with you both." Liam smiled at Damon. "Did you want a drink?"

"Not for me," Damon replied hastily. "Just tell me what this is about?"

"Hold your horses," Liam replied with a snigger. He puffed his chest out and pointed to the couch. "Take a seat and I'll be back soon," Liam said, disappearing into one of the rooms.

Damon shook his head. He strode towards the couch and parked his butt down.

Keegan went and joined him on the couch but at the opposite end. He could feel an unspoken anger firing off of Damon.

"So, K dog, any idea what this is about?" Damon asked.

"Not a clue," Keegan grumbled.

Damon leant forward and rested his elbows on his knees. He lowered his voice so Liam wouldn't be able to hear him, "Whatever he has to say just let me handle it, okay?"

Keegan nodded. As pissed off as he was for Damon getting it on with his father, Keegan was sort of glad Damon was here. If Liam were to bring up what they did in his bed, then it was a relief to have someone here to share the blame with.

"I wanted to tell you sorry about last night," Damon said. "I know that must have been weird to see."

Keegan bit his lip, willing himself not to respond.

"We didn't mean for it to happen. It just sort of came about." Damon tapped Keegan's knee. "Honest."

Keegan relented, turning to look at him. "So it just *sort of* came about after you and me hook up?"

Damon nodded.

"From where I was standing Damon, it looks an awful lot like you might be playing with my father's heart so he doesn't get angry if he finds out about what you and me did."

"Give me some credit, Keegan. I'm not that bad." Damon let out a frustrated breath. "You know I'd never hurt you or your father."

"I don't believe you."

"You're not jealous, are you?"

"What?" Keegan screwed his face up.

"Why would you think I would be jealous?"

"I'm just asking. You seem a little prickly." Damon stared back like Keegan was pitiful and deserving of sympathy.

"No, Damon. I can assure you that I am not jealous of you and Dad." Keegan cringed. "If you and him are happy doing what you're doing then that's fine by me." He squinted his eyes, feeling an oddly protective instinct come over him. "Just don't go messing with him."

"K dog. I am not messing with your dad. Matty and I have always been close." Damon scratched the stubble on his chin like he was lost in a memory. "I am just amazed it took us this long to realise we had more to give each other."

Gross! Keegan thought.

"I want only what's best for Matty. And right now, the best is me." The statement was overloaded with arrogance but Damon seemed oblivious to how he was sounding.

"Whatever," Keegan mumbled.

"Anyway, you don't need to worry about me or your father. You need to worry about yourself."

"Wat are you talking about?"

"That boyfriend of yours. I think you might be slumming it a little bit," Damon said. He laughed. "He ain't a bad-looking dude but you could have anyone you wanted, Keegan. Not some dropkick."

Before Keegan could respond the bedroom door opened and Liam reappeared.

"You have a boyfriend?" Liam said, sounding stunned. "Since when?"

"Garth isn't my boyfriend," Keegan blurted. He turned to face Damon. "And he isn't a dropkick."

"Wait. Are you talking about Garth Bridges?" Liam asked. "My brother's mate?"

Keegan nodded.

"I didn't know he was gay." Liam ran a hand through his hair.

"He's not gay," Keegan answered. "Not really."

"He looked pretty gay while you were kissing him last night," Damon said, laughing.

"So he is your boyfriend?" Liam prodded.

"Garth is not my boyfriend," Keegan insisted. "He's just a friend. That's all."

"And you two aren't together?" Liam asked. His eyes bounced from Keegan to Damon.

"No," Damon said firmly.

"Fucking in my bed was just you two having fun?" Liam's voice was a mixture of curiosity and disdain.

Damon sighed. "Look. I want to say sorry for what we did on your bed, Liam. If that's what this is about— dragging us here to give us a lecture—then I apologise. What we did wasn't cool. But as for the *fun* that is between me and

Keegan."

Liam folded his arms, standing tall in front of them both. "Is this the type of fun you do often?"

"Like I said, Liam, that doesn't concern you," Damon's voice remained firm.

Liam sniggered. "So you do have an arrangement?"

"No we don't," Keegan said quickly, hoping to cut Damon off before he got angry. "It was a one off."

"In the video though you both talk like you'd done it before," Liam responded.

Keegan shot Damon a look, begging him not to bite back. Damon inhaled loudly. "Okay, Liam. Is this all you wanted to talk about?"

"No. I umm…" Liam tugged at the neck of his singlet. "I wanted to see if you'd be keen on making a deal."

"A deal?" Damon asked.

Liam briefly stared at the floor, scuffing his foot on the carpet. "I wanted to see if you would be keen on one more round of fun, and if you were, then I'd get rid of the video."

What the fuck?

Keegan thought his heart would jump in his mouth.

"What do you mean get rid of the video?" Damon asked. "Keegan told me it had been streamed live by mistake and that people all over the place have already seen it."

Keegan stared at Liam. "That's what you told me."

"I know that's what I said to you but that isn't really the truth." Liam's face turned a sickly shade of guilt.

Damon laughed but it wasn't one based on anything funny being said. "Tell me, Liam. What is this *truth* you speak of?"

"I did leave the camera on that night after making a video of myself but it wasn't live streamed. It never got uploaded to the site."

"But you showed me the video on your phone," Keegan said.

"I know. After I found the video on my computer I uploaded it to my phone then deleted the file."

This was confusing as hell. Keegan didn't know what was going on. "Then why did you show Tony and Skippy the video and make me think that it was all over the net?"

"Because, Keegan, you and *him* fucked in my bed. Made a gross fucking mess leaving ya cum everywhere and pissed off leaving me to clean it up."

"Harden up, Liam," Damon hissed. "That's hardly the end of the world." He shook his head in disgust. "So you went and showed ya mates this video and led Keegan—your best mate—to believe that this video was all over the web?"

Liam didn't answer.

"You made Keegan think his whole life down there was over, embarrassed him to his friends, sent him running away from his home all because of some stupid fucking cum in your sheets." Damon looked like steam was about to come out of his ears. "You nasty prick."

Liam's eyes widened. "Look. I know how much of a dick that makes me, okay. But I am sorry. I really am. I was annoyed. I was pissed off and didn't handle it well."

Keegan just wanted to melt into a puddle and seep through the floor and be gone. This was too much. This was drama in its worst form.

"What was this about one more round of fun and getting rid of the video," Damon asked, his voice back at calm levels.

Liam blushed. "I want to see Keegan fuck you."

Whoa! Keegan's mouth gaped open.

"If that's what you want, watch the fucking video," Damon threw back.

"No, I wanna watch it happen in person… then I want to have a turn," Liam's voice wavered.

Keegan was in a room with two hot guys; one who wanted to watch him fuck the other then have a turn himself. This was the type of stuff he dreamed of. The type of hot and sexy porn he loved to watch, but it didn't feel hot and sexy in the moment. It felt wrong.

"You want me to get fucked by Keegan again and then let you have a go on me?"

Liam nodded. "And then I'll delete the video. No one will ever see it."

"I don't think—" Keegan started but Damon put his hand up, signalling him to stop talking.

"Where do you propose we do this?" Damon asked Liam.

"Are you serious?" Keegan squawked. "You want us both to fuck you?"

Damon stared at him with burning embers in his eyes. "Keegan. I just want that video gone." He looked up at Liam. "Where is your phone with this video."

"It's in the room. I figured we can use the bed in there and then I can delete the video in front of both of you."

Keegan was dumbfounded. He had wanted Liam to be gay for so long. Gay with him for so long. Now here Liam was wanting to do these sorts of things. Sharing Damon's arse between them.

Damon got to his feet. "Come on, K dog. Let's go do what we gotta do."

"But…"

"But nothing. Come on. If this is what Liam wants, then this is what Liam is getting."

You have got to be fucking kidding me!

Keegan sighed and stood up, following Damon and Liam into the bedroom. The bed was a king size. It appeared freshly made and by the pillow was a box of rubbers and sachets of lubricant. Liam had planned ahead.

"Shall we start?" Liam pointed at the bed. "You two get naked then after Keegan cums, I'll take over."

Damon smiled. "Sounds good to me." His eyes pounced around the room, landing on the bedside table. "Is that your phone?"

"Yeah," Liam answered. "I will delete the vid off of it once we're done."

Damon lowered his hands and started peeling his shirt off, revealing his hairy tanned chest. Suddenly he dropped his shirt then swung his fist right into Liam's face.

"Ough, fuck!" Liam screamed. Blood started gushing

out his nose. "You fucking prick!"

Damon stepped past him, going straight for the phone and picked it up. He stormed out of the room.

"What are you doing?" Keegan called out.

"Taking care of it," Damon yelled back.

Keegan turned and looked at Liam who sat on the bed, holding his bleeding face with one hand. He heard Damon stomping the ground in another room followed by the sound of a toilet flushing.

I guess that's you taking care of it.

Damon appeared back in the doorway, his face flaring angrily. "Now Liam. A word of advice. Never, and I mean NEVER try fucking with me. And don't you ever try fucking with the people I care about, which includes Keegan. If you ever fuck with us again then I will be breaking more than ya pretty little face." He stomped his foot on the floor. "You hear me?"

Liam grunted, nodding.

"Now I hope that was the only device with the video," Damon said.

"It was. It was the only copy, you fucking wanker."

"Good," Damon said calmly. "I want you to tell Keegan how much the phone cost and give him your account number so I can pay to replace the phone. But I stand by my words, don't ever fuck with me again. I have just started a relationship with someone I love like crazy and if he ever sees that video it would kill him."

Keegan looked at Damon standing there with a determined look on his face. The passion that had flowed through his vocal chords was undeniable. Damon flicked him a smile then left the room.

Keegan raced after him. "Damon, wait!"

Damon spun 'round. "Yeah?"

"You really love my dad like you say?"

Damon gave one firm nod of the head. "I do."

"I'm sorry I doubted you. I feel like an arsehole."

"Don't worry about it."

"Thanks for *taking care of it*," Keegan said, pointing

with his eyes to the next room.

"No worries, K dog. That's what families do. We fix things for each other."

Keegan hummed with happiness. Damon was right. They were family.

"Go help your mate out. And when you see your father tell him to call me."

Keegan nodded. "I will."

Damon gave him a thumbs up and walked out of the apartment. Keegan went back to check on Liam. He was still sat on the bed, holding his nose. Keegan knew he shouldn't feel bad for him but he did anyway. "Sorry about that," Keegan said.

Liam had his head tilted up, trying to stop the bleeding. "It's my own fault," he grumbled. "I was after a bang and I sure as fuck got it."

Keegan laughed. "Yeah. You got banged real good."

CHAPTER THIRTY-SIX

After ten minutes fussing around to stop Liam's nose from bleeding, they both went and sat back in the kitchenette of the compact hotel suite. Keegan's head was still spinning with questions as to how they wound up in such a bizarre situation, his heart still warm from Damon reinforcing the fact they were family.

Liam smiled at him from across the small table, blood stains were visible above his upper lip. "I bet I look a fucking mess."

Keegan scanned his mate's bloodied face. "Nar. It's not too bad. Your nose doesn't look crooked or anything So I don't think he broke it."

Liam touched the ridge of his nose tenderly. "Ouch," he hissed in pain. "It fucking feels like it." His eyes flickered at Keegan. "I guess I did deserve it though."

Keegan didn't want to say anything. The answer seemed obvious.

"I am sorry, Keegan. Sorry about lying to you and for being such a fuckwit to you at Tony's house that day."

"That's okay," Keegan answered, wanting to keep things peaceful. "I'd be annoyed too if someone used my bed to fuck in and didn't clean up."

Liam laughed. "You really think that's the reason why?"

Keegan did think the reason was a pathetic one but he had taken Liam at his word. "Is there another reason?"

Liam nodded. He lay back in his chair, spreading his legs out. "This is embarrassing to admit but the reason I got so annoyed was because I was jealous."

"Jealous of Damon? Do you like him or something?"

"No, Keegan. I was jealous of you. And not in the way you might be thinking," Liam said. "I don't think it's a secret that I am a competitive type."

"No, it's not." Keegan chuckled. "But what's that got to do with being jealous of me?"

"When I saw the video, I wasn't grossed out or nothing like I thought I would be. The video was hot. Like I ain't into guys or anything but what you did. The way you did it. It was fucking sexy."

This left Keegan a little confused. "If you found it hot, then doesn't that mean your maybe a little gay?"

"I'm not gay," he answered a little too forcefully. "I do think I could fuck a guy and probably enjoy it, but I'm not gay."

All Keegan could hear was the echo of Liam talking in a closet. "Okay."

"Yeah, I know how bullshit that sounds but what I liked about the video—the same thing I would enjoy about fucking a dude—is the control of it," Liam said. "You had Damon bent over my bed and gave him everything you had. You totally annihilated him, bro."

Keegan wanted to blush, he was proud of his sexual prowess being complimented.

"You totally fucking owned him," Liam continued. "And I would love to do that to someone. Especially a guy like Damon, someone who thinks he's a big hot shot who can punch anyone they please." He laughed. "It makes me wanna fuck him even more now."

"I don't think that will be happening this life time, sorry." Keegan grinned at his mate. "But why does all of this make you jealous?"

Liam nibbled on his lip, taking his time to respond. "Because you have done something I haven't. You know the sort of shit I like to watch online… and what you two did was sort of like that."

"To be fair, neither me or Damon were tied to a bed wearing rubber suits," Keegan joked.

"You know what I mean. You still had that whole vibe going on when you spat in his face and slapped his arse."

Keegan groaned and covered his face.

"Fuck. Don't be embarrassed, bro. I told you... that shit was hot."

Keegan smoothed his hand through his hair. "Let me get this right. You are jealous because I fucked someone in a way you haven't?"

Liam nodded. "I know it's mental but I always like to think I have one up on you but this time I didn't." He gave Keegan a bashful grin. "Fucked up I know."

"Nothing wrong with being fucked up," Keegan said. "All the best people are."

"Thanks, man."

"I actually thought maybe you were angry 'cos I never told you about me."

Liam laughed. "Keegan, I have known about you for a while."

"Really?" Keegan was shocked. "How did you know?"

"Hard to say. It was just a vibe I started getting. When you were around me I could feel it. There was something different about you this past year."

It was only in the last year he had taken such an interest in Liam. Keegan thought he had masked it so well. It turned out perhaps he hadn't. "You could tell?"

"Yep. I kept catching you sneaking little looks at me. At first I didn't think much of it but after a while I knew what they were about." Liam nodded. "I could tell you liked me."

"Shame," Keegan mumbled.

"No shame in it. I thought it was flattering." Liam smirked. "It means you have good taste."

"Good to see Damon didn't knock any of your vanity out."

"That will always be intact." Liam rubbed the side of his face, feeling up his own beauty.

"If you're not gay and you knew I liked you, why did you get me to make that video with you?"

"Maybe I liked seeing the effect I had on you." Liam stared at him, not shying away from his motives. "That was me having control."

Keegan couldn't doubt that. Liam certainly did have

control over his body that day.

"I was surprised when you chickened out after springing a boner though," Liam said nonchalantly. "If my dick was as big as yours, I wouldn't run away from showing it."

This was the first indication Keegan had ever had of Liam's cock size. It had been a source of endless wonder the past year whenever he had a wank, imagining what it looked like hard. Imagining how it would feel and taste. He began to feel a familiar yearning in his pants. "My cock's bigger than yours?" Keegan asked, feeling like he was crossing a line.

"Yeah buddy. You win that contest." Liam winked at him. "Not by much though."

"Good to know." He started fidgeting with his hands as a lingering silence drifted between them. Things were becoming weird again. Talking of cock size felt like he was doing something wrong.

Liam cleared his throat. "I'd let you see it, if that's what you want?"

"Don't bullshit," Keegan scoffed, playing it cool.

"No bullshit. If you want to see my cock then I don't mind showing you," Liam said.

Keegan wanted to scream *Yes!* But something was holding him back like he had been nailed in place.

Liam didn't wait for an answer; he stood up from his seat, dropped his shorts and briefs down past his knees then sat back down.

Keegan's eyes zoned in on Liam's pale white meat draped over shaved jiggly balls. Liam's cock wasn't completely soft, it was swollen to semi-erect status. Keegan took a breath, trying his best not to give in to the temptation in front of him. For the longest time he had wanted access to his best mate's cock and now he had it.

"You can touch it if you want," Liam said, spreading his legs wider.

"I don't know if I should," Keegan croaked, trying to blink the temptation away.

"I thought you liked me?" Liam grinned. "On the

video you sounded quite in love with me."

"I do like you, Liam. You're fucking gorgeous."

"So are you," Liam said. "For a guy." His dick pulsed, throbbing and growing larger.

"You have a nice cock," Keegan whispered as he continued staring.

"The girls tell me it tastes great too," Liam said crudely. "How about I let you suck it if you agree to be my bitch for the afternoon. Let me fuck you however I like…"

The wind in Keegan's lungs emptied. "I've never been fucked before."

"I would be the first to get inside your arse?"

Keegan swallowed. "You would."

Liam's cock was now fully erect, the news of Keegan having a virgin arse tipped his size to its fullest capacity. "You know you want to, Keegan."

"I-I dunno," Keegan stammered.

Liam locked eyes with Keegan and whispered in a voice equally sexy and commanding, "You are going to go get in the shower and get clean for me. When you're done you will come to the bedroom and lay down on the bed and I am going to fuck the shit out of you for the next two hours." His mouth curled up devilishly.

It was all so fucking derogatory like he was making Keegan swallow his own shit, but Liam's sultry voice, his piercing blue eyes, his hard dick; it all added together to make it worth it. Keegan gave a slight nod of the head, accepting his fate. If this was the only way he could ever have Liam then maybe it was worth having some submissive secrets of his own.

"I promise you'll enjoy it." Liam got to his feet, his pants still at his ankles. "Stand up," he ordered.

Keegan did as he was told.

"Before we get started I believe I owe you a little something," Liam said.

"What's that?"

"A nice big love bite on your neck."

Keegan flinched. *He fucking knew it was me!*

Liam tilted his head thoughtfully, as he ran a hand through Keegan's golden locks. "You thought I didn't know about you being the one who gave me that hideous root rash the night of your birthday." He laughed. "I was really shitfaced but I do remember it felt quite nice. Your good with your mouth."

Keegan blushed. "Thank you."

"It will be me thanking you when I'm fucking your face." Liam lowered his lips to Keegan's throat, trailing kisses up his neck.

He gasped as Liam sunk his teeth in and sucked with such hungry force it began to hurt.

Done with sucking, Liam released his fangs, kissing where he had bitten and blew softly. His warm breath tingled over Keegan's raw skin like medicine. "I think we're even now." Liam chuckled, admiring the bite mark he had just given. "Go jump in the shower and come meet me in the bedroom. I'll be waiting." He hitched his shorts up and wandered off, leaving Keegan alone to get his arse ready for wreck and ruin.

In the bathroom, Keegan found a clean white towel hanging behind the door. He threw it over his shoulder then went to turn the shower on. It roared to life with astonishing force, the water rampaging with the anger of a hurricane. As he waited for the water to warm up, he went and inspected the damage to his neck in the mirror. *Fucking hell!* It was brilliantly red. He knew that within a day it would turn a ghastly purple and look even worse.

Keegan lay the towel down on a small stool beside the shower. He stripped his clothes off, dumping them on the tiled floor. He groped his hard cock that was gagging for release. He only wished it was him fucking Liam and not the other way around.

But this is better than nothing, Keegan told himself. If being used brutally was the only way he could have a piece of Liam then he just had to accept it. Liam was the boss. Not Keegan.

What about Garth? Keegan felt bad, but it wasn't like

they were dating. Garth wouldn't turn down a chance encounter with some girl he had fancied for over a year. *Or would he?* Keegan cast his guilt aside, following his cock's instinct instead of his heart.

He was about to step into the shower when he noticed something bunched up on the ground in the corner of the bathroom.

What the fuck?

Keegan wandered over to the green streak on the floor. It was a pair of green silk boxers. *Skippy's mean greens!*

Keegan ripped open the small cabinet above the sink. There were three deodorants in all and three razors. Liam wasn't the only one staying here. He hadn't come all this way to just see Keegan and apologise or to have some sexy fun. Keegan realised that he was just a bloody item on a holiday to-do list.

It was the stub of a ticket on the bottom shelf that gave away the real reason for the trip. Keegan read the name printed on it. *Green day.* The fuckers had all come up to see the concert without him. He knew that if he went back out and checked in the other bedroom he would probably find two single beds where Tony and Skippy were staying. He put his clothes back on and marched into the room Liam was in. His mate was laying down on the bed, fully naked, wanking his hard cock. Liam let go of himself when he saw Keegan still unwashed, wearing a scowl on his face.

"What's wrong?" Liam asked.

"Did you come up to Auckland just to see me and try and patch things up," Keegan said heatedly. "Sorry…. I mean did you just come up to blackmail me and Damon."

"What are you on about?" Liam sat up, covering his crotch with his hands.

"Why are you in Auckland?"

Liam's eyes darted to the side. "What did you find in the bathroom?"

"It doesn't matter. Why are you in Auckland?"

Liam took a deep breath and gave a blunt honest answer, "I'm up here with Tony and Skippy. We arrived on

Thursday and went to the Green day concert last night. We've been fucking about doing touristy shit the past few days but the concert was the main reason we came up."

"I should have known," Keegan muttered.

Liam got off the bed and walked over to him. His beautiful dick bouncing like a hard arrow. "Keegan, I'm sorry. I didn't want to tell you in case you felt left out."

"Gee, funny that. Since I do sort of feel left out."

Liam rubbed his shoulder. "Yes, the concert was the main reason to come up here but so were you. I did go to visit you last week and talk, but you're mum told me you were staying with your dad. How do you think I even knew you were up here?" He sighed. "And yeah, the whole blackmail thing was crappy but I just... I hadn't intended that part. That only came to me in a moment of horny fuckery."

Keegan wanted to stay angry but he couldn't. He couldn't stay mad for long with Liam. He also knew what horny fuckery was like. It was the driving force for his two times with Damon. "And now? Is you wanting to fuck me another case of horny fuckery?"

"Probably." Liam grinned. "But that doesn't stop me really wanting do it. I know you want this too."

No. Keegan didn't want this. He didn't want to give himself away just for some guy who was horny and wanting to use him as an experiment. All that Keegan had in his head was Garth. He felt sick knowing the stuff he had already done with Liam, it felt like he had cheated on his *pretend boyfriend*. "I don't want this. I can't want this."

"Why not?"

"I think I have a boyfriend."

Liam laughed. "Piss off. No you don't."

"I sort of do. Garth and me..." Keegan's voice trailed off.

"Damon was right, wasn't he? You and Garth are an item."

"Not yet. But I really like him. I really do."

"More than me?" Liam smiled.

Keegan nodded. "Yes... even more than you."

Liam laughed and stepped back to sit on the bed. "Guess I should probably put my clothes back on then."

"Probably." Keegan groaned into his hands. "Garth's gonna be so fucked off when I tell him what I have done."

"Then don't tell him."

"Umm, I don't think I have much choice in the matter, Dracula." Keegan pointed to the mark on his neck.

Liam laughed. "True. But that's the only thing that happened. I can vouch for you if you need me to."

"Cheers," Keegan said. He knew he wouldn't be taking Liam up on the offer though. Garth would probably tell Liam to fuck off and not believe a word of it no matter how true it was. "Anyway, where's the other two?" Keegan asked, looking behind him towards the closed door of the other bedroom.

"Gone to Waiheke island for the day. I lied and told them I get sea sick so I couldn't go." He smiled. "I really did want to see you, Keegan. That wasn't a lie."

"I know." Keegan could see truth dwelling in Liam's blue eyes. "It's been good seeing you too. Even if it has been all sorts of... ." He whipped his eyes towards Liam's deflating cock. "Weird."

They looked at each other and began to laugh.

"So are we still mates?" Liam asked. "I feel like things aren't the same now. Like nothing will be normal again."

Liam was right. Things weren't the same. Their normal had abandoned them.

"Yeah, we're still mates," Keegan said. "I guess it might just take a while before we find a new normal between us."

Liam looked almost sad at accepting this. "Will you be coming home soon?"

Keegan thought this over. "Honestly. I don't know." He looked out the window at the urban landscape; the new scene of his life. "But I will keep in touch. I promise."

"You bloody better." Liam stood up again and wandered over. He opened his arms, motioning for a hug. Keegan stepped into his friends naked embrace. "I'm gonna really miss you, bro," Liam whispered.

Keegan squeezed him back. "Ditto."

As they parted from the embrace, Liam was smirking.

"What's so funny?" Keegan asked.

"Doesn't this feel like some tragic movie moment where we are meant to have learnt some important life-changing lesson?"

"It does a bit," Keegan agreed.

"Fuck knows what the lesson is though."

Keegan studied the room and his naked mate who had been so close to using him in degrading fashion. The room was warped between reality and fantasy. The answer was dripping all over them.

"Can't you see it?" Keegan chuckled. "The lesson is you and me watch too much bloody porn."

CHAPTER THIRTY-SEVEN

Matt rubbed his temples, closing his eyes in pain. He was left speechless from what he had just been told. It felt like an asteroid had just crash-landed, destroying his world. He peeled his lids open to see Jason staring back at him from across the table with cautious eyes.

"Why didn't you tell me about this as soon as you heard," Matt demanded.

"It wasn't my story to tell. It was between Keegan and Damon," Jason said, sounding uneasy.

Matt felt terrible for his son, wondering how horrible it would feel to know that such a private act was in the most public of places. It suddenly made sense why he had arrived in town unannounced and out of the blue. "I'm his father, you should have bloody told me." Matt smashed his fist on the table. "Fucking hell."

"You need to calm your farm, Matthew James Andrews. This isn't my fault. This has nothing to do with me," Jason snapped. "The only reason I am saying something now is I don't trust how Damon took photos of you. It strikes me as devious and somewhat well-timed."

Matt looked at his friend who glared back sternly. "I'm sorry, Jason. I don't mean to have a go at you. But I'm just…" Matt grabbed and pulled at his hair. "Grrr. Just so fucking unbelievably angry."

"I understand that," Jason said. "I'm sorry."

Sorry wasn't going to cut it. Not from Jason. Not from Damon. Not from anyone. Matt could feel his heart breaking but it wasn't what was most important. What was important was making sure Keegan was okay. He was consumed with worry—and anger. Boiling hot anger for Damon's disgusting behaviour. "Keegan is just a kid. How could he even do that? It is disgusting."

Jason looked hesitant to respond.

"How?" Matt cried.

"Keegan is eighteen, Matty. Not a small child. I don't think you can accuse Damon of what I think you may be insinuating."

"It's still wrong. It's a line you just don't cross." Matt let a hot breath escape his lips. "I gotta go see him."

"Hold your horses, Geronimo. You might want to calm down before you go all T Sizzle Bad Blood on his ass."

Matt knew Jason was right but the emotion boiling inside him was too much to control. He just wanted to get up and leave right that instant. Just as he was about to tell Jason he had to go, Garth appeared in the kitchen wearing no top and just a pair of his raggedy jeans.

"Everything okay?" Garth asked. "I thought I heard banging?" He looked at Jason and Matt with questioning eyes.

"Everything's fine and dandy," Jason lied through a smile.

"I thought you and Keegan had gone out," Matt asked, frowning.

"Only Keegan. He told me that he had to go help his grandfather with something," Garth answered, wiping a hand down his bare chest.

Jason shot Matt a questioning look.

"Umm did he?" Matt answered in a surprised tone.

Garth laughed, unpeeling Keegan's lie. "Guess he must be up to something he doesn't want us to know about then."

Matt cringed. "Must be."

Jason stood up. "Are you busy, Garth?"

"Nope. Just pissing about waiting for Keegan."

"Good," Jason said. "I don't suppose you could come help me with a wee chore. I need some help choosing the best alcoholic poisons for the wedding and who better to take along to help me choose than a handsome experienced bartender."

Garth grinned. "Sure. I'll just go put a top on."

With Garth gone, Jason shot Matt a knowing glance. "We will get out of your hair for a moment. I imagine you probably want to be alone to make a Damon voodoo doll."

"I do. The first pin will be going straight in his fucking cock."

"Promise me you won't do anything stupid."

Matt avoided his friend's eyes.

"I mean it, Matty. I don't want to be attending someone's funeral on a day that should be my wedding."

Garth came galloping back into the room, this time wearing a shirt. "Ready. I'm all yours."

"Ooo, don't get my hopes up, sugar" Jason flirted. He gave Matt a winsome smile. "I will call you later."

Matt nodded and watch them leave. He snuck into the lounge and peered through the window to see them drive off. As soon as Jason's car was gone, Matt ran to get his keys. "fuck sake," he hissed when he realised his father had taken the car. He cursed the fact that he had never bothered to buy a second vehicle. He went and called a taxi and let his mood brood like a destructive storm.

∞

Matt leapt out of the taxi and crossed the road towards Damon's apartment. Prickling at the back of his neck, Matt was wound up so tight he thought he might snap. His body singed with a heat that felt illegal like knives on a burning element. The taxi ride from Port Jackson had cost a small fortune but it felt worth it as he thundered up the stairs and saw the door to Damon's apartment come into sight.

He knocked with pulsating urgency. "Damon it's me. Open up." Matt pounded again.

Finally, Damon pulled the door open. Dressed casually, he looked like he had just got back from the gym, his body soppy with sweat. His smile was instant when he saw it was Matt. "Hey, you. I was about to call you."

Matt barged past, knocking Damon's shoulder as he marched to the centre of the apartment.

Damon laughed. "Is someone a little keen to have fun, aye?"

Matt snorted. "Piss off."

Damon shut the door and walked over to him. "What's with you?" He was still smiling but his forehead creased with a frown. "Is something wrong?"

"You could say that," Matt spat out, standing with his hands on his hips.

"Tell me what it is. I might be able to help."

Matt laughed wickedly. "No, Damon You can't help. You can only make things worse."

Damon narrowed his eyes.

"I know what you did, Damon." Matt felt his body tremble. "I know what you did with Keegan."

Damon looked like he was about to crack into a thousand pieces.

"You really are something else, aren't you?" Matt threw his arms in the air. "Nothing but a parasite who goes out of his way to fuck things up."

"Matty," Damon whispered. He took a step towards Matt, touching his shoulder.

Matt threw Damon's hand away. "Don't fucking touch me."

Damon stepped back like he was told to. "I'm sorry."

"Sorry isn't going to cut it this time, Damon. I may have been stupid enough twenty years ago to believe your bullshit apologies but not this time. This time you have gone and shown your true colours. Just a dirty sexual predator out for all he can get."

"It's not like that," Damon replied. "I know how fucking awful it is but I'm telling you the truth when I say I never planned it to happen... I'd never purposely hurt you."

"Well, you have, Damon. And you've hurt Keegan. Do you have any idea how that sort of thing could fuck with his head?"

"Keegan's a big boy, Matty. He knew what he was doing."

"Oh. So that makes it alright for you to go and fuck

him, does it?" Matt laughed callously. "You sick fuck."

Damon's face looked mushy; guilt and sadness rolled into one. "I am so sorry. I don't know what else I can say. I know I fucked up but that doesn't change how I feel about you." He went to step forward again but Matt moved away.

"Oh, so you really care about me, do you? Like so much that you took photos of me that I assume are being kept to be used against me if I ever try and tell people about how much of a filthy cunt you are."

Damon shook his head. "No." He went to say something else but stopped. He took a breath then started again, "Okay. That is why I took them in the first place but that was before I realised how much I care for you. I didn't know I felt these things until afterwards."

"Spare me the bullshit."

"The photos weren't even my idea. I asked Jenna for advice and she said I needed to have something to keep myself safe."

"Why does that not surprise me. She always was a schemey bitch and it seems you take after her."

Damon walked over to the kitchen counter and grabbed his phone. "I will delete them all now. No photos." He began scrolling through his phone with frantic swipes. "Deleted. All gone." He held his phone up to let Matt see but Matt turned his face away.

"I don't care, Damon. The pictures of me mean nothing. I am more concerned about the video of you and Keegan."

"There isn't a video," Damon said.

"There's no video?"

"Not anymore. I took care of it. The video is gone. I promise."

Matt was relieved to hear this but it didn't change how furious he was. "Good but that doesn't change the fact I never wanna see you again. You're fucking dead to me."

Damon clutched his chest, clawing at himself like a starving animal. "Matty, I don't think you understand how much I love you," His voice came out desperate and strained.

"I never thought I could be with someone properly but I know I can with you. You and me, Matty, are the real thing."

"No, we're not. You don't do the real thing, Damon. All you do is control people. You've done it your whole life... insist people do whatever you want them to. You can't handle not being the one in charge. If you had your way everyone would be under lock and key and only let out when you feel like." Matt glowered at him, releasing wrathful breaths.

Damon ignored Matt's seething anger warning him to stay away and crossed the space between them, he wrapped his arms around Matt and hugged tight.

Matt's pulse jerked in his throat and his skin puckered in goose bumps. "Get your filthy hands off of me. I don't want you near me."

Damon began to weep. "No," he spluttered. "I won't let you go 'till you forgive me."

"I said let go of me, Damon."

Damon's sniffles rolled into uncontrollable sobs, his tears wetting Matt's shirt. "Give me a chance to show you how much I care. I'll do anything you want. Anything!"

Matt wrestled his arms out of Damon's vice-like hug, pushing him away. "No! There is nothing that can fix this. You made me think you cared about me but all along you were using me. Waiting to blackmail me or humiliate me with those photos plastered around town or online."

Damon tore at his hair and groaned. "I just showed you, I deleted the photos. This isn't me playing games. I love you. I fucking love you." He wiped tears from his eyes and tried to reach out to hold him again.

Matt stepped back and shook his head. "Stay away from me," his voice warbled.

Damon ignored him and stepped forward. Matt curled his fingers into a ball of flesh and swung his fist in the air, punching Damon in the side of the face.

Damon's head jerked to the side and he wobbled on his feet. He looked at Matt with wounded damp eyes.

Matt waited for the stronger male to attack, and kick the shit out of him. Damon clutched his injury, crying some more. "Matty please. Don't do this." He dropped to the floor and grabbed hold of Matt's legs. "Don't go."

Matt heaved a sigh of frustration, trying to flick Damon off of him like dog shit under his shoe.

"I'll do anything," Damon pleaded. "I just want you to know how sorry I am." He began kissing Matt's leg. "Sorry." He kissed him again. "Sorry."

Matt was stunned by how pathetic Damon looked right now—crumpled on the floor with tear-filled eyes that begged forgiveness. Matt hurled a ball of spit in Damon's sad face. "LET GO!" Matt screamed. He shook his leg free, kicking Damon's head by accident in the process. He walked away as Damon began wailing for him to come back. Matt felt dizzy as he walked out of the apartment, slamming the door behind him.

He was shocked by his own anger. Stunned at his strength. Everything was surreal. Matt felt his knees start to give way and he collapsed against the wall of Damon's apartment, slowly sliding his back down the smooth surface 'till he was sat on the floor with bent knees, holding his head in his hands. He could faintly hear Damon's wailing of heartache through the door like a pained symphony. A flame in Matt's chest flared up; its heat burned away some invisible seal holding him together. It exploded, leaving his heart in scattered pieces. His eye sockets began to sting and his chest squeezed. Matt let it all out—tear after tear. Mourning the loss of a best mate and a chance at love.

CHAPTER THIRTY-EIGHT

Keegan wandered the sweaty city streets feeling like he and Liam had dodged a bullet. What they had nearly done together could have completely destroyed their already frayed friendship. As much as his body craved Liam, Keegan knew it wasn't right. It wasn't going to bring about anything good. And Keegan wanted good things. He wanted the best good he could find and he knew waiting for him at his father's house was where he would find it in the form of a messy-haired boy with cute dimples who seemed to think the world of him.

He didn't go home straight away. He took his time exploring the city, trying to clear the messy thoughts inside his head. As he made his way through the streams of strangers bustling outside the busy stores, a clarity dawned on him. He was walking away from a large chapter of his life. Not just Liam but everything about his life back home. As scary as that felt, this rush of change flooding his life was also incredibly exciting.

He had a whole new chapter about to be written. Keegan just hoped that the bright mark on his neck didn't dull the shine of his future, ripping away the one character he wanted by his side for the rest of the story.

The bus trip back to Port Jackson was tedious and felt like an eternity. When he finally arrived at the seaside suburb, he walked speedily to his father's home. Scared to come clean but eager to show Garth his heart's hand. When he got inside he found his father standing in the hallway with a dozy dumb look on his face.

"Hey, Dad." Keegan smiled about to walk past him

"Can we speak for a moment," his father asked, tapping Keegan on the shoulder.

"Umm, if you like." Keegan turned, following his

father into the lounge. His father stood in the centre of the room with sagging shoulders. He assumed that what was to follow was an awkward discussion about last night. Walking in on his father kissing Damon. "Everything okay, dad?"

"Yeah. Everything's fine," He smiled back affectionately.

Keegan decided to just cut to the chase. "Look, if it's about last night then I don't care about what you and Damon do together. If he makes you happy then that makes me happy."

"Thank you. But Damon and I…" His father paused, an odd gleam striking his eyes. "I'm glad you want me to be happy."

"Why wouldn't I. You're my dad."

His father nodded, his smile a faint arch of approval. "And I want you to know that if Garth makes you happy then I'm the same. I'm happy if you are. And he seems a nice guy."

"Yeah. He is." Keegan darted his eyes towards the door. His want to leave did not go unnoticed.

"Just one more thing." His father cleared his throat. "Have you given any thought to what you are doing for a job or study?"

"Not yet but I will do."

"I'm sorry Keegan but no 'will do'. Just do." His father's friendly face did not match the sternness of his words. "I expect you to have a job or be enrolled to study within a week. I am only prepared to keep helping you out if I see that you're willing to help yourself."

Keegan was stunned. He didn't expect his father to be so ballsy. "And if I don't?"

"Then you can come work for me. I am sure we can train you up in accounts or something."

Keegan grimaced. He didn't like the sound of that. "Oh god," he muttered.

His father laughed. "Use it as motivation to find something else then. But there are worse things in this life than being a bean counter's assistant."

"I guess so," Keegan said with a deflated voice. "Is Garth upstairs?"

"Uh no. He's swimming in the pool."

"Cool," Keegan said. He turned on his feet to go outside and find Garth.

"Hey, Keegan," his father called out. "One more thing."

"Yeah?"

"Did you need me to buy some fly spray for you to keep in your room."

Keegan wrinkled his forehead. "What?"

"The mosquitos up there look like real biters." His father tapped his neck, smirking.

Keegan blushed.

"Tell Garth to go easy with those sharp teeth of his," His father said. "Trust me. It's not a good look for job hunting."

"Mmph," Keegan exhaled through his nose. He gave his father a slight nod of the head and left the room. He had totally forgotten about that fucking mark. Thank god, his father spotted it and reminded him. He took a few deep breaths, going over in his head how best to explain its existence to Garth. He made his way to the kitchen and exited out the back door into the garden. The backyard was huge and with its pretty flowers and impressive old trees it would make the perfect setting for a wedding, he thought.

Most of the wide yard was grassed but towards the end of the lawn was the start of native trees and a small garden path that wound through it like some nature walk. Half way along the path a trellis fence covered in leafy vines fenced off what was the swimming area. Not an outdoor pool but a large shed that housed an indoor heated pool. Living across the road from the beach would have made an outdoor one pointless, but this way his father could swim the year round. Not that his father looked like much of a swimmer. It seemed an item that perhaps Karina's kids would have used and now it stood here pointlessly.

Keegan opened the latch of the trellis fence and

followed a now gravel path to the sheds entrance. He wasn't even inside before he could hear Garth's splashing and singing—horrendously again. Keegan smiled to himself at a noise so bad he imagined it could make dogs howl.

Inside, he saw Garth floating on his back, kicking his feet as he sang his happy song. Keegan took advantage of Garth not being able to see him, letting his eyes size his lover up from his toes to his wet locks.

"Hey, sexy," Keegan called out.

Garth stopped singing, flipping over in the water frantically. His eyes bulged and he sucked in a gust of air. "Fuck you gave me a fright."

"I can see that." Keegan chuckled. "Did you want me to get you a detective?"

"Huh?"

"Someone to help you track down those notes your voice can't find."

"Oh, Har. Har. Very funny, blondie." Garth grinned. He ducked his head under the water and started doing breaststroke towards the end of the pool.

Keegan bit down on his tongue, bracing himself for Garth to see the scandal on his neck. He felt like he was the one underwater, running out of oxygen. When Garth broke the surface, he shook his hair around like a wet dog, torpedoing water over the legs of Keegan's jeans. He looked up with a huge smile that instantly pulled back when he saw the mark.

"How's the water?" Keegan asked pointlessly.

Garth nodded, treading the water. "Pretty wet."

"Funny that."

"How was your granddad?" Garth asked. Before Keegan could come clean about his earlier lie, Garth added, "He looks like a brutal kisser."

"Yeah, about that." Keegan rubbed his neck. "I didn't go see Granddad."

"I sort of guessed that."

"I went to see Liam. He wanted to meet me to apologise about being such a dick to me back home."

"He sure said sorry by the looks." Garth let his head sink half under water, hiding his mouth from view.

"It was only a kiss. I swear. He wanted to do more, but I said no. I didn't want to."

Garth brought his head up again. "You don't have to explain yourself to me, blondie." He smiled but it didn't hide the sadness that floated in the pool with him.

"I do. I was a fucking moron. I don't know why I let him give me the love bite. You're the one I like."

Garth grabbed the concrete side of the pool and hoisted himself out of the water. He walked over to a blue towel sitting on a deck chair and started to dry himself off.

"I feel like I have really fucked up, Garth."

"What did you fuck up? It ain't like we are dating," Garth said, towelling his hair.

Keegan walked over to him and placed a hand to his shoulder. "I was kind of hoping we would." He exhaled through his nose. "You know… Date."

Garth stepped backwards, lowering the towel to dry off his legs. "You don't have to say shit you don't mean, Keegan. Its fine. I get it."

"But I do mean it."

Garth shook his head. "Like I said. It's okay. I get it."

"Get what?"

"You got what you wanted from me." Garth dropped the towel down and threw on his shirt. "You wanted to fuck me and you fucked me."

"I like you more than just a fuck." Keegan could tell by Garth's fake smile and wounded eyes that he was hurting.

"No you don't. If you did, then you wouldn't have lied about where you were going. You wouldn't have done what you did," his voice came out screechy. Keegan went to touch him again but Garth put his hand up stopping him and shook his head.

Garth dropped his face, trying to hide his eyes. When he looked back up Keegan could see the formation of tears waiting to shed. "I really liked you, Keegan. I trusted you." Garth mashed his lips together tightly. "I gave you a piece of me that… that I can never get back. I thought you were different. I thought you were special."

"Garth, I'm so sorry. I'll never lie again." Keegan felt his own eyes begin to burn.

"Nope. It's fine. You're eighteen. You wanna have fun. And fuck guys like Liam Corrigan. Why wouldn't you want to have fun with him. He's a fucking supermodel compared to me."

"No he's not. I think you're way hotter."

"Stop lying," Garth snapped. "We both know that's not true."

"I'm telling you that it is. Yes, Liam's hot but you're sexy. Probably the sexiest person I have ever met." Keegan meant every word but wanted to say more. "Everything about you is fucking sexy. Every inch of you turns me on. Wherever you are I want to be, you make a room sexy just by walking into it."

Garth looked like he was about to relent and smile but he frowned instead. "I think its best I go."

"Go where?" Keegan asked with urgent concern.

"Back home." Garth sniffed loudly, wiping his face. "I can't stay here forever. I have to go home and find a new place to live and get a job and all that shit."

"We can do that up here. You and me. Find a flat together."

Garth stared at him like he was playing the fantasy in his mind. "No," he said coldly, shattering the dream. "It's best I go."

"Please don't," Keegan whispered. He wanted to reach out to try and grab him one last time but the wild hurt in Garth's eyes told him not to even try.

Garth ran a hand through his wet hair, composing himself. "I am gonna go inside now and pack up. I want to say thank you for giving me one hell of a fun crazy week and for you and your father's hospitality."

Don't go. Don't do this. I am so fucking sorry! Keegan screamed internally. Garth's broken body language told him there was nothing he could say or do that would change his mind.

Garth offered a feeble smile. "I don't mean to be rude but is it okay if you stay here while I get my stuff."

Keegan gave a pained stare in return. His feelings sloshing around inside.

"I don't want to go inside and your father see me cry." Garth laughed pitifully. "And if you're around I think I might."

Seeing anyone sad was painful. But to see someone you didn't know capable of tears, well that was a sight sadder than a funeral. Keegan nodded, giving Garth what he wanted. He owed him that. "Okay," he whispered. "I'll stay here."

"Thanks, man. I'll only be ten minutes." Garth picked the rest of his clothes up and carried himself away in woeful steps.

Keegan watched him walk away, disappearing outside. He had no one to blame for this predicament but himself. His own stupid fucking self. He had wanted too much. Pushed too many limits with too many people.

Damon, Liam, Garth…

Now he had no one. He wanted to cry, but he didn't feel like he deserved to let himself shed a tear. He crouched down, rocking back and forwards on the balls of his feet and closed his eyes. He was now little more than a body bag with a beating heart. The beautiful glue that had held him together the past week was leaving and Keegan feared he might just come undone

CHAPTER THIRTY-NINE

The week was flying by and Matt was burying his feelings under the preparations for Jason's wedding—which was only two days away. He was busy tying brightly-coloured Chinese lanterns to tree limbs, adding another touch of daydream Jason had on his wish list. The backyard was looking unique to say the least. He had spent all morning trying these lanterns to trees and staking solar lights throughout the garden.

Garth had left unexpectedly over the weekend, leaving Keegan and Matt alone in the house. Matt didn't ask his son why Garth had gone. He suspected there was more to it than Garth's short line about needing to get back home for a job interview.

Keegan had moped about for two days looking as sad as Matt was feeling about Damon. Despite the bleak mood, Matt was enjoying the chance to be alone with Keegan a bit more, learning more about him; his favourite shows, music, food. Things like that.

Tonight, Matt was going to attempt Keegan's favourite dish; spicy tortillas. Chances were high he would fuck it up but then the Chinese takeaways was just down the road for an emergency backup meal.

The meal was to be in honour of Keegan's new job. The one that he was attending an interview for right that moment. Matt had pulled some strings with a former client who ran a small call centre in the city. It wasn't the job of the century but it was a very good starting point. Unbeknownst to Keegan the interview was a mere formality, unless he fucked up spectacularly then the job was his.

Matt lifted his shirt and wiped his brow. He drummed his fingers over his furry tummy dripping with sweat. It was hot today even with the slight summer breeze. The muggy air felt like breathing under water. He was tempted to strip his shirt off, expose his pale skin to the harsh rays of the sun but the sound of a car engine rolling into his driveway made him decide against it.

The noise of the car door slamming followed by a high-pitched zap of the vehicle locking told him it was Jason coming to inspect the makeshift venue. He didn't have to bother going and letting Jason in, this was one guest who had no problems walking in like he owned the place. Matt waited for his mate to stroll through the house and find him outside.

"Arigato, heeeey," Jason called out, waving a flimsy wrist covered in bright bangles.

Matt looked over at his pal wearing a mesh black top and mustard-coloured chinos. "Hey. Have you come to inspect the mess otherwise known as your big day."

"I sure have." Jason stopped in front of him, slowly nodding at the numerous lights and lanterns dotting the yard. "It looks perfect!"

Matt wasn't sure if this was the case. It looked tacky as fuck and he worried if Jason may just be being polite. "Are you sure?" He tried to word the state of the yard diplomatically. "You don't think it's a bit much?" Matt pointed to a rainbow-coloured wind wand that towered high into the sky. The kinetic piece of art drooped in the small breeze like a limp cock.

Jason giggled at the subtle hint. "Of course it's a bit much but that's just what I want." His smile crumbled as he squinted. "Have you heard from you know who?"

Matt felt his body go stiff. He shook his head. "Nope. The bad news is yesterday's news."

Jason nodded. "Are you okay about it?"

"Just like when you asked me yesterday and the day before and the days before that. Yes. I am fine, Jason." He knew his friend was only showing his worry but Matt wished he wouldn't. Each time Jason enquired it made him want to give in and make contact with the scoundrel of the century. In the heat of the moment, hitting Damon in the face and propelling himself out of the dickhead's life was simple. It was easy to do when running on raw emotion, but when the anger stopped stinging his blood, the adrenalin emptied out of his veins then all he had found himself left with was the sadness. An overwhelming grief, mourning for twenty years of friendship.

"I just want to make sure. You're fine." Jason said. "I worry about you."

"You really don't have to, Jason. I'm a big boy if you hadn't noticed."

Jason's eyes dropped to his crotch. "No need to turn the conversation dirty, girl."

Matt laughed. "I wasn't meaning that."

"Good, I would hate to have you trying to flirt with me only two days from my wedding, Matty."

"I can assure you that is not the case."

"Phew," Jason sighed. "It would be tough to break your heart when I tell you you're not my type," he teased.

"Piss off," Matt laughed. "You're not my type either."

"Who is your type?" Jason's eyes flickered. "Who is next on your hit list?"

"Nobody," Matt muttered. For the first time in his life he was embracing loneliness. Too scared to think about who or what came next.

"Really?" Jason squawked.

"Yes. Really."

Jason chewed his lip. "But if you were looking would they be male or female?"

Matt instinctively went to say female like Jason's question was absurd but he stopped the word leaving his lips. "Who knows," he said with a laboured breath.

"Interesting."

"Why is that interesting?" Matt frowned, puzzled by the look of delight on Jason's face.

"It means I may still be able to swap dirty stories with you about guys. It also means I may be able to fix you up with someone."

"No way. Don't even think about doing that." Matt gave Jason a stern look.

"Oh, why not? It'll be fun. Some of our friends are arriving from Sydney tomorrow for the wedding and a couple of them are mighty cute."

There was no way Matt was going to let Jason try and fix him up. He could only imagine the type of guy it would be. "No, Jason."

Jason slumped his shoulders. "Gee, way to ruin my fun."

"Your *fun* is supposed to be the getting married part, not worrying about finding me a date." Matt scanned the yard and the zany setup. "And you are sure this is what you want?"

Jason laughed. "Is this tragic fairy tale not how you envision a wedding, Matty pie?"

The concerned look on Matt's face must have answered for him.

"Matty, stop worrying about it. I know how it looks. If anything, I wish it were even more garish."

"But why? This is yours and Will's big day. I don't understand why you aren't going all out with something more... swanky. It's not like you both can't afford it."

Jason's lips curved thoughtfully. He pat Matt on the shoulder. "Because, sweet cheeks, have you seen me?" He tugged on his mesh top. "I'm not about the type of swanky you're thinking. The type of sanky Will's parents—who hate me for no good reason—will be expecting."

"So you are going out of your way to mess up your own wedding just to get at your in-laws?"

Jason laughed. "Not just that. I mean that is an indirect bonus, but it's also about giving my friends a day they won't forget. Imagine how many years they'll be able to tell everyone about the time they attended a wedding with a glitter speckled pony and a rainbow wind wand."

Matt smiled. He began to understand the appeal a bit more.

"And yes, it will be camp, and yes, it will be trashy as all out hell." Jason chuckled. "But while everyone is busy taking all that in, the only thing I will be focused on is Will and just how bloody lucky I am to be marrying my soul mate.

I don't care about the noise around us. I don't care if that pony shits up the whole joint. My eyes will only be on that dashing, sweet man with all the patience in the world who has put up with my bullshit all these years." He laughed softly as his eyes glossed over. "That is my moment. That is what is making my day so special. *Him*."

Matt was stunned. He had never heard Jason be so sentimental before. He was jealous and happy at the same time for his friend. It was in Jason's voice. The way he spoke. He really loved Will. The emotion struck a chord and Matt found himself wiping his cheek.

"You're not crying are you," Jason said; he looked almost uncomfortable. "Oh god, you are crying."

Matt snivelled away another tear. "That was just really fucking sweet."

"I swear, sometimes I wonder if you actually have an ovary in you somewhere."

Matt laughed, wiping his eyes dry. "Sorry. I can be a bit of a cry baby."

"Don't be sorry. It just means you care." Jason smiled and leaned in, giving him a hug. A hug that he really needed.

CHAPTER FORTY

Keegan wandered along the waterfront admiring the army of yachts in the harbour. It made sense why they called it the City of Sails, he thought. Walking through town in black dress pants and a choking business shirt was not how he wold normally dress, but he had just left from a job interview. He had been so nervous beforehand, but his father had told him to be confident or at least fake it. Keegan faked it.

He managed to blitz the typing and numeracy test and stumbled his way through the interview questions. He didn't think he had answered anything terribly but he was surprised when at the end of the questioning the manager shook his hand and welcomed him to the team. He would be starting next Monday and go into the training room for three weeks before "hitting the floor." Keegan was grateful and pleased with himself but he also suspected that it wasn't his own skill that landed him the job but the fact the woman was a former client from his father's firm.

The first thing he had done was call his mum once he got outside, telling her excitedly about how he had just gotten his first job. She squealed in delight for him, offering endless congratulations. He had worried she would be upset that this meant he wouldn't be coming home but when he asked if she minded she was adamant it didn't matter what she thought. That it was *his life* to lead and his decision.

Walking along, heading towards the transport station, Keegan wondered about his decisions. There was every chance that this job was the first step of having a future as sunny as the day beating down on him. But what good was a bright future when your mood was as black as night.

Since Garth had left, guilt had made itself at home in Keegan's chest; sapping him of his energy. He missed his *pretend boyfriend* like crazy. Garth had been the one to bring him up here, convincing Keegan to take a risk. And how did Keegan repay him? By shitting all over his feelings.

I really fucked up.

With Garth gone, Keegan had no option but to hang out with his father. The evenings in talking nonsense in the living-room while watching tele had been nice. A good opportunity to become more familiar with each other. Nothing too personal thank goodness. He had no desire to offer up what had happened with Garth or to ask his father about his romance with Damon. Their romance still had Keegan confused. Damon had made his feelings clear the day he punched Liam but Keegan had yet to hear his father voice similar emotions. Damon hadn't even been to visit since then and his name hadn't been spoken once. Perhaps his father was just too embarrassed to mention anything.

Keegan walked past a group of teenagers huddled together with leaned-in-heads and hushed voices. Seeing the bunch of friends looking like they were plotting naughty shit to do made him miss his own pals back home. He may have been surrounded by a sea of faces in a city of a million people but Keegan was sure he had never felt so alone in his whole life.

He wasn't just missing Garth. He was missing having mates. Any mates. Maybe once he started work he would make friends with co-workers. Maybe. Keegan ambled towards the bus station with his head dipped down like he had been defeated. Then an idea struck him. Maybe he did have a friend he could visit.

Damon...

He stood still and let the rush of people go around him as he deliberated if it were a good idea or not.

Does it matter? You're bored shitless and need to chat to someone who isn't your parent.

Keegan thought, *fuck it*. Even if the weirdness hadn't dissipated between them yet, Damon would still let him in and talk. Of that, Keegan was sure. He didn't care what they talked about. He just wanted to be with someone who would listen and be with someone he could listen to. With a bounce in his step, he headed away from the bus depot and zig zagged through the city streets towards Damon's apartment, hoping he was home.

∞

Trying to find Damon's place was like a loopy circle of trial and error. Keegan knew roughly where it was but not exactly. He was about to give up searching when he finally recognised a small grassy park lined with pohutukawa trees above a stone embankment. The line of trees was in full bloom, their stalky flowers bright red like fresh blood. Beneath the pretty image was a bearded man wearing a dark-green trench coat, rummaging through a bin. He cast Keegan a look that was as dirty as his unwashed face then carried on digging.

Across the road from the miniscule picnic spot—and apparently homeless takeout—was the old redbrick building that housed Damon's apartment. In a past life it must have been a factory of some kind where poor folk worked their fingers to the bone. Now it housed wealthy thirty-somethings like Damon living in executive pads. It seemed fucked-up to the extreme knowing how much money resided inside each of those apartments while below a man was about to eat from a bin. This city living was going to take some getting used to, Keegan thought.

He craned his neck, staring up to the top floor and saw Damon's balcony. While his father's home oozed money with its sheer size and sprawling garden, Damon's home oozed money thanks to its location and view. He lived just high enough up that from the large deck you could see out across Waitemta Harbour. It had been a few years since Keegan had been here when on a holiday with his mother but he remembered it well. The open plan living with two large bedrooms was filled with funky furniture and appliances, complimented by Damon's photography of nude models hanging from the walls. Everywhere you looked you saw tits and minge. As a horny fourteen-year-old he had never wanted to leave. It was strange to think how worked up he got over the nude women—jacking off whilst left alone in the apartment—when now he could only ever see himself sleeping with guys. It was stranger still when he took into account that it was Damon who had opened his eyes to the level of attraction he had for men.

Keegan crossed the road and made his way inside the building, climbing the stairs at a quick pace, keen to see if Damon was home. Outside Damon's door the place sounded dead-quiet. Keegan's heart sagged, disappointed that his father's best mate wouldn't be home. He knocked anyway and hoped for the best. To his delight the best did happen. The door opened and Damon appeared shirtless in just a pair of cargo pants. Keegan's eyes went straight to his face where around his left eye was a sore-looking black n blue bruise.

"What happened to your face," Keegan blurted.

"Nice to see you too, K dog." Damon motioned with his arm for Keegan to come inside. "Fancy a drink?"

"Yes, please." Keegan went and stood at the breakfast bar. Damon raided the fridge and came back with two Smirnoff blacks. "I'm hoping this is to your liking?"

Keegan didn't care that it was vodka. As long as it was cold then he would guzzle it down. "Thank you."

Damon led them over to the couch. "Come sit. How come I have this unexpected pleasure?"

"I was in town for a job interview so I figured I'd stop by and see how you are."

"That explains why you look so smart," Damon said, nodding in praise at Keegan's attire. "It suits you."

Keegan blushed. "Cheers." He leant forward, resting his elbows on his knees as he took another sip of his drink.

"What was the interview for?" Damon asked. "And how did it go?"

"A call centre job for an insurance company." Keegan grinned at Damon. "And I got it which is cool."

Damon slapped him on the back. "Well done, K dog. Look at you. Only been here a couple weeks and already scored yaself a good job."

"I wouldn't say it's a good job and I only got it I suspect because Dad knows the woman who runs the place."

"Don't sell yourself so short. They're lucky to have you."

"You reckon?"

"Absolutely. Your smart, polite and have the look that those places go for."

"But it's over the phone. Customers won't see me."

Damon laughed. "Just take the compliment, K dog. All that stuff matters when it comes to work. Phone-based or not. Good-looking people help add to their image." He twisted in his seat, smiling.

Keegan watched Damon scull back on his drink. His eye sure did look sore. He didn't want to be rude but he was concerned how it happened. "So how did you get a black eye?"

Damon kept his eyes aimed at the floor.

Out of nowhere a conspiracy theory attacked Keegan's brain. "It wasn't Liam was it? He didn't track you down and jump you?"

Damon laughed. "Piss off. You saw how easy I landed a hit on him. Sure, he's well on the way to being a challenge but he ain't there yet."

"Then how did it happen?"

Damon zipped his lip. He slumped his shoulders and sighed. "Do you honestly not know?"

"I wouldn't be asking if I already knew."

"Matty hasn't said a thing about it to you?"

"No. Did you walk into a wall or something?"

"Yeah. A wall called your dad's fist and boot."

"What the fuck? Dad did this to you?" Keegan shook his head. "No way."

Damon nodded. "Yep." He stroked his bruised face. "This here is your old man's handy work."

"That makes no sense. He would never hit you. He loves..." Keegan's voice dried out. He tried again. "You're his best mate."

"Not anymore." Damon gave Keegan a glare so sombre that it gave away what he was about to say, "He knows Keegan. He knows about us. What we did together."

Keegan's heart slammed in his chest. "Oh my god," he whispered.

"Yep. I assumed you had told him but I can tell now it mustn't have been you."

"It wasn't me. I would never say anything."

Damon chuckled. "But you have told someone, haven't you?"

Keegan looked away. Too guilty to answer.

"It's okay, K dog. I guess something like that isn't easy to keep to yourself. Especially at your age."

Suddenly Keegan felt like a pathetic little child. Incapable of keeping a secret. "It must have been Jason."

"That's what I was thinking. When I had dinner with your dad and Jason last week, he said some stuff that made me wonder if he knew."

"I'm so sorry. I didn't know the nasty little prick would say anything."

"Don't be too angry with him. Jason was just looking out for your dad."

"But it's still shitty. It's really fucking shitty that Dad would hit you." Keegan felt his body in shake in sympathetic anger. How dare his father hit Damon for what they had done. For something Keegan had started. "Dad's a fucking dick for hitting you. He deserves a smack back."

"Whoa, settle down, K dog. Your father does not deserve anything of the kind. He was hurt and he was mostly sticking up for you." Damon swallowed slowly. "What I did was wrong. Inexcusable. You're my best mate's son and I should have known better. That is something you just don't do."

"I practically forced you into it though that first night at the cabin. Tricked you into something you thought was innocent."

Damon let out a laugh that sounded almost mockful. "Yeah you did trick me, Keegan, but I still should have stopped it. I let it go too far." He threw his head back and groaned. "I now think I let it happen… I think I *wanted* it to happen."

Keegan grazed his eyes over Damon's chiselled chest. For a brief moment he wanted to reach out and touch him. Touch what he had enjoyed so much before.

But I can't.

It was wrong. Damon wasn't his to have. Damon belonged to his father.

"You said the other day that you love Dad, right?" Damon didn't respond so Keegan nudged his shoulder. "Right?"

"That's right."

"Do you still feel the same? And be honest. I need to know the truth."

Damon turned and met Keegan's demanding stare with moist green eyes. "I still feel the same. I still love him. I always will."

Keegan bit his lip, watching Damon shake with sadness.

"It took me so fucking long to work it out," Damon said, his voice rattling. "I feel like the world's biggest fucking retard that it took something like us—you and me—sleeping together to work out how I feel." He quickly added an apology, "Sorry. No offense."

"None taken."

"Like I enjoyed what we did. Both times." He chuckled. "You're a sexy lad, K dog, but my heart belongs somewhere else."

Keegan was grateful for the compliment but he didn't need it. All he needed to hear was Damon reiterate who he did love. "Stand up," Keegan blurted.

"What?" Damon frowned.

"Stand up. You are taking me back to Dad's place and we are sorting this out."

"I really don't think that's a good idea. I'm the last person Matty wants to see right now."

"I don't give a fuck what Dad *thinks* he wants. He's

got it wrong." Keegan embraced the rebel streak commanding him. "He loves you just as much as you love him and I am gonna make him see just that."

Damon bit his lip. "I dunno."

"Come on. You told me we're family. And if someone in my family is sad then I'll do what I can to make sure their happy." Keegan gave him a cheeky grin. "Even if it means hooking them up with another family member."

Damon laughed. "Crikey."

"Come on. What's the worst that could happen?"

"Another black eye," Damon joked.

"You could knock Dad over if you wanted, so that's not an issue."

"Yeah, but I could never hit your father even if I wanted to."

"Then if he tries to hit you just turn your face so he can balance you out with a bruise on the other side."

Damon rolled his eyes and giggled, "Fuck sake." He sat with a pensive look on his face, lost in a sea of *what ifs*.

The silence that followed was unbearable. Keegan needed to fix things. He needed to try and do something right for once. Something good for someone else where the thought hadn't originated from the backward brain in his cock.

"Please let me help you," Keegan said.

Damon finally relented and slapped his knee. "Alright, K dog. Let's do this." He nodded confidently. "But first, I need to go buy something and come back. Then we can go."

CHAPTER FORTY-ONE

Matt was inside cooling off. The heat had become too much for him so he had retreated to the couch where he lay stretched out in his dirty clothes. He tucked his nose under the top of his shirt and inhaled, instantly greeted with a light pong. He knew he needed to go take a shower but just thinking of shifting from the couch seemed too much effort. Hours of having his arms raised tying lanterns to trees had left his shoulders strained and his back aching.

The bright side to his body's pain was that outside was nearly finished. He now could have all day tomorrow off and then do the final touches on Saturday morning before the service began. He may have had taken the month off work, but it hadn't felt like it with the amount of planning and sweat that had gone in to getting his garden ready for Jason's big day.

Matt's eyes flicked across to the far wall of the lounge where a framed landscape picture hung prominently. It was a shot of Piha Beach along Auckland's wild west coast. The photo locked in time the sun's orange rays bouncing over the gritty black sand. Matt had always liked how it looked; this beach that could be as deadly as it was beautiful. He didn't have any connection to that coast but he had always had a fondness for this photograph. It had been a gift from Damon for his 21st birthday. It was one of the few items that had been packed up with him to London. It followed him around the world wherever he moved, always on a wall nearby to remind him of home and the wonderful friend who had taken it. His mate—*ex mate*—had always had a talent for capturing beauty. It seemed a waste that he only bothered now to photograph models. It was his landscapes Matt liked best. But then rolling hills and crashing water didn't pay the bills like rolling wet nudes. The longer he stared at the image the sadder he became thinking about his lost friendship.

The photo has to go.

He had just about dozed off when he heard the front door open, he shot up and stumbled to his feet. "Is that you, Keegan?" he called out.

Keegan appeared, walking briskly into the lounge. He was still dressed in the nice clothes he had worn to the interview. It was amazing how grown up he looked, Matt thought.

"Hey, Dad."

"So how did it go?" Matt asked pretending like he didn't know the outcome. "Did you get the job?"

"Yep. I start next Monday so you won't have to worry about me being a burden."

"Well done. Congratulations." Matt stepped forward and shook his son's hand. "And for the record I never thought you were a burden. I just wanted you to be on the right track."

"Yeah, I know."

"In honour of the good news I am going to try cooking your favourite food tonight."

"You're cooking McDonalds?"

Matt's face screwed up. "No. I thought your favourite food was tortillas?"

"Oh, yeah." Keegan nodded, smiling. "That's my other favourite."

"We can get McDonalds if you rather?" Matt went and sat back down on the couch waving his hand to fan his face. "It's up to you."

Keegan didn't respond, his lips began to curl into a regretful grin. "Dad…"

The way the word *dad* hung like it was clawing to the edge of a steep cliff sent a chill down Matt's spine. It was the pace and tone of the word that told Matt he was about to hear something his ears wouldn't enjoy. "Yes?"

"I have someone outside in the car who wants to see you. Someone who I think you need to talk with."

"Who?" Matt frowned. "It's like a sauna outside bring

them in before they cook."

"It's Damon."

Matt went rigid, his face turning to stone. "Why the hell is he with you?"

Keegan buried his hands in his pockets, swaying on his feet. "I know you know about me and him, Dad, and I think you should know that it wasn't Damon's fault. I was the one who started it."

Matt shot a hand in the air, shooing away Keegan's defence of Damon. "No, Keegan. *HE* is the one in the wrong. Not you."

"Dad. I am telling you he... he just isn't the bad guy here."

"I can assure you he is."

"If anyone is the bad guy here, it's you," Keegan said frostily.

"Why me?"

"For punching your best mate in the face and leaving him with a black eye."

Matt felt himself getting angry. How fucking dare Keegan try and lecture him. "You don't get to tell me what I can and cannot do, Keegan. I appreciate that Damon has been a big part of your life—more so than he should be apparently—but I am telling you now that I never want you bringing him here again, so go outside and tell him he is wasting his time."

Keegan scowled. "Fuck you."

"Excuse me??" Matt nearly choked on the audacity of Keegan's rudeness.

"I said, fuck you!" Keegan fired again. "You ditched me when I became an inconvenience to your precious life and goals and now you're ditching Damon because he's become an inconvenience to your life too."

Matt tried not to laugh at the stupidity of his son's comparison. "I think you'll find those are two very different scenarios, Keegan. And for the record I didn't *ditch you*." Matt sighed angrily. "I was young and stupid. Just like you're being now."

Keegan's nostrils flared. He looked wild. But as quick as the anger appeared it receded and he slowly nodded. "Okay. Well, if you don't go outside and talk to Damon then I will go grab my shit and go stay with him 'till Mum can come pick me up. I won't bother you ever again, Damon won't bother you ever again. You can stay here in this big empty house all on your own and rot."

Matt's heart squeezed in his chest. His head went muzzy. He was seething with anger but so scared he didn't know how to respond—afraid of what he could lose. Keegan had resorted to the only thing that would make him go outside and talk to Damon. *Blackmail.* He tugged on his hair, trying to contain a groan of pain. He had only just reconnected with his son. He didn't want to lose him now. He didn't want Damon to be the one to ruin everything. He took a deep breath, doing his best not to fall to pieces. "Are you saying that if I don't go outside now and talk to him that you won't ever talk to me again?"

Keegan didn't respond. He stood with his arms folded, acting staunch.

"That's not fair, Keegan." Matt's eyes began to water. "That's really not fair," his voice cracked. He stood up, wiping his face.

Keegan's macho act crumbled seeing how upset he had made him. "Dad, I'm sorry I didn't mean it."

Matt shook his head and walked past his son without saying a word.

"I'm sorry," Keegan spluttered like he was worried Matt was running away to cry.

Matt stormed out of the lounge, marching his way outside. He stood on the porch, holding a hand above his eyes to block out the sun. He squinted down at the cars lining the street. *There you are!* He spotted Damon's black sports car parked across the road. In snappy steps, he crossed the road and went to open the passenger side door and sat down.

"You wanted to talk to me," Matt gruffed, keeping his eyes set dead ahead.

"Are you okay, Matty?" Damon asked in a concerned

voice.

Matt shook his head. "Nope. My son just told me if I don't come speak with you he is moving back to Marie and never coming back. So well done on controlling him to do your dirty work."

"I never told him to say that," Damon said, sounding genuinely shocked. "I'd never encourage something like that."

"Yeah, right," Matt mumbled.

"Come on, Matty, give me some credit."

"Oh, I do. I give you plenty of credit, Damon. I give you the credit for tricking me into thinking you were my mate. I give you credit for playing with my heart and being a complete fuckhead."

"Matty, I know sorry doesn't fix all these things, but I want things to be good between us again. I understand if you don't want something serious. But I would just like us to be mates. I don't think I could ever be happy if I lost you completely."

Matt kept his eyes focused outside the car, worried that if he looked at Damon, he would grow as weak as his trembling knees were.

Damon touched his leg. "I am sorry. I am sorry, sorry, sorry, sorry, sorry a thousand times. I will do anything you want to make it right."

"There isn't anything that can make this right," Matt's voice warbled. "You slept with my son, Damon. Do you not even fathom what that means? What sort of betrayal that is?"

Damon pulled his hand away. "I would hate me too, if I were you."

"You said it." Matt chewed his lip, keeping prisoner the bad words wanting to escape.

"But if I were you I'd also forgive me," Damon said bluntly.

Matt finally gave in and turned to face him. "Bullshit."

"I would." Damon nodded. "If you had done the same thing, I would forgive you... if I knew you felt the way I do right now—how desperate I am to be with you."

"Here's the funny thing though, Damon. I would

NEVER do something like that. I am not that stupid or cruel."

"I know," Damon mumbled. "That's because you're a better person than me."

Matt laughed derisively. "Don't take the piss."

"I'm not taking the piss. I'm dead fucking serious, Matty." Damon's voice sounded strained. He sharpened his moss-green eyes, staring intensely back at Matt. "You are a better person than me. You're the best fucking person I have ever known. Do you think I would cry like I did the other day for anyone else?"

"How would I know," Matt lied. It had been a shock to see Damon cry. See him begging like a broken slave being dragged away from a beloved master. The tears. The pain in his voice. It had been raw and real. Matt knew this.

"I have never cried in front of anyone like that before." Damon curled his fingers into a fist, clutching at his knees. "Because I have never felt like *this* about anyone before. You're the first person who has ever made me want to settle down. Make me want to be part of something that was more than just me."

A small clink of armour fell away from Matt's heart. He was beginning to lose his nerve.

Damon continued, "I want to change so bad, Matty. I wanna bury my selfish life and everything about it but I need you to help me dig the hole."

Matt coughed, clearing the trickle of emotion choking his throat. "It ain't just about you sleeping with Keegan, Damon." He inhaled, wondering how to word his piece. "I don't agree with it. It's wrong as fuck. But I could probably get past that." He hated himself for saying this, but he was being honest. He could eventually forgive that. "The thing that makes me not want us to be *us* is you!"

"What do you mean?"

"I would love for us to be together the way you are saying but I don't think I am strong enough to take on the risk."

"There's no risk."

"Yes, there is." Matt's lip began to quiver. "If I let myself, I would just be completely under your spell and I don't think I could ever get out of it. And that scares the shit out of me."

"I don't see how that is a problem. That just means you love me." Damon smiled. "Just like I love you."

"But do you? What I worry about, Damon, is that this all a fucking ploy to try and have me under your control again. You live for control. That is why you have been single all your life because you need to have your own way. You can't share anything. You don't do compromise. And as a mate I have learned to accept that about you." Matt sighed, letting out a faint laugh. "Fuck. Sometimes I even admire that about you. But to date *that*—that is dangerous and like I said, I worry that this is you bringing out a secret weapon just to have me under your thumb once more. And as soon as you do you'll back off and go back to not giving a shit." Matt felt woozy from the waterfall of emotions that poured out of his mouth

"I know. You told me the other day I'm obsessed with control."

"Sorry for repeating myself," Matt said sarcastically.

"That's why I got you this." Damon dug his hand into his pocket and pulled out a tiny silver key. He grabbed Matt's wrist and placed it in the palm of his hand. "This is me giving you the control."

"I don't understand." Matt shrugged. "What's it for?"

Damon scanned the street, looking around. He lowered his voice and whispered, "This." His hands dropped to his pants and he pulled them down to show he was wearing some sort of metal contraption around his privates.

"What the hell is on your cock?" Matt squawked.

"Chastity belt." Damon grinned, pulling his pants back up.

Matt was shocked. He blinked a few times then burst out laughing. "You have gotta be kidding me. You have a chastity belt on?"

Damon winked. "Yep. And you have the key. My sex

life is in your hands."

"Wow," Matt muttered. "It looked like it's stabbing into you cock."

"Yeah that's the removable urethral insert." Damon tried sounding posh as he said it. "So I can still go for a piss whenever I want. But otherwise you're my owner."

"Oh god," Matt uttered with a smile. "But isn't it uncomfortable?"

"A bit. But I'll get used to it." Damon touched Matt's knee. "Even if it hurts it ain't up to me when it comes off." He waggled his eyebrows.

The mood had gone very quickly from one of doom to light-heartedness. Perhaps this is why he had been so reluctant to speak with Damon; the moment Matt came near his friend's presence it was always going to tear down his walls. "So I have the key that controls how and when you get laid?"

"Yep. I am giving up control."

"You know when I said that thing about control this isn't exactly what I meant."

"I know." Damon nodded. "That's why I got you this one too. The most important one." Damon reached into his pocket, fetching out another key he handed over.

"What the hell does this one belong to?" Matt worried what other contraptions may be attached to his mate's body.

Damon touched his chest and smiled. "My heart."

Whoa...

That was it. That was the fatal blow. The ice wall protecting Matt's feelings was blown to smithereens. His limbs went loose; he grabbed Damon's face and kissed him like the world were about to end.

When their lips finally parted, Damon grinned ear to ear. "Are we going to become an *us?*"

Matt nodded. "I think we've been *us* for years."

The smile that Damon gave back was heart-melting. "You've just made me so fucking happy, Matty."

Matt nodded. He looked Damon in the eyes and said, "Now come inside so I can get you out of that bloody device."

"Are you setting me free or just so horny you need me now?" Damon teased.

"Both. I don't want you living your life locked in a bloody cock cage just for me." Matt held up the second key, twisting his mouth into a smile. "I only need the one to your heart. I believe that controls the rest."

CHAPTER FORTY-TWO

The Wedding

Grey clouds in the morning had threatened rain but the sun saved the day, bursting through the gloomy sky 'till nothing but blue hung above. It was an hour before the wedding was due to start and the backyard was abuzz with last minute action to make sure everything was in place.

Keegan stood at the kitchen window watching Jason's nieces and nephews rush about arranging rows of white seats while their mother and grandmother barked orders at them to hurry up. The scene was a comical one, not because of the bossy Tuki women, but because of, Peanut—the Shetland pony on lend for the big day to double as a life-sized My Little Pony. Peanut trotted around the edge of the garden, rainbow braids through his mane, looking every bit the star. Keegan secretly was looking forward to Peanut taking a dump and seeing how Jason's mum and sister would react— hilariously, he imagined.

A rattling sound rounded the house as two young men walked past carrying crates of alcohol to go in the makeshift bar set up at the far end of the yard. The big day would be going well into the night and Keegan imagined it was going to get as messy as the camp cauldron Jason called a wedding.

He turned around when he heard his father's voice coming from the lounge. He strained his ears to try and make out what his father was saying.

"I just want to make sure it all goes well. The guests will be arriving in a couple hours and it still isn't all set up." His father's voice prattled.

"Relax, babe. You've done an amazing job. The place looks... how Jason wanted it to look," said Damon's voice, reluctant to say the word *great*.

Keegan quietly made his way through the kitchen and dining room to round the corner to the lounge. Damon had his arms around his father's waist, nuzzling his neck with tender kisses. Keegan's father leapt ford in fright when he saw Keegan watching them.

"Keegan," his father blurted, instantly turning red-faced.

Keegan grinned back at his father's embarrassment. It wasn't exactly a secret Damon and his father had patched things up and become more than just friends. The pathetic attempt at covering up the romance hadn't fooled Keegan. Since their talk in the car, Damon had stayed over both nights. His father had used the excuse that Damon was just too drunk to drive home and was staying in one of the guest rooms. One sneaky check inside the mentioned bedroom was all it took to debunk that fable; the bed with its covers and pillows in place had not been slept in.

"I didn't know you were there," His father said, smoothing his pants down. "Did you umm… need a hand getting ready?"

Keegan laughed at seeing how flustered his dad was. "I'm ready." He tugged on his fancy shirt. I'm eighteen and can dress myself."

"Of course. Of course." His father stared at the ground while Damon shot Keegan a wink.

"Dad. It's okay. You don't have to freak out. I know that you and Damon are together."

His father cringed. "You do?"

"Yep. So try not having a heart attack about it." Keegan smiled.

"See, Matty. I told you not to be so uptight," Damon said, returning his hands to Matt's waist. "Nobody cares."

"Sorry. I guess I need to learn to let go a bit more."

"Yes, you do," Damon replied. "You're too tense."

As soon as his father started to look like he was about to chill out and relax, his eyes darted towards the window, looking outside at a rusty old Toyota with a trailer attached to it carrying some gigantic monstrosity. "What the fuck," His father shrieked. He pulled Damon's hands off his waist and raced outside.

"What's set him off now," Damon grumbled. He glanced at Keegan. "With the way your dad's acting, anyone would think this was his bloody wedding."

"I know right." Keegan chuckled.

"Okay. Better go see what's setting him off this time," Damon said like he was faking a patience he didn't feel.

Keegan followed Damon outside where the heat of the day whacked him in the face. They walked down to the footpath and joined Keegan's father standing at the end of the trailer, inspecting what looked to be a large yellow cage.

Keegan's grandfather emerged from the car and greeted them all with a wide grin. "Ahhh. Good stuff. You strong lads can help me carry this out back. Don't worry though. She ain't as heavy as she looks."

"What is this?" Keegan's dad said, tapping the cage with his finger.

"The cage you wanted," The old man replied like the question had been a stupid one. "You know… for the bids."

"Umm, unless their pterodactyls, I imagine they might escape, don't ya think?" Keegan's father ran a hand through his black hair, sighing.

"What?" Keegan's grandfather frowned. "Pterodactyls?" His jaw dropped as he registered what that meant. "Oh dear."

"Yes. *Oh dear*. They will all fly away now," Keegan's father said.

"Let us know when you need us, Glen," A woman's voice called out. "We're just going to have a quick smoke."

They all looked across the road. Getting out of a car were three scantily dressed women. They waved back, smiling.

"And who are they," Keegan's father demanded.

The old man scuffed a shoe against the pavement and in a guilty voice whispered, "The pterodactyls."

"What?" Keegan's father shook his head.

"You said get birds, so I arranged some birds."

Damon and Keegan burst out laughing while Keegan's father looked like he was about to explode.

"Not *those* kinds of birds. I meant birds with feathers. With fucking wings." He started flapping his arms. He lowered his voice to a quieter level, "What made you think Jason would want female strippers?"

"Firstly, son. Britney, Chloe and Amber are not strippers. They are adult entertainers." The old man let loose a sly grin.

"I don't care what their working titles are, Dad. I can't have a fucking giant cage dragged onto my lawn and look like I'm holding three women prisoner."

"Are you sure, Matty?" Damon said, still laughing. "I think Peanut would enjoy some company."

Keegan's father turned and scowled. "Not funny, Damon."

"What's not funny," said a voice coming from the driveway. Keegan turned around and saw Jason in his white suit coming to join them.

"What's not funny, is my father ballsing up and ruining your wedding." Matt shot the old man a disapproving frown.

Jason looked confused. "What's happened?"

"Apparently someone thinks that when you say arrange the birds for the wedding that that means get ones with tits."

Jason spotted the three girls across the road smoking. He giggled. "Oh my lord. This is priceless."

"It's not priceless," Keegan's father fumed. "But don't worry, I'll take care of it."

Jason touched him on the arm. "Matty. Take a deep breath. It's okay. Nobody's going to die."

"No, but it's hardly adding to your perfect day." Keegan's father looked around at all of them trying not to laugh at his meltdown. He sighed and rolled his eyes. "I'm overreacting, aren't I?"

"No, no," Jason cooed. "You are just trying to help. You have done an amazing job, and everything is under control." Jason looked across the road at the girls and nudged Keegan's grandfather. "Glen. Ask the girls if they want to sit and join us for the wedding. Cage free. They can sit in the front row with Will's parents. It will do the Jenkins family good to see people flash more than just their ankles."

"Okie dokie," the old man replied and walked to speak with his *pterodactyls*.

"And, Matty, for the love of god, just go inside already and relax." Jason smiled at his friend. "As a wedding gift for me."

"Come on you," Damon said, grabbing Keegan's father by the hand. "Let's go get you this drink."

Keegan was about to follow after them but Jason stopped him. "Keegan. Can I ask you to do me a favour?"

He nodded. "Sure."

"We need someone to go help set up the garden bar. They delivered the drinks but haven't loaded the fridges for us."

"Okay. Not a problem."

"Thanks, sugar. I think you'll find it's a job you enjoy."

Keegan was about to question the odd statement but Jason raced off back inside before he could say anything. He trudged around to the quiet side of the house and let himself through a tall wooden gate. This private strip of garden was filled with fruit trees and citrus plants. A garden path wove through the leafy area, conveniently leading away from the house and the lawn where the wedding was to take place. He followed the cobbled steps 'till he came to a clearing and spotted the makeshift bar. He heard the rattling of bottles coming below the bench top. He was about to call out and say hello but then a shirtless body with a beautiful face rose above the bar, stopping Keegan in his tracks.

Garth! What the hell are you doing here?

Keegan tried to act cool with a brave smile on his face, which he struggled to stop from cracking at the edges.

Garth gave a nod of the head. "Blondie. Good to see you."

"What-what are you doing here?"

"I'm the bartender for today's wedding extravaganza." He raised his arms up and twirled around. "Whataya think?"

"You look really good," Keegan said honestly. Garth did look good in just black pants leaving his lean torso on display.

"Thanks."

Keegan shook his head, still amazed at seeing him. "But why are you here? I thought you had gone home."

"I was going to but when I left that day, I only got two blocks when I realised I couldn't afford the gas to get home."

"Oh," Keegan mumbled, feeling bad.

"It was alright though 'cos I went and saw Jason at his mum's place and asked to use the phone to ring my dad for a loan, but instead he convinced me to stay a bit longer and help him with the wedding and pay me to be the bartender for the day."

"That's nice of him."

"It was."

"You've been in Port Jackson this whole time?" Kegan asked.

"I have," Garth replied in a prickly tone. "Anyway, blondie, what was it you wanted?"

Keegan felt caught off guard. "Umm, Jason told me to come help stock the bar up."

"It's okay," Garth said. "I'm nearly finished." He turned his back and knelt down to continue stocking the row of fridges behind him.

Keegan stood there like a small child who had been dismissed. Garth wasn't being rude but he didn't appear in a hurry to be overly friendly either. Keegan walked forward and looked over the bar at Garth crouched over. "Garth."

"Yeah," he replied, not turning around.

"Can we talk."

"Can't talk. Too busy."

"Don't be like that," Keegan moaned. "I told you I was sorry." He didn't have to see to know that Garth was scowling.

"I know you did, blondie. We're all good. Don't worry about it."

Keegan drummed his fingers on the bench of the bar. As nice as the view was of the tip of Garth's arse crack, he was getting annoyed at being so ignored. "Garth. Just stand up and look at me."

Garth stopped what he was doing. His shoulders heaved as he took a deep breath before standing up and facing Keegan again. "What?"

Keegan stared Garth in his hazel eyes, eyes that wore a shield like he was fighting off an attack. "I wanted to say that I am sorry about what I did."

Garth smiled. A false one. "You don't have to apologise again. I told you we're all good."

Keegan shook his head. "No, we're not. We aren't all good until you agree to give me one more chance."

Garth rolled his eyes. "One more shot at what?"

"Being your *pretend boyfriend*." Keegan smiled. "Maybe this time we could drop the *pretend* part and just try being boyfriends."

"You don't want me like that, Keegan. You told me yourself that guys like Liam are your type. You like tidy-haired gym bunnies that look like they should be on a fucking magazine cover."

"Stop being so insecure," Keegan snapped. "It doesn't suit you. Especially when you have nothing at all to be insecure about.

"I'm not insecure," Garth muttered.

Keegan smiled "You are totally insecure."

Garth narrowed his eyes. He looked like he was about to hurl insults but in a split second his face softened. "You'd be insecure too if you liked someone who had a thing for Liam cunting Corrigan."

"You don't have to worry about that. I don't want to be with Liam. I want to be with you."

"Bullshit," Liam scoffed.

"I'm telling you the truth." Keegan dropped his eyes

to Garth's stomach, admiring the treasure trail dipping below his pants. "You're my favourite person in the world. You helped me while all my world was turning to shit. You went out of your way to try and make me feel better. And you do make me feel better. You make me feel so much fucking better when you're around. I haven't been able to stop thinking about you this whole week. Every morning I wake up and you're the first person I think of. When I go to bed you're the last face I see in my mind. All through the day I'm springing boner after boner thinking about how hot it was when we…" Keegan drew a breath. "What I am trying to say is… I miss you."

Garth blinked at him. He parted his lips and said, "So thinking of me gives you stiffys?"

Keegan laughed. "That's all you got from what I just said?"

Garth stared back with a cheeky grin and nodded.

"Yes, Garth. Thinking of you turns me on and gives me stiffys."

"Cool," Garth said nonchalantly.

"Just cool?"

"Yeah. That's cool."

Keegan felt like he was losing this battle of the heart. He summed up the courage to lay himself bare. "I want to be the person you fall in love with because I think I am pretty close to falling in love with you. I want you to be the one. My one." Keegan felt himself blush at his confession. "I will do anything you want to make things right. Anything."

"Anything?"

"Anything!" Keegan nodded firmly "I'll move back home if that's where you want to go. I'll cook you breakfasts every morning. I'll let you be in charge. If you want to be the one doing the fucking, then you can be the one fucking. I don't care. Just give me another chance."

"You'd let me fuck you? Everyday? Whenever I feel like it?" Garth's eyes narrowed seductively.

Keegan swallowed. "Yes. If that's what you want."

Garth motioned with his finger. "Come round here."

Keegan walked around and joined Garth on the other side of the bar.

"Take your top off," Garth growled.

Keegan didn't disobey. He peeled his shirt off. "Are you going to fuck me now? Right here?"

Garth exhaled through his nostrils. He placed a finger to Keegan's lips, signalling him to be quiet. He kissed Keegan gently on the neck, pecking all the way up to his ear. He then grazed his tongue back down just below Keegan's collarbone. Garth sank his teeth in, biting and sucking with force. He then went a little lower doing the same again; sucking and biting with sharp intent.

Keegan felt a tingle run up his spine from the traveling bites Garth was plating all over his chest. His hole quivered, expecting to be bent over the bar and fucked aggressively. He was scared as hell but he had offered Garth the chance to do this. He had given himself away if it meant they could be together. Keegan kept his eyes closed and waited for the last part of his virginity to be taken from him. Garth's mouth kept moving south below his nipples, crossing all over his abdomen. It went on and on and Keegan felt his chest and tummy covered in saliva from all the tongue and teeth action.

Garth started sniggering.

"What's so funny," Keegan whispered.

"Look for yourself."

Keegan opened his eyes and glanced down. Garth had covered his chest and stomach in bright love bites. His flesh was ravished completely. "What the fuck?" he shrieked. "I look like I'm covered in fucking birthmarks."

Garth smiled "I know right. I'm quite proud of myself."

Keegan went to get snotty but remembered he had said *anything*. He took a deep breath and unbuckled his belt, he pulled his pants down his legs and leant over the bar, pressing his face into the bench, so Garth could finish degrading him. "Just try and go slow. I know I said anything but I'm worried cos it's my first time."

Garth promptly crouched down and tugged Keegan's pants back up. "What are you doing, blondie?"

"Letting you fuck me."

"I'm not doing that."

"You're not?" Keegan suddenly felt embarrassed. He fiddled to do his belt back up. "I thought you liked me? Is there something turning you off?"

Garth placed his hands on Keegan's shoulders, locking him in place to stare him in the eyes. "I do like you, Keegan. I like you A LOT." He smiled kindly. "But I am not going to make you do something you're not ready for."

"But I said you could."

"But do you actually want me to?" Garth arched his eyebrows. "Do you want me to fuck you? Right here, right now?"

Keegan gently shook his head. "No," he whispered.

"Then why would I do it?" Garth leaned forward and kissed him on the lips. "I know you have this issue about sex being some sort of power game like it's a battle for who gets to be in control but that isn't what sex is about for me."

Keegan felt his cheeks burn even more from shame.

"Sure, sex can be like that, but I'd rather it be something we both enjoy. And yep I would love to fuck you but I'm not gonna force you to do shit you're not keen on." Garth kissed him again. "Now I'm not saying I ain't keen on getting freaky now and then, but I'd like to just have some nice stuff between us for a while. Think you can handle that?"

Keegan nodded. "I think I can handle that."

"Good." Garth stepped back and smiled as he inspected his handiwork. "Now I must say, I do have some motherfucking sharp teeth." He laughed.

"Ya think? I swear your part-werewolf."

"Watch out for the full moon, baby." Garth pretended to howl up at the sky.

"Why'd ya have to go and cover me like this anyway?" Keegan chuckled, still in disbelief at the amount of marks.

"Just to remind you that anything Liam—one bite—

Corrigan can do, I can do better."

Keegan found himself laughing at Garth's need to be competitive, which in a weird way he found adorable. "So are you and me…" he didn't want to say the word in case he jinxed it.

"Pretend boyfriends?" Garth winked.

The word *pretend* felt hideous but Keegan accepted it. "Yeah, are we?"

Garth bit his lip like he was thinking it over. He stepped forward and grabbed Keegan's crotch, groping his cock. "There's nothing pretend about my man." He smothered his mouth over Keegan's, slipping his tongue inside with such passion it felt like they were inventing their very own kiss. Keegan thought for a moment they would melt, merge into one person.

When they finally ran out of air, Garth pulled back, grinning. "I think I'm really gonna enjoy having a boyfriend."

Keegan smiled. "Me too."

"And you know the best part about being my boyfriend?"

"Sex on tap?"

Garth playfully whacked his side. "Other than that. It's helping me manage the bar today… shirtless."

"Say what?" Keegan balked.

"Yep. It's gonna get super busy after the ceremony so since you're my guy you can help me run the bar. But you have to keep your shirt off like me 'cos apparently Jason's friends need some eye candy to ogle while they drink."

"You have got to be fucking kidding," Keegan muttered. "Have you just seen what you did to my body?"

"I know. And I am gonna enjoy telling every single person who asks about the marks that it was me who gave you them. You know… 'cos I'm your boyfriend and they can't have you."

"You most definitely are." Keegan liked seeing how happy and proud Garth looked referring to him as his boyfriend. It made him happy and proud too. Garth was right. Sex wasn't a competition—aside from beating Liam apparently. It wasn't some dubious game where only one person had control. That wasn't what Keegan wanted. He wanted *this!* Garth and love.

He threw away the embarrassment at the prospect of working the bar—shirtless and love bite-ridden—and decided *fuck it.* The guests could say whatever they liked. In fact, the whole fucking world could say what it liked because Keegan's world would be right here beside him. Protecting him and loving him. *My boyfriend*

CHAPTER FORTY-THREE

The wedding turned out to be beautiful and perfect. Yes, having three strippers seated in the front row, Spice Girls music blaring and a life-sized My Little Pony named Peanut running riot was hilarious and bad taste, but it didn't take away from the love that had been at the altar. The truth in Jason and Will's words as they held each other's hands, staring into one another's eyes. It was beautiful. Truth like that always was.

Matt had tried hard not to cry but he failed. As his good friend made a commitment of love, he let happy tears roll down his cheeks. Normally he would blush from embarrassment at having his feelings spill into open air but he didn't hold back. The more they fell the better he felt. Damon had discreetly grabbed hold of his hand, squeezing gently and gave him a warm smile.

Matt appreciated the warm touch. He thought it was somewhat brave of Damon to sneak in some affection like that with so many people around. If it were up to Matt, he would tell the world about his love for Damon. Anybody who was lucky enough to be loved by such a fine person like Damon Harris would want the world to know. But out of respect for his best mate and lover—who he suspected would want things kept under wraps—Matt intended to remain silent. It was better to have a secret love than risk losing it and having none at all. Damon may have been fine with Keegan knowing about them but the wide community? Well, that was probably something the handsome photographer with a womanizing reputation would be afraid of, Matt assumed. It turned out he underestimated Damon. Completely.

After the grooms kissed and sealed their union, Jason addressed the crowd. "Now for those of you that know me well, I hate and I really do mean *hate* longwinded boring speeches, so I promise I will be as quick as I can." Jason looked out at the crowd of faces, smiling. "I want to thank every one of you for coming today and taking part in mine and Will's special day. It means a lot to us that you are here. Especially our dear friends who made the effort to fly over from Sydney and brave a New Zealand summer. I know you all came equipped with Antarctic jackets expecting snow. Sorry to disappoint you and your low expectations. But don't throw them out just yet cos you'll probably need them tomorrow." He chuckled and was met with friendly laughter. "Before I tell you all to go start drinking, I just wanted to say a huge thank you to my dear friend, Matthew." Jason pointed, singling him out. "Matty Pie, here, was kind enough to allow us to use his home today and he has done a tonne of work in helping get this carnival—me and my husband call a wedding—ready." He looked directly at Matt and with sincere eyes blew him a kiss. "I love you to pieces, Matty Pie. I know we haven't seen each other as much as I would like over the years, but I hope you know that you are family to me. I've always known I could count on my poverty peak sister and I am forever grateful for our friendship. Annnnd if anyone is ever lucky enough to marry you then I hope to return the favour and plan you the gayest brightest wedding ever, girl."

Matt smiled. His heart shone from the love his friend was sending. For once he accepted the gender bend and mouthed back, "Thanks, girl."

"I would be lucky indeed," Damon whispered quietly.

Matt felt butterflies in his stomach. Their wings flapping so hard he thought he would lift off the ground.

"So you messy bitches," Jason continued, "it's time to go hit the piss and have some fun." He pointed behind him to the rear of the garden. "If you head in that direction you will find a lovely wee bar with tasty refreshments." He sniggered. "And for the horny sluts amongst you, please also enjoy the shirtless bartenders I have there to serve you. But go easy on them since one of them is Matty's son and he is still teen meat." He waved his arms, encouraging people to go start the afterparty.

Oh god! Matt suddenly realised he hadn't seen Keegan since outside following the cage fiasco. "Bloody hell, Jason," he muttered to himself in a laugh.

"Marie will love to hear about this," Damon teased. "Her baby boy being pimped out to serve drinks half-naked."

Matt turned, frowning. "Don't you think it's a little awkward to be making jokes like that."

Damon looked surprised to hear him say this. His face settled to a look of knowing. "You're not worried about me and..." he knew better than to finish the sentence.

"I'm not worried about anything," Matt replied.

"Good." Damon lent forward and whispered in his ear, "You're the only man with the surname Andrews, I am interested in."

Before Matt could say anything, a booming voice shouted across the yard, "Damo!"

They both looked over and saw Will's brother, Todd. He made his way toward them looking just as smug as Matt always remembered him being. Todd had been Damon's best mate growing up here in port Jackson and together they had ruled high school. Matt had always envied the pair and wondered why they had stopped being friends. Damon had never told him why. Not that that mattered. Todd and Damon's fallout had helped bring about Damon and Matt's friendship and in a weird way he had always felt grateful to Todd for that. It didn't stop him from finding the guy a wanker of the first degree though. As he got closer it was apparent that Todd was still an attractive specimen but to Matt's relief some of the blond man's shine had faded; his hair appeared to be thinning and he was the owner of a fleshy beer pouch that poked out above his belt. The loss of some of his looks hadn't dampened any of his confidence though. He bowled right up, shaking Damon's hand with firmness, totally ignoring Matt's existence like it was high school all over again.

"Hey, Todd. How are you?" Damon replied, smiling back.

"Yeah, really good." Todd looked around at all the guests. "How could you not have yourself a good laugh with all these fucking fruits about."

"You mean your brother and his friends," Damon said coldly.

"Yeah. Nothing against them. They are what they are." He smiled looking Damon up and down. "You're looking good, Damo. Time has treated you well."

"Thanks, Todd." The lack of retuning the compliment was more than a little obvious.

"Did you end up settling down and having some little Damo's?"

Damon chuckled. "Nar, no little Damos. The world can only handle one of me. Yourself?"

"Single at the moment. Just split from my second Mrs last year. Fucking nightmare I tell you." He pointed over to Will and Jason who were talking to a girl who looked about ten. "That's my girl, Sophie. She adores her uncle Will so I decided to bring her along even though I probably shouldn't."

"Well, I guess it is his wedding so…" Damon frowned, his expression asking Todd why it's a big deal.

"Yeah, but you know. I didn't want her getting any funny ideas about this sort of stuff."

Fucking moron. Matt wanted to punch him but he was sure Jason wouldn't want a fist fight at his day of days.

"You mean funny ideas like you wanting to fuck me when we were teenagers?" Damon said crisply.

Whoa! He what? Matt wasn't sure if he had heard that right.

Todd's jaw dropped in shock, his calm exterior showing a slight crack. "Now, come on, Damo. We were young and stupid. Just boys being boys."

Damon smiled, reeling back from an argument. "I guess you're right. I'm just joshing ya."

Todd laughed. "It's really good to see you again."

"You remember Matt, don't you?" Damon said, bringing him into the conversation.

"Matt? Fatty Matty?" Todd looked stunned, only now making the connection that Jason's friend Matt was him. "Is this your place?"

Matt nodded.

Todd looked around the yard and back at the house. "Fuck. You did alright for yourself."

It felt nice to hear the surprise in Todd's voice but not as nice as Matt had have hoped. In that moment he decided an arsehole's opinion isn't worth shit.

"Yeah, Matty has done really well. Awesome job. Awesome kid. He probably did the best out of all of us."

"True," Todd said, nodding. "Are you two mates or something?" He half-grimaced.

Matt went to respond but Damon interrupted him, "Matt is my boyfriend."

Todd's eyes bulged. "Your what?"

"My boyfriend," Damon said proudly.

Matt was gobsmacked. He began to blush at Damon's ballsy confession. He never thought in a million years Damon would be so open.

"Your boyfriend?" Todd said, still sounding in disbelief.

Damon nodded. "Yep my boyfriend. We fuck every night. Don't we Matty?"

Matt tugged the collar of his shirt, mumbling.

"Fucking hell," Todd whispered.

Damon stepped behind Matt and laced his arms around his waist, patting his stomach. "If you remember from when we were younger and that prank we pulled on Matt, you'll know how lucky I am." Damon groped Matt's crotch. "He's a big boy, is my Matty."

Oh dear lord. Matt was simultaneously loving it while wishing he could be invisible. Damon kissed his cheek and hugged his arms around Matt's chest, squeezing him against his body.

"Okay. Well. Great catching up with you both," Todd spluttered and quickly walked off.

Damon laughed in Matt's ear. "Now that was fucking

343

classic."

"You're telling me," Matt said. "I-I can't believe you just did that."

"He's a prick. He deserves to have his self-hating homophobic arse rubbed in it."

Matt stepped out of the embrace and turned to face Damon. "So you don't mind people knowing about us?"

Damon shrugged and put his hands out like he was weighing gold. "Why would I mind introducing you as my boyfriend?"

"I just..." Matt petered out.

Damon stroked Matt's cheek. "Babe. I love you. And if its fine by you, then I would like to tell everybody how I feel."

"I'd like that."

"Good." Damon leaned in and kissed him. "So how about tomorrow we go have lunch with Jenna. I can't wait to tell her I have settled down. I think for once she will probably approve of my choice."

Matt smiled. "Lunch with your mum? Now that sounds awfully coupley"

"Yep. We can tell her the good news."

"I hope you didn't tell her that I called her a schemy bitch." Matt winced. "I was angry and I didn't really mean what I said."

Damon laughed. "Jenna is a schemy bitch. She would be the first person to agree with you on that."

Matt smiled, relieved. "Okay. It's a date."

"The first of many, babe." Damon kissed him again. They wandered off to get a drink from the bar, holding hands through the party.

∞

Matt lay in bed listening to the early morning drizzle. The pitter patter of raindrops against his bedroom window was soothing and he was grateful that they decided to fall today and not yesterday drowning out the wedding. He lay on his side, staring at the beautiful naked man sharing the bed with him.

Damon was still sleeping, lightly snoring. Suddenly he mashed his lips together like he was chewing and then grumbled. He rolled over, and as if he were running on autopilot, reached out and reeled Matt's body closer to his own; he hooked a leg over and draped his arm over Matt's waist—locking him in. Their chests were now pressed together, their dicks touching and the hairs of their body brushing; sparking like clothes just pulled out of a tumble dryer. It was as if the touch of their skin was a comforting sedative and Damon returned to his sleepy snores.

Matt closed his eyes and let himself get lost in the moment, remembering how hot last night had been. His rump was damp and he could still feel the traces of love inside him that Damon had given him in the most tender and sensual way. The most surprising part was when Damon had wanted love in him too.

"Fill me up, babe" Damon had said in a sexy growl not long after he had finished fucking Matt.

Matt couldn't believe it at first. Damon—control freak—Harris wanted a cock inside him.

"I wanna feel you inside me," he had whispered.

Matt did not deny his request.

Damon had lifted his legs, serving up his butthole and rested his feet over Matt's shoulders.

Matt took his time and very gently fed Damon every wide inch he had, giving him a humungous load that he shot deep inside. Within an hour, Damon asked for more. This time Damon lay on his side and Matt wriggled up behind him, grazing his cock along Damon's crack 'till he slipped his stiff prick back inside Damon's wet hole. They had finished their bouts of lovemaking with affectionate cuddling, absorbing the sexual scent in the room they had created with a fusion of their bodies.

As Matt now lay beside his lover he was overcome with pride at having such a wonderful man in his life. He kissed Damon on the forehead and whispered, "I love you."

"I love you too, babe," Damon whispered back, squeezing him tight.

"Sorry. I didn't mean to wake you."

"You didn't. I was getting thirsty anyway." He flicked his eyes over at the empty glass beside the bed. He groaned as he started to sit up to retrieve a fresh glass.

Matt placed a hand to Damon's chest. "Stay here. I'll go get it."

"Are you sure?" Damon's groggy eyes flickered.

"Yes." Matt kissed Damon's bristly cheek. "That's what I am here for. To bring the water." He scooted over the sheets and slid out of bed.

Damon chuckled. "My sister told me you'd bring the water."

Matt smiled, assuming Damon had just woken from a dream. He shoved on his boxers, walked 'round the bed and grabbed the glass. He made his way downstairs towards the kitchen. He almost dropped the glass in fright when he saw two shirtless figures sat at the table kissing.

"Shit," he murmured. "You boys gave me a fright.

Keegan looked back with a guilty grin. "Sorry, Dad."

"That's okay. It's not your fault your father's a scardy cat." He walked over to the sink, turned the tap on and filled the glass up. "How come you two are up so early. I saw how much you two were drinking while working the bar. I would have thought you would both have your heads hanging in a bucket this morning."

"Nar, my heads fine," Keegan said.

"His head's better than fine," Garth said cheekily, thinking Matt would be too old to pick up on the sexual innuendo. "The only thing we're drunk on is love."

Matt rolled his eyes. "You are definitely a charmer, Garth. I have to give you that." He looked at Keegan's punctured body from the numerous love bites. "A charmer with sharp teeth by the looks."

"Does he what," Keegan chuckled.

"I hope none of those are above the neckline, Keegan." Matt said grumpily. "Turning up to work on your first day covered in root rash is not a good look."

Keegan groaned in embarrassment. "You sound just like Mum."

"I'll take that as a compliment. It means I sound like a parent."

"Dad?" Keegan asked.

"Yeah."

"I was just wondering... would it be okay if Garth comes back to stay for a while? You know just 'till we have saved enough for a bond on a new flat."

Matt pretended to think it over even though it was always going to be a yes. "I can't see why not."

"Thank you, Mr Andrews," Garth said.

"Matt," he corrected.

"Thanks, Matt. I promise to be tidy and not bring girls home late at night," Garth said.

Keegan whacked Garth's arm and laughed. "I hope not."

"I love winding you up, blondie." Garth stroked Keegan's arm and the two boys kissed like Matt wasn't even there.

"Okay. I'll go now," Matt shuffled out of the room in awkward fashion. He was glad Keegan was happy. That was the most important thing. He was also glad that it was someone like Garth who made him happy. After his initial disproval of the messy-haired rascal, Matt had come to the conclusion that Garth was one of life's good guys and it was good guys Keegan needed on his team.

Just like the good guy I have waiting for me in bed.

Matt climbed the stairs and made his way back to his bedroom. He handed Damon the glass which he gulped back greedily before placing it back on the bedside table. Matt crawled in bed to snuggle beside his man. Damon wrapped him up in his arms and Matt breathed in his lover's musky scent. He loved the way Damon smelled. Even now covered in sweat he smelled clean. A purity that smelled like home and made him feel safe.

For years Matt's heart thrashed around like it was

some sort of toy in a pinball machine. Love never quite within his grasp. He wondered if that is how it was for everyone on the planet. Thrown about, waiting for some sort of love to stick and save us. We may chase our own paths and get hit around differently but something about the pursuit of love and its destination was unifying, Matt thought. The way it could uplift us, help us grow, sometimes hurt us, but most importantly heal us.

He hugged Damon tight, listening to their chests beating in time. Matt smiled. There was no more empty. No more lonely. Their crashing hearts had collided and become one.

The end

NOTE FROM THE AUTHOR

Thank you very much for taking the time out to read Submissive Secrets. I do hope you enjoyed it. If you have read the entire Crashing Hearts series then I hope that the initial overload of heat in book one now makes sense. Crashing Hearts is my way of highlighting that while sex is fun, important and all sorts of amazing things, it can become harmful if fantasy blurs reality.

Each book of the series I enjoyed writing for different reasons. Book One *Dubious Desire* is what I consider the ideal raunchy read. It contains the nerves and anticipation of first times and is heightened with the added taboo element of Keegan seducing a close family friend; a man who could do with being taken down a peg or two. While it may not have been overly kind or pleasant in parts it remained very realistic. But of course I would say that...

Book Two *I Kissed Him There* is my personal favorite of the series because of the different friendships, family relationships and the light touch of spirituality it has. Another reason this story is so special to me is because of its focus on inequality, which unfortunately is a growing issue in New Zealand; a country that is fast losing touch with its ideals of fairness.

And of course the final book *Submissive Secrets* I enjoyed creating because of how everything came together. To be honest, I was unsure of what path Submissive Secrets would take initially, but once the character Garth showed up again I knew exactly where things would lead. He really is one of my favorite characters I have ever written.

Anyway, thank you again for joining me on this journey. *Zane.*

Made in the USA
Middletown, DE
15 April 2018